CHICOT,

(LA DAM~ ~~ ~~~~UREAU)

A SEQUEL TO "MARGUERITE DE VALOIS."

The Second Volume in the Series of Historical
Stories known as the

"Valois Romances."

By ALEXANDRE DUMAS.

Translated from the latest French Edition.

A. L. BURT COMPANY, PUBLISHERS,
52-58 DUANE STREET, NEW YORK.

" Your highness mistakes your way," said Monsoreau.   "True," said the duke,
"thank you."—Page 373.   Chicot, the Jester.

CHICOT, THE JESTER.

CHAPTER I.

THE WEDDING OF ST. LUC.

On the evening of a Sunday, in the year 1578, a splendid fête was given in the magnificent hotel just built opposite the Louvre, on the other side of the water, by the family of Montmorency, who, allied to the royalty of France, held themselves equal to princes. This fête was to celebrate the wedding of François d'Epinay de St. Luc, a great friend and favorite of the king, Henri III., with Jeanne de Crossé-Brissac, daughter of the marshal of that name.

The banquet had taken place at the Louvre, and the king, who had been with much difficulty induced to consent to the marriage, had appeared at it with a severe and grave countenance. His costume was in harmony with his face; he wore that suit of deep chestnut, in which Clouet described him at the wedding of Joyeuse; and this kind of royal specter, solemn and majestic, had chilled all the spectators, but above all the young bride, at whom he cast many angry glances. The reason of all this was known to every one, but was one of those court secrets of which no one likes to speak.

Scarcely was the repast finished, when the king had risen abruptly, thereby forcing every one to do the same. Then St. Luc approached him, and said: "Sire, will your majesty do me the honor to accept the fête, which I wish to give to you this evening at the Hôtel Montmorency?" This was said in an imploring tone, but Henri, with a voice betraying both vexation and anger, had replied:

"Yes, monsieur, we will go, although you certainly do not merit this proof of friendship on our part."

Then Madame de St. Luc had humbly thanked the king, but he turned his back without replying.

"Is the king angry with you?" asked the young wife of her husband.

"I will explain it to you after, mon amie, when this anger shall have passed away."

"And will it pass away?"

"It must."

Mademoiselle de Brissac was not yet sufficiently Madame de St. Luc to insist further; therefore she repressed her curiosity, promising herself to satisfy it at a more favorable time.

They were, therefore, expecting St. Luc at the Hôtel Montmorency, at the moment in which our story commences. St. Luc had invited all the king's friends and all his own; the princes and their favorites, particularly those of the Duc d'Anjou. He was always in opposition to the king, but in a hidden manner, pushing forward those of his friends whom the example of La Mole and Coconnas had not cured. Of course, his favorites and those of the king lived in a state of antagonism, which brought on rencontres two or three times a month, in which it was rare that some one was not killed or badly wounded.

As for Catherine, she was at the height of her wishes; her favorite son was on the throne, and she reigned through him, while she pretended to care no more for the things of this world. St. Luc, very uneasy at the absence of all the royal family, tried to reassure his father-in-law, who was much distressed at this menacing absence. Convinced, like all the world, of the friendship of Henri for St. Luc, he had believed he was assuring the royal favor, and now this looked like a disgrace. St. Luc tried hard to inspire in them a security which he did not feel himself; and his friends, Maugiron, Schomberg, and Quelus, clothed in their most magnificent dresses, stiff in their splendid doublets, with enormous frills, added to his annoyance by their ironical lamentations.

"Eh! mon Dieu! my poor friend," said Jacques de Levis, Comte de Quelus, "I believe now that you are done for. The king is angry that you would not take his advice, and M. d'Anjou because you laughed at his nose."

"No, Quelus, the king does not come, because he has made a pilgrimage to the monks of the Bois de Vincennes ; and the Duc d'Anjou is absent, because he is in love with some woman whom I have forgotten to invite."

"But," said Maugiron, "did you see the king's face at dinner ? And as for the duke, if he could not come, his gentlemen might. There is not one here, not even Bussy."

"Oh ! gentlemen," said the Duc de Brissac, in a despairing tone, "it looks like a complete disgrace. Mon Dieu ! how can our house, always so devoted to his majesty, have displeased him ? "

The young men received this speech with bursts of laughter, which did not tend to soothe the marquis. The young bride was also wondering how St. Luc could have displeased the king. All at once one of the doors opened and the king was announced.

"Ah ! " cried the marshal, "now I fear nothing ; if the Duc d'Anjou would but come, my satisfaction would be complete."

"And I," murmured St. Luc ; "I have more fear of the king present than absent, for I fear he comes to play me some spiteful tricks."

But, nevertheless, he ran to meet the king, who had quitted at last his somber costume, and advanced resplendent in satin, feathers, and jewels. But at the instant he entered another door opened just opposite, and a second Henri III., clothed exactly like the first, appeared, so that the courtiers, who had run to meet the first, turned round at once to look at the second.

Henri III. saw the movement, and exclaimed :

"What is the matter, gentlemen ? "

A burst of laughter was the reply. The king, not naturally patient, and less so that day than usual, frowned ; but St. Luc approached, and said :

"Sire, it is Chicot, your jester, who is dressed exactly like your majesty, and is giving his hand to the ladies to kiss."

Henri laughed. Chicot enjoyed at his court a liberty similar to that enjoyed thirty years before by Triboulet at the court of François I., and forty years after by Longely at the court of Louis XIII. Chicot was not an ordinary jester. Before being Chicot he had been "De Chicot." He was a Gascon gentleman, who, ill-treated by M. de Mayenne on account of a rivalry in a love affair, in which Chicot had been victorious, had taken refuge at court, and prayed the king for his protection by telling him the truth.

"Eh, M. Chicot," said Henri, "two kings at a time are too much."

"Then," replied he, "let me continue to be one, and you play Duc d'Anjou ; perhaps.you will be taken for him, and learn something of his doings."

"So," said Henri, looking round him, "Anjou is not here."

"The more reason for you to replace him. It is settled, I am Henri, and you are François. I will play the king, while you dance and amuse yourself a little, poor king."

"You are right, Chicot, I will dance."

"Decidedly," thought De Brissac, "I was wrong to think the king angry ; he is in an excellent humor."

Meanwhile St. Luc had approached his wife. She was not a beauty, but she had fine black eyes, white teeth, and a dazzling complexion.

"Monsieur," said she to her husband, "why did they say that the king was angry with me ; he has done nothing but smile on me ever since he came?"

"You did not say so after dinner, dear Jeanne, for his look then frightened you."

"His majesty was, doubtless, out of humor then, but now——"

"Now, it is far worse ; he smiles with closed lips. I would rather he showed me his teeth. Jeanne, my poor child, he is preparing for us some disagreeable surprise. Oh ! do not look at me so tenderly, I beg ; turn your back to me. Here is Maugiron coming ; converse with him, and be amiable to him."

" That is a strange recommendation, monsieur."

But St. Luc left his wife full of astonishment, and went to pay his court to Chicot, who was playing his part with a most laughable majesty.

The king danced, but seemed never to lose sight of St. Luc. Sometimes he called him to repeat to him some pleasantry, which, whether droll or not, made St. Luc laugh heartily. Sometimes he offered him out of his comfit box sweetmeats and candied fruits, which St. Luc found excellent. If he disappeared for an instant, the king sent for him, and seemed not happy if he was out of his sight. All at once a voice rose above all the tumult.

" Oh !" said Henri, " I think I hear the voice of Chicot ; do you hear, St. Luc ?— the king is angry."

" Yes, sire, it sounds as though he were quarreling with some one."

" Go and see what it is, and come back and tell me."

As St. Luc approached he heard Chicot crying :

" I have made sumptuary laws, but if they are not enough I will make more ; at least they shall be numerous, if they are not good. By the horn of Beelzebub, six pages, M. de Bussy, are too much."

And Chicot, swelling out his cheeks, and putting his hand to his side, imitated the king to the life.

" What does he say about Bussy ?" asked the king, when St. Luc returned. St. Luc was about to reply, when the crowd opening, showed to him six pages, dressed in cloth of gold, covered with chains, and bearing on their breasts the arms of their masters, sparkling in jewels. Behind them came a young man, handsome and proud, who walked with his head raised and a haughty look, and whose simple dress of black velvet contrasted with the splendor of his pages. This was Bussy d'Amboise. Maugiron, Schomberg, and Quelus had drawn near to the king.

" See," said Maugiron, " here is the servant, but where is the master ? Are you also in disgrace with him, St. Luc ?"

" Why should he follow Bussy ? " said Quelus.

" Do you not remember that when his majesty did M. de

Bussy the honor to ask him if he wished to belong to him, he replied that, being of the House of Clermont, he followed no one, and belonged to himself."

The king frowned.

"Yes," said Maugiron, "whatever you say, he serves the Duc d'Anjou."

"Then it is because the duke is greater than the king."

No observation could have been more annoying to the king than this, for he detested the Duc d'Anjou. Thus, although he did not answer, he grew pale.

"Come, come, gentlemen," said St. Luc, trembling, "a little charity for my guests, if you please ; do not spoil my wedding day."

"Yes," said the king, in a mocking tone ; "do not spoil St. Luc's wedding-day."

"Oh !" said Schomberg, "is Bussy allied to the Brissacs ?—since St. Luc defends him."

"He is neither my friend nor relation, but he is my guest," said St. Luc. The king gave an angry look. "Besides," he hastened to add, "I do not defend him the least in the world."

Bussy approached gravely behind his pages to salute the king, when Chicot cried :

"Oh, la ! Bussy d'Amboise, Louis de Clermont, Comte de Bussy, do you not see the true Henri, do you not know the true king from the false ? He to whom you are going is Chicot, my jester, at whom I so often laugh."

Bussy continued his way, and was about to bow before the king, when he said :

"Do you not hear, M. de Bussy, you are called ?" and, amidst shouts of laughter from his minions, he turned his back to the young captain. Bussy reddened with anger, but he affected to take the king's remark seriously, and turning round towards Chicot :

"Ah ! pardon, sire," said he, "there are kings who resemble jesters so much, that you will excuse me, I hope, for having taken a jester for a king."

"Hein," murmured Henri, "what does he say ?"

"Nothing, sire," said St. Luc.

"Nevertheless, M. Bussy," said Chicot; "it was unpardonable."

"Sire, I was preoccupied."

"With your pages, monsieur," said Chicot; "you ruin yourself in pages, and, par la mordieu, it is infringing our prerogatives."

"How so? I beg your majesty to explain."

"Cloth of gold for them, while you a gentleman, a colonel, a Clermont, almost a prince, wear simple black velvet."

"Sire," said Bussy, turning towards the kings' minions, "as we live in a time when lackeys dress like princes, I think it good taste for princes to dress like lackeys."

And he returned to the young men in their splendid dress the impertinent smiles which they had bestowed on him a little before. They grew pale with fury, and seemed only to wait the king's permission to fall upon Bussy.

"Is it for me and mine that you say that?" asked Chicot, speaking like the king.

Three friends of Bussy's now drew near to him. These were Charles d'Antragues, François, Vicomte de Ribeirac, and Livarot. Seeing all this, St. Luc guessed that Bussy was sent by Monsieur to provoke a quarrel. He trembled more than ever, for he feared the combatants were about to take his house for a battle-field. He ran to Quelus, who already had his hand on his sword, and said, "In Heaven's name be moderate."

"Parbleu, he attacks you as well as us."

"Quelus, think of the Duc d'Anjou, who supports Bussy; you do not suppose I fear Bussy himself?"

"Eh! Mordieu, what need we fear; we belong to the king. If we get into peril for him he will help us."

"You, yes; but me," said St. Luc, piteously.

"Ah dame, why do you marry, knowing how jealous the king is in his friendships?"

"Good," thought St. Luc, "every one for himself; and as I wish to live tranquil during the first fortnight of my marriage, I will make friends with M. Bussy." And he advanced towards him. After his impertinent speech, Bussy had looked round the room to see if any one would

take notice of it. Seeing St. Luc approach, he thought
he had found what he sought.

"Monsieur," said he, "is it to what I said just now,
that I owe the honor of the conversation you appear to
desire?"

"Of what you have just said, I heard nothing. No, I
saw you, and wished to salute you, and thank you for the
honor you have done me by your presence here."

Bussy, who knew the courage of St. Luc, understood at
once that he considered the duties of a host paramount,
and answered him politely.

Henri, who had seen the movement said, "Oh, oh! I
fear there is mischief there; I cannot have St. Luc
killed. Go and see, Quelus; no, you are too rash—you,
Maugiron."

But St. Luc did not let him approach Bussy, but
came to meet him and returned with him to the king.

"What have you been saying to that coxcomb?" asked
the king.

"I, sire?"

"Yes, you."

"I said, good evening."

"Oh! was that all?"

St. Luc saw he was wrong. "I said, good evening;
adding, that I would have the honor of saying good morning to-morrow"

"Ah! I suspected it."

"Will your majesty keep my secret?" said St. Luc.

"Oh! parbleu, if you could get rid of him without
injury to yourself——"

The minions exchanged a rapid glance, which Henri III.
seemed not to notice.

"For," continued he, "his insolence is too much."

"Yes, yes," said St. Luc, "but some day he will find
his master."

"Oh!" said the king, "he manages the sword well.
Why does he not get bit by some dog?" And he threw a
spiteful glance on Bussy, who was walking about, laughing at all the king's friends.

" Corbleu ! " cried Chicot, " do not be so rude to my friends, M. Bussy, for I draw the sword, though I am a king, as well as if I was a common man."

" If he continue such pleasantries, I will chastise Chicot, sire," said Maugiron.

"No, no, Maugiron, Chicot is a gentleman. Besides, it is not he who most deserves punishment, for it is not he who is most insolent."

This time there was no mistaking, and Quelus made signs to D'O and D'Epernon, who had been in a different part of the room, and had not heard what was going on. " Gentlemen," said Quelus, "come to the council ; you, St. Luc, go and finish making your peace with the king."

St. Luc approached the king, while the others drew back into a window.

" Well," said D'Epernon, " what do you want ? I was making love, and I warn you, if your recital be not interesting I shall be very angry."

" I wish to tell you that after the ball I set off for the chase."

" For what chase ? "

" That of the wild boar."

" What possesses you to go, in this cold, to be killed in some thicket ? "

" Never mind, I am going."

" Alone ? "

" No, with Maugiron and Schomberg. We hunt for the king."

" Ah ! yes, I understand," said Maugiron and Schomberg.

" The king wishes a boar's head for breakfast to-morrow."

" With the neck dressed à l'Italienne," said Maugiron, alluding to the turn-down collar which Bussy wore in opposition to their ruffs.

" Ah, ah," said D'Epernon, " I understand."

" What is it ? " asked D'O, " for I do not."

" Ah ! look round you."

" Well ! "

" Did any one laugh at us here ? "

" Yes, Bussy."

" Well, that is the wild boar the king wants."

" You think the king——"

" He asks for it."

" Well, then, so be it.   But how do we hunt ?"

" In ambush ; it is the surest."

Bussy remarked the conference, and, not doubting that
they were talking of him, approached, with his friends.

" Look, Antragues, look, Ribeirac," said he, " how they
are grouped ; it is quite touching; it might be Euryale
and Nisus, Damon and Pythias, Castor and——.   But
where is Pollux ?"

" Pollux is married, so that Castor is left alone."

" What can they be doing ?"

" I bet they are inventing some new starch."

" No, gentlemen," said Quelus, " we are talking of the
chase."

" Really, Signor Cupid," said Bussy ; "it is very cold
for that.   It will chap your skin."

" Monsieur," replied Maugiron, politely, " we have warm
gloves, and doublets lined with fur."

" Ah ! that reassures me," said Bussy ; "do you go
soon ?"

" To-night, perhaps."

" In that case I must warn the king; what will he say
to-morrow, if he finds his friends have caught cold ?"

" Do not give yourself that trouble, monsieur," said
Quelus, " his majesty knows it."

" Do you hunt larks ?" asked Bussy, with an impertinent air.

" No, monsieur, we hunt the boar.   We want a head.
Will you hunt with us, M. Bussy ?"

" No, really, I cannot.   To-morrow I must go to the
Duc d'Anjou for the reception of M. de Monsoreau, to
whom monseigneur has just given the place of chief huntsman."

" But, to-night ?"

" Ah ! to-night, I have a rendezvous in a mysterious
house of the Faubourg St. Antoine."

"Ah! ah!" said D'Epernon, "is the Queen Margot here, incognito, M. de Bussy?"

"No, it is some one else."

"Who expects you in the Faubourg St. Antoine?"

"Just so, indeed I will ask your advice, M. de Quelus."

"Do so, although I am not a lawyer, I give very good advice."

"They say the streets of Paris are unsafe, and that is a lonely place. Which way do you counsel me to take?"

"Why, I advise you to take the ferry-boat at the Pré-aux-Clercs, get out at the corner, and follow the quay until you arrive at the great Châtelet, and then go through the Rue de la Tixanderie, until you reach the faubourg. Once at the corner of the Rue St. Antoine, if you pass the Hôtel des Tournelles without accident, it is probable you will arrive safe and sound at your mysterious house."

"Thanks for your route, M. de Quelus, I shall be sure to follow it." And saluting the five friends, he went away.

As Bussy was crossing the last saloon where Madame de St. Luc was, her husband made a sign to her. She understood at once, and going up, stopped him.

Oh! M. de Bussy," said she, "every one is talking of a sonnet you have made."

"Against the king, madame?"

"No, in honor of the queen; do tell it to me."

"Willingly, madame," and, offering his arm to her, he went off, repeating it.

During this time, St. Luc drew softly near his friends, and heard Quelus say:

"The animal will not be difficult to follow; thus then, at the corner of the Hôtel des Tournelles, opposite the Hôtel St. Pol."

"With each a lackey?" asked D'Epernon.

"No, no, Nogaret, let us be alone, and keep our own secret, and do our own work. I hate him, but he is too much a gentleman for a lackey to touch."

"Shall we go out all six together?"

"All five if you please," said St. Luc.

"Ah! it is true, we forgot your wife."

They heard the king's voice calling St. Luc.

"Gentlemen," said he, "the king calls me. Good sport, au revoir."

And he left them, but instead of going straight to the king, he ran to where Bussy stood with his wife.

"Ah! monsieur, how hurried you seem," said Bussy. "Are you going also to join the chase; it would be a proof of your courage, but not of your gallantry."

"Monsieur, I was seeking you."

"Really."

"And I was afraid you were gone. Dear Jeanne, tell your father to try and stop the king, whilst I say a few words tête-à-tête to M. Bussy." Jeanne went.

"I wish to say to you, monsieur," continued St. Luc, "that if you have any rendezvous to-night, you would do well to put it off, for the streets are not safe, and, above all, to avoid the Hôtel des Tournelles, where there is a place where several men could hide. This is what I wished to say; I know you fear nothing, but reflect."

At this moment they heard Chicot's voice crying, "St. Luc, St. Luc, do not hide yourself, I am waiting for you to return to the Louvre."

"Here I am, sire," cried St. Luc, rushing forward. Near Chicot stood the king, to whom one page was giving his ermine mantle, and another a velvet mask lined with satin.

"Sire," said St. Luc, "I will have the honor of lighting your majesties to your litters."

"No," said Henri, "Chicot goes one way, and I another. My friends are good-for-nothings, who have run away and left me to return alone to the Louvre. I had counted on them, and you cannot let me go alone. You are a grave married man, and must take me back to the queen. Come, my friend, my litter is large enough for two."

Madame de St. Luc, who had heard this, tried to speak, and to tell her father that the king was carrying away her husband, but he, placing his fingers on his mouth, motioned her to be silent.

"I am ready, sire," said he, "to follow you."

When the king took leave, the others followed, and

Jeanne was left alone. She entered her room, and knelt down before the image of a saint to pray, then sat down to wait for her husband's return. M. de Brissac sent six men to the Louvre to attend him back. But two hours after one of them returned, saying, that the Louvre was closed and that before closing, the captain of the watch had said, "It is useless to wait longer, no one will leave the Louvre to-night ; his majesty is in bed."

The marshal carried this news to his daughter.

CHAPTER II.

HOW IT IS NOT ALWAYS HE WHO OPENS THE DOOR, WHO ENTERS THE HOUSE.

THE Porte St. Antoine was a kind of vault in stone, similar to our present Porte St. Denis, only it was attached by its left side to buildings adjacent to the Bastile. The space at the right, between the gate and the Hôtel des Tournelles, was large and dark, little frequented by day, and quite solitary at night, for all passers-by took the side next to the fortress, so as to be in some degree under the protection of the sentinel. Of course, winter nights were still more feared than summer ones.

That on which the events which we have recounted, and are about to recount took place, was cold and black. Before the gate on the side of the city, was no house, but only high walls, those of the church of St. Paul, and of the Hôtel des Tournelles. At the end of this wall was the niche of which St. Luc had spoken to Bussy. No lamps lighted this part of Paris at that epoch. In the nights when the moon charged herself with the lighting of the earth, the Bastile rose somber and majestic against the starry blue of the skies, but on dark nights, there seemed only a thickening of the shadows where it stood. On the night in question, a practised eye might have detected in the angle of the wall of the Tournelles several black shades, which moved enough to show that they belonged to poor devils of human bodies, who seemed to find it difficult to preserve their natural warmth as they stood there. The sentinel from the Bastile, who could not see them on account of the darkness, could not hear them either, for they talked almost in whispers. However, the conversation did not want interest.

"This Bussy was right," said one ; " it is a night such as we had at Warsaw, when Henri was King of Poland, and if this continues we shall freeze."

"Come, Mangiron, you complain like a woman," replied another : " it is not warm, I confess ; but draw your mantle over your eyes, and put your hands in your pockets, and you will not feel it."

"Really, Schomberg," said a third, " it is easy to see you are German. As for me, my lips bleed, and my mustachios are stiff with ice."

"It is my hands," said a fourth ; " on my honor, I would not swear I had any."

"You should have taken your mamma's muff, poor Quelus," said Schomberg.

"Eh ! mon Dieu, have patience," said a fifth voice ; " you will soon be complaining you are hot."

"I see some one coming through the Rue St. Paul," said Quelus.

"It cannot be him ; he named another route."

"Might he not have suspected something, and changed it ?"

"You do not know Bussy ; where he said he should go, he would go, if he knew that Satan himself were barring his passage."

"However, here are two men coming."

" Ma foi ! yes."

"Let us charge," said Schomberg.

"One moment," said D'Epernon ; " do not let us kill good bourgeois, or poor women. Hold ! they stop."

In fact, they had stopped, and looked as if undecided.

"Oh, can they have seen us ?"

"We can hardly see ourselves !"

"See, they turn to the left; they stop before a house

they are seeking—they are trying to enter ; they will escape us !"

"But it is not him, for he was going to the Faubourg St. Antoine."

"Oh ! how do you know he told you right ?"

At this supposition they all rushed out, sword in hand, towards the gentlemen.

One of the men had just introduced a key into the lock ; the door had yielded and was about to open, when the noise of their assailants made them turn.

"What is this ? Can it be against us, Aurilly ?" said one.

"Ah, monseigneur," said the other, who had opened the door, "it looks like it. Will you name yourself, or keep incognito ?"

"Armed men—an ambush !"

"Some jealous lover ; I said the lady was too beautiful not to be watched."

"Let us enter quickly, Aurilly ; we are safer within doors."

"Yes, monseigneur, if there are not enemies within ; but how do you know——"

He had not time to finish. The young men rushed up ; Quelus and Maugiron made for the door to prevent their entering, while Schomberg, D'O, and D'Epernon prepared to attack in front. But he who had been called monseigneur turned towards Quelus, who was in front, and crossing his arms proudly, said :

"You attack a son of France, M. Quelus !"

Quelus drew back, trembling, and thunderstruck. "Monseigneur le Duc d'Anjou !" he cried.

"The Duc d'Anjou !" repeated the others.

"Well, gentlemen," cried the duke.

"Monseigneur," stammered D'Epernon, "it was a joke ; forgive us."

"Monseigneur," said D'O, "we did not dream of meeting your highness here !"

"A joke !" said the duke ; "you have an odd manner of joking, M. d'Epernon. Since it was not intended for me, whom did your jest menace ?"

" Monseigneur," said Schomberg ; " we saw St. Luc quit the Hôtel Montmorency and come this way ; it seemed strange to us, and we wished to see what took him out on his wedding night."

" M. de St. Luc—you took me for him ?"

" Yes, monseigneur."

" M. de St. Luc is a head taller then I am."

" It is true, monseigneur ; but he is just the height of M. Aurilly."

" And seeing a man put a key in a lock, we took him for the principal," added D'O.

" Monseigneur cannot suppose that we had the shadow of an ill-will towards him, even to disturb his pleasures ? "

As he listened, the duke, by a skilful movement, had, little by little, quitted the door, followed by Aurilly, and was now at some distance off.

" My pleasures ! " said he, angrily ; " what makes you think I was seeking pleasure ?"

" Ah, monseigneur, in any case pardon us, and let us retire," said Quelus.

" It is well ; adieu, gentlemen ; but first listen. I was going to consult the Jew Manasses, who reads the future ; he lives, as you know, in Rue de la Tournelle. In passing, Aurilly saw you and took you for the watch, and we, therefore, tried to hide ourselves in a doorway. And now you know what to believe and say ; it is needless to add, that I do not wish to be followed," and he turned away

" Monseigneur," said Aurilly, " I am sure these men have bad intentions ; it is near midnight, and this is a lonely quarter ; let us return home, I beg."

" No, no ; let us profit by their departure."

" Your highness is deceived ; they have not gone, but have returned to their retreat : look in the angle of the Hôtel des Tournelles. "

François looked, and saw that Aurilly was right ; it was evident that they waited for something, perhaps to see if the duke were really going to the Jew.

" Well, Monseigneur," continued Aurilly, " do you not think it will be more prudent to go home ?"

"Mordieu! yet it is annoying to give up.'

"Yes; but it can be put off. I told your highness that the house is taken for a year; we know the lady lodges on the first story. We have gained her maid, and have a key which opens the door: you may wait safely."

"You are sure that the door yielded?"

"Yes, at the third key I tried."

"Are you sure you shut it again?"

"Yes, monseigneur."

Aurilly did not feel sure, as he said, but he did not choose to admit it.

"Well, I will go; I shall return some other time." And the duke went away, promising to pay off the gentlemen for their interruption.

They had hardly disappeared, when the five companions saw approach a cavalier wrapped in a large cloak. The steps of his horse resounded on the frozen ground, and they went slowly and with precaution, for it was slippery.

"This time," said Quelus, "it is he."

"Impossible," said Maugiron.

"Why?"

"Because he is alone, and we left him with Livarot, Antragues, and Ribeirac, who would not have let him run such a risk."

"It is he, however; do you not recognize his insolent way of carrying his head?"

"Then," said D'O, "it is a snare."

"In any case, it is he; and so to arms!"

It was, indeed, Bussy, who came carelessly down the Rue St. Antoine, and followed the route given him by Quelus; he had, as we have seen, received the warning of St. Luc, and, in spite of it, had parted from his friends at the Hôtel Montmorency. It was one of those bravadoes delighted in by the valiant colonel, who said of himself, "I am but a simple gentleman, but I bear in my breast the heart of an emperor; and when I read in Plutarch the exploits of the ancient Romans, I think there is not one that I could not imitate." And besides, he thought that St. Luc, who was not ordinarily one of his friends, merely wished to get him laughed at for his precautions; and Bussy feared ridicule more than danger.

He had, even in the eyes of his enemies, earned a reputation for courage, which could only be sustained by the rashest adventures. Therefore, alone, and armed only with a sword and poniard, he advanced towards the house where waited for him no person, but simply a letter, which the Queen of Navarre sent him every month on the same day, and which he, according to his promise to the beautiful Marguerite, went to fetch himself, alone, and at night.

When he arrived at the Rue St. Catherine, his active eye discerned in the shade the forms of his adversaries. He counted them : "Three, four, five," said he, "without counting the lackeys, who are doubtless within call. They think much of me, it seems; all these for one man. That brave St. Luc did not deceive me; and were his even the first sword to pierce me I would cry, 'Thanks for your warning, friend.'" So saying, he continued to advance, only his arm held his sword under his cloak, of which he had unfastened the clasp.

It was then that Quelus cried, "To arms."

"Ah, gentlemen," said Bussy, "it appears you wish to kill me : I am the wild boar you had to hunt. Well, gentlemen, the wild boar will rip up a few of you; I swear it to you, and I never break my word."

"Possibly," said Schomberg; "but it is not right, M. Bussy d'Amboise, that you should be on horseback and we on foot." And as he spoke, the arm of the young man, covered with white satin, which glistened in the moonlight, came from under his cloak, and Bussy felt his horse give way under him. Schomberg had, with an address peculiar to himself, pierced the horse's leg with a kind of cutlass, of which the blade was heavier than the handle and which had remained in the wound. The animal gave a shrill cry and fell on his knees. Bussy, always ready, jumped at once to the ground, sword in hand.

"Ah!" cried he, "my favorite horse, you shall pay for this." And as Schomberg approached incautiously,

Bussy gave him a blow which broke his thigh. Schomberg uttered a cry.

"Well!" said Bussy, "have I kept my word? one already. It was the wrist of Bussy, and not his horse's leg, you should have cut."

In an instant, while Schomberg bound up his thigh with his handkerchief, Bussy presented the point of his long sword to his four other assailants, disdaining to cry for help, but retreating gradually, not to fly, but to gain a wall, against which to support himself, and prevent his being attacked behind, making all the while constant thrusts, and feeling sometimes that soft resistance of the flesh which showed that his blows had taken effect. Once he slipped for an instant. That instant sufficed for Quelus to give him a wound in the side.

"Touched," cried Quelus.

"Yes, in the doublet," said Bussy, who would not even acknowledge his hurt. And rushing on Quelus, with a vigorous effort, he made his sword fly from his hand. But he could not pursue his advantage, for D'O, D'Epernon, and Maugiron attacked him with fresh fury. Schomberg had bound his wound, and Quelus picked up his sword. Bussy made a bound backwards, and reached the wall. There he stopped, strong as Achilles, and smiling at the tempest of blows which rained around him. All at once he felt a cloud pass over his eyes. He had forgotten his wound, but these symptoms of fainting recalled it to him.

"Ah, you falter!" cried Quelus.

"Judge of it!" cried Bussy. And with the hilt of his sword he struck him on the temple. Quelus fell under the blow. Then furious—wild, he rushed forward, uttering a terrible cry. D'O and D'Epernon drew back, Maugiron was raising Quelus, when Bussy broke his sword with his foot, and wounded the right arm of D'Epernon. For a moment he was conqueror, but Quelus recovered himself, and four swords flashed again. Bussy felt himself lost. He gathered all his strength to retreat once more step by step. Already the perspiration was cold on his brow, and the ringing in his ears and the cloud over his eyes warned him that his strength was giving way. He sought for the wall with his left hand; to his astonishment, it yielded. It was a door not quite closed. Then he regained hope and strength for a last effort. For a second his blows were rapid and violent. Then he let himself glide inside the door, and pushed it to with a violent blow. It shut, and Bussy was saved. He heard the furious blows of his enemies on the door, their cries of rage, and wrathful imprecations. Then, the ground seemed to fail under his feet, and the walls to move. He made a few steps forward, and fell on the steps of a staircase. He knew no more, but seemed to descend into the silence and obscurity of the tomb.

CHAPTER III.

HOW IT IS SOMETIMES DIFFICULT TO DISTINGUISH A DREAM FROM THE REALITY.

BUSSY had had time, before falling, to pass his handkerchief under his shirt, and to buckle the belt of his sword over it, so as to make a kind of bandage to the open wound whence the blood flowed, but he had already lost blood enough to make him faint. However, during his fainting fit, this is what Bussy saw, or thought he saw. He found himself in a room with furniture of carved wood, with a tapestry of figures, and a painted ceiling. These figures, in all possible attitudes, holding flowers, carrying arms, seemed to him to be stepping from the walls. Between the two windows a portrait of a lady was hung. He, fixed to his bed, lay regarding all this. All at once the lady of the portrait seemed to move, and an adorable creature, clothed in a long white robe, with fair hair falling over her shoulders, and with eyes black as jet, with long lashes, and with a skin under which he seemed to see the blood circulate, advanced toward the bed. This woman was so beautiful, that Bussy made a violent effort to rise and throw himself at her feet. But he seemed to be confined in there by bonds like those which keep the dead body in the tomb, while the soul mounts to the skies. This forced him to look at the bed on which he was lying, and it seemed to him one of those magnificent beds sculptured in the reign of Francis I., to which were suspended hangings of white damask, embroidered in gold.

At the sight of this woman, the people of the wall and ceiling ceased to occupy his attention ; she was all to him, and he looked to see if she had left a vacancy in the frame. But suddenly she disappeared ; and an opaque body interposed itself between her and Bussy, moving slowly, and stretching its arms out as though it were playing blind-man's buff. Bussy felt in such a passion at this, that, had he been able, he would certainly have attacked this importunate vision ; but as he made a vain effort, the new-comer spoke :

"Well," said he, "have I arrived at last ? "

"Yes, monsieur," said a voice so sweet that it thrilled through Bussy, "and now you may take off your bandage."

Bussy made an effort to see if the sweet voice belonged to the lady of the portrait, but it was useless. He only saw the pleasant face of a young man, who had just, as he was told, taken off his bandage, and was looking curiously about him.

"To the devil with this man," thought Bussy, and he tried to speak, but fruitlessly.

"Ah, I understand now," said the young man, approaching the bed ; "you are wounded, are you not, my dear sir ? Well, we will try to cure you."

"Is the wound mortal ? " asked the sweet voice again, with a sad accent, which brought tears into the eyes of Bussy.

"I do not know yet, I am going to see ; meanwhile, he has fainted."

This was all Bussy heard, he seemed to feel a red-hot iron in his side, and then lost all consciousness. Afterwards, it was impossible for Bussy to fix the duration of this insensibility.

When he woke, a cold wind blew over his face, and harsh voices sounded in his ears ; he opened his eyes to see if it were the people of the tapestry speaking, and hoping to see the lady again, looked round him. But there was neither tapestry nor ceiling visible, and the portrait had also disappeared. He saw at his right only a man with a white apron spotted with blood ; at his left, a monk, who was raising his head ; and before him, an old woman mumbling her prayers. His wondering eyes next rested on a mass of stone before him, in which he recognized the Temple, and above that, the cold white sky, slightly tinted by the rising sun. He was in the street.

"Ah, thank you, good people," said he, "for the trouble you have taken in bringing me here. I wanted air, but you might have given it to me by opening the window, and I should have been better on my bed of white damask and gold than on the bare ground. But never mind, there is in my pocket, unless you have paid yourselves, which would have been prudent, some twenty golden crowns; take, my friends, take."

"But, my good gentleman," said the butcher, "we did not bring you here, but found you here as we passed."

"Ah, diable ! and the young doctor, was he here ?"

The bystanders looked at each other.

"It is the remains of delirium," said the monk. Then, turning to Bussy, "I think you would do well to confess," said he, "there was no doctor, poor young man ; you were here alone, and as cold as death."

Bussy then remembered having received a sword stroke, glided his hand under his doublet, and felt his handkerchief in the same place, fixed over his wound by his sword-belt.

"It is singular," said he.

Already profiting by his permission, the lookers-on were dividing his purse.

"Now, my friends," said he, "will you take me to my hôtel ?"

"Ah, certainly," said the old woman, "poor dear young man, the butcher is strong, and then he has his horse, on which you can ride."

"Yes, my gentleman, my horse and I are at your service."

"Nevertheless, my son," said the monk, "I think you would do well to confess."

"What are you called ?" asked Bussy.

"Brother Gorenflot."

"Well, Brother Gorenflot, I trust my hour has not yet arrived, and, as I am cold, I wish to get quickly home and warm myself."

"What is your hotel called ?"

"Hôtel de Bussy."

"How !" cried all, "you belong to M. de Bussy ?"

"I am M. de Bussy himself."

"Bussy," cried the butcher, "the brave Bussy, the scourge of the minions !"   And raising him, he was quickly carried home, whilst the monk went away, murmuring, "If it was that Bussy, I do not wonder he would not confess !"

When he got home, Bussy sent for his usual doctor, who found the wound not dangerous.

"Tell me," said Bussy, "has it not been already dressed?"

"Ma foi," said the doctor, "I am not sure."

"And was it serious enough to make me delirious ?"

"Certainly."

"Ah !" thought Bussy, "was that tapestry, that frescoed ceiling, that bed, the portrait between the windows, the beautiful blonde woman with black eyes, the doctor blindfolded, was this all delirium ? Is nothing true but my combat ? Where did I fight ? Ah, yes, I remember ; near the Bastile, by the Rue St. Paul. I leaned against a door, and it opened ; I shut it—and then I remember no more. Have I dreamed or not ? And my horse ! My horse must have been found dead on the place. Doctor, pray call some one."

The doctor called a valet. Bussy inquired, and heard that the animal, bleeding and mutilated, had dragged itself to the door of the hotel, and had been found there.

"It must have been a dream," thought he again : "how should a portrait come down from the wall and talk to a doctor with a bandage on his eyes ? I am a fool ; and yet when I remember she was so charming," and he began to

describe her beauties, till he cried out, " It is impossible
it should have been a dream ; and yet I found myself in
the street, and a monk kneeling by me.   Doctor," said he,
" shall I have to keep the house a fortnight again for this
scratch, as I did for the last ? "

" We shall see ; can you walk ? "

" I seem to have quicksilver in my legs."

" Try."

Bussy jumped out of bed, and walked quickly round his
room.

" That will do," said the doctor, " provided that you do
not go on horseback, or walk ten miles the first day."

" Capital ! you are a doctor ; however, I have seen
another to-night.   Yes, I saw him, and if ever I meet him,
I should know him."

" I advise you not to seek for him, monsieur ; one has
always a little fever after a sword wound ; you should know
that, who have had a dozen."

" Ah, mon Dieu ! " cried Bussy, struck with a new
idea, " did my dream begin outside the door instead of
inside ?   Was there no more a staircase and a passage, than
there was a bed with white and gold damask, and a portrait ?
Perhaps those wretches, thinking me dead, carried me to
the Temple, to divert suspicion, should any one have seen
them hiding.   Certainly, it must be so, and I have dreamed
the rest.   Mon Dieu ! if they have procured for me this
dream which torments me so, I swear to make an end of
them all."

" My dear seigneur," said the doctor, " if you wish to
get well, you must not agitate yourself thus."

" Except St. Luc," continued Bussy, without attending ;
" he acted as a friend, and my first visit shall be to him."

" Not before five this evening."

" If you wish it ; but, I assure you, it is not going out
and seeing people which will make me ill, but staying
quietly at home."

" Well, it is possible ; you are always a singular patient ;
act as you please, only I recommend you not to get another
wound before this one is healed."

Bussy promised to do his best to avoid it, and, after dressing, called for his litter to take him to the Hôtel Montmorency.

CHAPTER IV.

HOW MADAME DE ST. LUC HAD PASSED THE NIGHT.

LOUIS DE CLERMONT, commonly called Bussy d'Amboise, was a perfect gentleman, and a very handsome man. Kings and princes had sought for his friendship ; queens and princesses had lavished on him their sweetest smiles. He had succeeded La Mole in the affections of Queen Marguerite, who had committed for him so many follies, that even her husband, insensible so long, was moved at them ; and the Duke François would never have pardoned him, had it not gained over Bussy to his interests, and once again he sacrificed all to his ambition. But in the midst of all his successes of war, ambition, and intrigue, he had remained insensible ; and he who had never known fear, had never either known love.

When the servants of M. de St. Luc saw Bussy enter, they ran to tell M. de Brissac.

" Is M. de St. Luc at home ? " asked Bussy.

" No, monsieur."

" Where shall I find him ? "

" I do not know, monsieur. We are all very anxious about him, for he has not returned since yesterday."

" Nonsense."

" It is true, monsieur."

" But Madame de St. Luc ? "

" Oh, she is here."

" Tell her I shall be charmed if she will allow me to pay my respects to her."

Five minutes after, the messenger returned, saying Madame de St. Luc would be glad to see M. de Bussy.

When Bussy entered the room, Jeanne ran to meet him. She was very pale, and her jet black hair made her look more so ; her eyes were red from her sleepless night, and there were traces of tears on her cheeks.

"You are welcome, M. de Bussy," said she, "in spite of the fears your presence awakens."

"What do you mean, madame ? how can I cause you fear ?"

"Ah ! there was a meeting last night between you and M. de St. Luc ? confess it."

"Between me and St. Luc !"

"Yes, he sent me away to speak to you ; you belong to the Duc d'Anjou, he to the king. You have quarrelled— do not hide it from me. You must understand my anxiety. He went with the king, it is true—but afterwards ?"

"Madame, this is marvelous. I expected you to ask after my wound——"

"He wounded you ; he did fight, then ?"

"No, madame ; not with me at least ; it was not he who wounded me. Indeed, he did all he could to save me. Did he not tell you so ?"

"How could he tell me ? I have not seen him."

"You have not seen him ? Then your porter spoke the truth."

"I have not seen him since eleven last night."

"But where can he be ?"

"I should rather ask you."

"Oh, pardieu, tell me about it, it is very droll."

The poor woman looked at him with astonishment.

"No, it is very sad, I mean. I have lost much blood, and scarcely know what I am saying. Tell me this lamentable story, madame."

Jeanne told all she knew ; how the king had carried him off, the shutting of the doors of the Louvre, and the message of the guards.

"Ah ! very well, I understand," said Bussy.

"How ! you understand."

"Yes ; his majesty took him to the Louvre and once there he could not come out again."

"And why not ?"

"Ah ! that is a state secret."

" But my father went to the Louvre, and I also, and the guards said they did not know what we meant."

" All the more reason that he should be there."

" You think so ? "

" I am sure of it, and if you wish to be so also——"

" How ? "

" By seeing."

" Can I ? "

" Certainly."

" But if I go there, they will send me away, as they did before."

" Would you like to go in ? "

" But if he is not there ? "

" I tell you he is there. Come; but they will not let in the wife of St. Luc."

" You laugh at me, and it is very cruel in my distress."

" No, dear lady, listen. You are young, you are tall, and have black eyes; you are like my youngest page, who looked so well in the cloth of gold yesterday."

" Ah ! what folly, M. Bussy," cried Jeanne, blushing.

" I have no other method but this. If you wish to see St. Luc——"

" Oh ! I would give all the world to see him."

" Well, I promise that you shall without giving anything."

" Oh, but——"

" I told you how."

" Well, I will do it; shall I send for the dress ? "

" No, I will send you a new one I have at home; then you must join me this evening at the Rue St. Honoré. and we will go togeth r to the Louvre." Jeanne began to laugh, and gave her hand to Bussy.

" Pardon my suspicions," said she.

" Willingly," and taking leave he went home to prepare.

Bussy and Madame de St. Luc met at the appointed time; Jeanne looked beautiful in her disguise. At the end of the Rue St. Germain-l'Auxerrois they met a large party in which Bussy recognized the Duc d' Anjou and his train.

"Ah," said he, "we will make a triumphal entry into the Louvre."

"Eh! monseigneur," cried he to the duke.

The prince turned. "You, Bussy!" cried he joyfully, "I heard you were badly wounded, and I was going to your hotel."

"Ma foi, monseigneur, if I am not dead, it is thanks to no one but myself. You got me into nice situations; that ball at St. Luc's was a regular snare, and they have nearly drained all the blood out of my body."

"They shall pay for it, Bussy; they shall pay dearly."

"Yes, you say so," said Bussy, with his usual liberty, "and you will smile on the first you meet."

"Well! accompany me to the Louvre, and you shall see."

"What shall I see, monseigneur?"

"How I will speak to my brother."

"You promise me reparation?"

"I promise you shall be content. You hesitate still, I believe."

"Monseigneur, I know you so well."

"Come, I tell you."

"This is good for you," whispered Bussy to Jeanne. "There will be a quarrel between the brothers, and meanwhile you can find St. Luc."

"Well," said he to the prince, "I follow you; if I am insulted, at least I can always revenge myself."

And he took his place near the duke, while his page kept close to him.

"Revenge yourself; no, Bussy," said the prince, "I charge myself with it. I know your assassins," added he, in a low tone.

"What! your highness has taken the trouble to inquire?"

"I saw them."

"How so?" cried Bussy, astonished.

"Oh! I had business myself at the Porte St. Antoine. They barely missed killing me in your place. Ah! I did not know it was you they were waiting for, or else——"

" Well ?"

" Had you this new page with you ?" asked the prince, without finishing his sentence.

" No, I was alone, and you ?"

" I had Aurilly with me ; and why were you alone ?"

" Because I wish to preserve my name of the brave Bussy."

" And they wounded you ?"

" I do not wish to give them the pleasure of knowing it, but I had a severe wound in the side."

" Ah ! the wretches ; Aurilly said he was sure they were bent on mischief."

" How ! you saw the ambush, you were with Aurilly, who uses his sword as well as his lute, you thought they had bad intentions, and you did not watch to give aid ?"

" I did not know who they were waiting for."

" Mort diable ! when you saw the king's friends, you might have known it was against some friends of yours. Now, as there is hardly any one but myself who has courage to be your friend, you might have guessed that it was I."

" Oh ! perhaps you are right, my dear Bussy, but I did not think of all that."

When they entered, " Remember your promise," said Bussy, " I have some one to speak to."

" You leave me, Bussy ?"

" Yes, I must, but if I hear a great noise I will come to you, so speak loud."

Then Bussy, followed by Jeanne, took a secret staircase, traversed two or three corridors, and arrived at an ante-chamber.

" Wait here for me," said he to Jeanne.

" Ah, mon Dieu ! you leave me alone."

" I must, to provide for your entrance."

CHAPTER V.

HOW MADAME DE ST. LUC PASSED THE SECOND NIGHT OF HER MARRIAGE.

BUSSY went straight to the sleeping-room of the king. There were in it two beds of velvet and satin, pictures, relics, perfumed sachets from the East, and a collection of beautiful swords. Bussy knew the king was not there, as his brother had asked to see him, but he knew that there was next to it a little room which was occupied in turn by all the king's favorites, and which he now expected to find occupied by St. Luc, whom the king in his great affection had carried off from his wife. Bussy knocked at the ante-chamber common to the two rooms. The captain of the guards opened.

"M. de Bussy!" cried he.

"Yes, myself, dear M. de Nancey; the king wishes to speak to M. de St. Luc."

"Very well, tell M. de St. Luc the king wants him."

"What is he doing?"

"He is with Chicot, waiting for the king's return from his brother."

"Will you permit my page to wait here?"

"Willingly, monsieur."

"Enter, Jean," said Bussy, and he pointed to the em-brasure of a window, where she went to hide herself. St. Luc entered, and M. de Nancey retired.

"What does the king want now?" cried St. Luc, angrily; "ah! it is you, M. de Bussy."

"I, and before everything, let me thank you for the service you rendered me."

"Ah! it was quite natural; I could not bear to see a brave gentleman assassinated: I thought you killed."

"It did not want much to do it, but I got off with a wound, which I think I repaid with interest to Schomberg and D'Epernon. As for Quelus, he may thank the bones of his head : they are the hardest I ever knew."

"Ah ! tell me about it, it will amuse me a little."

"I have no time now, I come for something else. You are ennuyé——"

"To death."

"And a prisoner ?"

"Completely. The king pretends no one can amuse him but mo. He is very good, for since yesterday I have made more grimaces than his ape, and been more rude than his jester."

"Well, it is my turn to render you a service : can I do it ?"

"Yes, go to the Marshal de Brissac's, and reassure my poor little wife, who must be very uneasy, and must think my conduct very strange."

"What shall I say to her ?"

"Morbleu ! tell her what you see ; that I am a prisoner, and that the king talks to me of friendship like Cicero, who wrote on it ; and of virtue like Socrates, who practised it. It is in vain I tell him I am ungrateful for the first, and incredulous as to the last : he only repeats it over again."

"Is that all I can do for you ?"

"Ah, mon Dieu ! I fear so."

"Then it is done."

"How so ?"

"I guessed all this, and told your wife so."

"And what did she say ?"

"At first she would not believe ; but I trust now," continued he, glancing towards the window, "she will yield to evidence. Ask me something more difficult."

"Then, bring here the griffin of Signor Astolfo, and let me mount en croupe, and go to my wife."

"A more simple thing would be to take the griffin to your wife and bring her here."

"Here !"

"Yes, here."

"To the Louvre, that would be droll."

"I should think so. Then you would be ennuyé no longer ?"

"Ma foi! no , but if this goes on much longer, I believe I shall kill myself."

"Well! shall I give you my page ?"

"To me ?"

"Yes, he is a wonderful lad."

"Thank you, but I detest pages."

"Bah! try him."

"Bussy, you mock me."

"Let me leave him."

"No."

"I tell you, you will like him."

"No, no, a hundred times, no."

"Hola, page, come here."

Jeanne came forward, blushing.

"Oh !" cried St. Luc, recognizing her, in astonishment.

"Well ! shall I send him away ? "

"No, no. Ah Bussy, I owe you an eternal friendship."

"Take care, you cannot be heard, but you can be seen."

"It is true," said St. Luc, retreating from his wife.

Indeed, M. de Nancey was beginning to wonder what was going on, when a great noise was heard from the gallery.

"Ah ! mon Dieu !" cried M. de Nancey, "there is the king quarreling with some one."

"I really think so," replied Bussy, affecting inquietude; "can it be with the Duc d'Anjou, who came with me ?"

The captain of the guard went off in the direction of the gallery.

"Have I not managed well ? " said Bussy to St. Luc.

"What is it ?"

"M. d'Anjou and the king are quarrelling ; I must go to them. You profit by the time to place in safety the page I have brought you ; is it possible ? "

"Oh, yes ; luckily I declared I was ill and must keep my room."

"In that case, adieu, madame, and remember me in your prayers." And Bussy went off to the gallery, where the king, red with fury, swore to the duke, who was pale with anger, that in the scene of the preceding night Bussy was the aggressor.

"I affirm to you, sire," cried the duke, "that D'Epernon, Schomberg and Quelus were waiting for him at the Hôtel des Tournelles."

"Who told you so?"

"I saw them with my own eyes."

"In that darkness! The night was pitch dark."

"I knew their voices."

"They spoke to you?"

"They did more, they took me for Bussy, and attacked me."

"You?"

"Yes, I."

"And what were you doing there?"

"What does that matter to you?"

"I wish to know; I am curious to-day."

"I was going to Manasses."

"A Jew?"

"You go to Ruggieri, a poisoner."

"I go where I like: I am the king. Besides, as I said, Bussy was the aggressor."

"Where?"

"At St. Luc's ball."

"Bussy provoked five men? No, no, he is brave, but he is not mad."

"Par la mordieu! I tell you I heard him. Besides, he has wounded Schomberg in the thigh, D'Epernon in the arm, and half killed Quelus."

"Ah! really I did not know; I compliment him on it."

"I will make example of this brawler."

"And I, whom your friends attack, in his person and in my own, will know if I am your brother, and if——"

At this moment Bussy, dressed in pale-green satin, entered the room.

"Sire!" said he, "receive my humble respects."

3

"Pardieu! here he is," cried Henri.

"Your majesty, it seems, was doing me the honor of speaking of me."

"Yes, and I am glad to see that, in spite of what they told me, your look shows good health."

"Sire, blood drawn improves the complexion, so mine ought to be good this morning."

"Well, since they have wounded you, complain, and I will do you justice."

"I complain of nothing, sire."

Henri looked astonished. "What did you say?" said he to the duke.

"I said that Bussy had received a wound in his side."

"Is it true, Bussy?"

"The first prince of the blood would not lie, sire."

"And yet you do not complain?"

"I shall never complain, sire, until they cut off my right-hand, and prevent my revenging myself, and then I will try to do it with the left."

"Insolent," murmured Henri.

"Sire," said the duke, "do justice; we ask no better. Order an inquiry, name judges, and let it be proved who prepared the ambush and the intended murder."

Henri reddened. "No," said he, "I prefer this time to be ignorant where the wrong lies, and to pardon every one. I wish these enemies to make peace, and I am sorry that Schomberg and D'Epernon are kept at home by their wounds. Say, M. d'Anjou, which do you call the most forward to fight of all my friends, as you say you saw them?"

"Sire, it was Quelus."

"Ma foi! yes," said Quelus, "his highness is right."

"Then," said Henri, "let MM. Bussy and Quelus make peace in the name of all."

"Oh! Oh!" said Quelus," what does that mean, sire?"

"It means that you are to embrace here, before me."

Quelus frowned.

"Ah, signor," cried Bussy, imitating a pantaloon, "will you not do me this favor?"

Even the king laughed. Then, approaching Quelus,

Bussy threw his arms round his neck, saying, "The king wishes it."

"I hope it engages us to nothing," whispered Quelus.

"Be easy," answered Bussy, "we will meet soon."

Quelus drew back in a rage, and Bussy, making a pirouette, went out of the gallery.

CHAPTER VI.

LE PETIT COUCHER OF HENRI III.

AFTER this scene, beginning in tragedy and ending in comedy, the king, still angry, went to his room, followed by Chicot, who asked for his supper.

"I am not hungry," said the king.

"It is possible, but I am."

The king did not seem to hear. He unclasped his cloak, took off his cap, and, advancing to the passage which led to St. Luc's room, said to Chicot, "Wait here for me till I return."

"Oh! do not be in a hurry," said Chicot. No sooner was the king gone, than Chicot opened the door and called "Hola!"

A valet came. "The king has changed his mind," said Chicot, "he wishes a good supper here for himself and St. Luc, above all, plenty of wine, and despatch."

The valet went to execute the orders, which he believed to be the king's. Henri meanwhile had passed into St. Luc's room. He found him in bed, having prayers read to him by an old servant who had followed him to the Louvre, and shared his captivity. In a corner, on an armchair, his head buried in his hands, slept the page.

"Who is that young man?" asked the king.

"Did not your majesty authorize me to send for a page."

"Yes, doubtless."

"Well, I have profited by it."

"Oh!"

"Does your majesty repent of having allowed me this little indulgence?"

"No, no, on the contrary, amuse yourself, my son. How are you?"

"Sire, I have a fever."

"Really, your face is red; let me feel your pulse, I am half a doctor."

St. Luc held out his hand with visible ill-humor.

"Oh!" said the king, "intermittent—agitated."

"Yes, sire, I am very ill."

"I will send you my doctor."

"Thank you, sire, but I hate Miron."

"I will watch you myself. You shall have a bed in my room, and we will talk all night."

"Oh!" cried St Luc, "you see me ill, and you want to keep me from sleeping. That is a singular way to treat your patient, doctor."

"But you cannot be left alone, suffering as you are."

"Sire, I have my page, Jean."

"But he sleeps."

"That is what I like best, then he will not disturb me."

"Well, come and assist at my going to bed."

"Then I shall be free to come back to bed?"

"Perfectly."

"Well, so be it. But I shall make a bad courtier, I assure you; I am dying with sleep."

"You shall yawn at your case."

"Sire, if your majesty will leave me, I will be with you in five minutes."

"Well, then, five minutes, but no longer."

As soon as the door was shut, the page jumped up. "Ah! St. Luc," cried she, "you are going to leave me again. Mon Dieu! I shall die of fright here, if they discover me."

"My dear Jeanne, Gaspard here will protect you."

"Had I not better go back?"

"If you really wish it, Jeanne," said St. Luc, sadly, "you shall. But if you are as good as you are beautiful, if you have any feeling in your heart for me, you will wait here a little. I shall suffer so much from my head and nerves that the king will not long keep so sad a companion."

"Go, then," said Jeanne, "and I will wait."

"My dear Jeanne, you are adorable. Trust me to returns as soon as possible. Besides, I have an idea, which I will tell you when I return."

"An idea which will restore your liberty?"

"I hope so."

"Then go."

"Gaspard," said St. Luc, "prevent any one from entering here, and in a quarter of an hour lock the door, and bring me the key to the king's room. Then go home, and tell them not to be uneasy about Madame la Comtesse, and come back to-morrow."

Then St. Luc kissed his wife's hand, and went to the king, who was already growing impatient. Jeanne, alone and trembling, hid behind the curtains of the bed. When St. Luc entered he found the king amidst a perfect carpet of flowers, of which the stalks had been cut off—roses, jasmine, violets, and wall-flowers, in spite of the severe weather, formed an odorous carpet for Henry III. The chamber, of which the roof was painted, had in it two beds, one of which was so large as to occupy a third of the room. It was hung with gold and silk tapestry, representing mythological figures and the windows had curtains to match. From the center of the ceiling hung, suspended by a golden chain, a silver gilt lamp, in which burned a perfumed oil. At the side of the bed was a golden satyr, holding in his hand a candelabrum, containing four rose-color wax candles, also perfumed.

The king, with his naked feet resting on the flowers, was seated on a chair of ebony inlaid with gold; he had on his knees seven or eight young spaniels, who were licking his hands. Two servants were curling his hair, his mustachios, and beard, a third was covering his face with a kind of cream, which had a most delightful scent.

"Here," cried Chicot, "the grease and the combs, I will try them too."

"Chicot," said Henri, "your skin is too dry, and will

use too much cream, and your beard is so hard, it will break my combs. Well, my son," said he, turning to St. Luc, "how is your head?"

St. Luc put his hand to his head and groaned.

"Imagine!" continued Henri, "I have seen Bussy d'Amboise."

"Bussy!" cried St. Luc, trembling.

"Yes, those fools! five of them attacked him, and let him escape. If you had been there, St. Luc——"

"I should probably have been like the others."

"Oh! no, I wager you are as good as Bussy. We will try to-morrow."

"Sire, I am too ill for anything."

Henri, hearing a singular noise, turned round, and saw Chicot eating up all the supper that had been brought for two.

"What the devil are you doing, M. Chicot?" cried Henri.

"Taking my cream internally, since you will not allow me to do it outwardly."

"Go and fetch my captain of the guards," said Henri.

"What for?" asked Chicot, emptying a porcelain cup of chocolate.

"To pass his sword through your body."

"Ah! let him come, we shall see!" cried Chicot, putting himself in such a comical attitude of defense that every one laughed.

"But I am hungry," cried the king; "and the wretch has eaten up all the supper."

"You are capricious, Henri; I offered you supper and you refused. However, your bouillon is left; I am no longer hungry, and I am going to bed."

"And I also," said St. Luc, "for I can stand no longer."

"Stay, St. Luc," said the king, "take these," and he offered him a handful of little dogs.

"What for?"

"To sleep with you; they will take your illness from you."

"Thanks, sire," said St. Luc, putting them back in their basket, "but I have no confidence in your receipt."

"I will come and visit you in the night, St. Luc."

"Pray do not, sire, you will only disturb me," and saluting the king, he went away. Chicot had already disappeared, and there only remained with the king the valets, who covered his face with a mask of fine cloth, plastered with the perfumed cream, in which were holes for the eyes, nose, and mouth ; a cap of silk and silver fixed it on the forehead and ears. They next covered his arms with sleeves made of wadded silk, and then presented him with kid gloves, also greased inside.

These mysteries of the royal toilet finished, they presented to him his soup in a golden cup. Then Henri said a prayer, a short one that night, and went to bed.

When settled there, he ordered them to carry away the flowers, which were beginning to make the air sickly, and to open the window for a moment. Then the valet closed the doors and curtains, and called in Narcissus, the king's favorite dog, who, jumping on the bed, settled himself at once on the king's feet. The valet next put out the wax-lights, lowered the lamp, and went out softly.

Already, more tranquil and nonchalant than the lazy monks of his kingdom in their fat abbeys, the King of France no longer remembered that there was a France.—He slept.

Every noise was hushed, and one might have heard a bat fly in the somber corridors of the Louvre.

CHAPTER VII.

HOW, WITHOUT ANY ONE KNOWING WHY, THE KING WAS CONVERTED BEFORE THE NEXT DAY.

THREE hours passed thus.

Suddenly, a terrible cry was heard, which came from the king's room.

All the lights in his room were out, and no sound was to be heard except this strange call of the king's. For it was he who had cried.

Soon was heard the noise of furniture falling, porcelain breaking, steps running about the room, and the barking of dogs—mingled with new cries. Almost instantly lights burned, swords shone in the galleries, and the heavy steps of the Guards were heard.

" To arms !" cried all, " the king calls."

And the captain of the guard, the colonel of the Swiss, and some attendants, rushed into the king's room with flambeaux.

Near an overturned chair, broken cups, and disordered bed, stood Henri, looking terrified and grotesque in his night-dress. His right hand was extended, trembling like a leaf in the wind, and his left held his sword, which he had seized mechanically.

He appeared dumb through terror, and all the spectators, not daring to break the silence, waited with the utmost anxiety.

Then appeared, half dressed and wrapped in a large cloak, the young queen, Louise de Lorraine, blonde and gentle, who led the life of a saint upon earth, and who had been awakened by her husband's cries.

" Sire," cried she, also trembling, " what is the matter ? Mon Dieu ! I heard your cries, and I came."

" It—it is nothing," said the king, without moving his eyes, which seemed to be looking in the air for some form invisible to all but him.

" But your majesty cried out ; is your majesty suffering ?" asked the queen.

Terror was so visibly painted on the king's countenance, that it began to gain on the others.

" Oh, sire !" cried the queen again, " in Heaven's name do not leave us in this suspense. Will you have a doctor ? "

" A doctor, no," cried Henri, in the same tone, " the body is not ill, it is the mind ; no doctor—a confessor."

Every one looked round ; nowhere was there to be seen any traces of what had so terrified the king. However, a confessor was sent for ; Joseph Foulon, superior of the convent of St. Généviève, was torn from his bed, to come to the king. With the confessor, the tumult ceased, and silence was reestablished ; every one conjectured and wondered—the king was confessing.

The next day the king rose early, and began to read prayers, then he ordered all his friends to be sent for. They sent to St. Luc, but he was more suffering than ever. His sleep, or rather his lethargy, had been so profound, that he alone had heard nothing of the tumult in the night, although he slept so near. He begged to be left in bed. At this deplorable recital, Henri crossed himself, and sent him a doctor.

Then he ordered that all the scourges from the convent should be brought to him, and, going to his friends, distributed them, ordering them to scourge each other as hard as they could.

D'Epernon said that as his right arm was in a sling, and he could not return the blows he received, he ought to be exempt, but the king replied that that would only make it the more acceptable to God.

He himself set the example. He took off his doublet, waistcoat, and shirt, and struck himself like a martyr. Chicot tried to laugh, as usual, but was warned by a terrible look, that this was not the right time, and he was forced to take a scourge like the others.

All at once the king left the room, telling them to wait for him. Immediately the blows ceased, only Chicot continued to strike D'O, whom he hated, and D'O returned it as well as he could. It was a duel with whips.

The king went to the queen, gave her a pearl necklace worth 25,000 crowns, and kissed her, which he had not done for a year. Then he asked her to put off her royal ornaments and put on a sack.

Louise, always good, consented, but asked why her husband gave her a necklace, and yet made such a request.

"For my sins," replied he.

The queen said no more, for she knew, better than any one, how many he had to repent of.

Henri returned, which was a signal for the flagellation to recommence. In ten minutes the queen arrived, with her sack on her shoulders. Then tapers were distributed

to all the court, and barefooted, through the snow, all the
courtiers and fine ladies went to Montmartre, shivering.
At five o'clock the promenade was over, the convents had
received rich presents, the feet of all the court were swollen,
and the backs of the courtiers sore. There had been tears,
cries, prayers, incense, and psalms. Every one had suffered, without knowing why the king, who danced the
night before, scourged himself to-day. As for Chicot, he
had escaped at the Porte Montmartre, and, with Brother
Gorenflot, had entered a public-house, where he had eaten
and drank. Then he had rejoined the procession and returned to the Louvre.

In the evening the king, fatigued with his fast and his
exercise, ordered himself a light supper, had his shoulders
washed, and then went to visit St. Luc.

"Ah!" cried he, "God has done well to render life so
bitter."

"Why so, sire?"

"Because then man, instead of fearing death, longs
for it."

"Speak for yourself, sire, I do not long for it at all."

"Listen, St. Luc, will you follow my example?"

"If I think it a good one."

"I will leave my throne, and you your wife, and we will
enter a cloister. I will call myself Brother Henri——"

"Pardon, sire, if you do not care for your crown, of
which you are tired, I care very much for my wife, whom
I know so little. Therefore I refuse."

"Oh! you are better."

"Infinitely better, sire; I feel quite joyous, and disposed
for happiness and pleasure."

"Poor St. Luc!" cried the king, clasping his hands.

"You should have asked me yesterday, sire, then I was
ill and cross. I would have thrown myself into a well for
a trifle. But this evening it is quite a different thing. I
have passed a good night and a charming day. Mordieu,
vive la joie!"

"You swear, St. Luc."

"Did I, sire? but I think you swear sometimes."

"I have sworn, St. Luc, but I shall swear no more."

"I cannot say that ; I will not swear more than I can help, and God is merciful."

"You think He will pardon me ?"

"Oh ! I speak for myself, not for you, sire. You have sinned as a king, I as a private man, and we shall, I trust, be differently judged."

The king sighed. "St. Luc," said he, "will you pass the night in my room ?"

"Why, what should we do ?"

"We will light all the lamps, I will go to bed, and you shall read prayers to me."

"No, thank you, sire."

"You will not ?"

"On no account."

"You abandon me, St. Luc !"

"No, I will stay with your majesty, if you will send for music and ladies, and have a dance."

"Oh, St. Luc, St. Luc !"

"I am wild to-night, sire, I want to dance and drink."

"St. Luc," said the king, solemnly, "do you ever dream ?"

"Often, sire."

"You believe in dreams ?"

"With reason."

"How so ?"

"Dreams console for the reality. Last night I had a charming dream."

"What was it ?"

"I dreamed that my wife——"

"You still think of your wife ?"

"More than ever, sire ; well, I dreamed that she, with her charming face —for she is pretty, sire——"

"So was Eve, who ruined us all."

"Well, my wife had procured wings and the form of a bird, and so, braving locks and bolts, she passed over the walls of the Louvre, and came to my window, crying, "Open, St. Luc, open, my husband."

"And you opened ?"

"I should think so."

"Worldly."

"As you please, sire."

"Then you woke?"

"No, indeed, the dream was too charming; and I hope to-night to dream again; therefore I refuse your majesty's obliging offer. If I sit up, let me at least have something to pay me for losing my dream. If your majesty will do as I said——"

"Enough, St. Luc. I trust Heaven will send you a dream to-night which will lead you to repentance."

"I doubt it, sire, and I advise you to send away this libertine St. Luc, who is resolved not to amend."

"No, no, I hope, before to-morrow, grace will have touched you as it has me. Good night, I will pray for you."

CHAPTER VIII.

HOW THE KING WAS AFRAID OF BEING AFRAID.

WHEN the king left St. Luc, he found the court, according to his orders, in the great gallery. Then he gave D'O, D' Epernon and Schomberg an order to retire into the provinces, threatened Quelus and Maugiron to punish them if they quarreled any more with Bussy, to whom he gave his hand to kiss, and then embraced his brother François.

As for the queen, he was prodigal in politeness to her.

When the usual time for retiring approached, the king seemed trying to retard it. At last ten o'clock struck.

"Come with me, Chicot," then said he, "good night, gentlemen."

"Good night, gentlemen," said Chicot, "we are going to bed. I want my barber, my hairdresser, my valet de chambre, and, above all, my cream."

"No," said the king, "I want none of them to-night; Lent is going to begin."

"I regret the cream," said Chicot.

The king and Chicot entered the room, which we already know.

"Ah ça! Henri," said Chicot, "I am the favorite to-night. Am I handsomer than that Cupid, Quelus?"

"Silence, Chicot, and you, gentlemen of the toilette, go out."

They obeyed, and the king and Chicot were left alone.

"Why do you send them away?" asked Chicot, "they have not greased us yet. Are you going to grease me with your own royal hand? It would be an act of humility."

"Let us pray," said Henri.

"Thank you, that is not amusing. If that be what you called me here for, I prefer to return to the bad company I have left. Adieu, my son. Good night."

"Stay," said the king.

"Oh! this is tyranny. You are a despot, a Phalaris, a Dionysius. All day you have made me tear the shoulders of my friends with cow-hide, and now we are to begin again. Do not let us do it, Henri, when there's but two, every blow tells."

"Hold your tongue, miserable chatterer, and think of repentance."

"I repent! And of what? Of being jester to a monk. Confiteor—I repent, mea culpa, it is a great sin."

"No sacrilege, wretch."

"Ah! I would rather be shut up in a cage with lions and apes, than with a mad king. Adieu, I am going."

The king locked the door.

"Henri, you look sinister; if you do not let me go, I will cry, I will call, I will break the window, I will kick down the door."

"Chicot," said the king, in a melancholy tone, "you abuse my sadness."

"Ah! I understand, you are afraid to be alone. Tyrants always are so. Take my long sword, and let me take the scabbard to my room."

At the word "afraid," Henri shuddered, and he looked nervously around, and seemed so agitated and grew so pale, that Chicot began to think him really ill, and said,—

"Come, my son, what is the matter, tell your troubles to your friend Chicot."

The king looked at him and said, " Yes, you are my friend, my only friend."

"There is," said Chicot, "the abbey of Valency vacant."

"Listen, Chicot, you are discreet."

"There is also that of Pithiviers, where they make such good pies."

"In spite of your buffooneries, you are a brave man."

"Then do not give me an abbey, give me a regiment."

"And even a wise one."

"Then do not give me a regiment, make me a counselor ; but no, when I think of it, I should prefer a regiment, for I should be always forced to be of the king's opinion."

"Hold your tongue, Chicot, the terrible hour approaches."

" Ah ! you are beginning again."

" You will hear."

" Hear what ? "

" Wait, and the event will show you. Chicot, you are brave ! "

"I boast of it, but I do not wish to try. Call your captain of the guard, your Swiss, and let me go away from this invisible danger."

" Chicot, I command you to stay."

" On my word, a nice master. I am afraid, I tell you. Help ! "

" Well, drôle, if I must, I will tell you all."

" Ah ! " cried Chicot, drawing his sword, " once warned, I do not care ; tell, my son, tell. Is it a crocodile ? my sword is sharp, for I use it every week to cut my corns." And Chicot sat down in the armchair with his drawn sword between his legs.

"Last night," said Henri, "I slept——" ·

" And I also," said Chicot.

"Suddenly a breath swept over my face."

" It was the dog, who was hungry, and who licked your cream."

"I half woke, and felt my beard bristle with terror under my mask."

"Ah! you make me tremble deliciously."

"Then," continued the king, in a trembling voice, "then a voice sounded through the room, with a doleful vibration."

"The voice of the crocodile! I have read in Marco Polo, that the crocodile has a voice like the crying of children; but be easy, my son, for if it comes, we will kill it."

"'Listen! miserable sinner,' said the voice——"

"Oh! it spoke; then it was not a crocodile."

"'Miserable sinner,' said the voice, 'I am the angel of God.'"

"The angel of God!"

"Ah! Chicot, it was a frightful voice."

"Was it like the sound of a trumpet?"

"'Are you there?' continued the voice, 'do you hear, hardened sinner; are you determined to persevere in your iniquities?'"

"Ah, really; he said very much the same as other people, it seems to me."

"Then, Chicot, followed many other reproaches, which I assure you were most painful."

"But tell me what he said, that I may see if he was well informed?"

"Impious! do you doubt?"

"I? all that astonishes me is, that he waited so long to reproach you. So, my son, you were dreadfully afraid?"

"Oh, yes, the marrow seemed to dry in my bones."

"It is quite natural; on my word, I do not know what I should have done in your place. And then you called?"

"Yes."

"And they came?"

"Yes."

"And there was no one here?"

"No one."

"It is frightful."

"So frightful, that I sent for my confessor."

"And he came?"

" Immediately."

" Now, be frank, my son ; tell the truth for once. What did he think of your revelation ? "

" He shuddered."

" I should think so."

" He ordered me to repent, as the voice told me."

" Very well. There can be no harm in repenting. But what did he think of the vision ? "

" That it was a miracle, and that I must think of it seriously. Therefore, this morning——"

" What have you done "

" I gave 100,000 livres to the Jesuits."

" Very well."

" And scourged myself and my friends."

" Perfect ! but after ? "

" Well, what do you think of it, Chicot ? It is not to the jester I speak, but to the man of sense, to my friend."

" Ah, sire, I think your majesty had the nightmare."

" You think so ? "

" Yes, it was a dream, which will not be renewed, unless your majesty thinks too much about it."

" A dream ? No, Chicot, I was awake, my eyes were open."

" I sleep like that."

" Yes, but then you do not see, and I saw the moon shining through my windows, and its light on the amethyst in the hilt of my sword, which lay in that chair where you are."

" And the lamp ? "

" Had gone out."

" A dream, my son."

" Why do you not believe, Chicot ? It is said that God speaks to kings, when He wishes to effect some change on the earth."

" Yes, he speaks, but so low that they never hear Him."

" Well, do you know why I made you stay ?—that you might hear as well as I."

" No one would believe me if I said I heard it."

"My friend, it is a secret which I confide to your known fidelity."

"Well, I accept. Perhaps it will also speak to me."

"Well, what must I do?"

"Go to bed, my son."

"But——"

"Do you think that sitting up will keep it away?"

"Well, then, you remain."

"I said so."

"Well, then, I will go to bed."

"Good."

"But you will not?"

"Certainly not, I will stay here."

"You will not go to sleep?"

"Oh, that I cannot promise; sleep is like fear, my son, a thing independent of will."

"You will try, at least?"

"Be easy; I will pinch myself. Besides, the voice would wake me."

"Do not joke about the voice."

"Well, well, go to bed."

The king sighed, looked round anxiously, and glided tremblingly into bed. Then Chicot established him in his chair, arranging round him the pillows and cushions.

"How do you feel, sire?" said he.

"Pretty well; and you?"

"Very well; good night, Henri."

"Good night, Chicot; do not go to sleep."

"Of course not," said Chicot, yawning fit to break his jaws.

And they both closed their eyes, the king to pretend to sleep, Chicot to sleep really.

4

CHAPTER IX.

HOW THE ANGEL MADE A MISTAKE AND SPOKE TO CHICOT, THINKING IT WAS THE KING.

THE king and Chicot remained thus for some time. All at once the king jumped up in his bed. Chicot woke at the noise.

"What is it?" asked he in a low voice.

"The breath on my face."

"As he spoke, one of the wax lights went out, then the other, and the rest followed. Then the lamp also went out, and the room was lighted only by the rays of the moon. At the same moment they heard a hollow voice, saying, apparently from the end of the room,—

"Hardened sinner, art thou there?"

"Yes," said Henri, with chattering teeth.

"Oh!" thought Chicot, "that is a very hoarse voice to come from heaven; nevertheless, it is dreadful."

"Do you hear?" asked the voice.

"Yes, and I am bowed down to the earth."

"Do you believe you obeyed me by all the exterior mummeries which you performed yesterday, without your heart being touched?"

"Very well said," thought Chicot. He approached the king softly.

"Do you believe now?" asked the king, with clasped hands.

"Wait."

"What for?"

"Hush! leave your bed quietly, and let me get in."

"Why?"

"That the anger of the Lord may fall first on me."

"Do you think He will spare me for that?"

"Let us try," and he pushed the king gently out and got into his place.

"Now, go to my chair, and leave all to me."

Henri obeyed; he began to understand.

"You do not reply," said the voice; "you are hardened in sin."

"Oh! pardon! pardon!" cried Chicot, imitating the king's voice. Then he whispered to Henri, "It is droll that the angel does not know me."

"What can it mean?"

"Wait."

"Wretch!" said the voice.

"Yes, I confess," said Chicot; "I am a hardened sinner, a dreadful sinner."

"Then acknowledge your crimes, and repent."

"I acknowledge to have been a great traitor to my cousin Condé, whose wife I seduced."

"Oh! hush," said the king, "that is so long ago."

"I acknowledge," continued Chicot, "to have been a great rogue to the Poles, who chose me for king, and whom I abandoned one night, carrying away the crown jewels. I repent of this."

"Ah!" whispered Henri again: "that is all forgotten."

"Hush! let me speak."

"Go on," said the voice.

"I acknowledge having stolen the crown from my brother D'Alençon, to whom it belonged of right, as I had formerly renounced it on accepting the crown of Poland."

"Knave!" said the king.

"Go on," said the voice.

"I acknowledge having joined my mother, to chase from France my brother-in-law, the King of Navarre, after having destroyed all his friends."

"Ah!" whispered the king, angrily.

"Sire, do not let us offend God, by trying to hide what He knows as well as we do."

"Leave politics," said the voice.

"Ah!" cried Chicot, with a doleful voice, "is it my private life I am to speak of?"

"Yes."

"I acknowledge, then, that I am effeminate, idle, and hypocritical."

" It is true."

" I have ill-treated my wife—such a worthy woman."

" One ought to love one's wife as one's self, and prefer her to all things," said the voice, angrily.

" Ah !" cried Chicot, " then I have sinned deeply."

" And you have made others sin by your example."

" It is true."

" Especially that poor St. Luc ; and if you do not send him home to-morrow to his wife, there will be no pardon for you."

" Ah !" said Chicot to the king, "the voice seems to be friendly to the house of Cossé."

" And you must make him a duke, to recompense him for his forced stay."

" Peste !" said Chicot ; " the angel is much interested for M. de St. Luc."

" Oh !" cried the king, without listening, " this voice from on high will kill me."

" Voice from the side, you mean," said Chicot.

" How ! voice from the side ?"

" Yes ; can you not hear that the voice comes from that wall, Henri ?—the angel lodges in the Louvre."

" Blasphemer !"

" Why, it is honorable for you; but you do not seem to recognize it.   Go and visit him ; he is only separated from you by that partition."

A ray of the moon falling on Chicot's face, showed it to the king so laughing and amused, that he said, " What ! you dare to laugh ?"

" Yes, and so will you in a minute.   Be reasonable, and do as I tell you.   Go and see if the angel be not in the next room."

" But if he speak again ?"

" Well, I am here to answer.   He is vastly credulous. For the last quarter of an hour I have been talking, and he has not recognized me.   It is not clever !"

Henri frowned.   " I begin to believe you are right, Chicot," said he.

" Go, then."

Henri opened softly the door which led into the corridor. He had scarcely entered it, when he heard the voice redoubling its reproaches, and Chicot replying.

"Yes," said the voice, "you are as inconstant as a woman, as soft as a Sybarite, as irreligious as a heathen."

"Oh!" whined Chicot, "is it my fault if I have such a soft skin—such white hands—such a changeable mind? But from to-day I will alter—I will wear coarse linen——"

However, as Henri advanced, he found that Chicot's voice grew fainter, and the other louder, and that it seemed to come from St. Luc's room, in which he could see a light. He stooped down and peeped through the keyhole, and immediately grew pale with anger.

"Par la mordieu!" murmured he, "is it possible that they have dared to play such a trick?"

This is what he saw through the keyhole. St. Luc, in a dressing-gown, was roaring through a tube the words which he had found so dreadful, and beside him, leaning on his shoulder, was a lady in white, who every now and then took the tube from him, and called through something herself, while stifled bursts of laughter accompanied each sentence of Chicot's, who continued to answer in a doleful tone.

"Jeanne de Cossé in St. Luc's room! A hole in the wall! such a trick on me! Oh! they shall pay dearly for it!" And with a vigorous kick he burst open the door.

Jeanne rushed behind the curtains to hide herself, while St. Luc, his face full of terror, fell on his knees before the king, who was pale with rage.

"Ah!" cried Chicot, from the bed, "Ah! mercy! —Holy Virgin! I am dying!"

Henri, seizing, in a transport of rage, the trumpet from the hands of St. Luc, raised it as if to strike. But St. Luc jumped up and cried—

"Sire, I am a gentleman; you have no right to strike me!"

Henri dashed the trumpet violently on the ground. Some one picked it up; it was Chicot, who, hearing the noise, judged that his presence was necessary as a mediator.   He ran to the curtain, and, drawing out poor Jeanne, all trembling—

"Oh !" said he, " Adam and Eve after the Fall.   You send them away, Henri, do you not ?"

"Yes."

" Then I will be the exterminating angel."

And throwing himself between the king and St. Luc, and waving the trumpet over the heads of the guilty couple, said—

" This is my Paradise, which you have lost by your disobedience ; I forbid you to return to it."

Then he whispered to St. Luc, who had his arm round his wife—

"If you have a good horse, kill it, but be twenty leagues from here before to-morrow."

CHAPTER X.

HOW BUSSY WENT TO SEEK FOR THE REALITY OF HIS DREAM.

WHEN Bussy returned home again, he was still thinking of his dream.

" Morbleu !" said he, " it is impossible that a dream should have left such a vivid impression on my mind.   I see it all so clearly ;—the bed, the lady, the doctor.   I must seek for it—surely I can find it again."   Then Bussy, after having the bandage of his wound resettled by a valet, put on high boots, took his sword, wrapped himself in his cloak, and set off for the same place where he had been nearly murdered the night before, and nearly at the same hour.

He went in a litter to the Rue Roi-de-Sicile, then got out, and told his servants to wait for him.   It was about nine in the evening, the curfew had sounded, and Paris was deserted.   Bussy arrived at the Bastile, then he sought for the place where his horse had fallen, and thought he had found it : he next endeavored to repeat his movements of the night before, retreated to the wall, and examined every door to find the corner against which he had leaned, but all the doors seemed alike.

"Pardieu!" said he, "if I were to knock at each of these doors, question all the lodgers, spend a thousand crowns to make valets and old women speak, I might learn what I want to know. There are fifty houses; it would take me at least five nights."

As he spoke, he perceived a small and trembling light approaching.

This light advanced slowly, and irregularly, stopping occasionally, moving on again, and going first to the right, then to the left, then, for a minute, coming straight on, and again diverging. Bussy leaned against a door, and waited. The light continued to advance, and soon he could see a black figure, which, as it advanced, took the form of a man, holding a lantern in his left hand. He appeared to Bussy to belong to the honorable fraternity of drunkards, for nothing else seemed to explain the eccentric movements of the lantern. At last he slipped over a piece of ice, and fell. Bussy was about to come forward and offer his assistance, but the man and the lantern were quickly up again, and advanced directly towards him, when he saw, to his great surprise, that the man had a bandage over his eyes.

"Well!" thought he, "it is a strange thing to play at blind man's buff with a lantern in your hand. Am I beginning to dream again? And, good heavens! he is talking to himself. If he be not drunk or mad, he is a mathematician."

This last surmise was suggested by the words that Bussy heard.

"488, 489, 490," murmured the man, "it must be near here." And then he raised his bandage, and finding himself in front of a house, examined it attentively.

"No, it is not this," he said. Then, putting back his bandage, he recommenced his walk and his calculations.

"491, 492, 493, 494; I must be close." And he raised his bandage again, and, approaching the door next to that against which Bussy was standing, began again to examine.

" Hum ! " said he, " it might, but all these doors are so alike."

" The same reflection I have just made," thought Bussy.

However, the mathematician now advanced to the next door, and going up to it, found himself face to face with Bussy.

" Oh ! " cried he, stepping back.

" Oh ! " cried Bussy.

" It is not possible."

" Yes ; but it is extraordinary.   You are the doctor ? "

" And you the gentleman ? "

" Just so."

" Mon Dieu ! how strange."

" The doctor," continued Bussy, " who yesterday dressed a wound for a gentleman ? "

" Yes, in the right side."

" Exactly so.   You had a gentle, light, and skilful hand."

" Ah, sir, I did not expect to find you here."

" But what were you looking for ? "

" The house."

" Then you do not know it ? "

" How should I ?   They brought me here with my eyes bandaged."

" Then you really came here ? "

" Either to this house or the next."

" Then I did not dream ? "

" Dream ? "

" I confess I feared it was all a dream."

" Ah ! I fancied there was some mystery."

" A mystery which you must help me to unravel."

" Willingly."

" What is your name ? "

" Monsieur, to such a question I ought, perhaps, to reply by looking fierce, and saying, ' Yours, monsieur, if you please ; but you have a long sword, and I only a lancet ; you seem to me a gentleman, and I cannot appear so to you, for I am wet and dirty.   Therefore, I reply frankly : I am called Rémy-le-Haudouin."

"Very well, monsieur; I thank you. I am Louis de Clermont, Comte de Bussy."

"Bussy d'Amboise! the hero Bussy!" cried the young doctor, joyfully. "What, monsieur, you are that famous Bussy——?"

"I am Bussy," replied he. "And now, wet and dirty as you are, will you satisfy my curiosity?"

"The fact is," said the young man, "that I shall be obliged, like Epaminondas the Theban, to stay two days at home, for I have but one doublet and trousers. But, pardon, you did me the honor to question me, I think?"

"Yes, monsieur, I asked you how you came to this house?"

"M. le Comte, this is how it happened; I lodge in the Rue Beauboillis, 502 steps from here. I am a poor surgeon, not unskilful, I hope."

"I can answer for that."

"And who has studied much but without any patients. Seven or eight days ago, a man having received behind the Arsenal a stab with a knife, I sewed up the wound, and cured him. This made for me some reputation in the neighborhood, to which I attribute the happiness of having been last night awoke by a pretty voice."

"A woman's?"

"Yes, but, rustic as I am, I knew it to be the voice of a servant. I know them well."

"And what did you do?"

"I rose and opened my door, but scarcely had I done so, when two little hands, not very soft, but not very hard, put a bandage over my eyes, without saying anything."

"'Oh!' she said, 'come, do not try to see where you are going, be discreet, here is your recompense;' and she placed in my hand a purse."

"Ah! and what did you say?"

"That I was ready to follow my charming conductress. I did not know if she were charming or not, but I thought that the epithet, even if exaggerated, could do no harm."

"And you asked no more?"

"I had often read these kinds of histories in books, and

I had remarked that they always turned out well for the doctor. Therefore I followed, and I counted 498 paces."

" Good ; then this must be the door."

" It cannot be far off, at all events, unless she led me by some détour, which I half suspect."

" But did she pronounce no name ? "

" None."

" But you remarked something ? "

" All that one could with one's fingers, a door with nails, then a passage, and then a staircase——"

" On the left ? "

" Yes ; and I counted the steps. Then I think we came to a corridor, for they opened three doors."

" Well ? "

" Then I heard another voice, and that belonged to the mistress, I am sure ; it was sweet and gentle."

" Yes, yes, it was her."

" Good, it was hers."

" I am sure of it."

" Then they pushed me into the room where you were, and told me to take off my bandage, when I saw you——"

" Where was I ? "

" On a bed."

." A bed of white and gold damask ? "

" Yes."

" In a room hung with tapestry ? "

" Just so."

" And a painted ceiling ? "

" Yes, and between two windows——"

" A portrait ? "

" Yes."

" Representing a woman about nineteen ? "

" Yes."

" Blonde, and beautiful as an angel ? "

" More beautiful."

" Bravo ! what did you do then ? "

" I dressed your wound."

" And, ma foi ! very well."

" As well as I could."

" Admirably ! this morning it was nearly well."

" It is thanks to a balm I have composed, and which appears to me sovereign, for many times, not knowing who to practise upon, I have made wounds on myself, and they were always well in two or three days."

" My dear M. Rémy, you are a charming doctor. Well, afterwards ? "

" You fainted again. The voice asked me how you were."

" From whence ? "

" From a room at the side."

" So you did not see her ? "

" No."

" And you replied ? "

" That the wound was not dangerous, and in twenty-four hours would be well."

" She seemed pleased ? "

" Charmed ; for she cried, ' I am very glad of that.' "

" My dear M. Rémy, I will make your fortune. Well ? "

" That was all ; I had no more to do ; and the voice said, ' M. Rémy——' "

" She knew your name ? "

" Yes ; ' M. Rémy,' said she, ' be a man of honor to the last ; do not compromise a poor woman carried away by an excess of humanity. Take your bandage, and let them take you straight home.' "

" You promised ? "

" I gave my word."

" And you kept it ? "

" As you see, for I am seeking now."

" You are an honest man, and here is my hand," cried Bussy.

" Monsieur, it will be an eternal glory for me to have touched the hand of Bussy d'Amboise. However, I have a scruple. There were ten pistoles in the purse."

" Well ? "

" It is too much for a man who charges five sous for his visits, when he does not give them gratis, and I was seeking the house——"

"To return the purse?"

"Just so."

"My dear M. Rémy, it is too much delicacy; you have earned the money well, and may surely keep it."

"You think so?" said Rémy, well pleased.

"But I also am in your debt; indeed, it was I who ought to have paid you, and not the lady. Come, give me your confidence. What do you do in Paris?"

"What do I do? I do nothing; but I would if I had a connection."

"Well, that is just right; I will give you a patient. Will you have me? I am famous practise; for there is scarcely a day when I do not deface God's noblest work for others, or they for me. Will you undertake the care of all the holes I make in the skin of others or others in mine?"

"Ah, M. le Comte! this honor."

"No; you are just the man I want. You shall come and live with me; you shall have your own rooms, and your own servants; accept, or you will really annoy me."

"M. le Comte, I am so overjoyed, I cannot express it. I will work—I will make a connection——"

"But, no, I tell you, I keep you for myself and my friends. Now, do you remember anything more?"

"Nothing."

"Ah, well! help me to find out, if it be possible."

"I will."

"And you, who are a man of observation, how do you account for it, that after being doctored by you, I found myself by the Temple, close to the ditch."

"You!"

"Yes, I. Did you help to take me there?"

"Certainly not, and I should have opposed it if they had consulted me; for the cold might have done you much harm."

"Then I can tell nothing. Will you search a little more with me?"

"I will if you wish it; but I much fear it will be useless for all these houses are alike."

"Well, we must come again by day."

"Yes ; but then we shall be seen."

"Then we must inquire."

"We will, monseigneur."

"And we shall unravel the mystery. Be sure, Rémy, now there are two of us to work."

;

CHAPTER XI.

M. BRYAN DE MONSOREAU.

IT was more than joy, it was almost delirium, which agitated Bussy when he had acquired the certainty that the lady of his dream was a reality, and had, in fact, given him that generous hospitality of which he had preserved the vague remembrance in his heart. He would not let the young doctor go, but, dirty as he was, made him get into the litter with him ; he feared that if he lost sight of him, he too would vanish like a dream. He would have liked to talk all night of the unknown lady, and explain to Rémy how superior she was even to her portrait ; but Rémy, beginning his functions at once, insisted that he should go to bed : fatigue and pain gave the same counsel and these united powers carried the point.

The next day, on awaking, he found Rémy at his bedside. The young man could hardly believe in his good fortune, and wanted to see Bussy again to be sure of it.

"Well !" said he, "how are you, M. le Comte ?"

"Quite well, my dear Esculapius ; and you, are you satisfied ? "

"So satisfied, my generous protector, that I would not change places with the king. But I now must see the wound."

"Look." And Bussy turned round for the young surgeon to take off the bandage. All looked well ; the wound was nearly closed. Bussy, quite happy, had slept well, and sleep and happiness had aided the doctor.

"Well," said Bussy, "what do you say ? "

"I dare not tell you that you are nearly well, for fear you should send me back to the Rue Beauheillis, five hundred paces from the famous house."

"Which we will find, will we not, Rémy?"

"I should think so."

"Well, my friend, look on yourself as one of the house, and to-day, while you move your things, let me go to the fête of the installation of the new chief huntsman."

"Ah! you want to commit follies already."

"No, I promise to be very reasonable."

"But you must ride."

"It is necessary."

"Have you a horse with an easy pace?"

"I have four to choose from."

"Well, take for to-day the one you would choose for the lady of the portrait you know."

"Know! Ah, Rémy, you have found the way to my heart forever; I feared you would prevent me from going to this chase, or rather this imitation of one, and all the ladies of the Court, and many from the City, will be admitted to it. Now, Rémy, this lady may be there. She certainly is not a simple bourgeoise—those tapestries, that bed, so much luxury as well as good taste, show a woman of quality, or, at least, a rich one. If I were to meet her there!"

"All is possible," replied Rémy, philosophically.

"Except to find the house," sighed Bussy. "Or to penetrate when we have found it."

"Oh! I have a method."

"What is it?"

"Get another sword wound."

"Good; that gives me the hope that you will keep me."

"Be easy, I feel as if I had known you for twenty years, and could not do without you."

The handsome face of the young doctor grew radiant with joy.

"Well, then," said he, "it is decided; you go to the chase to look for the lady, and I go to look for the house."

"It will be curious if we each succeed."

There had been a great chase commanded in the Bois de
Vincennes, for M. de Monsoreau to enter on his functions
of chief huntsman. Most people had believed, from the
scene of the day before, that the king would not attend,
and much astonishment was expressed when it was announced that he had set off with his brother and all the
court. The rendezvous was at the Point St. Louis. It
was thus they named a cross-road where the martyr king
used to sit under an oak-tree and administer justice.
Every one was therefore assembled here at nine o'clock,
when the new officer, object of the general curiosity, unknown as he was to almost every one, appeared on a magnificent black horse. All eyes turned towards him.

He was a man about thirty-five, tall, marked by the
smallpox, and with a disagreeable expression. Dressed in
a jacket of green cloth braided with silver, with a silver
shoulder belt, on which the king's arms were embroidered
in gold ; on his head a cap with a long plume ; in his left
hand a spear, and in his right the éstortuaire * destined
for the king, M. de Monsoreau might look like a terrible
warrior, but not certainly like a handsome cavalier.

" Fie ! what an ugly figure you have brought us, monseigneur," said Bussy, to the Duc d'Anjou, " are these the
sort of gentlemen that your favor seeks for out of the
provinces ? Certainly, one could hardly find such in Paris,
which is nevertheless as well stocked with ugliness. They
say that your highness made a great point of the king's
appointing this man."

" M. de Monsoreau has served me well, and I recompense him," replied the duke.

" Well said, monseigneur, it is rare for princes to be
grateful ; but if that be all, I also have served you well,
and should wear the embroidered jacket more gracefully,
I trust, than M. de Monsoreau. He has a red beard, I
see also, which is an additional beauty."

---

* The éstortuaire was a stick, which the chief huntsman presented to the king, to put aside the branches of the trees when
he was going at full gallop.

"I never knew that a man must be an Apollo, or Antinous, to fill an office at court.

"You never heard it ; astonishing !"

"I consult the heart and not the face—the services rendered and promised."

"Your highness will say I am very envious ; but I search, and uselessly, I confess, to discover what service this Monsoreau can have rendered you."

"You are too curious, Bussy," said the duke, angrily.

"Just like princes," cried Bussy, with his ordinary freedom, "they ask you everything ; but if you ask a question in return, you are too curious."

"Well ! go and ask M. de Monsoreau, himself."

"Ah ! you are right. He is but a simple gentleman, and if he do not reply, I shall know what to say."

"What ?"

"Tell him he is impertinent." And, turning from the prince, Bussy approached M. de Monsoreau, who was in the midst of the circle.

Bussy approached, gay and smiling, and his hat in his hand.

"Pardon, monsieur, but you seem all alone. Is it that the favor which you enjoy has already made you enemies ?"

"I do not know, monsieur, but it is probable. But, may I ask, to what I owe the honor that you do me in invading my solitude ?"

"Ma foi, to the great admiration that M. le Duc d'Anjou has inspired in me for you."

"How so ?"

"By recounting to me the exploit for which you were made chief huntsman."

M. de Monsoreau grew so frightfully pale, that the marks in his face looked like black spots on his yellow skin ; at the same time he looked at Bussy in a manner that portended a violent storm. Bussy saw that he had done wrong ; but he was not a man to draw back ; on the contrary, he was one of those who generally repair an indiscretion by an impertinence.

"You say, monsieur," said Monsoreau, "that the Duke recounted to you my last exploit?"

"Yes, monsieur, but I should much like to hear the story from your own lips."

M. de Monsoreau clasped his dagger tighter in his hand, as though he longed to attack Bussy.

"Ma foi, monsieur," said he, "I was quite disposed to grant your request, and recognize your courtesy, but unfortunately here is the king arriving, so we must leave it for another time."

Indeed, the king, mounted on his favorite Spanish horse, advanced rapidly towards them. He loved handsome faces, and was therefore little pleased with that of M. de Monsoreau. However, he accepted, with a good grace, the éstortuaire which he presented to him, kneeling, according to custom. As soon as the king was armed, the chase commenced.

Bussy watched narrowly every one that passed, looking for the original of the portrait, but in vain; there were pretty, even beautiful and charming women, but not the charming creature whom he sought for. He was reduced to conversation, and the company of his ordinary friends. Antragues, always laughing and talking, was a great amusement.

"We have a frightful chief huntsman," said he to Bussy, "do you not think so?"

"I find him horrible; what a family it must be if his children are like him. Do you know his wife?"

"He is not married."

"How do you know?"

"From Madame de Vendron, who finds him very handsome, and would willingly make him her fourth husband. See how she keeps near him."

"What property has he?"

"Oh! a great deal in Anjou."

"Then he is rich?"

"They say so, but that is all; he is not of very good birth. But see, there is M. le Duc d'Anjou calling to you."

"Ah! ma foi, he must wait. I am curious about this

man. I find him singular, I hardly know why. And such an odd name."

"Oh! it comes from Mons Soricis ; Livarot knows all about that.—Here, Livarot ; this Monsoreau——"

"Well."

"Tell us what you know about him——"

"Willingly. Firstly, I am afraid of him."

"Good, that is what you think ; now tell us what you know."

"Listen. I was going home one night——"

"It begins in a terrible manner."

"Pray let me finish. It was about six months ago, I was returning from my uncle D'Entragues, through the wood of Méridor, when all at once I heard a frightful cry, and I saw pass, with an empty saddle, a white horse, rushing through the wood. I rode on, and at the end of a long avenue, darkened by the approaching shades of night, I saw a man on a black horse ; he seemed to fly. Then I heard again the same cry, and I distingushed before him on the saddle a woman, on whose mouth he had his hand. I had a gun in my hand—you know I aim well, and I should have killed him, but my gun missed fire."

"Well ?"

"I asked a woodcutter who this gentleman on the black horse was, and he said, ' M. de Monsoreau.' "

"Well," said Antragues, "it is not so uncommon to carry away a woman, is it, Bussy ? "

"No ; but, at least, one might let them cry out."

"And who was the woman ? "

"That I do not know ; but he has a bad reputation."

"Do you know anything else about him ? "

"No ; but he is much feared by his tenantry. However, he is a good hunter, and will fill his post better than St. Luc would have done, for whom it was first destined."

"Do you know where St. Luc is ? "

"No ; is he still the king's prisoner ? "

"Not at all ; he set off at one o'clock this morning to visit his country house with his wife."

"Banished ? "

" It looks like it."

" Impossible ! "

" True as the gospel ; Marshal de Brissac told me so this morning."

" Well ! it has served M. de Monsoreau——"

" Ah ! I know now."

" Know what ? "

" The service that he rendered to the duke."

" Who ? St. Luc ? "

"No ; Monsoreau."

" Really."

" Yes, you shall see ; come with me," and Bussy, followed by Livarot and Antragues, galloped after the Duc d'Aujou.

" Ah, monseigneur," said he, " what a precious man M. de Monsoreau is."

" Ah ! really ; then you spoke to him ? "

" Certainly."

" And asked him what he had done for me ? "

" Certainly ; that was all I spoke to him for."

" And what did he say ? "

" He courteously confessed that he was your purveyor."

" Of game ? "

" No ; of women."

" What do you mean, Bussy ? " cried the duke angrily.

" I mean, monseigneur, that he carries away women for you on his great black horse, and that as they are ignorant of the honor reserved for them, he puts his hand on their mouths to prevent their crying out."

" The duke frowned, and ground his teeth with anger, grew pale, and galloped on so fast, that Bussy and his companions were left in the rear.

" Ah ! ah ! it seems that the joke is a good one," said Antragues.

" And so much the better, that every one does not seem to find it a joke," said Bussy.

" A moment after, they heard the duke's voice calling Bussy. He went, and found the duke laughing.

" Oh ! " said he, " it appears that what I said was droll."

"I am not laughing at what you said."

"So much the worse; I should have liked to have made a prince laugh, who hardly ever does so."

"I laugh at your inventing a false story to find out the true one."

"No, I told you the truth."

"Well, then, as we are alone, tell me your little history. Where did it happen?"

"In the wood of Méridor."

The duke grew pale again, but did not speak.

"Decidedly," thought Bussy, "the duke is mixed up with that story. Pardien! monseigneur," said he, "as M. de Monsoreau seems to have found the method of pleasing you so well, teach it to me."

"Pardieu! yes, Bussy, I will tell you how. Listen; I met, by chance, at church, a charming woman, and as some features of her face, which I only saw through a veil, recalled to me a lady whom I had much loved, I followed her, and found out where she lived. I have gained over her servant, and have a key of the house."

"Well, monseigneur, all seems to go well for you."

"But they say she is a great prude, although free, young, and beautiful."

"Ah! you are romancing."

"Well, you are brave, and love me?"

"I have my days."

"For being brave?"

"No, for loving you."

"Well, is this one of the days?"

"I will try and make it one, if I can serve your highness."

"Well, I want you to do for me what most people do for themselves."

"Make love to her, to find out if she be a prude?"

"No, find out if she has a lover. I want you to lay in wait and discover who the man is that visits her."

"There is a man then?"

"I fear so."

"Lover, or husband?"

"That is what I want to know."

"And you want me to find out?"

"If you will do me that great favor——"

"You will make me the next chief huntsman."

"I have never yet done anything for you."

"Oh! you have discovered that at last."

"Well, do you consent?"

"To watch the lady?"

"Yes."

"Monseigneur, I confess I do not like the commission."

"You offered to do me a service, and you draw back already!"

"Because you want me to be a spy."

"I ask you as a friend."

"Monseigneur, this is a sort of thing that every man must do for himself, even if he be a prince."

"Then you refuse?"

"Ma foi! yes."

The duke frowned. "Well, I will go myself," said he, "and if I am killed or wounded, I shall say that I begged my friend Bussy to undertake the task, and that for the first time he was prudent."

"Monseigneur, you said to me the other night, 'Bussy, I hate all those minions of the king's who are always laughing at and insulting us; go to this wedding of St. Luc's, pick a quarrel and try to get rid of them.' I went; they were five and I was alone. I defied them all; they laid wait for me, attacked me all together, and killed my horse, yet I wounded three of them. To-day you ask me to wrong a woman. Pardon, monseigneur, but that is past the service which a prince should exact from a gallant man, and I refuse."

"So be it.; I will do my work myself, or with Aurilly, as I have done already."

"Oh!" said Bussy, with a sudden thought.

"What?"

"Were you engaged on it the night when you saw the ambush laid for me?"

"Just so."

"Then your beautiful unknown lives near the Bastile."

"Opposite the Rue St. Catherine. It is a dangerous place, as you know."

"Has your highness been there since?"

"Yesterday."

"And you saw?"

"A man spying all about and who at last stopped at her door."

"Was he alone?"

"Yes, at first. Afterwards he was joined by another, with a lantern in his hand."

"Ah!"

"Then they began to talk together, and at last, tired of waiting, I went away. And before I venture into the house where I might be killed——"

"You would like one of your friends to try it."

"They would not have my enemies, nor run the same risk; and then they might report to me——"

"In your place I would give up this woman."

"No, she is too beautiful."

"You said you hardly saw her."

"I saw her enough to distinguish splendid blonde hair, magnificent eyes, and such a complexion!"

"Ah! ah!"

"You understand! one does not easily renounce such a woman."

"No, I feel for you."

"You jest."

"No, on my word, and the proof is, that if you will give me my instructions, I will watch this evening."

"You retract your decision?"

"There is no one but the pope infallible; now tell me what I am to do."

"You will have to hide a little way off, and if a man enter, follow him to find out who he is?"

"But if, in entering, he close the door behind him?"

"I told you I had a key."

"Ah! true; then there is only one more thing to fear, that I should follow a wrong man to a wrong door."

" You cannot mistake ; this door is the door of an alley, and at the end of the alley there is a staircase ; mount twelve steps, and you will be in a corridor."

" How do you know all this, if you have never been in ? "

" Did I not tell you I had gained over the servant ? She told me all."

" Mon Dieu ! how convenient it is to be a prince. I should have had to find out all for myself, which would have taken me an enormous time, and I might have failed after all."

" Then you consent ? "

" Can I refuse your highness ? But will you come with me to show me the house ? "

" Useless ; as we return from the chase, we will make a detour, and pass through the Porte St. Antoine, and I will point it out to you."

" Very well, and what am I to do to the man if he comes? "

" Only follow him till you learn who he is. I leave to you your mode of action. And not a word to any one."

" No, on my honor."

" And you will go alone ? "

" Quite."

" Well, then, it is settled ; I show you the door on our way home ; then you come with me, and I give you the key."

Bussy and the prince then rejoined the rest. The king was charmed with the manner in which M. de Monsoreau had conducted the chase.

" Monseigneur," then said M. de Monsoreau to the duke, " I owe my place and these compliments to you."

" But you know that you must go to-night to Fontainebleau, where the king will hunt to-morrow and the day after."

" I know, monseigneur ; I am prepared to start to-night."

" Ah, M. de Monsoreau, there is no more rest for you," said Bussy, " you wished to be chief huntsman, and you are so, and now you will have at least fifty nights' rest less than other men. Luckily you are not married."

At this joke, Monsoreau's face was covered once more with that hideous paleness which gave to him so sinister an aspect.

CHAPTER XII.

HOW BUSSY FOUND BOTH THE PORTRAIT AND THE ORIGINAL.

THE chase terminated about four o'clock in the evening, and at five all the court returned to Paris. As they passed by the Bastile, the duke said to Bussy, " Look to the right, at that little wooden house with a statue of the Virgin before it; well, count four houses from that. It is the fifth you have to go to, just fronting the Rue St. Catherine."

" I see it ; and look ! at the sound of the trumpets announcing the king, all the windows are filled with gazers."

" Except the one I show you, where the curtains remain closed."

" But there is a corner lifted," said Bussy, with a beating heart.

" Yes, but we can see nothing. The lady is well guarded. However, that is the house."

When Bussy returned, he said to Rémy, " Have you discovered the house ? "

" No, monseigneur."

" Well, I believe I have been more lucky."

" How so, monsieur, have you been seeking ? '

" I passed through the street."

" And you recognized the house ? "

" Providence, my dear friend, has mysterious ways."

" Then you are sure ? "

" Not sure, but I hope."

" And when shall I know if you are right ? "

" To-morrow morning."

" Meanwhile, do you want me ? "

" No, my dear Rémy."

" Shall I not follow you ? "

" Impossible."

" Be prudent, monseigneur."

" Ah ! the recommendation is useless, my prudence is
well known."

Bussy dined like a man who does not know when he
will sup, then, at eight o'clock, choosing the best of his
swords, and attaching, in spite of the king's orders, a pair
of pistols to his belt, went in his litter to the corner of
the Rue St. Paul.

He easily recognized the house again, and then, wrapped
in his cloak, hid at the corner of the street, determined to
wait for two hours, and at the end of that time, if no one
came, to act for himself. He had scarcely been there ten
minutes, when he saw two cavaliers coming. One of them
dismounted, gave his horse to the other, who was probably
a lackey, and who went away with the horses, and advanced
towards the house pointed out to Bussy, and, after glancing
round to see if he were observed, opened the door and went
in. Bussy waited two or three minutes, and then followed
him. He advanced slowly and softly, found the staircase,
and went up. In the corridor he stopped, for he heard a
voice say, " Gertrude, tell your mistress that it is I, and
that I must come in."

This was said in an imperious tone, and, a minute after,
Bussy heard a woman's voice say :

" Pass into the drawing-room, Monsieur, and madame
will come to you."

Then he heard the sound of a door shutting. He made
a few steps silently, and extending his hand, felt a door ;
he went in, found a second in which was a key ; he turned
it, and entered the room tremblingly. The room in which
he found himself was dark, except from the light shining
from another. By this he could see two windows, hung
with tapestry, which sent a thrill of joy through the
young man's heart. On the ceiling he could faintly see
the mythological figures ; he extended his hand, and felt
the sculptured bed. There was no more doubt, he was
in the room where he had awakened the night of his
wound.

Bussy hid behind the bed-curtains to listen. He heard

in the adjoining room the impatient step of the unknown; from time to time he stopped, murmuring between his teeth, "Will she come?"

Presently a door opened, and the rustling of a silk dress struck on Bussy's ear. Then he heard a woman's voice, expressive at once of fear and disdain, saying:

"Here I am, monsieur, what do you want now?"

"Madame," replied the man, "I have the honor of telling you that, forced to set off to-morrow morning for Fontainebleau, I come to pass the night with you."

"Do you bring me news of my father?"

"Madame, listen to me——"

"Monsieur, you know what we agreed yesterday, when I consented to become your wife, that, before all things, either my father should come to Paris, or I should go to him."

"Madame, as soon as I return from Fontainebleau, I give you my word of honor, but meanwhile——"

"Oh! monsieur, do not close the door, it is useless; I will not pass a single night under the same roof with you until you bring me my father." And the lady, who spoke thus, whistled through a silver whistle, which was then the manner of calling servants.

Immediately the door opened, and a young, vigorous-looking girl entered. As she went in, she left the door open, which threw a strong light into the room where Bussy was hid, and between the two windows he saw the portrait. Bussy now crept noiselessly along to where he could peep into the room. However carefully he moved, the floor creaked. At the noise the lady turned, she was the original of the portrait. The man, seeing her turn, turned also; it was M. de Monsoreau.

"Ah!" thought Bussy, "the white horse, the woman carried away, there is some terrible history."

Bussy, as we have said, could see them both; she, standing up, pale and disdainful. He, not pale, but livid, agitated his foot impatiently.

"Madame," said he, at last, "do not hope to continue with me this character of a persecuted woman; you are at Paris, in my house, and, still more, you are Comtesse de Monsoreau, that is to say, my wife."

"If I am your wife, why refuse to conduct me to my father? Why continue to hide me from the eyes of the world?"

"You have forgotten the Duc d'Anjou, madame."

"You assured me that, once your wife, I should have no more to fear from him."

"That is to say——"

"You promised me that."

"But still, madame, I must take precautions."

"Well, monsieur, when you have taken them, return to me."

"Diana," said the count, who was growing visibly angry, "Diana, do not make a jest of this sacred tie."

"Act so, monsieur, that I can have confidence in the husband, and I will respect the marriage."

"Oh! this is too much!" cried the count. "I am in my own house, you are my wife, and this night you shall be mine."

Bussy put his hand on his sword-hilt, and made a step forward, but Diana did not give him time to appear.

"Stay," said she, drawing a poignard from her belt, "here is my answer." And rushing into the room where Bussy was, she shut the door and locked it, while Monsoreau exhausted himself in menaces and in blows on the door.

"If you break this door you will find me dead on the threshold."

"And be easy, madame, you shall be revenged," said Bussy.

Diana was about to utter a cry, but her fear of her husband was strong enough to restrain her. She remained pale and trembling, but mute.

M. de Monsoreau struck violently with his foot, but convinced that Diana would execute her menace, went out of the drawing-room, shutting the door violently behind him. Then they heard him going down the stairs.

"But you, monsieur," said Diana, turning to Bussy, "who are you, and how came you here?"

"Madame," said Bussy, opening the door; and kneeling before her, "I am the man whose life you preserved. You cannot think that I come to your house with any bad designs." As the light streamed in, Diana recognized him at once.

"Ah! you here, monsieur," cried she, clasping her hands, "you were here—you heard all?"

"Alas! yes, madame."

"But who are you? your name, monsieur?"

"Madame, I am Louis de Clermont, Comte de Bussy."

"Bussy! you are the brave Bussy!" cried Diana, filling with joy the heart of the young man. "Ah! Gertrude!" cried she, turning to her servant, who, hearing her mistress talking to some one, had entered in terror, "Gertrude, I have no more to fear, for from this time I place myself under the safeguard of the most noble and loyal gentleman in France." Then holding out her hand to Bussy:

"Rise, monsieur," said she, "I know who you are, now you must know who I am."

CHAPTER XIII.

WHO DIANA WAS.

BUSSY rose, bewildered at his own happiness, and entered with Diana into the room which M. de Monsoreau had just quitted. He looked at Diana with astonishment and admiration; he had not dared to hope that the woman whom he had sought for, would equal the woman of his dream, and now the reality surpassed all that he had taken for a caprice of his imagination. Diana was about nineteen, that is to say in the first éclat of that youth and beauty which gives the purest coloring to the flower, the finest flavor to the fruit. There was no mistaking the looks of Bussy; Diana felt herself admired. At last she broke the silence.

"Monsieur," said she, "you have told me who you are, but not how you came here."

"Madame, the cause of my presence here will come naturally out of the recital you have been good enough to promise me; I am sure of it, from some words of your conversation with M. de Monsoreau."

"I will tell you all, monsieur; your name has been sufficient to inspire me with full confidence, for I have always heard of it as of that of a man of honor, loyalty, and courage."

Bussy bowed, and Diana went on.

"I am the daughter of the Baron de Méridor—that is to say, the only heiress of one of the noblest and oldest names in Anjou."

"There was," said Bussy, "a Baron de Méridor, who, although he could have saved himself, came voluntarily and gave up his sword at the battle of Pavia, when he heard that the king was a prisoner, and begged to accompany Francis to Madrid, partook his captivity, and only quitted him to come to France and negotiate his ransom."

"It was my father, monsieur, and if ever you enter the great hall of the Château de Méridor you will see, given in memory of this devotion, the portrait of Francis I., painted by Leonardo da Vinci."

"Ah!" said Bussy, "in those times kings knew how to recompense their followers."

"On his return from Spain my father married. His two first children, sons, died. This was a great grief to the Baron de Méridor. When the king died, my father quitted the court, and shut himself with his wife in the Château de Méridor. It was there that I was born, ten years after the death of my brothers.

"Then all the love of the baron was concentrated on the child of his old age; his love for me was idolatry. Three years after my birth I lost my mother, and, too young to feel my loss, my smiles helped to console my father. As I was all to him, so was he also all to me. I attained my sixteenth year without dreaming of any other world than that of my sheep, my peacocks, my swans, and my doves, without imagining that this life would change, or wishing that it should.

· "The castle of Méridor was surrounded by vast forests, belonging to the Duc d'Anjou ; they were filled with deer and stags, whom no one thought of tormenting, and who had grown quite familiar to me ; some of them would even come when I called them, and one, a doe, my favorite Daphné, my poor Daphné, would come and eat out of my hand.

"One spring I had missed her for a month, and was ready to weep for her as for a friend, when she reappeared with two little fawns. At first they were afraid of me, but seeing their mother caress me, they soon learned to do the same.

"About this time we heard that the Duc d'Anjou had sent a governor into the province, and that he was called the Comte de Monsoreau. A week passed, during which every one spoke of the new governor. One morning the woods resounded with the sound of the horn, and the barking of dogs. I ran to the park, and arrived just in time to see Daphné, followed by her two fawns, pass like lightning, pursued by a pack of hounds. An instant after, mounted on a black horse, M. de Monsoreau flew past me.

"I cried out and implored pity for my poor protégée, but he did not hear me. Then I ran after him, hoping to meet either the count or some of his suite and determined to implore them to stop this chase, which pierced my heart. I ran for some time without knowing where, for I had lost sight of both dogs and hunters.

"Soon I could not even hear them, so I sat down at the foot of a tree, and began to cry. I had been there about a quarter of an hour, when I heard the chase again. The noise came nearer and nearer, and, darting forward, I saw my poor Daphné again ; she had but one fawn with her now, the other had given way through fatigue. She herself was growing visibly tired, and the distance between her and the hounds was less than when I saw her first.

"As before, I exerted myself in vain to make myself heard. M. de Monsoreau saw nothing but the animal he was chasing ; he passed more quickly than ever, with his horn to his mouth, which he was sounding loudly. Behind him, two or three hunters animated the dogs with horn and voice. All passed me like a tempest, and disappeared in the forest. I was in despair, but I ran on once more, and followed a path which I knew led to the castle of Beaugé, belonging to the Duc d'Anjou, and which was about six miles from the castle of Méridor. It was not till I arrived there that I remembered that I was alone, and far from home.

" I confess that a vague terror seized me, and that then only I thought of the imprudence and folly of my conduct. I followed the border of the lake, intending to ask the gardener (who, when I had come there with my father, had often given me bouquets) to take me home, when all at once I heard the sound of the chase again. I remained motionless, listening, and I forgot all else. Nearly at the same moment the doe reappeared, coming out of the wood on the other side of the lake, but pursued so closely that she must be taken immediately. She was alone, her second fawn had fallen, but the sight of the water seemed to reanimate her, and she plunged in as if she would have come to me. At first she swam rapidly, and I looked at her with tears in my eyes, and almost as breathless as herself ; insensibly her strength failed her, while the dogs seemed to grow more and more earnest in their pursuit. Soon some of them reached her, and, stopped by their bites, she ceased to advance. At this moment, M. de Monsoreau appeared at the border of the lake, and jumped off his horse. Then I collected all my strength to cry for pity, with clasped hands. It seemed to me that he saw me, and I cried again. He heard me, for he looked at me ; then he ran towards a boat, entered it, and advanced rapidly towards the animal, who was fighting among the dogs. I did not doubt that, moved by my voice, he was hastening to bring her succor, when all at once I saw him draw his hunting knife, and plunge it into the neck of the poor animal. The blood flowed out, reddening the water at the lake, while the poor doe uttered a doleful cry, beat the water with her feet, reared up, and then fell back dead.

"I uttered a cry almost as doleful as hers, and fell fainting on the bank. When I came to myself again, I was in bed, in a room of the château of Beaugé, and my father, who had been sent for, standing by me. As it was nothing but over-excitement, the next morning I was able to return home ; although I suffered for three or four days. Then my father told me, that M. de Monsoreau, who had seen me, when I was carried to the castle, had come to ask after me ; he had been much grieved when he heard that he had been the involuntary cause of my accident and begged to present his excuses to me, saying, that he could not be happy until he had his pardon from my own lips.

" It would have been ridiculous to refuse to see him, so, in spite of my repugnance, I granted his request. He came the next day ; I felt that my behavior must have seemed strange, and I excused it on the ground of my affection for Daphne. The count swore twenty times, that had he known I had any interest in his victim, he would have spared her with pleasure ; but his protestations did not convince me, nor remove the unfavorable impression I had formed of him. When he took leave, he asked my father's permission to come again. He had been born in Spain and educated at Madrid, and it was an attraction for my father to talk over the place where he had been so long a prisoner. Besides, the count was of good family, deputy-governor of the province, and a favorite, it was said, of the Duc d'Anjou ; my father had no motive for refusing his request, and it was granted. Alas ! from this moment ceased, if not my happiness, at least my tranquillity. I soon perceived the impression I had made on the count ; he began to come every day, and was full of attentions to my father, who showed the pleasure he took in his conversation, which was certainly that of a clever man.

" One morning my father entered my room with an air graver than usual, but still evidently joyful. ' My child,' said he, ' you always have said you did not wish to leave me.'

" ' Oh ! my father,' cried I, ' it is my dearest wish.'

" ' Well, my Diana,' continued he, embracing me, ' it only depends now on yourself to have your wish realized.' I guessed what he was about to say, and grew dreadfully pale.

" ' Diana, my child, what is the matter ?' cried he.

" ' M. de Monsoreau, is it not ?' stammered I. ' Well ?' said he, astonished. ' Oh ! never, my father, if you have any pity for your daughter, never——'

" ' Diana, my love,' said he, ' it is not pity I have for you, but idolatry ; you know it ; take a week to reflect, and if then——'

" ' Oh ! no, no,' cried I, ' it is useless ; not a day, not a minute ! No, no, no !' and I burst into tears. My father adored me, and he took me in his arms, and gave me his word that he would speak to me no more of this marriage.

" Indeed, a month passed, during which I neither heard of nor saw M. de Monsoreau. One morning we received an invitation to a grand fête which M. de Monsoreau was to give to the Duc 'd'Anjou, who was about to visit the province whose name he bore. To this was added a personal invitation from the prince, who had seen my father at court. My first impulse was to beg my father to refuse, but he feared to offend the prince, so we went. M. de Monsoreau received us as though nothing had passed, and behaved to me exactly as he did to the other ladies.

" Not so the duke. As soon as he saw me, he fixed his eyes on me, and scarcely ever removed them. I felt ill at ease under these looks, and begged my father to go home early. Three days after M. de Monsoreau came to Méridor ; I saw him from the windows, and shut myself up in my own room. When he was gone, my father said nothing to me, but I thought he looked gloomy.

" Four days passed thus, when, as I was returning from a walk, the servants told me that M. de Monsoreau was with my father, who had asked for me several times, and had desired to be immediately informed of my return. Indeed, no sooner had I entered my room, than my father came to me.

" ' My child,' said he, ' a motive which I cannot explain

to you, forces me to separate myself from you for some days. Do not question me, but be sure that it is an urgent one, since it determines me to be a week, a fortnight, perhaps a month, without seeing you.' I trembled, I knew not why, but I fancied that the visits of M. de Monsoreau boded me no good.

" ' Where am I to go, my father ? ' asked I.

" ' To the château of Lude, to my sister, where you will be hidden from all eyes. You will go by night.' 'And do you not accompany me ? ' 'No, I must stay here, to ward off suspicion ; even the servants must not know where you are going.' ' But then, who will take me there ? ' ' Two men whom I can trust.' ' Oh ! mon Dieu ! father,' I cried. The baron embraced me. ' It is necessary, my child,' said he.

" I knew my father's love for me so well that I said no more, only I asked that Gertrude, my nurse, should accompany me. My father quitted me, telling me to get ready.

" At eight o'clock (it was dark and cold, for it was the middle of winter) my father came for me. We descended quietly, crossed the garden, when he opened himself a little door leading to the forest, and there we found a litter waiting, and two men ; my father spoke to them, then I got in, and Gertrude with me.

" My father embraced me once more, and we set off. I was ignorant what danger menaced me, and forced me to quit the castle of Méridor. I did not dare to question my conductors, whom I did not know. We went along quietly, and the motion of the litter at last sent me to sleep, when I was awoke by Gertrude, who, seizing my arm, cried out, ' Oh, mademoiselle, was is the matter ? "

" I passed my head through the curtains. We were surrounded by six masked cavaliers, and our men, who had tried to defend me, were disarmed. He who appeared the chief of the masked men approached me, and said, ' Reassure yourself, mademoiselle, no harm will be done to you, but you must follow us.'

" ' Where ? ' I asked. ' To a place,' he replied, ' where,

far from having anything to complain of, you will be treated like a queen.' 'Oh! my father! my father!' I cried. 'Listen, mademoiselle,' said Gertrude, 'I know the environs, and I am strong; we may be able to escape.' 'You must do as you will with us, gentlemen,' said I, 'we are but two poor women, and cannot defend ourselves.' One of the men then took the place of our conductor, and changed the direction of our litter."

Here Diana stopped a moment, as if overcome with emotion.

"Oh, continue, madame, continue," cried Bussy.

It was impossible for Diana not to see the interest she inspired in the young man; it was shown in his voice, his gestures, his looks. She smiled, and went on.

"We continued our journey for about three hours, then the litter stopped. I heard a door open, we went on, and I fancied we were crossing a drawbridge. I was not wrong, for, on looking out of the litter, I saw that we were in the courtyard of a castle. What castle was it? We did not know. Often, during the route, we had tried to discover where we were, but seemed to be in an endless forest. The door of our litter was opened, and the same man who had spoken to us before asked us to alight. I obeyed in silence. Two men from the castle had come to meet us with torches; they conducted us into a bedroom richly decorated, where a collation waited for us on a table sumptuously laid out.

"'You are at home here, madame,' said the same man, 'and the room for your servant is adjoining. When you wish for anything, you have but to strike with the knocker on this door, and some one, who will be constantly in the antechamber, will wait on you.' This apparent attention showed that we were guarded. Then the man bowed and went out, and we heard him lock the door behind him.

"Gertrude and I were alone. She was about to speak, but I signed her to be silent, for perhaps some one was listening. The door of the room which had been shown us as Gertrude's was open, and we went in to examine it. It was evidently the dressing-room to mine, and was also locked. We were prisoners. Gertrude approached me, and said in a low tone : ' Did demoiselle remark that we only mounted five steps after leaving the court ?' ' Yes,' said I. ' Therefore we are on the ground floor.' ' Doubtless.' ' So that——' said she, pointing to the window. ' Yes, if they are not barred.' ' And if mademoiselle had courage.' ' Oh ! yes, I have.'

" Gertrude then took a light, and approached the window. It opened easily, and was not barred ; but we soon discovered the cause of this seeming negligence on the part of our captors. A lake lay below us, and we were guarded by ten feet of water better than by bolts and bars. But in looking out I discovered where we were. We were in the château of Beaugé, where they had brought me on the death of my poor Daphné. This castle belonged to the Duc d'Anjou, and a sudden light was thrown upon our capture. We shut the window again, and I threw myself, dressed, on my bed, while Gertrude slept in a chair by my side. Twenty times during the night I woke, a prey to sudden terror ; but nothing justified it, excepting the place where I found myself, for all seemed asleep in the castle, and no noise but the cry of the birds interrupted the silence of the night. Day appeared, but only to confirm my conviction that flight was impossible without external aid ; and how could that reach us ? About nine they came to take away the supper and bring breakfast. Gertrude questioned the servants, but they did not reply. Our morning passed in fruitless plans for escape, and yet we could see a boat fastened to the shore, with its oars in it. Could we only have reached that, we might have been safe.

" They brought us our dinner in the same way, put it down, and left us. In breaking my bread I found in it a little note. I opened it eagerly, and read, ' A friend watches over you. To-morrow you shall have news of him and of your father.' You can imagine my joy. The rest of the day passed in waiting and hoping. The second night passed as quietly as the first ; then came the hour of breakfast, waited for impatiently, for I hoped to find another note. I was not wrong, it was as follows :—'The person who had you carried off will arrive at the castle of Beaugé at ten o'clock this evening ; but at nine, the friend who watches over you will be under your windows with a letter from your father, which will command the confidence you, perhaps, might not otherwise give. Burn this letter.

"I read and re-read this letter, then burned it as I was desired. The writing was unknown to me, and I did not know from whom it could have come. We lost ourselves in conjectures, and a hundred times during the morning we went to the window to see if we could see any one on the shores of the lake, but all was solitary. An hour after dinner, some one knocked at our door, and then entered. It was the man who had spoken to us before. I recognized his voice ; he presented a letter to me.

"'Whom do you come from ?' asked I. 'Will mademoiselle take the trouble to read, and she will see.' 'But I will not read this letter without knowing whom it comes from.' 'Mademoiselle can do as she pleases ; my business is only to leave the letter,' and putting it down, he went away. 'What shall I do ?' asked I of Gertrude. 'Read the letter, mademoiselle ; it is better to know what to expect.' I opened and read."

Diana, at this moment, rose, opened a desk, and from a portfolio drew out the letter. Bussy glanced at the address and read, "To the beautiful Diana de Méridor."

Then looking at Diana, he said—

"It is the Duc d'Anjou's writing."

"Ah !" replied she, with a sigh, "then he did not deceive me."

Then, as Bussy hesitated to open the letter—

"Read," said she, "chance has initiated you into the most secret history of my life, and I wish to keep nothing from you."

Bussy obeyed and read—

"An unhappy prince, whom your divine beauty has struck to the heart, will come at ten o'clock to-night to apologize for his conduct towards you—conduct which he himself feels has no other excuse than the invincible love he entertains for you.

"FRANÇOIS."

"Then this letter was really from the duke?" asked Diana.

"Alas! yes; it is his writing and his seal."

Diana sighed. "Can he be less guilty than I thought?" said she.

"Who, the prince?"

"No, M. de Monsoreau."

"Continue, madame, and we will judge the prince and the count."

"This letter, which I had then no idea of not believing genuine, rendered still more precious to me the intervention of the unknown friend who offered me aid in the name of my father; I had no hope but in him. Night arrived soon, for it was in the month of January, and we had still four or five hours to wait for the appointed time. It was a fine frosty night; the heavens were brilliant with stars, and the crescent moon lighted the country with its silver beams. We had no means of knowing the time, but we sat anxiously watching at Gertrude's window. At last we saw figures moving among the trees, and then distinctly heard the neighing of a horse.

"It is our friends,' said Gertrude. 'Or the prince,' replied I. 'The prince would not hide himself.' This reflection reassured me. A man now advanced alone: it seemed to us that he quitted another group who were left under the shade of the trees. As he advanced, my eyes made violent efforts to pierce the obscurity, and I thought I recognized first the tall figure, then the features, of M. de Monsoreau. I now feared almost as much the help as the danger. I remained mute, and drew back from the window. Arrived at the wall, he secured his boat, and I saw his head at our window. I could not repress a cry.

"'Ah, pardon,' said he, 'but I thought you expected me.' 'I expected some one, monsieur, but I did not know it was you. A bitter smile passed over his face.

'Who else,' said he, 'except her father, watches over the honor of Diana de Méridor?' 'You told me, monsieur, in your letter, that you came in my father's name.' 'Yes, mademoiselle, and lest you should doubt it, here is a note from the baron,' and he gave me a paper. I read—

"'MY DEAR DIANA,—M. de Monsoreau can alone extricate you from your dangerous position, and this danger is immense. Trust, then, to him as to the best friend that Heaven can send to us. I will tell you later what from the bottom of my heart I wish you to do to acquit the debt we shall contract towards him,

"'Your father, who begs you to believe him, and to have pity on him, and on yourself,

"'BARON DE MÉRIDOR.'

"I knew nothing against M. de Monsoreau; my dislike to him was rather from instinct than reason. I had only to reproach him with the death of a doe, a very light crime for a hunter. I then turned towards him. 'Well?' said he. 'Monsieur, I have read my father's letter, it tells me you will take me from hence, but it does not tell me where you will take me.' 'Where the baron waits for you.' 'And where is that?' 'In the castle of Méridor.' 'Then I shall see my father?' 'In two hours.'

"'Ah! monsieur, if you speak truly——' I stopped. The count waited for the end of my sentence. 'Count on my gratitude,' said I in a trembling tone, for I knew what he might expect from my gratitude. 'Then, mademoiselle,' said he, 'you are ready to follow me?' I looked at Gertrude. 'Reflect that each minute that passes is most precious,' said he, 'I am nearly half an hour behind time now; it will soon be ten o'clock, and then the prince will be here.' 'Alas! yes.' 'Once he comes, I can do nothing for you but risk without hope that life which I now risk to save you.' "Why did not my father come?' I asked. 'Your father is watched. They know every step he takes.' 'But you——' 'Oh! I am different; I am the prince's friend and confidant.' 'Then if you are his friend——' 'Yes, I betray him for you; it is true, as I told you just now, I am risking my life to save you.' This seemed so true, that although I still felt repugnance, I could not express it. ' I wait,' said the count, 'and stay ; if you still doubt, look there.' I looked, and saw on the opposite shore a body of cavaliers advancing. ' It is the duke and his suite,' said he, ' in five minutes it will be too late.'

" I tried to rise, but my limbs failed me. Gertrude raised me in her arms and gave me to the count. . I shuddered at his touch, but he held me fast and placed me in the boat. Gertrude followed without aid. Then I noticed that my veil had come off, and was floating on the water. I thought they would track us by it, and I cried, ' My veil ; catch my veil. The count looked at it and said, ' No, no, better leave it.' And seizing the oars, he rowed with all his strength. We had just reached the bank when we saw the windows of my room lighted up. 'Did I deceive you ? Was it time ?' said M. de Monsoreau. ' Oh ! yes, yes,' cried I, ' you are really my saviour.'

" The lights seemed to be moving about from one room to the other. We heard voices, and a man entered who approached the open window, looked out, saw the floating veil, and uttered a cry. ' You see I did well to leave the veil,' said the count, ' the prince believes that to escape him you threw yourself into the lake.' I trembled at the man who had so instantaneously conceived this idea."

CHAPTER XIV.

THE TREATY.

THERE was a moment's silence. Diana seemed almost overcome. Bussy was already vowing eternal vengeance against her enemies. She went on :

" Scarcely had we touched the shore, when seven or eight men ran to us. They were the count's people, and I thought I recognized among them the two men who had escorted me when I left Méridor. A squire held t

horses, a black one for the count and a white one for
me. The count helped me to mount, and then jumped
on his own horse. Gertrude mounted en croupe behind
one of the men, and we set off at full gallop. The count
held the bridle of my horse. I said to him that I was
a sufficiently good horsewoman to dispense with this, but
he replied that the horse was inclined to run away. When
we had gone about ten minutes, I heard Gertrude's voice
calling to me, and turning, I saw that four of the men
were taking her by a different path from that which we
were following. 'Gertrude,' cried I, 'why does she not
come with me?' 'It is an indispensable precaution,'
said the count; 'if we are pursued we must leave two
tracks, and they must be able to say in two places that
they have seen a woman carried away by men. There is
then a chance that M. d'Anjou may take a wrong road,
and go after your servant instead of you.' Although spe-
cious, this reply did not satisfy me, but what could I do?
Besides, the path which the count was following was the
one which led to the Château de Méridor. In a quarter
of an hour, at the rate at which we are going, we should
have been at the castle, when all at once, when we came
to a cross road which I knew well, the count, instead of
following the road to the castle, turned to the left, and
took a road which led away from it. I cried out, and in
spite of our rapid pace had already my hand on the pommel
in order to jump off, when the count, seizing me round the
waist, drew me off my horse, and placed me on the saddle
before him. This action was so rapid that I had only time
to utter a cry. M. de Monsoreau put his hand on my
mouth, and said, 'Mademoiselle, I swear to you, on my
honor, that I only act by your father's orders, as I will
prove to you at the first halt we make. If this proof appears to you insufficient, you shall then be free.' 'But,
monsieur, cried I, pushing away his hand, 'you told me
you were taking me to my father!' 'Yes, I told you so,
because I saw that you hesitated to follow me, and a moment's more hesitation would have ruined us both, as you
know. Now, do you wish to kill your father? Will you

march straight to your dishonor ? If so, I will take you
to Méridor.' 'You spoke of a proof that you acted in the
name of my father.' 'Here it is,' said the baron, giving
me a letter, 'keep it, and read it at the first stoppage.
If, when you have read it, you wish to return to Méridor,
you are free ; but if you have any respect for your father's
wishes you will not.' 'Then, monsieur,' I replied, 'let us
reach quickly our stopping-place, for I wish to know if
you speak the truth.' 'Remember, you follow me freely.
'Yes, as freely as a young girl can who sees herself placed between her father's death and her own dishonor on the one
hand, and on the other the obligation to trust herself to
the word of a man whom she hardly knows. Never mind,
I follow you freely, monsieur, as you shall see if you
will give me my horse again.' The count called to one of
his men to dismount and give me his horse. 'The white
mare cannot be far,' said he to the man ; 'seek her in
the forest and call her, she will come like a dog to her
name or to a whistle ; you can rejoin us at La Châtre.' I
shuddered in spite of myself. La Châtre was ten leagues
from Méridor, on the road to Paris. 'Monsieur,' said
I, 'I accompany you, but at La Châtre we make our
conditions.' 'Mademoiselle, at La Châtre you shall give
me your orders.' At daybreak we arrived at La Chatre,
but instead of entering the village we went by a cross-road
to a lonely house. I stopped. 'Where are we going ?' I
asked. 'Mademoiselle,' said the count, 'I appeal to yourself. Can we, in flying from a prince next in power to
the king, stop in an ordinary village inn, where the first
person would denounce us ?' 'Well,' said I, 'go on.'
We resumed our way. We were expected, for a man had
ridden on before to announce our arrival. A good fire
burned in a decent room, and a bed was prepared. 'This
is your room,' said the count, 'I will await your orders.'
He went out and left me alone. My first thought was for
my letter. Here it is, M. de Bussy ; read."

Bussy took the letter and read :

"My beloved Diana—As I do not doubt that, yielding to my prayer, you have followed the Comte de Monsoreau, he must have told you that you had the misfortune to please M. le Duc d'Anjou, and that it was this prince who had you forcibly carried away and taken to the castle of Beaugé ; judge by this violence of what the prince is capable, and with what you were menaced. Your dishonor I could not survive ; but there is a means of escape—that of marrying our noble friend. Once Countess of Monsoreau, the count would protect his wife. My desire is, then, my darling daughter, that this marriage should take place as soon as possible, and if you consent, I give you my paternal benediction, and pray God to bestow upon you every treasure of happiness.

"Your father, who does not order, but entreats,

"BARON DE MÉRIDOR."

"Alas !" said Bussy, "if this letter be from your father, it is but too positive."

"I do not doubt its being from him, and yet I read it three times before deciding. At last I called the count. He entered at once ; I had the letter in my hand. 'Well, have you read it ?' said he. 'Yes,' I replied. 'Do you still doubt my devotion and respect ?' 'This letter imposes belief on me, monsieur ; but in case I yield to my father's wishes, what do you propose to do ?' 'To take you to Paris, mademoiselle ; that is the easiest place to hide you.' 'And my father ?' 'As soon as there is no longer danger of compromising you, you know he will come to you wherever you are. 'Well, monsieur, I am ready to accept your protection on the conditions you impose.'

"'I impose nothing, mademoiselle,' answered he, 'I simply offer you a method of safety.' 'Well, I will accept this safety on three conditions.' 'Speak, mademoiselle.' 'The first is, that Gertrude shall return to me.' She is here. 'The second is, that we travel separately to Paris.' 'I was about to propose it to you.' 'And the third is, that our marriage, unless I myself acknowledge some urgent necessity for it, shall only take place in presence of my father.'

'It is my earnest desire; I count on his benediction to draw upon us that of heaven.'

"I was in despair. I had hoped for some opposition to my wishes. 'Now, mademoiselle,' said he, 'allow me to give you some advice.' 'I listen, monsieur.' 'Only to travel by night.' 'Agreed.' 'To let me choose the route, and the places where you should stop. All my precautions will be taken with the sole aim of escaping the Duc d'Anjou.' 'I have no objection to make, monsieur.' 'Lastly, at Paris, to occupy the lodging I shall prepare for you, however simple and out of the way it may be.' 'I only ask to live hidden, monsieur, the more out of the way, the better it will suit me.' 'Then, as we are agreed on all points, mademoiselle, it only remains for me to present to you my humble respects, and to send to you your femme de chambre.' 'On my side, monsieur, be sure that if you keep all your promises, I will keep mine.' 'That is all I ask,' said the count, 'and the promise makes me the happiest of men.'

"With these words, he bowed and went out. Five minutes after, Gertrude entered. The joy of this good girl was great; she had believed herself separated from me forever. I told her all that had passed. As I finished, we heard the sound of a horse's hoofs. I ran to the window; it was M. de Monsoreau going away. He had fulfilled two articles of the treaty. We passed all the day in that little house, served by our hostess; in the evening the chief of our escort appeared, and asked me if I were ready. I said yes, and five minutes after, we set off. At the door I found my white mare. We traveled all night, and stopped at daybreak. I calculated we had gone about thirty-five miles, but my horse had a very easy pace, and on leaving the house a fur cloak had been thrown over me to protect me from the cold. It took us seven days to reach Paris in this manner, and I saw nothing of the count. We entered the city at night, and the first object I saw, after passing through the gate, was an immense monastery; then we crossed the river, and in ten minutes we were in the Place de la Bastile. Then a

man, who seemed to be waiting for us, advanced and said,
'It is here.' The chief of our escort jumped off his horse,
and presented me his hand to dismount also. A door was
open, and the staircase lighted by a lamp. ' Madame,' said
the man to me, 'you are now at home. At this door
finishes the mission I received; may I flatter myself I
have fulfilled it according to your wishes?' 'Yes, monsieur,' said I, 'I have only thanks to give you. Offer
them in my name to all your men; I would wish to reward
them in a better manner, but I possess nothing.' 'Do
not be uneasy about that, madame,' said he, 'they are
largely recompensed.'

"Then the little troop went away, and we went up the
stairs of our house, and found ourselves in a corridor.
Three doors were open; we entered the middle one, and
found ourselves in the room where we now stand. On
opening the door of my bedroom, to my great astonishment I found my own portrait there. It was one which
had hung at Méridor, and the count had doubtless begged
it of my father. I trembled at this new proof that my
father regarded me already as his wife.

"Nothing was wanting in the room; a fire burned in
the grate, and a supper was ready in the sitting-room.
I saw with satisfaction that it was laid for one only, and
yet when Gertrude said, 'Well, mademoiselle, you see
the count keeps his promises.'—'Alas! yes,' replied I
with a sigh, for I should have preferred that by breaking
his word he should have given me an excuse to break mine.
After supper, we examined the house, but found no one
in it. The next day Gertrude went out, and from her I
learned that we were at the end of the Rue St. Antoine,
near the Bastile. That evening, as we were sitting down
to supper, some one knocked. I grew pale.

"'If it be the count?' asked Gertrude. 'You must open
to him; he has kept his promises, and I must keep mine.'
A moment after he entered. "Well, madame,' said he,
'have I kept my word?' 'Yes, monsieur, and I thank you
for it.' 'Then you will receive me?' said he, with an ironical smile. 'Enter, monsieur,' said I, 'have you any news?'

'Of what, madame?' 'Of my father, firstly?' 'I have
not been to Méridor and have not seen the baron.' 'Then
of Beaugé, and the Duc d'Anjou?' 'I have been to
Beaugé, and have spoken to the duke.' 'What does he
say?' 'He appears to doubt.' 'Of what?' 'Of your
death.' 'But you confirmed it?' 'I did all I could.'
'Where is the duke?' I then asked. 'He returned to
Paris yesterday. One does not like to stay in a place
where one has the death of a woman to reproach one's self
with.' 'Have you seen him in Paris?' 'I have just
left him.' 'Did he speak of me?' 'I did not give him
time; I spoke incessantly of a promise which he made to
me.' 'What is it?' 'He promised me as a reward for
services rendered to him, to make, me chief huntsman.'
'Ah, yes,' said I, thinking of my poor Daphné 'you
are a terrible hunter, I know.' 'It is not for, that
reason I obtain it, but the duke dare not be ungrateful to
me.'

"'Can I write to my father? said I. 'Doubtless; but
your letters may be intercepted.' 'Am I forbidden to go
out?' 'Nothing is forbidden; but I beg to point out to
you that you may be followed.' 'At least I must go on
Sunday to mass.' 'It would be better not; but if you do,
I advise you to go to St. Catherine.' 'Where is that?'
'Just opposite you.' There was a silence. Then I said,
'When shall I see you again, monsieur?' 'When I have
your permission to come.' 'Do you need it?' 'Certainly,
as yet I am a stranger to you.' 'Monsieur,' said I, half
frightened at this unnatural submission, 'you can return
when you like, or when you think you have anything important to communicate.'

"''Thanks, madame,' said he,' I will use your permission,
but not abuse it. I know you do not love me, and I will
not abuse a situation which forces you to receive me. You
will, I trust, gradually become accustomed to the thought,
and be willing, when the moment shall arrive, to become
my wife.' 'Monsieur, said I, ' I appreciate your delicacy
and frankness. I will use the same frankness. I had a
prejudice against you, which I trust that time will cure'

'Permit me,' said he, ' to partake this anticipation and live in the hopes of that happy moment.' Then bowing respectfully, he went out."

CHAPTER XV.

THE MARRIAGE.

" A STRANGE man," said Bussy.

" Yes, is he not, monsieur ? When he was gone I felt sadder and more frightened than ever. This icy respect, this ironical obedience, this repressed passion, which now and then showed itself in his voice, frightened me more than a will firmly expressed, and which I could have opposed, would have done. The next day was Sunday ; I had never in my life missed divine service, so I took a thick veil and went to St. Catherine's, followed by Gertrude, and no one seemed to remark us.

" The next day the count came to announce to me that the duke had fulfilled his promise, and had obtained for him the place of chief huntsman, which had been promised to M. de St. Luc. A week passed thus : the count came twice to see me, and always preserved the same cold and submissive manner. The next Sunday I went again to the church. Imprudently, in the midst of my prayers, I raised my veil. I was praying earnestly for my father, when Gertrude touched me on the arm. I raised my head, and saw with terror M. le Duc d'Anjou leaning against the column, and looking earnestly at me. A man stood by him."

" It was Aurilly," said Bussy.

" Yes, that was the name that Gertrude told me afterwards. I drew my veil quickly over my face, but it was too late : he had seen me, and if he had not recognized me, at least my resemblance to her whom he believed dead had struck him. Uneasy, I left the church, but found him standing at the door, and he offered to me the holy water

as I passed. I feigned not to see him, and went on. We
soon discovered that we were followed. Had I known anything of Paris, I would have attempted to lead them wrong,
but I knew no more of it than from the church to the
house, nor did I know any one of whom I could ask a quarter
of an hour's hospitality ; not a friend, and only one protector, whom I feared more than an enemy."

"Oh ! mon Dieu !" cried Bussy, "why did not Heaven,
or chance, throw me sooner in your path ?"

Diana thanked the young man with a look.

"But pray go on," said Bussy, "I interrupt you, and
yet I am dying to hear more."

"That evening M. de Monsoreau came. I did not know
whether to tell him of what had happened, but he began,
'You asked me if you could go to mass, and I told you you
were free, but that it would be better not to do so. You
would not believe me : you went this morning to St.
Catherine's, and by a fatality the prince was there and saw
you.' 'It is true, monsieur ; but I do not know if he recognized me.' 'Your face struck him ; your resemblance
to the woman he regrets appeared to him extraordinary,
he followed you home, and made inquiries, but learned
nothing, for no one knew anything.' 'Mon Dieu !' cried
I. 'The duke is persevering,' said he. 'Oh ! he will
forget me, I hope.'

"'No one forgets you who has once seen you,' said he.
'I did all I could to forget you, and I have not succeeded.' And the first passionate look that I had seen
flashed from the eyes of the count. I was more terrified by
it than I had been by the sight of the prince. I remained
mute. 'What will you do ?' asked the count. 'Can I
not change my abode—go to the other end of Paris, or,
better still, return to Anjou ?' 'It will be useless ; the
duke is a terrible bloodhound, and now he is on your track,
he will follow you wherever you go till he finds you.'
'Oh ! mon Dieu ! you frighten me.' 'I tell you the simple
truth.' 'Then what do you advise me to do ?' 'Alas !'
said he, with a bitter irony. 'I am a man of poor imagination, I had formed a plan, but it does not suit you ;

I can find no other.' 'But the danger is perhaps less pressing than you imagine.'

"'The future will show us, madame,' said the count, rising. 'I can but add that the Comtesse de Monsoreau would have the less to fear from the prince, as my new post places me under the direct protection of the court.' I only replied by a sigh. He smiled bitterly, and as he went down-stairs I heard him giving vent to oaths. The next day, when Gertrude went out, she was accosted by a young man whom she recognized as the one who had accompanied the prince, but she remained obstinately silent to all his questions. This meeting inspired me with profound terror; I feared that M. de Monsoreau would not come, and that they would invade the house in his absence. I sent for him, he came at once. I told him all about the young man, whom I described.

"'It was Aurilly;' he said, 'and what did Gertrude answer?' 'She did not answer at all.' 'She was wrong,' said he. 'Why?' 'We must gain time.' 'Time?' 'Yes, I am now dependent on the Duc d'Anjou; in a fort-night, in a week perhaps, he will be in my power. We must deceive him to get him to wait.' 'Mon Dieu!' 'Certainly; hope will make him patient. A complete refusal will push him to extremities.' 'Monsieur, write to my father; he will throw himself at the feet of the king. He will have pity on an old man.' 'That is according to the king's humor, and whether he be for the time friendly or hostile to the duke. Besides, it would take six days for a messenger to reach your father, and six days for him to come here. In twelve days, if we do not stop him, the duke will have done all he can do.'

"'And how to stop him?' I cried. A smile passed over the lips of M. de Monsoreau at this first appeal to his protection. 'Madame,' said he, 'will you permit me to pass two or three hours in your room? I may be seen going out, and would rather wait till dark.' I signed him to sit down. We conversed; he was clever and had traveled much, and at the end of the time I understood, better than I had ever done before, the influence he had

7

obtained over my father. When it grew dark, he rose and took leave. Gertrude and I then approached the window, and could distinctly see two men examining the house. The next day, Gertrude, when she went out, found the same young man in the same place. He spoke to her again, and this time she answered him. On the following day she told him that I was the widow of a counselor, who, being poor, lived in retirement. He tried to learn more, but could extract nothing further from her. The next day, Aurilly, who seemed to doubt her story, spoke of Anjou, of Beaugé, and Méridor. Gertrude declared these names to be perfectly unknown to her. Then he avowed that he came from the Duc d'Anjou, who had seen and fallen in love with me ; then came magnificent offers for both of us, for her, if she would introduce the prince into my house, and for me, if I would receive him.

" Every evening M. de Monsoreau came, to hear what was going on, and remained from eight o'clock to midnight, and it was evident that his anxiety was great. On Saturday evening he arrived pale and agitated.

" ' You must promise to receive the duke on Tuesday or Wednesday,' said he. ' Promise ! and why ? ' ' Because he has made up his mind to come in, and he is just now on the best terms with the king ; we have nothing to expect from him.' ' But before then will anything happen to help me ?' ' I hope so. I expect from day to day the event which is to place the duke in my power. But to-morrow I must leave you, and must go to Monsoreau.' ' Must you ?' cried I with a mixture of joy and terror. ' Yes, I have there a rendezvous which is indispensable to bring about the event of which I speak.' ' But if you fail, what are we to do ?' ' What can I do against a prince, if I have no right to protect you, but yield to bad fortune ?'

" ' Oh ! my father ! my father !' cried I. The count looked at me. ' What have you to reproach me with ?' said he. ' Nothing, on the contrary.' ' Have I not been a devoted friend, and as respectful as a brother ?' ' You have behaved throughout like a gallant man.' ' Had I not your promise ?' ' Yes.' ' Have I once recalled it to you ?' 'No.' 'And yet you prefer to be the mistress of the duke, to being my wife?' 'I do not say so, monsieur.' 'Then decide.' 'I have decided.' 'To be Countess of Monsoreau?' 'Rather than mistress of the duke.' 'The alternative is flattering. But, meanwhile, let Gertrude gain time until Tuesday.' The next day Gertrude went out, but did not meet Aurilly. We felt more frightened at his absence than we had done at his presence. Night came, and we were full of terror. We were alone and feeble, and for the first time I felt my injustice to the count."

"Oh! madame!" cried Bussy, "do not be in a hurry to think so, his conduct conceals some mystery, I believe."

"All was quiet," continued Diana, "until eleven o'clock. Then five men came out of the Rue St Antoine, and hid themselves by the Hôtel des Tournelles. We began to tremble; were they there for us? However, they remained quiet, and a quarter of an hour passed; then we saw two other men approach. By the moonlight Gertrude recognized Aurilly. 'Alas! mademoiselle; it is they,' cried she. 'Yes,' cried I, trembling, 'and the five others are to help them.' 'But they must force the door,' said Gertrude, 'perhaps the neighbors will come and help us.' 'Oh! no, they do not know us, and they will not fight against the duke. Alas! Gertrude, I fear we have no real defender but the count.' 'Well! then, why do you always refuse to marry him?' I sighed."

CHAPTER XVI.

THE MARRIAGE.

"THE two men approached the window. We gently opened it a little way, and heard one say, 'Are you sure it is here?' 'Yes, monseigneur, quite sure,' said the other. 'It is the fifth house from the corner of the Rue St. Paul.' 'And you are sure of the key?' 'I took the pattern of

the lock.' I seized Gertrude's arm in terror. 'And once
inside,' he went on, 'the servant will admit us ; your
highness has in your pocket a golden key as good as this
one.' 'Open, then.' We heard the key turn in the
lock, but all at once the ambushed men rushed forward,
crying, 'à mort! à mort!' I could not understand this,
only I saw that unexpected help had come to us, and I fell
on my knees, thanking Heaven. But the prince had only
to name himself, when every sword went back into the
scabbard, and every foot drew back."

"Yes, yes," said Bussy, "it was for me they came, not
for the prince."

"However, this attack caused the prince to retire, and
the five gentlemen went back to their hiding-place. It
was evident that the danger was over for that night, but
we were too unquiet to go to bed. Soon we saw a man on
horseback appear, and then the five gentlemen immediately
rushed on him. You know the rest, as the gentleman
was yourself."

"On the contrary, madame, I know only that I fought
and then fainted."

"It is useless to say," continued Diana, with a blush,
"the interest that we took in the combat so unequal, but
so valiantly sustained. Each blow drew from us a shudder,
a cry, and a prayer. We saw your horse fall, and we
thought you lost, but it was not so ; the brave Bussy
merited his reputation. At last, surrounded, menaced on
all sides, you retreated like a lion, facing your foes, and
came to lean against our door ; the same idea came to both
of us, to go down and open to you, and we ran towards
the staircase ; but we had barricaded the door, and it took
us some minutes to move the furniture, and as we arrived
on the stairs, we heard the door shut. We stopped, and
looked at each other, wondering who had entered. Soon
we heard steps, and a man appeared, who tottered, threw
up his arms, and fell on the first step. It was evident that
he was not pursued, but had put the door, so luckily left
open by the duke, between him and his adversaries. In
any case we had nothing to fear ; it was he who needed

our help. Gertrude ran and fetched a lamp, and we found you had fainted, and carried you to the bed. Gertrude had heard of a wonderful cure made by a young doctor in the Rue Beautrellis, and she offered to go and fetch him. 'But,' said I, 'he might betray us.' 'I will take precautions' said she. She took money and the key, and I remained alone near you, and—praying for you."

"Alas!" said Bussy, "I did not know all my happiness, madame."

"In a quarter of an hour Gertrude returned, bringing the young doctor with his eyes bandaged."

"Yes, it was at that moment I recovered my senses and saw your portrait, and thought I saw you enter," said Bussy.

"I did so; my anxiety was stronger than my prudence. The doctor examined your wound and answered for your life."

"All that remained in my mind," said Bussy, "like a dream, and yet something told me," added he, laying his hand upon his heart, "that it was real."

"When the surgeon had dressed your wound, he drew from his pocket a little bottle containing a red liquor, of which he put some drops on your lips. He told me it was to counteract the fever and produce sleep, and said that the only thing then was to keep you quiet. Gertrude then bandaged his eyes again, and took him back to the Rue Beautrellis, but she fancied he counted the steps."

"He did so, madame."

"This supposition frightened us. We feared he would betray us, and we wished to get rid of every trace of the hospitality we had shown you. I gathered up my courage; it was two o'clock, and the streets were deserted; Gertrude was strong, and I aided her, and between us we carried you to the Temple. Luckily we met no one, but when we returned, I fainted with emotion."

"Oh! madame!" cried Bussy, "how can I ever repay you for what you have done for me?"

There was a moment's silence, and they heard the clock of St. Catherine's church strike. "Two o'clock," cried Diana, "and you here!"

"Oh! madame, do not send me away without telling me all. Suppose that God had given you a brother, and tell this brother what he can do for his sister."

"Alas! nothing now; it is too late."

"What happened the next day?" said Bussy; "what did you do on that day when I thought constantly of you, without feeling sure if you were not a vision of my delirium?"

"During that day, Gertrude went out, and met Aurilly. He was more pressing than ever. He said nothing of the night before, but asked for an interview for his master. Gertrude appeared to consent, but she asked until the Wednesday—that is to-day—to decide. Aurilly promised that his master would wait until then. That evening, M. de Monsoreau returned. We told him all, except about you.

"'Yes,' said he, 'I heard of all this. Then he has a key.' 'Can we not change the lock?' 'He will get another key.' 'Put on bolts?' 'He will come with ten men and force the door. 'But the event which was to give you full power over him?' 'Is postponed indefinitely.' I stood in despair. 'Monsieur,' said I, 'the duke has promised to wait till Wednesday; I ask you to wait till Tuesday.' 'Tuesday evening I will be here, madame,' and without another word he went out. I followed him with my eyes, but instead of going away he stood in the corner by the Hôtel des Tournelles, and seemed determined to watch me all night. Every proof of devotion he gave me was like a knife in my heart. The two days passed rapidly, but what I suffered it is impossible to describe. When Tuesday evening came, I felt exhausted, and all emotion seemed dead within me.

"Gertrude went to the window. 'Madame,' cried she, 'four men! I see four men! They approach, they open the door—they enter! It is, doubtless, the duke and his followers.' For an answer, I drew my poniard, and placed it near me on the table. 'See,' said I. An instant after, Gertrude returned, 'It is the count,' said she. He entered. 'Gertrude tells me,' said he, 'that you took me for the duke, and were ready to kill yourself.' It was the first time I had ever seen him moved. Gertrude was wrong to tell you,' said I. 'You know that I am not alone.' 'Gertrude saw four men.' 'You know who they are?'. 'I presume one is a priest, and the others witnesses.' 'Then, you are ready to become my wife?' 'It was so agreed; only I stipulated that except in an urgent case, I would only marry you in the presence of my father.' 'I remember; but do you not think the case urgent?' 'Yes, and the priest may marry us, but, until I have seen my father, I will be your wife only in name.'

"The count frowned, and bit his lips. 'I do not wish to coerce you,' said he; 'you are free; but look here.' I went to the window, and saw a man wrapped in a cloak, who seemed trying to get into the house."

"Oh! mon dieu!" cried Bussy; "and this was yesterday?"

"Yes, about nine o'clock. Presently, another man, with a lantern, joined him. I thought it was the duke and his followers.

"'Now,' said, M de Monsoreau, 'shall I go or stay?' I hesitated a moment, in spite of my father's letter and of my given word, but those two men there——"

"Oh! unhappy that I am," cried Bussy, "it was I and Rémy, the young doctor."

"You!" cried Diana.

"Yes, I; I, who, more and more convinced of the reality of my dream, sought for the house where I had been, and the woman, or rather angel, who had appeared to me. Oh! I am unfortunate. Then," continued he, after a pause, "you are his wife?"

"Since yesterday."

There was a fresh silence.

"But," said Diana at last, "how did you enter this house?"

Bussy silently showed his key.

"A key! where did you get it?"

"Had not Gertrude promised the prince to enter to-night? He had seen M. de Monsoreau here, and also myself, and fearing a snare, sent me to find out."

"And you accepted this mission ? "

" It was my only method' of penetrating to you. Will you reproach me for having sought at once the greatest joy and the greatest grief of my life ? "

" Yes, for it is better that you should see me no more, and forget me."

" No, madame ; God has brought me to you, to deliver you from the toils in which your enemies have taken you. I vow my life to you. You wish for news of your father ? "

" Oh, yes ! for, in truth, I know not what has become of him."

"Well, I charge myself with finding out ; only think of him who henceforth will live but for you."

" But this key ? "

" This key I restore to you, for I will receive it only from your hands ; but I pledge you my word as a gentleman, that never sister could trust in a brother more devoted and respectful."

"I trust to the word of the brave Bussy. Here, monsieur," and she gave back the key.

" Madame, in a fortnight we will know more ;" and, saluting Diana with a respect mingled with love and sadness, Bussy took leave. Diana listened to his retreating steps with tears in her eyes.

CHAPTER XVII.

HOW HENRI III. TRAVELED, AND HOW LONG IT TOOK HIM TO GET FROM PARIS TO FONTAINEBLEAU.

THE sun, which shone four or five hours after the events which we have just recorded had taken place, saw, by his pale light, Henri III. set off for Fontainebleau, where a grand chase was projected. A crowd of gentlemen, mounted on good horses and wrapped in their fur cloaks, then a number of pages, after them lackeys, and then Swiss, followed the royal litter. This litter, drawn by eight mules

richly caparisoned, was a large machine, about fifteen feet
long and eight wide, on four wheels, furnished inside with
cushions and curtains of silk brocade. In difficult places
they substituted for the mules an indefinite number of
oxen.

This machine contained Henri III., his doctor, and his
chaplain, Chicot, four of the king's favorites, a pair of
large dogs, and a basket of little ones, which the king held
on his knees, and which was suspended from his neck by
a golden chain. From the roof hung a gilded cage containing turtle doves, quite white, with a black ring round
their necks. Sometimes the collection was completed by
the presence of two or three apes. Thus this litter was
commonly termed the Noah's Ark.

Quelus and Maugiron employed themselves with plait-
ing ribbons, a favorite diversion of that time; and Chicot
amused himself by making anagrams on the names of all
the courtiers. Just as they passed the Place Maubert,
Chicot rushed out of the litter, and went to kneel down
before a house of good appearance.

"Oh!" cried the king, "if you kneel, let it be before
the crucifix in the middle of the street, and not before the
house. What do you mean by it?"

But Chicot, without attending, cried out in a loud voice:

"Mon Dieu! I recognize it, I shall always recognize it—
the house where I suffered! I have never prayed for
vengeance on M. de Mayenne, author of my martyrdom,
nor on Nicholas David, his instrument. No; Chicot is
patient, Chicot can wait, although it is now six years that
this debt has been running on, and in seven years the interest is doubled. May, then, my patience last another year,
so that instead of fifty blows of a stirrup-leather which I received in this house by the orders of this assassin of a Lorraine prince, and which drew a pint of blood, I may owe a
hundred blows and two pints of blood! Amen, so be it!"

"Amen!" said the king.

Chicot then returned to the litter, amidst the wondering
looks of the spectators.

"Why, Chicot, what does all this mean?" said the king.

"Sire, it means that Chicot is like the fox—that he licks the stones where his blood fell, until against those very stones he crushes the heads of those who spilt it."

"Explain yourself."

"Sire, in that house lived a girl whom Chicot loved, a good and charming creature, and a lady. One evening when he went to see her, a certain prince, who had also fallen in love with her, had him seized and beaten, so that Chicot was forced to jump out of window ; and as it was a miracle that he was not killed, each time he passes the house he kneels down and thanks God for his escape."

"You were, then, well beaten, my poor Chicot ?"

"Yes, sire, and yet not as much as I wished."

"Why—for your sins ?"

"No, for those of M. de Mayenne."

"Oh ! I understand ; your intention is to render to Cæsar——"

"Not to Cæsar, sire—Cæsar is the great general, the valiant warrior, the eldest brother, who wishes to be king of France. No, you must settle with him ; pay your debts, and I will pay mine."

Henri did not like to hear his cousin of Guise spoken of, and this made him serious. It was three o'clock in the afternoon when they arrived at Juvisy and the great hotel of the " Cour de France."

Chicot, looking out of the litter, saw at the door of the hotel several men wrapped in cloaks. In the midst of them was a short, stout person, whose large hat almost covered his face. They went in quickly on seeing the litter, but not before the look of this person had had time to excite Chicot's attention. Therefore he jumped out, and asking a page for his horse, which was being led, let the royal litter go on to Essones, where the king was to sleep, while he remained behind, and, cautiously peeping in through a window, saw the men whom he had noticed sitting inside. He then entered the hotel, went into the opposite room, asked for a bottle of wine, and placed himself so that, although he could not be seen, no one could pass by without his seeing them.

"Ah!" said he to himself, "shall I be forced to make my payment sooner than I expected?"

Soon Chicot found that by keeping the door open he could both see into the room and hear what was said.

"Gentlemen," said the short fat man to his companions, "I think it is time to set out; the last lackey of the cortége is out of sight, and I believe now that the road is safe."

"Perfectly so, monseigneur," replied a voice which made Chicot tremble, and which came from the mouth of a person as tall as the other was short, as pale as he was red, and as obsequious as he was arrogant.

"Ah! M. Nicolas," said Chicot, "tu quoque, that is good. It will be odd if I let you slip this time!"

Then the short man came out, paid the bill, and, followed by the others, took the road to Paris. Chicot followed them at a distance. They entered by the Porte St. Antoine, and entered the Hôtel Guise. Chicot waited outside a full hour, in spite of cold and hunger. At last the door reopened, but, instead of seven cavaliers wrapped in their cloaks, seven monks came out, with their hoods over their faces, and carrying immense rosaries.

"Oh!" said Chicot, "is, then, the Hôtel Guise so embalmed in sanctity that wolves change into lambs only by entering it? This becomes more and more interesting."

And he followed the monks as he had followed the cavaliers, for he believed them to be the same.

The monks passed over the bridge of Notre Dame, crossed the city and the petit pont, and went up the Rue St. Geneviève.

"Oh!" said Chicot, as he passed the house where he had kneeled in the morning, "are we returning to Fontainebleau? In that case I have made a round."

However, the monks stopped at the door of the Abbey of St. Geneviève, in the porch of which stood another monk, who examined every one's hand.

"Why," said Chicot, "it seems that to be admitted to night into the abbey one must have clean hands!"

Then he saw, with astonishment, monks appear from

every street leading to the abbey, some alone, some walking in pairs, but all coming to the abbey.

"Ah!" said Chicot, "is there a general chapter at the abbey to-night? I have never seen one, and I should like it much."

The monks entered, showing their hands, or something in them, and passed on.

"I should like to go also," thought Chicot; "but for that I want two things—a monk's robe, for I see no layman here, and then this mysterious thing which they show to the porter, for certainly they show something. Ah, Brother Gorenflot, if you were here!"

The monks continued to arrive, till it seemed as if half Paris had taken the frock.

"There must be something extraordinary to-night," thought Chicot. "I will go and find Gorenflot at the Corne d'Abondance; he will be at supper."

CHAPTER XVIII.

BROTHER GORENFLOT.

To the beautiful day had succeeded a beautiful evening, only, as the day had been cold, the evening was still colder. It was one of those frosts which make the lights in the windows of an hotel look doubly tempting. Chicot first entered the dining-room, and looked around him, but not finding there the man he sought for, went familiarly down to the kitchen. The master of the establishment was superintending a frying-pan full of whitings. At the sound of Chicot's step he turned.

"Ah! it is you, monsieur," said he, "good evening, and a good appetite to you."

"Thanks for the wish, but you know I cannot bear to eat alone."

"If necessary, monsieur, I will sup with you."

"Thanks, my dear host, but though I know you to be an excellent companion, I seek for some one else."

"Brother Gorenflot, perhaps?"

"Just so; has he begun supper?"

"No, not yet; but you must make haste nevertheless, for in five minutes he will have finished."

"Monsieur!" cried Chicot, striking his head.

"Monsieur, it is Friday, and the beginning of Lent."

"Well, and what then?" said Chicot, who did not hold a high opinion of Gorenflot's religious austerity.

Boutromet shrugged his shoulders. "Decidedly, something must be wrong," said Chicot, "five minutes for Gorenflot's supper! I am destined to see wonders to-day."

Chicot then advanced towards a small private room, pushed open the door, and saw within the worthy monk, who was turning negligently on his plate a small portion of spinach, which he tried to render more savory by the introduction into it of some cheese. Brother Gorenflot was about thirty-eight years of age and five feet high. However, what he wanted in height, he made up in breadth, measuring nearly three feet in diameter from shoulder to shoulder, which, as every one knows, is equal to nine feet of circumference. Between these Herculean shoulders rose a neck of which the muscles stood out like cords. Unluckily this neck partook of the same proportions; it was short and thick, which at any great emotion might render Brother Gorenflot liable to apoplexy. But knowing this, perhaps, he never gave way to emotions, and was seldom so disturbed as he was when Chicot entered his room.

"Ah, my friend! what are you doing?" cried Chicot, looking at the vegetables and at a glass filled with water just colored with a few drops of wine.

"You see, my brother, I sup," replied Gorenflot in a powerful voice.

"You call that supper, Gorenflot! Herbs and cheese?"

"We are in the beginning of Lent, brother; we must think of our souls," replied Gorenflot, raising his eyes to heaven.

Chicot looked astounded; he had so often seen Gorenflot feast in a different manner during Lent.

"Our souls!" said he; "and what the devil have herbs and water to do with them?"

"We are forbidden to eat meat on Wednesdays and Fridays."

"But when did you breakfast?"

"I have not breakfasted, my brother," said the monk.

"Not breakfasted! Then what have you done?"

"Composed a discourse," said Gorenflot proudly.

"A discourse, and what for?"

"To deliver this evening at the abbey."

"That is odd."

"And I must be quick and go there, or perhaps my audience will grow impatient."

"Chicot thought of the infinite number of monks he had seen going to the abbey, and wondered why Gorenflot, whom certainly he had never thought eloquent, had been chosen to preach before M. de Mayenne and the numerous assemblage. "When are you to preach?" said he.

"At half-past nine."

"Good; it is still a quarter to nine, you can give me a few minutes. Ventre de biche! we have not dined together for a week."

"It is not our fault, but I know that your duties keep you near our King Henry III., while my duties fill up my time."

"Yes, but it seems to me that is so much the more reason why we should be merry when we do meet."

"Yes, I am merry," said Gorenflot, with a piteous look, "but still I must leave you."

"At least, finish your supper."

Gorenflot looked at the spinach, and sighed, then at the water, and turned away his head.

"Do you remember," said Chicot, "the little dinner at the Porte Montmartre, where, while the king was scourging himself and others, we devoured a teal from the marshes of the Grange-Batelière, with a sauce made with crabs, and we drank that nice Burgundy wine; what do you call it?"

"It is a wine of my country, La Romanée."

"Yes, yes, it was the milk you sucked as a baby, worthy son of Noah."

"It was good," said Gorenflot, "but there is better."

"So says Claude Boutromet, who pretends that he has in his cellar fifty bottles to which that is paltry."

"It is true."

"True, and yet you drink that abominable red water. Fie!" And Chicot, taking the glass, threw the contents out of window.

"There is a time for all, my brother," said Gorenflot, "and wine is good when one has only to praise God after it, but water is better when one has a discourse to pronounce."

"Opinions differ, for I, who have also a discourse to pronounce, am going to ask for a bottle of Romanée. What do you advise me to take with it, Gorenflot?"

"Not these herbs, they are not nice." Chicot, seizing the plate, threw it after the water, and then cried, "Maître Claude."

The host appeared.

"M. Claude, bring me two bottles of your Romanée, which you call so good."

"Why two bottles," said Gorenflot, "as I do not drink it?"

"Oh! if you did I would have four or six, but if I drink alone, two will do for me."

"Indeed; two bottles are reasonable, and if you eat no meat with it, your confessor will have nothing to reproach you with."

"Oh, of course not; meat on a Friday in Lent!" And going to the larder, he drew out a fine capon.

"What are you doing, brother?" said Gorenflot, following his movements with interest.

"You see I am taking this carp."

"Carp!" cried Gorenflot.

"Yes, a carp," said Chicot, showing him the tempting bird.

"And since when has a carp had a beak?"

"A beak! do you see a beak? I only see a nose."

"And wings?"

"Fins!"

"Feathers?"

" Scales, my dear Gorenflot, you are drunk."

" Drunk ! I, who have only eaten spinach and drunk water ? "

" Well, your spinach has overloaded your stomach, and your water has mounted to your head."

" Parbleu ! here is our host, he shall decide."

" So be it, but first let him uncork the wine."

M. Boutromet uncorked a bottle and gave a glass to Chicot. Chicot swallowed and smacked his lips.

"Ah !" said he, " I have a bad memory, I cannot remember if it be better or worse than that at Montmartre. Here, my brother, enlighten me," said he, giving a little to the monk, who was looking on with eager eyes.

Gorenflot took the glass, and drank slowly the liquor it contained.

" It is the same wine," said he, "but I had too little to tell whether it be better or worse."

" But I want to know, and if you had not a sermon to preach, I would beg you to drink a little more."

" If it will give you pleasure, my brother."

Chicot half filled the monk's glass. Gorenflot drank it with great gravity.

" I pronounce it better," said he.

" You flatter our host."

" A good drinker ought, at the first draught, to recognize the wine, at the second, the quality, and, at the third, the age."

" Oh ! I should like to know the age of this wine."

" Give me a few drops more, and I will tell you."

Chicot filled his glass. He drank it off, and then said, " 1561."

" Right," cried Claude Boutromet, " it was 1561."

" Brother Gorenflot," cried Chicot, " they have beatified men at Rome who were worth less than you."

" A little habit," said Gorenflot, modestly.

" And talent ; for I flatter myself I have the habit, and I could not do it. But what are you about ? "

" Going to my assembly."

" Without eating a piece of my carp ? "

" Ah ! true ; you know still less of eating than drinking. M. Boutromet, what is the name of this animal ? "

The innkeeper looked astonished.   " A capon," said he.

" A capon ! " cried Chicot, with an air of consternation.

" Yes, and a fine one."

" Well !" said Gorenflot, triumphantly.

" Well ! it seems I was wrong, but as I wish to eat this capon, and yet not sin, be so kind, brother, as to throw a few drops of water upon it, and christen it a carp."

" Ah ! ah ! "

" Yes, I pray you, save me from mortal sin."

" So be it," cried Gorenflot, " but there is no water."

" Oh ! the intention is all ; baptize it with wine, my brother ; the animal will be less Catholic but quite as good." And Chicot refilled the monk's glass.   The first bottle was finished.

" In the name of Bacchus, Momus, and Comus, trinity of the great saint Pantagruel, I baptize thee, carp," said Gorenflot.

" Now," said Chicot, " to the health of the newly baptized ; may it be cooked to perfection, and may M. Boutromet add to the excellent qualities which it has received from nature."

" To his health," cried Gorenflot, interrupting a hearty laugh to swallow his wine.

" M. Claude, put this carp at once on the spit, cover it with fresh butter, with shalots in it, and put some toast in the frying-pan, and serve it hot."   Gorenflot approved with a motion of his head.

" Now, M. Boutromet, some sardines and a tunny fish, meanwhile ; it is Lent, and I wish to make a maigre dinner.   And let me have two more bottles of wine."

The smell of the cookery began to mount to the brain of the monk.   Yet he made a last effort to rise.

" Then you leave me, after all ? " said Chicot.

" I must," said Gorenflot, raising his eyes to heaven.

" It is very imprudent of you to go to pronounce a discourse fasting."

8

" Why ? "

" Because your strength will fail you.   Galen, has said it.
Pulmo hominis facile deficit."

" Alas ! yes."

" You see, then ? "

" Luckily, I have zeal."

" Ah ! but that is not enough ; I advise you to eat some
sardines, and drink a little of this nectar."

" A single sardine, then, and one glass."   Chicot gave
him the sardine, and passed him the bottle.   He himself
took care to keep sober.

" I feel myself less feeble," said Gorenflot.

" Oh ! you must feel quite strong before you go, and so
I advise you to eat the fins of the carp."   And as they en-
tered with the pullet, Chicot cut off a leg and thigh, which
Gorenflot soon despatched.

" What a delicious fish ! " said Gorenflot.   Chicot cut off
the other leg and gave it to Gorenflot, while he ate the
wings.

" And famous wine," said he, uncorking another
bottle.

Having once commenced, Gorenflot could not stop.   His
appetite was enormous ; he finished the bird, and then
called to Boutromet.   " M. Claude," said he, " I am
hungry ; did you not offer me omelet just now ? "

" Certainly."

" Well, bring it."

" In five minutes."

" Ah ! " said Gorenflot, " now I feel in force ; if the
omelet were here, I could eat it at a mouthful, and I swallow this wine at a gulp."   And he swallowed a quarter of
the third bottle.

" Ah ! you were ill before."

" I was foolish, friend ; that cursed discourse weighed
on my mind ; I have been thinking of it for days."

" It ought to be magnificent."

" Splendid."

" Tell me some of it while we wait for the omelet."

" No, no ; not a sermon at table."

"We have beautiful discourses at the court, I assure you."

"About what?"

"About virtue."

"Ah! yes, he is a very virtuous man, our King Henri III."

"I do not know if he be virtuous; but I know that I have never seen anything there to make me blush."

"You blush!"

At this moment M. Boutromet entered with the omelet and two more bottles.

"Bring it here," cried the monk, with a smile, which showed his thirty-two teeth.

"But, friend, I thought you had a discourse to pronounce."

"It is here," cried Gorenflot, striking his forehead.

"At half-past nine."

"I lied; it was ten."

"Ten! I thought the abbey shut at nine."

"Let it shut; I have a key."

"A key of the abbey!"

"Here, in my pocket."

"Impossible; I know the monastic rules. They would not give the key to a simple monk."

"Here it is," said Gorenflot, showing a piece of money.

"Oh, money! you corrupt the porter to go in when you please, wretched sinner! But what strange money!"

"An effigy of the heretic, with a hole through his heart."

"Yes, I see it is a tester of the Béarn king's, and here is a hole."

"A blow with a dagger. Death to the heretic. He who does it is sure of Paradise."

"He is not yet drunk enough;" so thought Chicot; and he filled his glass again.

"To the mass!" cried Gorenflot, drinking it off.

Chicot remembered the porter looking at the hands of the monks, and said—

"Then, if you show this to the porter——"

" I enter."

"Without difficulty ?"

" As this wine into my stomach." And the monk absorbed a new dose."

" And you pronounce your discourse ?"

" And I pronounce my discourse. I arrive—do you hear ? The assembly is numerous and select. There are barons, counts, and dukes."

" And even princes ?"

" And even princes. I enter humbly among the faithful of the Union——"

"The Union—what does that mean ?"

" I enter ; they call Brother Gorenflot, and I advance——"

At these words the monk rose. "And I advance," continued he, trying to do so, but at the first step he rolled on the floor.

" Bravo !" cried Chicot ; "you advance, you salute the audience and say——"

"No, it is my friends who say, Brother Gorenflot—a fine name for a leaguer, is it not ? "

" A leaguer," thought Chicot : "what truths is this wine going to bring out ? "

"Then I begin." And the monk rose, and leaned against the wall.

" You begin," said Chicot, holding him up.

" I begin, ' My brothers, it is a good day for the faith, a very good day, my brothers ; it is a very good day for the faith.'"

After this, as Chicot loosed his hold, Gorenflot fell full length again on the floor, and before many minutes a loud snoring was heard.

" Good," said Chicot, "he is in for twelve hours' sleep. I can easily undress him."

He then untied the monk's robe, and pulled it off ; then rolled Gorenflot in the tablecloth, and covered his head with a napkin, and hiding the monk's frock under his cloak, passed into the kitchen.

" M. Boutromet," said he, "here is for our supper, and

for my horse; and pray do not wake the worthy Brother
Gorenflot, who sleeps sound."

"No, no; be easy, M. Chicot."

Then Chicot ran to the rue St. Etienne, put on the
monk's robe, took the tester in his hand, and at a quarter
to ten presented himself, not without a beating heart, at
the wicket of the Abbey St. Geneviève.

CHAPTER XIX.

HOW CHICOT FOUND OUT THAT IT WAS EASIER TO GO IN THAN OUT OF THE ABBEY.

CHICOT, from the cloak and other things under the
monk's robe, looked much larger across the shoulders than
usual. His beard was of the same color as Gorenflot's,
and he had so often amused himself with mimicking the
monk's voice and manner of speaking that he could do it
perfectly. Now, every one knows that the beard and the
voice are the only things which are recognizable from
under the depths of a monk's hood. Chicot exhibited his
coin, and was admitted without difficulty, and then followed two other monks to the chapel of the convent. In
this chapel, built in the eleventh century, the choir was
raised nine or ten feet above the rest of the building, and
you mounted into it by two lateral staircases, while an iron
door between them led from the nave to the crypt, into
which you had to descend again. In this choir there was a
portrait of St. Geneviève, and on each side of the altar.
were statues of Clovis and Clotilda.

Three lamps only lighted the chapel, and the imperfect
light gave a greater solemnity to the scene. Chicot was
glad to find that he was not the last, for three monks entered after in gray robes, and placed themselves in front
of the altar. Soon after, a little monk, doubtless a lad
belonging to the choir, came and spoke to one of these
monks, who then said, aloud,—

" We are now one hundred and thirty-six."

Then a great noise of bolts and bars announced that the door was being closed. The three monks were seated in armchairs, like judges. The one who had spoken before now rose and said—

" Brother Monsoreau, what news do you bring to the Union from the province of Anjou ? "

Two things made Chicot start, the first was the voice of the speaker, the second the name of Monsoreau, known to the court only the last few days. A tall monk crossed the assembly, and placed himself in a large chair, behind the shadow of which Chicot had kept himself.

" My brothers," said a voice which Chicot recognized at once as that of the chief huntsman, " the news from Anjou is not satisfactory ; not that we fail there in sympathy, but in representatives. The progress of the Union there had been confided to the Baron de Méridor, but he in despair at the recent death of his daughter, has, in his grief, neglected the affairs of the league, and we cannot at present count on him. As for myself, I bring three new adherents to the association. The council must judge whether these three, for whom I answer, as for myself, ought to be admitted into the Union."

A murmur of applause followed and as Monsoreau regained his seat,—" Brother la Hurière," cried the same monk, " tell us what you have done in the city of Paris."

A man now took the chair and said, " My brothers, you know I am devoted to the Catholic faith, and I have given proofs of this devotion on the great day of its triumph. Yes, my brothers, I glory in saying that I was one of the faithful of our great Henri de Guise, and that I followed his orders strictly. I have now noted all the heretics of the Quartier St. Germain l'Auxerrois, where I shall hold the hotel of the Belle-Etoile, at your service, my brothers. Now, although I no longer thirst for the blood of heretics as formerly, I do not delude myself as to the real object of the holy Union which we are forming. If I am not deceived, brothers, the extinction of private heretics is not all we aim at. We wish to be sure that we shall never be governed by a heretic prince. Now, my friends, what is our situation? Charles IX., who was zealous, died without children; Henri III. will probably do the same, and there remains only the Duc d'Anjou, who not only has no children either, but seems cold towards us."

"What makes you accuse the prince thus?" said the monk who always spoke.

"Because he has not joined us."

"Who tells you so, since there are new adherents?"

"It is true; I will wait; but after him, who is mortal, and has no children, to whom will the crown fall? To the most ferocious Huguenot that can be imagined, to a renegade, a Nebuchadnezzar?" Here the acclamations were tremendous.

"To Henri of Béarn," continued he, "against whom this association is chiefly directed—to Henri, who the people at Pau, or Tarbes, think is occupied with his love affairs, but who is in Paris!"

"In Paris! impossible!" cried many voices.

"He was here on the night when Madame de Sauve was assassinated, and perhaps is here still."

"Death to the Béarnais!" cried several.

"Yes, doubtless, and if he came to lodge at the Belle-Etoile, I answer for him; but he will not come. One does not catch a fox twice in the same hole. He will lodge with some friend, for he has friends. The important thing is to know them. Our union is holy, our league is loyal, consecrated and blessed by the Pope; therefore I demand that it be no longer kept secret, but that we go into the houses and canvass the citizens. Those who sign will be our friends, the others our enemies, and if a second St. Bartholomew come, which seems to the faithful to be more necessary daily, we shall know how to separate the good from the wicked."

Thunders of acclamation followed. When they were calm, the monk who always spoke said,—

"The proposition of Brother la Hurière, whom the union thanks for his zeal, will be taken into consideration by the superior council."

La Hurière bowed, amidst fresh applause.

"Ah ! ah !" thought Chicot, " I begin to see clearly into all this. The Guises are forming a nice little party, and some fine morning Henri will find that he has nothing left, and will be politely invited to enter a monastery. But what will they do with the Duc d'Anjou ? "

" Brother Gorenflot, " then cried the monk.

No one replied.

" Brother Gorenflot, " cried the little monk, in a voice which made Chicot start ; for it sounded like a woman's. However, he rose, and speaking like the monk, said,—

" Here I am ; I was plunged in profound meditation." He feared not to reply, for the members had been counted, and therefore the absence of a member would have provoked an examination. Therefore, without hesitation, he mounted the chair and began.

" My brothers, you know that I purvey for the convent, and have the right of entering every dwelling. I use this privilege for the good of religion. My brothers," continued he, remembering Gorenflot's beginning, " this day, which unites us, is a good one for the faith. Let us speak freely, my brothers, since we are in the house of God.

"What is the kingdom of France ? A body. 'Omnis civitas corpus est.' What is the first requisite of a body ? Good health. How do we preserve this ? By prudent bleedings at times. Now it is evident that the enemies of our religion are too strong ; we must therefore once more bleed that great body we call society. This is what is constantly said to me by the faithful, who give me ham, eggs, or money for the convent."

Several murmurs of approbation interrupted Chicot, then he went on.

" Some may object that the church abhors blood. But they do not say what blood, and I wager that it is not the blood of heretics it abhors. And then another argument ; I said, ' the church ;' but are we the church ? Brother Monsoreau, who spoke so well just now, has, I doubt not, his huntsman's knife in his belt. Brother la Hurière manages the spit ; I, myself, who speak to you—I, Jacques

Gorenflot, have carried the musket in Champagne. It now remains to us to speak of our chiefs, of whom it seems to me, poor monk as I am, that there is something to say. Certainly, it is very well and prudent to come at night under a monk's robe, to hear Brother Gorenflot preach ; but it appears to me that their duties do not stop there. So much prudence may make the Huguenots laugh. Let us play a part more worthy of the brave people we are. What do we want ? The extinction of heresy. Well, that may be cried from the housetops, it seems to me. Why not march in holy procession, displaying our good cause, and our good partisans, but not like the thieves, who keep looking round them to see if the watch is coming. Who is the man who will set the example ? Well, it is I, Jacques Gorenflot ; I, unworthy brother of the order of St. Geneviève, poor and humble purveyor of the convent. It shall be I, who with a cuirass on my back, a helmet on my head, and a musket on my shoulder, will march at the head of all good Catholics who will follow me. This I would do, were it only to make those chiefs blush, who, while defending the Church, hide, as if their cause was a bad one."

This speech, which corresponded with the sentiments of many there, was received with shouts of applause ; and the more so, as up to this time Gorenflot had never shown any enthusiasm for the cause. However, it was not the plan of the chiefs to let this enthusiasm proceed. One of the monks spoke to the lad, who cried in his silvery voice, " My brothers, it is time to retire ; the sitting is over."

The monks rose, all determined to insist on the procession at the next meeting. Many approached the chair to felicitate the author of this brilliant speech ; but Chicot, fearful of being recognized, threw himself on his knees and buried his head in his hands, as if in prayer. They respected his devotions, and went towards the door. However, Chicot had missed his chief aim. What had made him quit the king was the sight of M. de Mayenne and Nicolas David, on both of whom he had, as we know, vowed vengeance ; and although the duke was too great a

man to be attacked openly, Nicolas David was not, and
Chicot was so good a swordsman as to feel sure of success
if he could but meet him.   He therefore began to watch
each monk as he went out, and perceived to his terror
that each, on going out, had to show some sign again.
Gorenflot had told him how to get in, but not how to get
out again.

CHAPTER XX.

HOW CHICOT, FORCED TO REMAIN IN THE ABBEY, SAW AND HEARD THINGS VERY DANGEROUS TO SEE AND HEAR.

CHICOT hastened to get down from his chair, and to
mix among the monks so as to discover, if possible, what
signs they used.   By peeping over their shoulders, he
found out that it was a farthing, with a star cut in the
middle.   Our Gascon had plenty of farthings in his pocket,
but unluckily none with a star in it.   Of course, if when
on coming to the door he was unable to produce the
necessary signs, he would be suspected and examined.
He gained the shade of a pillar, which stood at the corner of a confessional, and stood there wondering what he
should do.   An assistant cried, "Is every one out, the
doors are about to be shut."
No one answered ; Chicot peeped out and saw the chapel
empty, with the exception of the three monks, who still
kept their seats in front of the choir.
" Provided they do not shut the windows, it is all I ask,"
thought Chicot.
"Let us examine," said the young lad to the porter.
Then the porter lifted a taper, and, followed by the young
lad, began to make the tour of the church. There was not
a moment to lose. Chicot softly opened the door of the
confessional, slipped in, and shut the door after him.
They passed close by him, and he could see them through
the spaces of the sculpture.

"Diable!" thought he, "he cannot stay here all night, and once they are gone, I will pile chairs upon benches, Pelion on Ossa, and get out of the window. Ah! yes, but when I have done that, I shall be, not in the street, but in the court. I believe it will be better to pass the night in the confessional ; Gorenflot's robe is warm."

"Extinguish the lamps," now cried the lad ; and the porter with an immense extinguisher put out the lamps, and left the church dark, except for the rays of the moon which shone through the windows. The clock struck twelve.

"Ventre de biche!" said Chicot, "Henri, if he were here, would be nicely frightened ; but, luckily, I am less timid. Come, Chicot, my friend, good night and sleep well."

Then Chicot pushed the inside bolt, made himself as comfortable as he could, and shut his eyes. He was just falling asleep, when he was startled by a loud stroke on a copper bell, and at the same time the lamp in the choir was relighted, and showed the three monks still there.

"What can this mean ?" thought Chicot, starting up. Brave as he was, Chicot was not exempt from superstitious fears. He made the sign of the cross, murmuring, "Vade retro, Satanas !" But as the lights did not go out at the holy sign, Chicot began to think he had to deal with real monks and real lights ; but at this moment one of the flagstones of the choir raised itself slowly, and a monk appeared through the opening, after which the stone shut again. At this sight Chicot's hair stood on end, and he began to fear that all the priors and abbés of St. Geneviève, from Opsat, dead in 533, down to Pierre Boudin, predecessor of the present superior, were being resuscitated from their tombs, and were going to raise with their bony heads the stones of the choir. But this doubt did not last long.

"Brother Monsoreau," said one of the monks to him who had just made so strange an appearance.

"Yes, monseigneur," said he.

"Open the door that he may come to us."

Monsoreau descended to open the door between the staircases, and at the same time the monk in the middle lowered his hood, and showed the great scar, that noble sign by which the Parisians recognized their hero.

"The great Henri of Guise himself!" thought Chicot, "whom his very imbecile majesty believes occupied at the siege of La Charité.   Ah! and he at the right is the Cardinal of Lorraine, and he at the left M. de Mayenne—a trinity not very holy, but very visible."

"Did you think he would come?" said La Balafré to his brothers.

"I was so sure of it, that I have under my cloak wherewith to replace the holy vial."

And Chicot perceived, by the feeble light of the lamp, a silver gilt box, richly chased.   Then about twenty monks, with their heads buried in immense hoods, came out of the crypt, and stationed themselves in the nave.   A single one, conducted by M. de Monsoreau, mounted the staircase, and placed himself at the right of M. de Guise.

Then M. de Guise spoke.   "Friends," said he, "time is precious; therefore I go straight to the point.   You have heard just now, in the first assembly, the complaints of some of our members, who tax with coldness the principal person among us, the prince nearest to the throne.   The time is come to render justice to this prince; you shall hear and judge for yourselves whether your chiefs merit the reproach of coldness and apathy made by one of our brothers, the monk Gorenflot, whom we have not judged it prudent to admit into our secret."

At this name, pronounced in a tone which showed bad intentions towards the warlike monk, Chicot in his confessional could not help laughing quietly.

"Monsieur," said the duke, now turning towards the mysterious personages at his right, "the will of God appears to me manifest; for since you have consented to join us, it shows that what we do is well done.   Now, your highness, we beg of you to lower your hood, that your faithful friends may see with their own eyes that you keep the promise which I made in your name, and which they hardly dared to believe."

The mysterious personage now lowered his hood, and Chicot saw the head of the Duc d'Anjou appear, so pale that, by the light of the lamp, it looked like that of a marble statue.

"Oh, oh!" thought Chicot, "the duke is not yet tired of playing for the crown with the heads of others!"

"Long live Monseigneur le Duc d'Anjou!" cried the assembly.

The duke grew paler than ever.

"Fear nothing, monseigneur," said Henri de Guise; our chapel is deaf, and its doors are well closed."

"My brothers," said the Comte de Monsoreau, "his highness wishes to address a few words to the assembly."

"Yes, yes!" cried they.

"Gentlemen," began he, in a voice so trembling that at first they could hardly distinguish his words, "I believe that God, who often seems insensible and deaf to the things of this world, keeps, on the contrary, His piercing eyes constantly on us, and only remains thus careless in appearance in order to remedy, by some great blow, the disorders caused by the foolish ambitions of men. I also have kept my eyes, if not on the world, at least on France. What have I seen there? The holy religion of Christ shaken to its foundation by those who sap all belief, under the pretext of drawing nearer to God, and my soul has been full of grief. In the midst of this grief, I heard that several noble and pious gentlemen, friends of our old faith, were trying to strengthen the tottering altar. I threw my eyes around me, and saw on one side the heretics, from whom I recoiled with horror; on the other side the elect, and I am come to throw myself into their arms. My brothers, here I am."

The applause and bravos resounded through the chapel. Then the cardinal, turning to the duke, said:

"You are amongst us of your own free will?"

"Of my free will, monsieur."

"Who instructed you in the holy mystery?"

"My friend, the Comte de Monsoreau, a man zealous for religion."

"Then," said the Duc de Guise, "as your highness has

joined us, have the goodness to tell us what you intend to
do for the league."

"I intend to serve the Catholic religion in all its extent."

"Ventre de biche!" thought Chicot, "why not propose
this right out to the king? It would suit him excellently
—processions, macerations, extirpation of heresy, fagots,
and auto-da-fés! Go on, worthy brother of his majesty,
noble imbecile, go on!"

And the duke, as if sensible of the encouragement, proceeded: "But the interests of religion are not the sole
aim which you gentlemen propose. As for me, I see
another; for when a gentleman has thought of what he
owes to God, he then thinks of his country, and he asks
himself if it really enjoys all the honor and prosperity
which it ought to enjoy. I ask this about our France,
and I see with grief that it does not. Indeed, the state
is torn to pieces by different wills and tastes, one as powerful as the other. It is, I fear, to the feebleness of the
head, which forgets that it ought to govern all for the
good of its subjects, or only remembers this royal princi-
ple at capricious intervals, when the rare acts of energy
are generally not for the good, but the ill of France, that
we must attribute these evils. Whatever be the cause,
the ill is a real one, although I accuse certain false friends
of the king rather than the king himself. Therefore I
join myself to those who by all means seek the extinction
of heresy and the ruin of perfidious counselors."

This discourse appeared profoundly to interest the
audience, who, throwing back their hoods, drew near to
the duke.

"Monseigneur," said the Duc de Guise, "in thanking
your royal highness for the words you have just uttered, I
will add that you are surrounded by people devoted not
only to the principles which you profess, but to the person
of your highness; and if you have any doubt, the conclusion
of this sitting will convince you."

"Monseigneur," said the cardinal, "if your highness
still experiences any fear, the names of those who now surround you will, I hope, reassure you. Here is M. le Gou-

verneur d'Aunis, M. d'Antragues, M. de Ribeirac, and M. de
Livarot, and gentlemen whom your highness doubtless
knows to be as brave as loyal. Here are, besides, M. de
Castillon, M. le Baron de Lusignan, MM. Cruce and Leclerc,
all ready to march under the guidance of your highness, to
the emancipation of religion and the throne. We shall,
then, receive with gratitude the orders that you will give us."

Then M. de Mayenne said: "You are by your birth,
and by your wisdom, monseigneur, the natural chief of
the Holy Union, and we ought to learn from you what our
conduct should be with regard to the false friends of his
majesty of whom you just now spoke."

"Nothing more simple," replied the prince, with that
feverish excitement which in weak natures supplies the
place of courage to weak minds ; "when venomous plants
grow in a field, we root them up. The king is surrounded,
not with friends, but with courtiers, who ruin him, and
cause a perpetual scandal in France and all Christendom."

"It is true," said the Duc de Guise, in a gloomy tone.

"And," said the cardinal, "these courtiers prevent us,
who are his majesty's true friends, from approaching him
as we have the right to do by our birth and position."

"Let us, then," said M. de Mayenne, "leave the heretics to the vulgar leaguers ; let us think of those who
annoy and insult us, and who often fail in respect to the
prince whom we honor, and who is our chief."

The Duc d'Anjou grew red.

"Let us destroy," continued Mayenne, "to the last
man, that cursed race whom the king enriches, and let
each of us charge ourselves with the life of one. We are
thirty here ; let us count."

"I," said D'Antragues, "charge myself with Quelus."

"I with Maugiron," said Livarot.

"And I with Schomberg," said Ribeirac.

"Good !" said the duke ; "and there is Bussy, my brave
Bussy, who will undertake some of them."

"And us !" cried the rest.

M. de Monsoreau now advanced. "Gentlemen," said
he, "I claim an instant's silence. We are resolute men,

and yet we fear to speak freely to each other ; we are in
telligent men, and yet we are deterred by foolish scruples.
Come, gentlemen, a little courage, a little hardihood, a
little frankness.   It is not of the king's minions that we
think ; there does not lie our difficulty.   What we really
complain of is the royalty which we are under, and which
is not acceptable to a French nobility ; prayers and des-
potism, weakness and orgies, prodigality for fêtes which
make all Europe laugh, and parsimony for everything
that regards the state and the arts.   Such conduct is not
weakness or ignorance—it is madness."

A dead silence followed this speech.   Every one trembled
at the words which echoed his own thoughts.   M. de Monsoreau went on.

"Must we live under a king, foolish, inert, and lazy, at
a time when all other nations are active, and work glori-
ously, while we sleep ?   Gentlemen, pardon me for saying
before a prince, who will perhaps blame my temerity (for
he has the prejudices of family), that for four years we
have been governed, not by a king, but by a monk."

At these words the explosion so skilfully prepared and as
skilfully kept in check, burst out with violence.

"Down with the Valois !" they cried, "down with
Brother Henri !   Let us have for chief a gentleman, a
knight, rather a tyrant than a monk."

"Gentlemen !" cried the Duc d'Anjou, hypocritically,
"let me plead for my brother, who is led away.   Let me
hope that our wise remonstrances, that the efficacious intervention of the power of the League, will bring him
back into the right path."

"Hiss, serpent, hiss," said Chicot to himself.

"Monseigneur," replied the Duc de Guise, "your highness has heard, perhaps rather too soon, but still you have
heard, the true meaning of the association.   No ! we are
not really thinking of a league against the Béarnais, nor
of a league to support the Church, which will support itself : no, we think of raising the nobility of France from
its abject condition.   Too long we have been kept back by
the respect we feel for your highness, by the love which

we know you to have for your family. Now, all is re-
vealed, monseigneur, and your highness will assist at the
true sitting of the League. All that has passed is but
preamble."

"What do you mean, M. le Duc ?" asked the prince,
his heart beating at once with alarm and ambition.

"Monseigneur, we are united here, not only to talk,
but to act. To-day we choose a chief capable of honoring
and enriching the nobility of France ; and as it was the
custom of the ancient Franks when they chose a chief to
give him a present worthy of him, we offer a present to the
chief whom we have chosen."

All hearts beat, and that of the prince most of any ; yet
he remained mute and motionless, betraying his emotion
only by his paleness.

"Gentlemen," continued the duke, taking something
from behind him, "here is the present that in your name
I place at the feet of the prince."

"A crown !" cried the prince, scarcely able to stand,
"a crown to me, gentlemen ?"

"Long live François III. !" cried all the gentlemen,
drawing their swords.

"I ! I !" cried the Duke, trembling with joy and terror.
"It is impossible ! My brother still lives ; he is the
anointed of the Lord."

"We depose him," said the duke, "waiting for the
time when God shall sanction, by his death, the election
which we are about to make, or rather, till one of his
subjects, tired of this inglorious reign, forestalls by poison
or the dagger the justice of God."

"Gentlemen !" said the duke, feebly.

"Monseigneur," then said the cardinal, " to the scruple
which you so nobly expressed just now, this is our answer.
Henri III. was the anointed of the Lord, but we have de-
posed him ; it is you who are going to be so. Here is a
temple as venerable as that of Rheims ; for here have re-
posed the relics of St Geneviève, patroness of Paris ; here
has been embalmed the body of Clovis, our first Christian
king ; well, monseigneur, in this holy temple, I, one of

the princes of the Church, and who may reasonably hope
to become one day its head, I tell you, monseigneur, that
here, to replace the holy oil, is an oil sent by Pope Gregory XIII. Monseigneur, name your future archbishop
of Rheims, name your constable, and in an instant, it is
you who will be king, and your brother Henri, if he do
not give you up the crown, will be the usurper. Child,
light the altar."

Immediately, the lad, who was evidently waiting, came
out, and presently fifty lights shone round the altar and
choir.

Then was seen on the altar a miter glittering with precious stones, and a large sword ornamented with flour-de-
lis. It was the archbishop's miter and the constable's
sword. At the same moment the organ began to play the
Veni Creator. This sudden stroke, managed by the three
Lorraine princes, and which the Duc d'Anjou himself did
not expect, made a profound impression on the spectators.
The courageous grew bolder than ever, and the weak
grew strong. The Duc d'Anjou raised his head, and with
a firmer step than might have been expected, walked to
the altar, took the miter in the left hand and the sword in
the right, presented one to the cardinal and the other to
the duke. Unanimous applause followed this action.

"Now, gentlemen," said the prince to the others,
"give your names to M. de Mayenne, grand Master of
France, and the day when I ascend the throne, you shall
have the cordon bleu."

"Mordieu!" thought Chicot, "what a pity I cannot
give mine; I shall never have such another opportunity."

"Now to the altar, sire," said the cardinal.

"Monsieur de Monsoreau my colonel, MM. de Ribeirac
and d'Antragues my captains, and M. Livarot, my lieutenant of the guards, take your places."

Each of those named took the posts which, at a real
coronation, etiquette would have assigned to them. Meanwhile, the cardinal had passed behind the altar to put on
his pontifical robes; soon he reappeared with the holy vial.
Then the lad brought to him a Bible and a cross. The

cardinal put the cross on the book and extended them towards the Duc d'Anjou, who put his hand on them, and
said,—

"In the presence of God, I promise to my people to
maintain and honor our holy religion as a Christian king
should. And may God and His saints aid me !"

Then the Duc de Guise laid the sword before the altar,
and the cardinal blessed it and gave it to the prince.

"Sire," said he, "take this sword, which is given to you
with the blessing of God, that you may resist your enemies,
and protect and defend the holy Church, which is confided to you. Take this sword that, with it, you may
exercise justice, protect the widow and the orphan, repair
disorders, so that, covering yourself with glory by all the
virtues, you will be a blessing to your people."

Then the prince returned the sword to the Duc de Guise,
and knelt down. The cardinal opened the gold box, and,
with the point of a golden needle, drew out some holy
oil ; he then said two prayers, and taking the oil on his
finger, traced with it a cross on the head of the prince,
saying, "Ungo dein regem de oleo sanctificato, in nomine
Patris et Filii et Spiritus Sancti."

The lad wiped off the oil with an embroidered handkerchief. Then the cardinal took the crown, and, holding it
over the head of the prince, said, "God crown thee with the
crown of glory and justice." Then, placing it, "Receive
this crown, in the name of the Father, the Son, and the Holy
Ghost."

All brandished their swords and cried, " Long live
François III."

"Sire," said the cardinal, " you reign henceforth over
France."

"Gentlemen," said the prince, " I shall never forget
the names of the thirty gentlemen who first judged me
worthy to reign over them ; and now adieu, and may God
have you in His holy keeping."

The Duc de Mayenne led away the new king, while the
other two brothers exchanged an ironical smile.

CHAPTER XXI.

HOW CHICOT LEARNED GENEALOGY.

WHEN the Duc d'Anjou was gone, and had been followed by all the others, the three Guises entered the vestry. Chicot, thinking of course this was the end, got up to stretch his limbs, and then, as it was nearly two o'clock, once more disposed himself to sleep.

But to his great astonishment, the three brothers almost immediately came back again, only this time without their frocks. On seeing them appear, the lad burst into so hearty a fit of laughing, that Chicot could hardly help laughing also.

" Do not laugh so loud, sister," said the Duc de Mayenne ; " they are hardly gone out, and might hear you."

As he spoke, the seeming lad threw back his hood, and displayed a head as charming and intelligent as was ever painted by Leonardo da Vinci. Black eyes, full of fun, but which could assume an expression almost terrible in its seriousness, a little rosy mouth, and a round chin terminating the perfect oval of a rather pale face. It was Madame de Montpensier, a dangerous syren, who had the soul of a demon with the face of an angel.

" Ah, brother cardinal," cried she, " how well you acted the holy man ! I was really afraid for a minute that you were serious ; and he letting himself be greased and crowned. Oh, how horrid he looked with his crown on !"

" Never mind," said the duke, " we have got what we wanted, and François cannot now deny his share. Monsoreau, who doubtless had his own reasons for it, led the thing on well, and now he cannot abandon us, as he did La Mole and Coconnas."

Chicot saw that they had been laughing at M. d'Anjou, and as he detested him, would willingly have embraced them for it, always excepting M. de Mayenne, and giving his share to his sister.

" Let us return to business," said the cardinal, " is all well closed ? "

" Oh, yes ! " said the duchess, " but if you like I will go and see."

" Oh, no ; you must be tired."

" No ; it was too amusing."

" Mayenne, you say he is here ? "

" Yes."

" I did not see him."

" No, he is hidden in a . confessional."

These words startled Chicot fearfully.

" Then he has heard and seen all ? " asked the duke.

" Never mind, he is one of us."

" Bring him here, Mayenne."

Mayenne descended the staircase and came straight to where Chicot was hiding. He was brave, but now his teeth chattered with terror. " Ah," thought he, trying to get out his sword from under his monk's frock, " at least I will kill him first ! " The duke had already extended his hand to open the door, when Chicot heard the duchess say :

" Not there, Mayenne ; in that confessional to the left."

" It was time," thought Chicot, as the duke turned away, " but who the devil can the other be ? "

" Come out, M. David," said Mayenne, " we are alone."

" Here I am, monseigneur," said he, coming out.

" You have heard all ? " asked the Duc de Guise.

" I have not lost a word, monseigneur."

" Then you can report it to the envoy of his Holiness Gregory XIII. ? "

" Everything."

" Now, Mayenne tells me you have done wonders for us ; let us see."

" I have done what I promised, monseigneur ; that is to say, found a method of seating you, without opposition, on the throne of France ! "

" They also ! " thought Chicot ; " every one wants then to be King of France ! "

Chicot was gay now, for he felt safe once more, and he

had discovered a conspiracy by which he hoped to ruin his two enemies.

" To gain a legitimate right is everything," continued Nicolas David, " and I have discovered that you are the true heirs, and the Valois only a usurping branch."

" It is difficult to believe," said the duke, " that our house, however illustrious it may be, comes before the Valois."

" It is nevertheless proved, monseigneur," said David, drawing out a parchment. ˙ The duke took it.

" What is this ?" said he.

" The genealogical tree of the house of Lorraine."

" Of which the root is ?"

" Charlemagne, monseigneur."

" Charlemagne !" cried the three brothers, with an air of incredulous satisfaction, " Impossible !"

" Wait, monseigneur ; you may be sure I have not raised a point to which any one may give the lie. What you want is a long lawsuit, during which you can gain over, not the people, they are yours, but the parliament. See, then, monseigneur, here it is. Ranier, first Duc de Lorraine, contemporary with Charlemagne ;—Guibert, his son ;—Henri, son of Guibert——"

" But——" said the duke.

" A little patience, monseigneur. Bonne——"

" Yes," said the duke, " daughter of Ricin, second son of Ranier."

" Good ; to whom married ?"

" Bonne ?"

" Yes."

" To Charles of Lorraine, son of Louis IV., King of France."

" Just so. Now add, ' brother of Lothaire, despoiled of the crown of France by the usurper, Hugh Capet.'"

" Oh ! oh !" said the duke and the cardinal.

" Now, Charles of Lorraine inherited from his brother Lothaire. Now, the race of Lothaire is extinct, therefore you are the only true heirs of the throne."

" What do you say to that, brother ?" cried the cardinal.

" I say, that unluckily there exists in France a law they call the Salic law, which destroys all our pretensions."

" I expected that objection, monseigneur," said David, but what is the first example of the Salic law ? "

" The accession of Philippe de Valois, to the prejudice of Edward of England."

" What was the date of that accession ? "

" 1328," said the cardinal.

" That is to say, 341 years after the usurpation of Hugh Capet, 240 years after the extinction of the race of Lothaire. Then, for 240 years your ancestors had already had a right to the throne before the Salic law was invented. Now, every one knows that the law cannot have any retrospective effect."

" You are a clever man, M. David," said the Duc de Guise.

" It is very ingenious," said the cardinal.

" It is very fine," said Mayenne.

" It is admirable," said the duchess ; " then I am a princess royal. I will have no one less than the Emperor of Germany for a husband."

" Well ; here are your 200 gold crowns which I promised you."

" And here are 200 others," said the cardinal, " for the new mission with which we are about to charge you."

" Speak, monseigneur, I am ready."

" We cannot commission you to carry this genealogy yourself to our holy Father, Gregory XIII."

" Alas ! no ; my will is good, but I am of too poor birth."

" Yes, it is a misfortune. We must therefore send Pierre de Gondy on this mission."

" Permit me to speak," said the duchess. " The Gondys are clever, no doubt, but ambitious, and not to be trusted."

" Oh ! reassure yourself. Gondy shall take this, but mixed with other papers, and not knowing what he carries. The Pope will approve, or disapprove, silently, and Gondy will bring us back the answer, still in ignorance of what he brings. You, Nicolas David, shall wait for him at Chalons, Lyons, or Avignon, according to your instructions. Thus you alone will know our true secret."

Then the three brothers shook hands, embraced their sister, put on again their monk's robes, and disappeared. Behind them the porter drew the bolts, and then came in and extinguished the lights, and Chicot heard his retreating steps fainter and fainter, and all was silent.

" It seems now all is really over," thought Chicot, and he came out of the confessional. He had noticed in a corner a ladder destined to clean the windows. He felt about until he found it, for it was close to him, and by the light of the moon placed it against the window. He easily opened it, and striding across it and drawing the ladder to him with that force and address which either fear or joy always gives, he drew it from the inside to the outside. When he had descended, he hid the ladder in a hedge, which was planted at the bottom of the wall, jumped from tomb to tomb, until he reached the outside wall over which he clambered. Once in the street he breathed more freely ; he had escaped with a few scratches from the place where he had several times felt his life in danger. He went straight to the Corne d'Abondance, at which he knocked. It was opened by Claude Boutromet himself, who knew him at once, although he went out dressed as a cavalier, and returned attired as a monk.

" Ah ! is it you ? " cried he.

Chicot gave him a crown, and asked for Gorenflot.

The host smiled, and said, "Look !"

Brother Gorenflot lay snoring just in the place where Chicot had left him.

CHAPTER XXII.

HOW M. AND MADAME DE ST. LUC MET WITH A TRAVELING COMPANION.

THE next morning, about the time when Gorenflot woke from his nap, warmly rolled in his frock, our reader, if he had been traveling on the road from Paris to Angers, might have seen a gentleman and his page, riding quietly side by side. These cavaliers had arrived at Chartres the evening before, with foaming horses, one of which had fallen with fatigue, as they stopped. They entered the inn, and half an hour after set out on fresh horses. Once in the country, still bare and cold, the taller of the two approached the other, and said, as he opened his arms :

"Dear little wife, embrace me, for now we are safe."

Then Madame de St. Luc, leaning forward and opening her thick cloak, placed her arms round the young man's neck and gave him the long and tender kiss which he had asked for. They stayed the night in the little village of Courville four leagues only from Chartres, but which from its isolation seemed to them a secure retreat ; and it was on the following morning that they were, as we said, pursuing their way. This day, as they were more easy in their minds, they traveled no longer like fugitives, but like schoolboys seeking for moss, for the first few early flowers, enjoying the sunshine and amused at everything."

"Morbleu !" cried St. Luc, at last, "how delightful it is to be free. Have you ever been free, Jeanne ?"

"I ?" cried she, laughing, "never ; it is the first time I ever felt so. My father was suspicious, and my mother lazy. I never went out without a governess and two lackeys, so that I do not remember having run on the grass, since, when a laughing child, I ran in the woods of Méridor with my dear Diana, challenging her to race, and rushing through the branches. But you, dear St. Luc ; you were free, at least ?"

"I, free ? "

"Doubtless, a man."

"Never.   Brought up with the Duc d'Anjou, taken by
him to Poland, brought back to Paris, condemned never to
leave him by the perpetual rule of etiquette ; pursued ,if I
tried to go away, by that doleful voice, crying, 'St. Luc,
my friend, I am ennuyé, come and amuse me.'   Free,
with that stiff corset which strangled me, and that great
ruff which scratched my neck !   No, I have never been
free till now, and I enjoy it."

"If they should catch us, and send us to the Bastile ? "

"If they only put us there together, we can bear it."

"I do not think they would.   But there is no fear, if you
only knew Méridor, its great oaks, and its endless thickets,
its rivers, its lakes, its flower-beds and lawns ; and, then,
in the midst of all, the queen of this kingdom, the beautiful, the good Diana.   And I know she loves me still ; she
is not capricious in her friendships.   Think of the happy
life we shall lead there."

"Let us push on ; I am in haste to get there," and they
rode on, stayed the night at Mans, and then set off for
Méridor.   They had already reached the woods and thought
themselves in safety, when they saw behind them a cavalier advancing at a rapid pace.   St. Luc grew pale.

"Let us fly," said Jeanne.

"Yes ; let us fly, for there is a plume on that hat which
disquiets me ; it is of a color much in vogue at the court,
and he looks to me like an ambassador from our royal
master."

But to fly was easier to say than to do ; the trees grew so
thickly that it was impossible to ride through them but
slowly, and the soil was so sandy that the horses sank into
it at every step.   The cavalier gained upon them rapidly,
and soon they heard his voice crying,—

"Eh, monsieur, do not run away ; I bring you something you have lost."

"What does he say ? " asked Jeanne.

"He says we have lost something."

"Eh ! monsieur," cried the unknown, again, "you left

a bracelet in the hotel at Courville. Diable! a lady's portrait; above all, that of Madame de Cossé. For the sake of that dear mamma, do not run away."

. "I know that voice," said St. Luc.

"And then he speaks of my mother."

"It is Bussy!"

"The Comte de Bussy, our friend," and they reined up their horses.

"Good morning, madame," said Bussy, laughing, and giving her the bracelet.

"Have you come from the king to arrest us?"

"No, ma foi, I am not sufficiently his majesty's friend for such a mission. No, I found your bracelet at the hotel, which showed me that you preceded me on my way."

"Then," said St. Luc, "it is chance which brings you on our path."

"Chance, or rather Providence."

Every remaining shadow of suspicion vanished before the sincere smile and bright eyes of the handsome speaker.

"Then you are traveling?" asked Jeanne.

"I am."

"But not like us?"

"Unhappily, no."

"I mean in disgrace. Where are you going?"

"Towards Angers, and you?"

"We also."

"Ah! I should envy your happiness if envy were not so vile."

"Eh! M. de Bussy, marry, and you will be as happy as we are," said Jeanne; "it is so easy to be happy when you are loved."

"Ah! madame, every one is not so fortunate as you."

"But you, the universal favorite."

"To be loved by every one is as though you were loved by no one, madame."

"Well, let me marry you, and you will know the happiness you deny."

"I do not deny the happiness, only that it does not exist for me."

"Shall I marry you ? "

" If you marry me according to your taste, no ; if according to mine, yes."

" Are you in love with a woman whom you cannot marry ?"

" Comte," said Bussy, "beg your wife not to plunge daggers in my heart."

"Take care, Bussy ; you will make me think it is with her you are in love."

" If it were so, you will confess, at least, that I am a lover not much to be feared."

"True," said St. Luc, remembering how Bussy had brought him his wife. " But confess, your heart is occupied."

" I avow it."

" By a love, or by a caprice ?" asked Jeanne.

" By a passion, madame."

" I will cure you."

" I do not believe it."

" I will marry you."

" I doubt it."

" And I will make you as happy as you ought to be."

" Alas ! madame, my only happiness now is to be unhappy."

" I am very determined."

" And I also."

" Well, will you accompany us ?"

" Where are you going ? "

" To the château of Méridor."

The blood mounted to the cheeks of Bussy, and then he grew so pale, that his secret would certainly have been betrayed, had not Jeanne been looking at her husband with a smile. Bussy therefore had time to recover himself, and said,—

" Where is that ? "

" It is the property of one of my best friends."

" One of your best friends, and—are they at home ?"

" Doubtless," said Jeanne, who was completely ignorant of the events of the last two months : " but have you never heard of the Baron de Méridor, one of the richest noble-men in France, and of——"

"Of what ?"

"Of his daughter, Diana, the most beautiful girl pos-sible ?"

Bussy was filled with astonishment, asking himself by what singular happiness he found on the road people to talk to him of Diana de Méridor to echo the only thought which he had in his mind.

"Is this castle far off, madame ?" asked he.

"About seven leagues, and we shall sleep there to-night ; you will come, will you not ?"

"Yes, madame."

"Come, that is already a step towards the happiness I promised you."

"And the baron, what sort of a man is he ?"

"A perfect gentleman, a preux chevalier, who, had he lived in King Arthur's time, would have had a place at his round table."

"And," said Bussy, steadying his voice, "to whom is his daughter married ?"

"Diana married ?"

"Would that be extraordinary ?"

"Of course not, only I should have been the first to hear of it."

"Bussy could not repress a sigh. "Then," said he, "you expect to find Mademoiselle de Méridor at the château with her father ?"

"We trust so."

They rode on a long time in silence, and at last Jeanne cried :

"Ah ! there are the turrets of the castle. Look, M. de Bussy, through that great leafless wood, which in a month, will be so beautiful ; do you not see the roof ?"

"Yes," said Bussy, with an emotion which astonished himself ; "and is that the château of Méridor ?"

And he thought of the poor prisoner shut up in the Rue St. Antoine.

CHAPTER XXIII.

THE OLD MAN.

Two hours after they reached the castle. Bussy had been debating within himself whether or not to confide to his friends what he knew about Diana. But there was much that he could tell to no one, and he feared their questions, and besides, he wished to enter Méridor as a stranger.

Madame de St. Luc was surprised, when the report sounded his horn to announce a visit, that Diana did not run as usual to meet them, but instead of her appeared an old man, bent and leaning on a stick, and his white hair flying in the wind. He crossed the drawbridge, followed by two great dogs, and when he drew quite near, said in a feeble voice,—

"Who is there, and who does a poor old man the honor to visit him?"

"It is I, Seigneur Augustin!" cried the laughing voice of the young woman.

But the baron, raising his head slowly, said, "You? I do not see. Who is it?"

"Oh, mon Dieu!" cried Jeanne, "do you not know me? It is true, my disguise——"

"Excuse me," said the old man, "but I can see little; the eyes of old men are not made for weeping, and if they weep too much, the tears burn them."

"Must I tell you my name? I am Madame de St. Luc."

"I do not know you."

"Ah! but my maiden name was Jeanne de Cossé-Brissac."

"Ah, mon Dieu!" cried the old man, trying to open the gate with his trembling hands. Jeanne, who did not understand this strange reception, still attributed it only to his declining faculties; but, seeing that he remembered her, jumped off her horse to embrace him, but as she did so she felt his cheek wet with tears.

" Come," said the old man, turning towards the house, without even noticing the others. The château had a strange sad look ; all the blinds were down, and no one was visible.

" Is Diana unfortunately not at home ? " asked Jeanne.

The old man stopped, and looked at her with an almost terrified expression. " Diana ! " said he. At this name the two dogs uttered a mournful howl. " Diana ! " repeated the old man ; " do you not, then, know ? "

And his voice, trembling before, was extinguished in a sob.

" But what has happened ? " cried Jeanne, clasping her hands.

" Diana is dead ! " cried the old man, with a torrent of tears.

" Dead ! " cried Jeanne, growing as pale as death.

" Dead," thought Bussy ; " then he has let him also think her dead. Poor old man ! how he will bless me some day ! "

" Dead ! " cried the old man again ; " they killed her."

" Ah, my dear baron ! " cried Jeanne, bursting into tears, and throwing her arms round the old man's neck.

" But," said he at last, " though desolate and empty, the old house is none the less hospitable. Enter."

Jeanne took the old man's arm, and they went into the dining-hall, where he sunk into his armchair. At last, he said, " You said you were married ; which is your husband ? "

M. de St. Luc advanced and bowed to the old man, who tried to smile as he saluted him ; then, turning to Bussy, said, " And this gentleman ? "

" He is our friend, M. Louis de Clermont, Comte de Bussy d'Amboise, gentleman of M. le Duc d'Anjou."

At these words the old man started up, threw a withering glance at Bussy, and then sank back with a groan.

" What is it ? " said Jeanne.

" Does the baron know you, M. de Bussy ? " asked St. Luc.

"It is the first time I ever had the honor of seeing M. de Méridor," said Bussy, who alone understood the effect which the name of the Duc d'Anjou had produced on the old man.

"Ah! you a gentleman of the Duc d'Anjou!" cried the baron, "of that monster, that demon, and you dare to avow it, and have the audacity to present yourself here!"

"Is he mad?" asked St. Luc of his wife.

"Grief must have turned his brain," replied she, in terror.

"Yes, that monster!" cried he again; "the assassin who killed my child! Ah, you do not know," continued he, taking Jeanne's hands; "but the duke killed my Diana, my child—he killed her!"

Tears stood in Bussy's eyes, and Jeanne said:

"Seigneur, were it so, which I do not understand, you cannot accuse M. de Bussy of this dreadful crime—he, who is the most noble and generous gentleman living. See, my good father, he weeps with us. Would he have come had he known how you would receive him? Ah, dear baron, tell us how this catastrophe happened."

"Then you did not know?" said the old man to Bussy.

"Eh, mon Dieu! no," cried Jeanne, "we none of us know."

"My Diana is dead, and her best friend did not know it! Oh, it is true! I wrote to no one; it seemed to me that everything must die with her. Well, this prince, this disgrace to France, saw my Diana, and, finding her so beautiful, had her carried away to his castle of Beaugé to dishonor her. But Diana, my noble and sainted Diana, chose death instead. She threw herself from the window into the lake, and they found nothing but her veil floating on the surface." And the old man finished with a burst of sobs which overwhelmed them all.

"Oh, comte," cried St. Luc, "you must abandon this infamous prince; a noble heart like yours cannot remain friendly to a ravisher and an assassin!"

But Bussy instead of replying to this, advanced to M. de Méridor.

"M. le Baron," said he, "will you grant me the honor of a private interview ?"

"Listen to M. de Bussy, dear seigneur," said Jeanne ; "you will see that he is good and may help you."

"Speak, monsieur," said the baron, trembling.

Bussy turned to St. Luc and his wife, and said :

"Will you permit me ?"

The young couple went out, and then Bussy said : "M. le Baron, you have accused the prince whom I serve in terms which force me to ask for an explanation. Do not mistake the sense in which I speak ; it is with the most profound sympathy, and the most earnest desire to soften your griefs, that I beg of you to recount to me the details of this dreadful event. Are you sure all hope is lost ?"

"Monsieur, I had once a moment's hope. A noble gentleman, M. de Monsoreau, loved my poor daughter, and interested himself for her."

"M. de Monsoreau ! Well, what was his conduct in all this !"

"Ah, generous ; for Diana had refused his hand. He was the first to tell me of the infamous projects of the duke ; he showed me how to baffle them, only asking, if he succeeded, for her hand. I gave my consent with joy; but alas ! it was useless—he arrived too late—my poor Diana had saved herself by death !"

"And since then, what have you heard of him ?"

"It is a month ago, and the poor gentleman has not dared to appear before me, having failed in his generous design."

"Well, monsieur," said Bussy, "I am charged by the Duc d'Anjou to bring you to Paris, where his highness desires to speak to you."

"I !" cried the baron, "I see this man ! And what can the murderer have to say to me ?"

"Who knows ? To justify himself perhaps."

"No, M. de Bussy, no, I will not go to Paris ; it would be too far away from where my child lies in her cold bed."

"M. le Baron," said Bussy firmly, "I have come ex-

10

pressly to take you to Paris, and it is my duty to do so."

" Well, I will go," cried the old man, trembling with anger ; " but wo to those who bring me. The king will hear me, or, if he will not, I will appeal to all the gentlemen of France. Yes, M. de Bussy, I will accompany you."

" And I, M. le Baron," said Bussy, taking his hand, " recommend to you the patience and calm dignity of a Christian nobleman. God is merciful to noble hearts, and you know not what He reserves for you. I beg you also, while waiting for that day, not to count me among your enemies, for you do not know what I will do for you. Till to-morrow, then, baron, and early in the morning we will set off."

" I consent," replied the old baron, moved by Bussy's tone and words ; " but meanwhile, friend or enemy, you are my guest, and I will show you to your room."

CHAPTER XXIV.

HOW RÉMY-LE-HAUDOUIN HAD, IN BUSSY'S ABSENCE, ESTABLISHED A COMMUNICATION WITH THE RUE ST. ANTOINE.

M. AND MADAME DE ST. LUC could hardly recover from their surprise. Bussy, holding secret interviews with M. de Méridor, and then setting off with him for Paris, appearing to take the lead in a matter which at first seemed strange and unknown to him, was to the young people an inexplicable phenomenon. In the morning the baron took leave of his guests, begging them to remain in the castle. Before Bussy left, however, he whispered a few words to Madame de St. Luc, which brought the color to her cheeks, and smiles to her eyes.

It was a long way from Méridor to Paris, especially for the old baron, covered with wounds from all his battles, and for his old horse, whom he called Jarnac. Bussy studied earnestly during the journey to find his way to the heart of the old man by his care and attentions, and without doubt he succeeded, for on the sixth morning, as they arrived at Paris, M. de Méridor said :

" It is singular, count, but I feel less unquiet at the end than at the beginning of my journey."

" Two hours more, M. le Baron, and you shall have judged me as I deserve."

" Where are we going—to the Louvre ?"

" Let me first take you to my hotel, that you may refresh yourself a little, and be fit to see the person to whom I am leading you."

The count's people had been very much alarmed at his long absence, for he had set off without telling any one but Rémy. Thus their delight on seeing him again was great, and they all crowded round him with joyous exclamations. He thanked them, and then said, " Now assist this gentleman to dismount, and remember that I look upon him with more respect than a prince."

When M. de Méridor had been shown to his room, and had had some refreshment, he asked if they should set out.

" Soon, baron ; and be easy—it will be a happiness for you as well as for us."

" You speak in a language which I do not understand."

Bussy smiled, and left the room to seek Rémy.

" Well ! dear Hippocrates !" said he, " is there anything new ?"

" Nothing ; all goes well."

" Then the husband has not returned ?"

" Yes, he has, but without success. It seems there is a father who is expected to turn up to make the dénouement.

" Good," said Bussy, " but how do you know all this ?"

" Why, monseigneur, as your absence made my position a sinecure, I thought I would try to make some little use of my time ; so I took some books and a sword to a little room which I hired at the corner of the Rue St. Antoine, from whence I could see the house that you know."

" Very good."

" But as I feared, if I were constantly watching, to pass for a spy, I thought it better to fall in love."

" In love ? "

" Oh yes, desperately with Gertrude ; she is a fine girl, only two inches taller than myself, and who recounts capitally."

"Recounts ? "

" Yes ; through her I know all that passes with her mistress. I thought you might not dislike to have communications with the house."

"Rémy, you are a good genius, whom chance, or rather Providence, has placed in my way. Then you are received in the house ? "

" Last night I made my entrance on the points of my toes, by the door you know."

" And how did you manage it ? "

" Quite naturally. The day after you left, I waited at my door till the lady of my thoughts came out to buy provisions, which she does every morning. She recognized me, uttered a cry, and ran away."

" Then ? "

" Then I ran after her, but could hardly catch her, for she runs fast ; but still, petticoats are always a little in the way. 'Mon Dieu !' cried she. 'Holy Virgin !' said I. 'The doctor !' 'The charming housekeeper.' She smiled, but said, 'You are mistaken, monsieur, I do not know you.' 'But I know you,' I replied, 'and for the last three days I have lived but for you, and I adore you so much, that I no longer live in the Rue Beautreillis, but at the corner of this street, and I changed my lodging only to see you pass in and out.'"

" So that now you are——"

" As happy as a lover can be—with Gertrude."

" Does she suspect you come from me ? "

" Oh no, how should the poor doctor know a great lord like M. de Bussy. No, I said, 'And how is your young master ?' 'What young master ?' 'The one I cured.' 'He is not my master.' 'Oh ! I thought, as he was in your mistress's bed——' 'Oh ! no, poor young man ! we have only seen him once since.' 'Do you know his name ?' 'Oh ! yes ; he is the Seigneur de Bussy.' 'What ! the

brave Bussy?' 'Yes himself.' 'And your mistress?'
'Oh! she is married!' 'Yes, but still she may think
sometimes of a handsome young man when she has seen
him lying wounded in her bed.' 'Oh, to be frank, I do
not say she does not think of him; we talk of him very
often.' 'What do you say about him?' I asked. 'I recount all I hear about his prowess, and I have even taught
her a little song about him, which she sings constantly.'"

Bussy pressed the young man's hand; he felt supremely
happy.

CHAPTER XXV.

THE FATHER AND DAUGHTER.

ON descending into the court, M. de Méridor found a
fresh horse, which Bussy had had prepared for him; another waited for Bussy, and attended by Rémy, they
started. As they went along, the baron could not but ask
himself by what strange confidence he had accompanied,
almost blindly, the friend of the prince to whom he owed
all his misfortunes. Would it not have been better to
have braved the Duc d'Anjou, and instead of following
Bussy where it pleased him to lead, to have gone at once
to the Louvre, and thrown himself at the feet of the king?
What could the prince say to him? How could he console him? Could soft words heal his wound?

When they stopped, "What," said the baron, "does the
Duc d'Anjou live in this humble house?"

"Not exactly, monsieur, but if it is not his dwelling, it is
that of a lady whom he has loved."

A cloud passed over the face of the old gentleman.
"Monsieur," said he, "we provincials are not used to the
easy manners of Paris; they annoy us. It seems to me
that if the Duc d'Anjou wishes to see the Baron de Méridor,
it ought to be at his palace, and not at the house of one
of his mistresses."

"Come, come, baron!" said Bussy, with his smile,

which always carried conviction with it, "do not hazard
false conjectures.   On my honor, the lady whom you are
going to see is perfectly virtuous and worthy in all respects."

"Who is she then ?"

"She is—the wife of a friend of yours."

"Really ! but then, monsieur, why did you say the duke
loved her ?"

"Because I always speak truth.   But enter, and you
shall see accomplished all I have promised you."

"Take care ; I wept for my child, and you said, 'Console yourself, monsieur, the mercy of God is great ;' to
promise me a consolation to my grief was almost to promise
me a miracle."

"Enter, monsieur," said Bussy, with his bright smile.

Bussy went in first, and, running up to Gertrude, said,
"Go and tell Madame de Monsoreau that M. de Bussy is
here, and desires to speak to her.   But," continued he, in
a low voice, "not a word of the person who accompanies
me."

"Madame de Monsoreau !" said the old man in astonishment.   But as he feebly mounted the staircase, he heard
the voice of Diana crying,—

"M. de Bussy, Gertrude ?   Oh ! let him come in !"

"That voice !" cried the baron, stopping.   "Oh ! mon
Dieu ! mon Dieu !"

At that moment, as the baron tremblingly held on to
the banister, and looked around him, he saw at the top of
the staircase, Diana, smiling, and more beautiful that ever.
At this sight the old man uttered a cry and would have
fallen, had he not caught hold of Bussy, who stood by
him.

"Diana alive ! Diana, oh, my God !"

"Mon Dieu ! M. de Bussy !" cried Diana, running down,
"what is the matter with my father ?"

"He thought you dead, madame, and he wept, as a
father must weep for a daughter like you."

"How !" cried Diana ; "and no one undeceived him ?"

"No one."

"No," cried the old men, recovering a little, "no one, not even M. de Bussy."

"Ungrateful," said Bussy.

"Oh! yes! you are right; for this moment repays me for all my griefs. Oh! my Diana! my beloved Diana!" cried he, drawing his daughter to him with one hand, and extending the other to Bussy. But all at once he cried, "But you said I was to see Madame de Monsoreau. Where is she?"

"Alas! my father!" cried Diana.

Bussy summoned up all his strength. "M. de Monsoreau is your son-in-law," he said.

"What! my son-in-law! and every one—even you, Diana—left me in ignorance."

"I feared to write, my father; he said my letters would fall into the hands of the prince. Besides, I thought you knew all."

"But why all these strange mysteries?"

"Ah, yes, my father; why did M. de Monsoreau let you think me dead, and not let you know I was his wife?"

The baron, overwhelmed, looked from Bussy to Diana. "M. de Monsoreau my son-in-law!" stammered he.

"That cannot astonish you, father; did you not order me to marry him?"

"Yes, if he saved you."

"Well! he did save me," said Diana, sinking on to a chair, "not from misfortune, but from shame."

"Then why did he let me think you dead? I, who wept for you so bitterly. Why did he let me die of despair, when a single word would have restored me?"

"Oh! there is some hidden mystery," cried Diana; "my father, you will not leave me again; M. de Bussy, you will protect us."

"Alas! madame! it belongs to me no more to enter into your family secrets. Seeing the strange maneuvers of your husband, I wished to bring you a defender; you have your father, I retire."

"He is right," said the old man, sadly.

"M. de Monsoreau feared the Duc d'Anjou, and so does M. de Bussy."

Diana cast a glance at the young man. He smiled and said, "M. le Baron, excuse, I beg, the singular question I am about to ask ; and you also, madame, for I wish to serve you. M. le Baron, ask Madame de Monsoreau if she be happy in the marriage which she has contracted in obedience to your orders."

Diana burst into tears for her only answer. The eyes of the baron filled also, for he began to fear that his friendship for M. de Monsoreau had tended to make his daughter unhappy.

"Now !" said Bussy,"is it true that you voluntarily promised him your daughter's hand ?"

"Yes, if he saved her."

"And he did save her. Then, monsieur, I need not ask if you mean to keep your promise."

"It is a law for all, and above all for gentlemen ; you know that, M. de Bussy. My daughter must be his."

"Ah !" cried Diana, " would I were dead !"

"Madame, " said Bussy, " you see I was right, and that I can do no more here. M. le Baron gives you to M. de Monsoreau, and you yourself promised to marry him when you should see your father again safe and well."

"Ah ! you tear my heart, M. de Bussy," cried Diana, approaching the young man ; " my father does not know that I fear this man, that I hate him ; my father sees in him only my saviour, and I think him my murderer."

"Diana ! Diana !" cried the baron, " he saved you."

"Yes," cried Bussy, "but if the danger were less great than you thought ; what do we know ? There is some mystery in all this, which I must clear up. But I protest to you, that if I had had the happiness to be in the place of M. de Monsoreau, I would have saved your young and beautiful daughter without exacting a price for it."

"He loved her," said M. de Méridor, trying to excuse him.

"And I, then——" cried Bussy ; and, although he

stopped, frightened at what he was about to say, Diana heard and understood.

"Well!" cried she, reddening, "my brother, my friend, can you do nothing for me?"

"But the Duc d'Anjou," said the baron.

"I am not aware of those who fear the anger of princes," said Bussy; "and, besides, I believe the danger lies not with him, but with M. de Monsoreau."

"But if the duke learns that Diana is alive, all is lost."

"I see," said Bussy, "you believe M. de Monsoreau more than me. Say no more; you refuse my aid; throw yourself, then, into the arms of the man who has already so well merited your confidence. Adieu, baron; adieu, madame, you will see me no more."

"Oh!" cried Diana, taking his hand. "Have you seen me waver for an instant; have you ever seen me soften towards him? No. I beg you, on my knees, M. de Bussy, not to abandon me."

Bussy seized her hands, and all his anger melted away like snow before the sun.

"Then so be it, madame," said he; "I accept the mission, and in three days—for I must have time to go to Chartres to the prince—you shall see me again." Then, in a low tone to her, he said, "We are allied against this Monsoreau; remember that it was not he who brought you back to your father, and be faithful to me."

CHAPTER XXVI.

HOW BROTHER GORENFLOT AWOKE, AND THE RECEPTION HE MET WITH AT HIS CONVENT.

CHICOT, after seeing with pleasure that Gorenflot still slept soundly, told M. Boutromet to retire and to take the light with him, charging him not to say anything of his absence. Now M. Boutromet, having remarked that, in all transactions between the monk and Chicot, it was the latter who paid, had a great deal of consideration for him, and promised all he wished. Then, by the light of the fire

which still smouldered, he wrapped Gorenflot once more
in his frock, which he accomplished without eliciting any
other signs of wakefulness than a few grunts, and afterwards making a pillow of the table-cloth and napkins, lay
down to sleep by his side. Daylight, when it came, succeeded in at last awakening Gorenflot, who sat up, and
began to look about him, at the remains of their last night's
repast, and at Chicot, who, although also awake, lay pre-
tending to snore, while, in reality, he watched.

"Broad daylight!" said the monk. "Corbleu, I must
have passed the night here. And the abbey! Oh, dear!
How happy he is to sleep thus!" cried he, looking at Chicot.
"Ah! he is not in my position," and he sighed. "Shall
I wake him to ask for advice? No, no, he will laugh
at me; I can surely invent a falsehood without him. But
whatever I invent, it will be hard to escape punishment.
It is not so much the imprisonment, it is the bread and
water I mind. Ah! if I had but some money to bribe the
brother jailer."

Chicot, hearing this, adroitly slipped his purse from his
pocket and put it under him. This precaution was not
useless, for Gorenflot, who had been looking about him,
now approached his friend softly, and murmuring:

"Were he awake, he would not refuse me a crown, but
his sleep is sacred, and I will take it," advanced, and began
feeling his pockets. "It is singular," said he, "nothing
in his pockets. Ah! in his hat, perhaps."

While he searched there Chicot adroitly emptied out his
money, and stuffed the empty purse into his breeches'
pocket.

"Nothing in the hat," said the monk. "Ah! I forgot,"
and thrusting in his hand, he drew from the pocket the
empty purse. "Mon Dieu," cried he, "empty! and who
will pay the bill?"

This thought terrified him so much that he got up and
made instantly for the door, through which he quickly
disappeared. As he approached the convent, his fears
grew strong, and seeing a concourse of monks standing
talking on the threshold, he felt inclined to fly. But some

of them approached to meet him ; he knew flight was
hopeless, and resigned himself.   The monks seemed at first
to hesitate to speak to him, but at last one said :

"Poor dear brother !"

Gorenflot sighed, and raised his eyes to Heaven.

"You know the prior waits for you ?"

"Ah ! mon Dieu !"

"Oh ! yes ; he ordered that you should be brought to
him as soon as you came in."

"I feared it," said Gorenflot.   And more dead than
alive, he entered the convent, whose doors closed on him.
They led him to the prior.   Gorenflot did not dare to raise
his eyes, finding himself alone with his justly irritated
superior.

"Ah ! it is you at last," said the abbé.

"Reverend sir——"

"What anxiety you have given me."

"You are too good, my father," said Gorenflot, astonished at this indulgent tone.

"You feared to come in after the scene of last night ?"

"I confess it."

"Ah, dear brother, you have been very imprudent."

"Let me explain, father."

"There is no need of explanations ; your sally——"

"Oh ! so much the better, " thought Gorenflot.

"I understand it perfectly.   A moment of enthusiasm
carried you away ; enthusiasm is a holy virtue, but virtues,
exaggerated become almost vices, and the most honorable
sentiments, when carried to excess, are reprehensible."

"Pardon, my father," said Gorenflot, timidly, "but I
do not understand.   Of what sally do you speak ?"

"Of yours last night."

"Out of the convent ?"

"No ; in it.   I am as good a Catholic as you, but your
audacity frightened me."

Gorenflot was puzzled.   "Was I audacious ?" asked he.

"More than that—rash."

"Alas ! you must pardon me, my father.   I will endeav-
or to correct myself."

" Yes ; but meanwhile, I fear the consequences for you and for all of us. Had it passed among ourselves, it would have been nothing."

" How, is it known to others ? "

" Doubtless ; you know well there were more than a hundred laymen listening to your discourse."

" My discourse ! " said Gorenflot, more and more astonished.

" I allow it was fine, and that the universal applause must have carried you on, but to propose to make a procession through the streets of Paris, with a helmet on your head and a partisan on your shoulder, appealing to all good Catholics, was rather too strong, you will allow."

Gorenflot looked bewildered.

" Now," continued the prior, " this religious fervor, which burns so strongly in your heart, will injure you in Paris. I wish you therefore to go and expend it in the provinces."

" An exile ! " cried Gorenflot.

" If you remain here, much worse may happen to you, my dear brother."

" What? "

" Perpetual imprisonment, or even death."

Gorenflot grew frightfully pale ; he could not understand how he had incurred all this by getting tipsy in an inn, and passing the night out of the convent.

" By submitting to this temporary exile, my dear brother, not only will you escape this danger, but you will plant the banner of our faith in the provinces, where such words are less dangerous than here, under the eyes of the king. Set off at once, then, brother ; perhaps the archers are already out to arrest you."

" The archers, I ! " said Gorenflot.

" I advise you to go at once."

" It is easy to say ' go,' but how am I to live ? "

" Oh ! nothing more easy. You will find plenty of partisans who will let you want for nothing. But go, in Heaven's name, and do not come back till you are sent for." And the prior, after embracing him, pushed him to the door. There he found all the community waiting for him, to touch his hands or his robe.

"Adieu!" said one, embracing him, "you are a holy man; do not forget me in your prayers."

"I, a holy man!" thought Gorenflot.

"Adieu, brave champion of the faith," said another.

"Adieu, martyr," said a third, "the light will soon come."

Thus was he conducted to the outside of the convent, and as he went away he exclaimed, "Devil take me, but either they are all mad, or I am."

CHAPTER XXVII.

HOW BROTHER GORENFLOT REMAINED CONVINCED THAT HE WAS A SOMNAMBULIST, AND BITTERLY DEPLORED THIS INFIRMITY.

UNTIL the day when this unmerited persecution fell on Brother Gorenflot, he had led a contemplative and easy life, diverting himself on occasions at the Corne d'Abondance, when he had gained a little money from the faithful. He was one of those monks for whom the world began at the prior of the convent, and finished at the cook. And now he was sent forth to seek for adventures. He had no money; so that when out of Paris and he heard eleven o'clock (the time for dinner at the convent) strike, he sat down in dejection. His first idea was to return to the convent, and ask to be put in confinement, instead of being sent into exile, and even to submit to the discipline, provided they would insure him his repasts. His next was more reasonable. He would go to the Corne d'Abondance, send for Chicot, explain to him the lamentable situation into which he had helped to bring him, and obtain aid from this generous friend. He was sitting absorbed in these reflections, when he heard the sound of a horse's feet approaching. In great fear, he hid behind a tree until the traveler should have passed; but a new idea struck him. He would endeavor to obtain some money for his dinner.

So he approached tremblingly, and said, "Monsieur, if five paters, and five aves for the success of your projects would be agreeable to you——"

"Gorenflot!" cried the cavalier.

"M. Chicot!"

"Where the devil are you going?"

"I do not know. And you?"

"Oh! I am going straight before me."

"Very far?"

"Till I stop. But you—what are you doing outside the barriers?"

"Alas! M. Chicot! I am proscribed," said Gorenflot, with an enormous sigh.

"What?"

"Proscribed, I tell you. My brothers reject me from their bosom: I am anathematized, excommunicated."

"Bah! what for?"

"Listen, M. Chicot; you will not believe me, perhaps, but I do not know."

"Perhaps you were met last night gadding about."

"Do not joke; you know quite well what I was doing last night."

"Yes, from eight till ten, but not from ten till three."

"How, from ten till three?"

"Yes, at ten you went out."

"I?"

"Yes, and I asked you where you were going."

"And what did I say?"

"That you were going to pronounce a discourse."

"There was some truth in that," murmured Gorenflot.

"Yes, and you even told me part of it; it was very long, and there were terrible things against the king in it."

"Bah!"

"So terrible, that I should not wonder if you were arrested for them."

"M. Chicot, you open my eyes; did I seem quite awake when I spoke?"

"I must say you seemed very strange; you looked like a man who talks in his sleep."

"Yet, I feel sure I awoke this morning at the Corne d'Aboundance."

"Well, of course; you came in again at three o'clock. I know; you left the door open, and made me cold."

"It is true, then?"

"True! ask M. Boutromet."

"M. Boutromet?"

"Yes, he opened to you on your return. And you were so full of pride when you came in, that I said to you,— 'Fie, compère; pride does not become mortals, more especially monks.'"

"And of what was I proud?"

"Of the success your discourse had met with, and the compliments paid to you by the Duc de Guise and M. de Mayenne."

"Now I understand all."

"That is lucky. Then you confess you went to the assembly; what did you call it? Oh! the Holy Union."

Gorenflot groaned. "I am a somnambulist," he said.

"What does that mean?"

"It means, that with me mind is stronger than matter; so that while the body sleeps, the spirit wakes, and sometimes is so powerful that it forces the body to obey."

"Ah! compère, that sounds much like magic; if you are possessed, tell me so frankly; for, really a man who walks and makes discourses in his sleep in which he attacks the king is not natural. Vade retro, Satanas!"

"Then," cried Gorenflot, "you abandon me also. Ah! I could not have believed that of you."

Chicot took pity on him. "What did you tell me just now?" said he.

"I do not know; I feel half mad, and my stomach is empty."

"You spoke of traveling."

"Yes, the holy prior sends me."

"Where to?"

"Wherever I like."

"I also am traveling, and will take you with me."

Gorenflot looked bewildered.

"Well! do you accept?" continued Chicot.

"Accept! I should think so. But have you money to travel with?"

"Look," said Chicot, drawing out his purse.

Gorenflot jumped for joy.

"How much?" said he.

"One hundred and fifty pistoles."

"And where are we going?"

"You shall see."

"When shall we breakfast?"

"Immediately."

"What shall I ride?"

"Not my horse; you would kill it."

"Then what must I do?"

"Nothing more simple; I will buy you an ass."

"You are my benefactor, M. Chicot. Let the ass be strong. Now, where do we breakfast?"

"Here; look over this door and read."

Gorenflot looked up, and saw, "Here eggs, ham, eel-pies, and white wine may be had!" At this sight, Goren-flot's whole face expanded with joy.

"Now," said Chicot, "go and get your breakfast, while I go and look for an ass for you."

CHAPTER XXVIII.

HOW BROTHER GORENFLOT TRAVELED UPON AN ASS, NAMED PANURGE, AND LEARNED MANY THINGS HE DID NOT KNOW BEFORE.

WHAT made Chicot so indifferent to his own repast was, that he had already breakfasted plentifully. Therefore, he sat Gorenflot down to eggs and bacon, while he went among the peasants to look for an ass. He found a pacific creature, four years old, and something between an ass and a horse; gave twenty-two livres for it, and brought it to Gorenflot, who was enchanted at the sight of it, and christened it Panurge. Chicot, seeing by the look of the table that there would be no cruelty in staying his companion's repast, said,—

"Come, now we must go on; at Mélun we will lunch."

Gorenflot got up, merely saying, "At Mélun, at Mélun."

They went on for about four leagues, then Gorenflot lay down on the grass to sleep, while Chicot began to calculate.

"One hundred and twenty leagues, at ten leagues a day, would take twelve days." It was as much as he could reasonably expect from the combined forces of a monk and an ass. But Chicot shook his head. "It will not do," he said, "if he wants to follow me, he must do fifteen."

He pushed the monk to wake him, who, opening his eyes, said, "Are we at Mélun? I am hungry."

"Not yet, compère, and that is why I woke you; we must get on; we go too slow, ventre de biche!"

"Oh, no, dear M. Chicot; it is so fatiguing to go fast. Besides, there is no hurry: am I not traveling for the propagation of the faith, and you for pleasure? Well, the slower we go, the better the faith will be propagated, and the more you will amuse yourself. My advice is to stay some days at Mélun, where they make excellent eelpies. What do you say, M. Chicot?"

"I say, that my opinion is to go as fast as possible; not to lunch at Mélun, but only to sup at Montereau, to make up for lost time."

Gorenflot looked at his companion as if he did not understand.

"Come, let us get on," said Chicot.

The monk sat still and groaned.

"If you wish to stay behind and travel at your case, you are welcome."

"No, no!" cried Gorenflot, in terror; "no, no, M. Chicot; I love you too much to leave you!"

"Then to your saddle at once."

Gorenflot got on his ass this time sideways, as a lady sits, saying it was more comfortable; but the fact was that,

11

fearing they were to go faster, he wished to be able to hold
on both by mane and tail.

Chicot began to trot, and the ass followed. The first
moments were terrible for Gorenflot, but he managed to
keep his seat. From time to time Chicot stood up in
his stirrups and looked forward, then, not seeing what he
looked for, redoubled his speed.

"What are you looking for, dear M. Chicot?"

"Nothing; but we are not getting on."

"Not getting on! we are trotting all the way."

"Gallop then!" and he began to canter.

Panurge again followed; Gorenflot was in agonies.

"Oh, M. Chicot!" said he, as soon as he could speak,
"do you call this traveling for pleasure? It does not
amuse me at all."

"On! on!"

"It is dreadful!"

"Stay behind then!"

"Panurge can do no more; he is stopping."

"Then adieu, compère!"

Gorenflot felt half inclined to reply in the same manner,
but he remembered that the horse, whom he felt ready to
curse, bore on his back a man with a hundred and fifty
pistoles in his pocket, so he resigned himself, and beat his
ass to make him gallop once more.

"I shall kill my poor Panurge!" cried he dolefully,
thinking to move Chicot.

"Well, kill him," said Chicot quietly, "and we will
buy another."

All at once Chicot, on arriving at the top of a hill, reined
in his horse suddenly. But the ass, having once taken it
into his head to gallop, was not so easily stopped, and
Gorenflot was forced to let himself slide off and hang on
to the donkey with all his weight before he could stop
him.

"Ah, M. Chicot!" cried he, "what does it all mean?
First we must gallop fit to break our necks, and then we
must stop short here!"

Chicot had hidden himself behind a rock, and was

eagerly watching three men who, about two hundred yards in advance, were traveling on quietly on their mules, and he did not reply.

- "I am tired and hungry!" continued Gorenflot angrily.

"And so am I," said Chicot; "and at the first hotel we come to we will order a couple of fricasseed chickens, some ham, and a jug of their best wine."

"Really, is it true this time?"

"I promise you, compère."

"Well, then, let us go and seek it. Come, Panurge, you shall have some dinner."

Chicot remounted his horse, and Gorenflot led his ass. The much-desired inn soon appeared, but, to the surprise of Gorenflot, Chicot caused him to make a detour and pass round the back. At the front door were standing the three travelers.

CHAPTER XXIX.

HOW BROTHER GORENFLOT CHANGED HIS ASS FOR A MULE, AND HIS MULE FOR A HORSE.

However, Gorenflot's troubles were near their end for that day, for after the detour they went on a mile, and then stopped at a rival hotel. Chicot took a room which looked on to the high-road, and ordered supper. But even while he was eating he was constantly on the watch. However, at ten o'clock, as he had seen nothing, he went to bed, first, however, ordering that the horse and the ass should be ready at daybreak.

"At daybreak?" uttered Gorenflot, with a deep sigh.

"Yes; you must be used to getting up at that time."

"Why so?"

"For matins."

"I had an exemption from the superior." Chicot ordered Gorenflot's bed to be placed in his room. With daylight he was up and at the window, and before very long he saw three mules coming along. He ran to Gorenflot and shook him.

" Can I not have a moment's rest ? " cried the monk, who had been sleeping for ten hours.

" Be quick ; get up and dress, for we are going."

" But the breakfast ? "

" Is on the road to Monteran."

" Where is Monterau ? "

" It is the city where we breakfast, that is enough for you. Now, I am going down to pay the bill, and if you are not ready in five minutes, I go without you."

A monk's toilet takes not long ; however, Gorenflot took six minutes, and when he came down Chicot was starting. This day passed much like the former one, and by the third, Gorenflot was beginning to get accustomed to it, when towards the evening, Chicot lost all his gaiety. Since noon he had seen nothing of the three travelers ; therefore he was in a very bad humor. They were off at daybreak and galloped till noon, but all in vain ; no mules were visible. Chicot stopped at a turnpike, and asked the man if he had seen three travelers pass on mules.

" Not to-day," was the reply, " yesterday evening about seven."

" What were they like ? "

" They looked like a master and two servants ! "

" It was them," said Chicot ; " ventre de biche ! they have twelve hours' start of me. But courage ! "

" Listen, M. Chicot ! " said Gorenflot, " my ass can do no more, even your horse is almost exhausted." Chicot looked, and saw, indeed, that the poor animals were trembling from head to foot.

" Well ! brother," said he, " we must take a resolution. You must leave me."

" Leave you ; why ? "

" You go too slow."

" Slow ! why, we have galloped for five hours this morning."

" That is not enough."

" Well, then, let us go on ; the quicker we go, the sooner we shall arrive, for I suppose we shall stop at last."

" But our animals are exhausted."

" What shall we do then ? "

" Leave them here, and take them as we come back. "

" Then how are we to proceed ? "

" We will buy mules. "

" Very well," said Gorenflot with a sigh. Two mules were soon found, and they went so well that in the evening Chicot saw with joy those of the three travelers, standing at the door of a farrier's. But they were without harness, and both master and lackeys had disappeared. Chicot trembled. " Go," said he, to Gorenflot, " and ask if those mules are for sale, and where their owners are." Gorenflot went, and soon returned, saying that a gentleman had sold them, and had afterwards taken the road to Avignon.

" Alone ? "

" No, with a lackey. "

" And where is the other lackey ? "

" He went towards Lyons. "

" And how did they go on ? "

" On horses which they bought. "

" Of whom ? "

" Of a captain of troopers who was here, and they sold their mules to a dealer, who is trying to sell them again to those Franciscan monks whom you see there. "

" Well, take our two mules and go and offer them to the monks instead ; they ought to give you the preference. "

" But, then, how shall we go on ? "

" On horseback, morbleu. "

" Diable ! "

" Oh ! a good rider like you. You will find me again on the Grand Place." Chicot was bargaining for some horses, when he saw the monk reappear, carrying the saddles and bridles of the mules.

" Oh ! you have kept the harness ? "

" Yes. "

" And sold the mules ? "

" For ten pistoles each. "

" Which they paid you ? "

" Here is the money. "

"Ventre de biche! you are a great man, let us go on."

"But I am thirsty."

"Well, drink while I saddle the beasts, but not too much."

"A bottle."

"Very well."

Gorenflot drank two, and came to give the rest of the money back to Chicot, who felt half inclined to give it to him, but reflecting that if Gorenflot had money he would no longer be obedient, he refrained. They rode on, and the next evening Chicot came up with Nicolas David, still disguised as a lackey, and kept him in sight all the way to Lyons, whose gates they all three entered on the eighth day after their departure from Paris.

CHAPTER XXX.

HOW CHICOT AND HIS COMPANION INSTALLED THEMSELVES AT THE HOTEL OF THE CROSS, AND HOW THEY WERE RECEIVED BY THE HOST.

CHICOT watched Nicolas David into the principal hotel of the place, and then said to Gorenflot, "Go in and bargain for a private room, say that you expect your brother, then come out and wait about for me, and I will come in when it is dark, and you can bring me straight to my room. Do you understand?"

"Perfectly."

"Choose a good room, as near as possible to that of the traveler who has just arrived; it must look on to the street, and on no account pronounce my name."

Gorenflot acquitted himself marvelously of the commission. Their room was only separated by a partition from that of Nicolas David.

"You deserve a recompense," said Chicot to him, "and you shall have sherry wine for supper."

"I never got tipsy on that wine; it would be agreeable."

"You shall to-night. But now ramble about the town."

" But the supper ? "

" I shall be ready against your return ; here is a crown meanwhile."

. Gorenflot went off quite happy, and then Chicot made, with a gimlet, a hole in the partition at about the height of his eye. Through this, he could hear distinctly all that passed, and he could just see the host talking to Nicolas David, who was professing to have been sent on a mission by the king, to whom he professed great fidelity. The host did not reply, but Chicot fancied he could see an ironical smile on his lip whenever the king's name was mentioned.

" Is he a leaguer ? " thought Chicot ; " I will find out."

When the host left David he came to visit Chicot, who said, " Pray sit down, monsieur, and before we make a definitive arrangement, listen to my history. You saw me this morning with a monk ? "

" Yes, monsieur."

" Silence ! that monk is proscribed."

" What ! is he a disguised Huguenot ? "

Chicot took an offended air. " Huguenot, indeed ! he is my relation, and I have no Huguenot relations. On the contrary, he is so fierce an enemy of the Huguenots, that he has fallen into disgrace with his majesty Henri III., who protects them, as you know."

The host began to look interested. " Silence," said he.

" Why, have you any of the king's people here ? "

" I fear so ; there is a traveler in there."

" Then we must fly at once, for proscribed, menaced——"

" Where will you go ? "

" We have two or three addresses given to us by an innkeeper we know, M. la Hurière."

" Do you know La Hurière ? "

" Yes, we made his acquaintance on the night of St. Bartholomew."

" Well, I see you and your relation are holy people ; I also know La Hurière. Then you say this monk——"

"Had the imprudence to preach against the Huguenots, and with so much success that the king wanted to
put him in prison."

"And then ?"

"Ma foi, I carried him off."

"And you did well."

"M. de Guise offered to protect him."

"What ! the great Henri ?"

"Himself ; but I feared civil war."

"If you are friends of M. de Guise, you know this ;"
and he made a sort of masonic sign by which the leaguers
recognized each other.

Chicot, who had seen both this and the answer to it
twenty times during that famous night, replied, "And
you this ?"

"Then," said the innkeeper, "you are at home here ;
my house is yours, look on me as a brother, and if you
have no money——"

Chicot drew out his purse. The sight of a well-filled
purse is always agreeable, even to a generous host.

"Our journey," continued Chicot, "is paid for by the
treasurer of the Holy Union, for we travel to propagate
the faith. Tell us of an inn where we may be safe."

"Nowhere more so than here, and if you wish it, the
other traveler shall turn out."

"Oh ! no ; it is better to have your enemies near, that
you may watch them. But, what makes you think he is
our enemy ?"

"Well ! first he came disguised as a lackey, then he put
on an advocate's dress, and I am sure he is no more an advocate than he is a lackey, for I saw a long rapier under
his cloak. Then he avowed he had a mission from the
king !"

"From Herod, as I call him."

"Sardanapalus."

"Bravo !"

"Ah ! I see we understand each other."

"Then we are to remain here ?"

"I should think so."

"Not a word about my relation."

"Of course not."

"Nor of me."

"Oh, no! But hush! here is some one."

"Oh, it is the worthy man himself!"

The host turned to Gorenflot, and made a sign of the leaguers. Gorenflot was struck with terror and astonishment.

"Reply, my brother," said Chicot; "he is a member."

"Of what?"

"Of the Holy Union," said Bernouillet, in a low tone.

"You see all is safe; reply," said Chicot.

Gorenflot replied, to the great joy of the innkeeper.

"But," said Gorenflot, who did not like the conversation, "you promised me some sherry."

"Sherry, Malaga, Alicant—every wine in my cellar is at your disposal."

Gorenflot looked at Chicot in amazement.

For three following days Gorenflot got drunk, first on sherry, next on Malaga, then on Alicant; afterwards he declared he liked Burgundy best, and returned to that. Meanwhile, Chicot had never stirred from his room, and had constantly watched Nicolas David, who, having appointed to meet Pierre de Gondy at this inn, would not leave the house. On the morning of the sixth day he declared himself ill, and the next day worse. Bernouillet came joyfully to tell Chicot.

"What! do you think him in danger?"

"High fever, my dear brother; he is delirious, and tried to strangle me and beat my servants. The doctors do not understand his complaint."

"Have you seen him?"

"Yes; I tell you he tried to strangle me."

"How did he seem?"

"Pale and furious, and constantly crying out."

"What?"

"Take care of the king! they want to hurt the king! Then he constantly says that he expects a man from Avignon, and wishes to see him before he dies."

As for Gorenflot, he grew visibly fatter every day, so much so, that he announced to Chicot with terror one day that the staircase was narrowing. Neither David, the League, nor religion occupied him ; he thought of nothing but how to vary his dinner and wine, so that Bernouillet often exclaimed in astonishment, "To think that that man should be a torrent of eloquence ! "

CHAPTER XXXI.

HOW THE MONK CONFESSED THE ADVOCATE, AND THE ADVOCATE THE MONK.

At last M. Bernouillet came into Chicot's room, laughing immoderately.

"He is dying," said he, "and the man has arrived from Avignon."

"Have you seen him ? "

"Of course."

"What is he like ? "

"Little and thin."

"It is he," thought Chicot; and he said, "Tell me about his arrival."

"An hour ago I was in the kitchen, when I saw a great horse, ridden by a little man, stop before the door. 'Is M. Nicolas here ?' asked he. 'Yes, monsieur,' said I. 'Tell him that the person he expects from Avignon is here.' 'Certainly, monsieur, but I must warn you that he is very ill.' 'All the more reason for doing my bidding at once.' 'But he has a malignant fever.' 'Oh, pray, then, be quick !' 'How ! you persist ?' 'I persist.' 'In spite of the danger !' 'In spite of everything I must see him.' So I took him to the room, and there he is now. Is it not odd ? "

"Very droll."

"I wish I could hear them."

"Go in."

"He forbade me to go in, saying he was going to confess."

"Listen at the door."

Bernouillet went, and Chicot went also to his hole : but they spoke so low that he could hear nothing, and in a few minutes Gondy rose and took leave. Chicot ran to the window, and saw a lackey waiting with a horse, which M. de Gondy mounted and rode off.

"If he only has not carried off the genealogy. Never mind, I shall soon catch him if necessary ; but I suspect it is left here. Where can Gorenflot be ?"

M. Bernouillet returned, saying, "He is gone."

"The confessor ?"

"He is no more a confessor than I am."

"Will you send me my brother as soon as he comes in."

"Even if he be drunk ?"

"Whatever state he is in."

Bernouillet went, and Chicot remained in a state of indecision as to what to do, for he thought, "If David is really so ill, he may have sent on the despatches by Gondy." Presently he heard Gorenflot's voice, singing a drinking song as he came up the stairs.

"Silence, drunkard !" said Chicot.

"Drunkard, indeed !"

"Yes ; but come here and speak seriously, if you can."

"What is it now ?"

"It is, that you never think of the duties of your profession, that you wallow in greediness and drunkenness, and let religion go where it pleases."

Gorenflot looked astonished. "I !" he gasped.

"Yes, you ; you are disgraceful to see ; you are covered with mud ; you have been drunk in the streets."

"It is too true !"

"If you go on so, I will abandon you."

"Chicot, my friend, you will not do that ? Am I very guilty ?"

"There are archers at Lyons."

"Oh, pity ! my dear protector, pity !"

"Are you a Christian or not ?"

"I not a Christian!"

"Then do not let aneighbor die without confession."

"I am ready, but I must drink first, for I am thirsty."
Chicot passed him a jug of water, which he emptied.

"Now who am I to confess?"

"Our unlucky neighbor who is dying."

"Let them give him a pint of wine with honey in
it."

"He needs spiritual aid as well as temporal. Go to
him."

"Am I fit?" said Gorenflot, timidly.

"Perfectly."

"Then I will go."

"Stay; I must tell you what to do."

"Oh! I know."

"You do not know what I wish."

"What you wish?"

"If you execute it well, I will give you one hundred
pistoles to spend here."

"What must I do?"

"Listen; your robe gives you authority; in the name
of God and the King, summon him to give up the papers
he has just received from Avignon."

"What for?"

"To gain one hundred pistoles, stupid."

"Ah! true; I go."

"Wait a minute. He will tell you he has confessed."

"But if he has?"

"Tell him he lies; that the man who has just left him
is no confessor, but an intriguer like himself."

"But he will be angry."

"What does that matter, since he is dying?"

"True."

"Well; one way or the other, you must get hold of
those papers."

"If he refuses?"

"Refuse him absolution, curse him, anathematize
him——"

"Oh, I will take them by force."

" Good ; and when you have got them, knock on the wall."

" And if I cannot get them ? "

" Knock also."

" Then, in any case I am to knock ? "

" Yes."

Gorenflot went, and Chicot placed his ear to the hole in the wall. When Gorenflot entered, the sick man raised himself in his bed, and looked at him with wonder.

" Good day, brother," said Gorenflot.

" What do you want, my father ? " murmured the sick man, in a feeble voice.

" My son, I hear you are in danger, and I come to speak to you of your soul."

" Thank you, but I think your care is needless ; I feel better."

" You think so ? "

" I am sure of it."

" It is a ruse of Satan, who wishes you to die without confession."

" Then he will be deceived, for I have just confessed."

" To whom ? "

" To a worthy priest from Avignon."

" He was not a priest."

" Not ! "

" No."

" How do you know ? "

" I knew him."

" You knew the man who has just gone ? "

" Yes ; and as you are not better, and this man was not a priest, you must confess."

" Very well," replied the patient, in a stronger voice, " but I will chose to whom I will confess."

" You will have no time to send for another priest, and I am here."

" How ! no time, when I tell you I am getting well ? "

Gorenflot shook his head. "I tell you, my son, you are condemned by the doctors and by Providence ; you may think it cruel to tell you so, but it is what we must all come to sooner or later.   Confess, my son, confess."

"But I assure you, father, that I feel much stronger."

"A mistake, my son, the lamp flares up at the last, just before it goes out. Come, confess all your plots, your intrigues, and machinations!"

"My intrigues and plots!" cried David, frightened at this singular monk, whom he did not know, but who seemed to know him so well.

"Yes; and when you have told all that, give me up the papers, and perhaps God will let me absolve you."

"What papers?" cried the sick man, in a voice as strong as though he were quite well.

"The papers that the pretended priest brought you from Avignon."

"And who told you that he brought me papers?" cried the patient, putting one leg out of bed.

Gorenflot began to feel frightened, but he said firmly, "He who told me knew well what he was saying; give me the papers, or you shall have no absolution."

"I laugh at your absolution," cried David, jumping out of bed, and seizing Gorenflot by the throat, "and you shall see if I am too ill to strangle you."

Gorenflot was strong, and he pushed David back so violently that he fell into the middle of the room. But he rose furious, and seizing a long sword, which hung on the wall behind his clothes, presented it to the throat of Gorenflot, who sank on a chair in terror.

"It is now your turn to confess," said he, "speak, or you die."

"Oh!" cried Gorenflot, "then you are not ill—not dying."

"It is not for you to question, but to answer."

"To answer what?"

"Who are you?"

"You can see that."

"Your name?"

"Brother Gorenflot."

"You are then a real monk?"

"I should think so."

"What brings you to Lyons?"

"I am exiled."

"What brought you to this inn?"

"Chance."

"How long have you been here?"

"A fortnight."

"Why did you watch me?"

"I did not."

"How did you know that I had the papers?"

"Because I was told so."

"Who told you?"

"He who sent me here."

"Who was that?"

"I cannot tell you."

"You must."

"Oh! oh! I will cry out."

"And I will kill."

Gorenflot cried out, and a spot of blood appeared on the point of the sword.

"His name?" cried David.

"Oh! I can hold out no more."

"Speak."

"It was Chicot."

"The king's jester!"

"Himself."

"And where is he?"

"Here!" cried a voice, and Chicot appeared at the door with a drawn sword in his hand.

CHAPTER XXXII.

HOW CHICOT USED HIS SWORD.

NICOLAS DAVID, in recognizing him whom he knew to be his mortal enemy, could not repress a movement of terror, during which Gorenflot slipped a little to the side, crying out, "Help, friend! come to my aid!"

"Ah, Monsieur David, it is you!" said Chicot; "I

am delighted to meet you again!" Then, turning to Gorenflot, he said, "My good Gorenflot, your presence as monk was very necessary just now, when we believed monsieur dying; but now that he is so well, it is with me he must deal; therefore, do me the favor to stand sentinel on the threshold, and prevent any one from coming in to interrupt our little conversation." Gorenflot, who asked no better than to go, was soon out of the room; but David, having now recovered from his surprise, and confident in his skill as a swordsman, stood waiting for Chicot, with his sword in his hand and a smile on his lips.

"Dress yourself, monsieur," said Chicot; "I do not wish to take any advantage of you. Do you know what I have come to seek in this room?"

"The rest of the blows which I have owed you on account of the Duc de Mayenne, since that day when you jumped so quickly out of the window."

"No, monsieur; I know the number, and will return them. Be easy. What I have come for is a certain genealogy which M. Pierre de Gondy took to Avignon, without knowing what he carried, and, equally in ignorance, brought back to you just now."

David turned pale. "What genealogy?" he said.

"That of M. de Guise, who descends, as you know, in a direct line from Charlemagne."

"Ah, you are a spy! I thought you only a buffoon."

"Dear M. David, I will be both if you wish it: a spy to hang you, and a buffoon to laugh at it after."

"To hang me!"

"High and dry, monsieur; I hope you do not lay claim to be beheaded like a gentleman."

"And how will you do it?"

"Oh, very easily; I will relate the truth, for I must tell you, dear M. David, that I assisted last month at the meeting held in the convent of St. Geneviève."

"You!"

"Yes; I was in the confessional in front of yours, and it was very uncomfortable there, especially as I was obliged to wait to go out until all was finished. Therefore I heard all, saw the coronation of M. d'Anjou, which was not very amusing ; but then the genealogy was delightful."

"Ah ! you know about the genealogy ?" cried David, biting his lips with anger.

"Yes, and I found it very ingenious, especially that part about the Salic law ; only it is a misfortune to have so much intellect, one gets hung for it ; therefore, feeling myself moved with tender pity for so ingenious a man, I said to myself, 'Shall I let this brave M. David be hung ?' and I took the resolution of traveling with, or rather behind, you. I followed you, therefore, not without trouble, and at last we arrived at Lyons. I entered the hotel an hour after you, and have been in the adjoining room ; look, there is only a partition between, and, as you may imagine, I did not travel all the way from Paris to Lyons to lose sight of you now. I pierced a little hole, through which I had the pleasure of watching you when I liked, and I confess I gave myself this pleasure several times a day. At last you fell ill ; the host wished to get rid of you, but you were determined to wait here for M. de Gondy. I was duped by you at first, for you might really have been ill, so I sent you a brave monk, to excite you to repentance ; but, hardened sinner that you are, you tried to kill him, forgetting the Scripture maxim, 'He who strikes with the sword shall perish with the sword.' Then I came to you, and said, 'We are old friends ; let us arrange the matter.'"

"In what manner ?"

"It would be a pity that such a man as you should disappear from the world ; give up plots, trust me, break with the Guises, give me your papers, and, on the faith of a gentleman, I will make your peace with the king."

"While, on the contrary, if I do not give them to you ?"

"Ah ! then, on the faith of a gentleman, I will kill you ! But if you give them to me, all shall be forgotten. You do not believe me, perhaps, for your nature is bad, and you think my resentment can never be forgotten. But, although it is true that I hate you, I hate M. de Mayenne more ; give me what will ruin him, and I will save you. And then, perhaps, you will not believe this either, for

12

you love nothing ; but I love the king, foolish and corrupt-
ed as he is, and I wish that he should reign tranquilly—
which is impossible with the Mayennes and the genealogy
of Nicolas David. Therefore, give me up the genealogy,
and I promise to make your name and your fortune."

David never moved.

"Well," said Chicot, "I see all that I say to you is but
wasted breath ; therefore, I go to get you hanged.   Adieu,
M. David,"and he stepped backwards towards the door.

"And you think I shall let you go out," cried the advocate.

"No, no, my fine spy ; no, no, Chicot, my friend, those
who know of the genealogy must die.   Those who menace
me must die."

"You put me quite at my ease ; I hesitated only because I am sure to kill you.   Crillon, the other day, taught
me a particular thrust, only one, but that will suffice.
Come, give me the papers, or I will kill you ; and I will tell
you how—I will pierce your throat just where you wished
to bleed Gorenflot."

Chicot had hardly finished, when David rushed on him
with a savage laugh.   The two adversaries were nearly
matched in height, but Chicot, who fenced nearly every
day with the king, had become one of the most skilful
swordsmen in the kingdom.   David soon began to perceive
this, and he retreated a step.

"Ah ! ah !" said Chicot, "now you begin to understand.   Once more ; the papers."

David, for answer, threw himself again upon Chicot,
and a new combat ensued.   At last Chicot called out,—

"Here is the thrust," and as he spoke, he thrust his
rapier half through his throat.

David did not reply, but fell at Chicot's feet, pouring
out a mouthful of blood.   But by a natural movement he
tried to drag himself towards his bed, so as to defend his
secret to the last.

"Ah !" cried Chicot, "I thought you cunning, but I
see you are a fool.   I did not know where the papers were,
and you have shown me——" and while David rolled in the

agonies of death, he ran to the bed, raised the mattress, and found under it a roll of parchment. At the moment in which he unrolled it to see if it was the document he sought, David raised himself in a rage and then fell back dead. Chicot saw with joy that he held what he wanted. The Pope had written at the bottom, "Fiat ut voluit Deus; Deus jura hominum fecit." After placing it in his breast, he took the body of the advocate, who had died without losing more blood, the nature of the wound making him bleed inwardly, put it back in the bed, turned the face to the wall, and, opening the door, called Gorenflot.

"How pale you are!" said the monk, as he entered.

"Yes, the last moments of that man caused me some emotion."

"Then he is dead?"

"Yes."

"He was so well just now."

"Too well; he swallowed something difficult of digestion, and died of it."

"The wretch wanted to strangle me, a holy man, and he is punished for it."

"Pardon him, you are a Christian."

"I do, although he frightened me much."

"You must do more; you must light the lamps, and say some prayers by his bed."

"Why?"

"That you may not be taken prisoner as his murderer."

"I, a murderer! it was he who tried to murder me."

"Mon Dieu! yes, and as he could not succeed, his rage made him break a blood-vessel. But till your innocence is established they might annoy you much."

"I fear you are right."

"Then do what I tell you. Install yourself here, and recite all the prayers you know, or do not know; then, when evening comes, go out and call at the ironmonger's at the corner of the street. There you will find your horse; mount him, and take the road to Paris; at Villeneuve-le-Roi sell him, and take Panurge back."

"Ah! that good Panurge; I shall be delighted to see him again. But how am I to live?"

Chicot drew from his pocket a handful of crowns and put them into the large hand of the monk.

"Generous man!" cried Gorenflot. "Let me stay with you at Lyons; I love Lyons."

"But I do not stay here; I set off at once, and travel too rapidly for you to follow me."

"So be it, then."

Chicot installed the monk by the bed, and went downstairs to the host.

"M. Bernouillet," said he, "a great event has taken place in your house."

"What do you mean?"

"The hateful royalist, the enemy of our religion upstairs, received to-day a messenger from Rome."

"I know that: it was I who told you."

"Well, our holy father, the Pope, had sent him to this conspirator, who, however, probably did not suspect for what purpose."

"And why did he come?"

"Go up-stairs, lift up the bedclothes, look at his neck, and you will see."

"You frighten me."

"I say no more. The Pope did you honor in choosing your house for the scene of his vengeance."

Then Chicot put ten crowns into the hand of the host, and went down to the stable to get out the horses. M. Bernouillet went up and found Gorenflot praying. He looked as directed, and found the wound.

"May every enemy of our religion die thus," said he to Gorenflot.

"Amen," replied the monk.

These events passed about the same time that Bussy brought the Baron de Méridor back to his daughter.

CHAPTER XXXIII.

HOW THE DUC D'ANJOU LEARNED THAT DIANA WAS NOT DEAD.

THE month of April had arrived. The great cathedral of Chartres was hung with white, and the king was standing barefooted in the nave. The religious ceremonies, which were for the purpose of praying for an heir to the throne of France, were just finishing, when Henri, in the midst of the general silence, heard what seemed to him a stifled laugh. He turned round to see if Chicot were there, for he thought no one else would have dared to laugh at such a time. It was not, however, Chicot who had laughed at the sight of the two chemises of the Holy Virgin which were said to have such a prolific power, and which were just being drawn from their golden box ; but it was a cavalier who had just stopped at the door of the church, and who was making his way with his muddy boots through the crowd of courtiers in their penitents' robes and sacks. Seeing the king turn, he stopped for a moment, and Henri, irritated at seeing him arrive thus, threw an angry glance at him. The newcomer, however, continued to advance until he reached the velvet chair of M. le Duc d'Anjou, by which he knelt down. He, turning round, said, "Bussy !"

"Good morning, monseigneur."

"Are you mad ?"

"Why so ?"

"To come here to see this nonsense."

"Monseigneur, I wish to speak to you at once."

"Where have you been for the last three weeks ?"

"That is just what I have to tell you."

"Well, you must wait until we leave the church."

"So much the worse."

"Patience, here is the end."

Indeed, the king was putting on one of these chemises, and the queen another. Then they all knelt down, and afterwards the king, taking off his holy tunic, left the church.

"Now, monseigneur," said Bussy, "shall we go to your house?"

"Yes, at once, if you have anything to tell me."

"Plenty of things which you do not expect."

When they were in the hotel the duke said, "Now sit down and tell me all; I feared you were dead."

"Very likely, monseigneur."

"You left me to look after my beautiful unknown. Who is this woman, and what am I to expect?"

"You will reap what you have sown, monseigneur—plenty of shame."

"What do you mean?" cried the duke.

"What I said."

"Explain yourself, monsieur; who is this woman?"

"I thought you had recognized her."

"Then it was her?"

"Yes, monseigneur."

"You saw her?"

"Yes."

"And she spoke to you?"

"Certainly. Doubtless you had reason to think her dead, and you perhaps hoped she was so."

The duke grew pale.

"Yes, monseigneur," continued Bussy, "although you pushed to despair a young girl of noble race, she escaped from death; but do not breathe yet, do not think yourself absolved, for, in preserving her life, she found a misfortune worse than death."

"What is it? what has happened to her?"

"Monseigneur, a man preserved her honor and saved her life, but he made her pay for this service so dearly that she regrets his having rendered it."

"Finish."

"Well, monseigneur, Mademoiselle de Méridor, to escape becoming the mistress of the Duc d'Anjou, has thrown herself into the arms of a man whom she detests, and is now Madame de Monsoreau."

At these words the blood rushed furiously into the duke's face.

"Is this true?" said he.

"Pardieu! I said it," said Bussy, haughtily.

"I did not mean that; I did not doubt your word, Bussy, I wondered only if it were possible that one of my gentlemen had had the audacity to interfere between me and a woman whom I honored with my love."

"And why not?"

"Then you would have done so?"

"I would have done better; I would have warned you that your honor was being lost."

"Listen, Bussy," said the prince, becoming calmer, "I do not justify myself, but M. de Monsoreau has been a traitor towards me."

"Towards you?"

"Yes, he knew my intentions."

"And they were?"

"To try and make Diana love me."

"Love you!"

"Yes, but in no case to use violence."

"Those were your intentions?" said Bussy, with an ironical smile.

"Certainly, and these intentions I preserved to the last, although M. de Monsoreau constantly combated them."

"Monseigneur, what do you say! This man incited you to dishonor Diana?"

"Yes."

"By his counsels?"

"By his letters. Would you like to see them?"

"Oh! if I could believe that!"

"You shall see."

And the duke, opening a little cabinet, and taking out a letter, said, "Since you doubt your prince's words, read."

Bussy took it and read,—

" MONSEIGNEUR,

"Be quite easy; the coup-de-main can be executed without risk, for the young person sets off this evening to pass a week with an aunt who lives at the château of Lude . I charge myself with it, and you need take no trouble As for the scruples of the young lady, be sure that they wil' vanish in the presence of your highness : meanwhile I act ; and this evening she will be at the château of Beaugé.

"Your highness's respectful servant,
"BRYAN DE MONSOREAU."

" Well, what do you say, Bussy ? "

" I say that you are well served, monseigneur."

" You mean betrayed."

" Ah, true ; I forgot the end."

" The wretch ! he made me believe in the death of a woman——"

" Whom he stole from you ; it is black enough."

" How did he manage ? "

" He made the father believe you the ravisher, and offered himself to rescue the lady, presented himself at the chateau of Beaugé with a letter from the Baron de Méridor, brought a boat to the windows, and carried away the prisoner ; then shut her up in the house you know of, and by constantly working upon her fears, forced her to become his wife."

" Is it not infamous ? "

" Only partly excused by your conduct, monseigneur."

" Ah ! Bussy, you shall see how I will revenge myself ! "

" Princes do not revenge themselves, they punish," said Bussy.

" How can I punish him ? "

" By restoring happiness to Madame de Monsoreau."

" But can I ? "

" Certainly."

" How ? "

" By restoring her to liberty. The marriage was forced, therefore it is null."

"You are right."

"Get it set aside, then, and you will have acted like a gentleman and a prince."

"Ah, ah!" said the prince, "what warmth! you are interested in it, Bussy."

"I! not at all, except that I do not wish people to say that Louis de Clermont serves a perfidious prince and a man without honor."

"Well, you shall see. But how to do it?"

"Nothing more easy; make her father act."

"But he is buried in Anjou."

"Monseigneur, he is here in Paris."

"At your house?"

"No, with his daughter. Speak to him, monseigneur, that he may see in you, not what he does now, an enemy, but a protector—that he who now curses your name may bless you."

"And when can I see him?"

"As soon as you return to Paris."

"Very well."

"It is agreed, then?"

"Yes."

"On your word as a gentleman?"

"On my faith as a prince."

"And when do you return?"

"This evening; will you accompany me?"

"No, I go first; where shall I meet your highness?"

"To-morrow; at the king's levée."

"I will be there, monseigneur."

Bussy did not lose a moment, and the distance that took the duke fifteen hours to accomplish, sleeping in his litter, the young man, who returned to Paris, his heart beating with joy and love, did in five, to console the baron and Diana the sooner.

CHAPTER XXXIV.

HOW CHICOT RETURNED TO THE LOUVRE, AND WAS RE-
CEIVED BY THE KING HENRI III.

ALL was quiet at the Louvre, for the king, fatigued
with his pilgrimage, had not yet risen, when two men presented themselves together at the gates.

"M. Chicot," cried the younger, "how are you this
morning?"

"Ah, M. de Bussy."

"You come for the king's levée, monsieur?"

"And you also, I presume?"

"No; I come to see M. le Duc d'Anjou. You know I
have not the honor of being a favorite of his majesty's."

"The reproach is for the king, and not for you."

"Do you come from far? I heard you were traveling."

"Yes, I was hunting. And you?"

"Yes, I have been in the provinces; and now will you
be good enough to render me a service?"

"I shall be delighted."

"Well, you can penetrate into the Louvre, while I remain in the ante-chamber; will you tell the duke I am
waiting for him?"

"Why not come in with me?"

"The king would not be pleased."

"Bah!"

"Diable! he has not accustomed me to his most gracious smiles."

"Henceforth, for some time, all that will change."

"Ah, ah! are you a necromancer, M. Chicot?"

"Sometimes; come, take courage, and come in with
me."

They entered together; one went towards the apartments of the Duc d'Anjou, and the other to those of the
king.

Henri was just awake, and had rung, and a crowd of

valets and friends had rushed in; already the chicken broth and the spiced wine were served, when Chicot entered, and without saying a word, sat down to eat and drink.

"Par la mordieu!" cried the king, delighted, although he affected anger; "it is that knave of a Chicot, that fugitive, that vagabond!"

"What is the matter, my son?" said Chicot, placing himself on the immense seat, embroidered with fleur-de-lis, on which the king was seated.

"Here is my misfortune returned," said Henri; "for three weeks I have been so tranquil."

"Bah! you always grumble. One would think you were one of your own subjects. Let me hear, Henriquet, how you have governed this kingdom in my absence."

"Chicot!"

"Have you hung any of your curled gentlemen? Ah! pardon, M. Quelus, I did not see you."

"Chicot, I shall be angry," said the king; but he ended by laughing, as he always did; so he went on: "But what has become of you? Do you know that I have had you sought for in all the bad parts of Paris?"

"Did you search the Louvre?"

Just then M. de Monsoreau entered.

"Ah! it is you, monsieur," said the king; "when shall we hunt again?"

"When it shall please your majesty; I hear there are plenty of wild boars at St. Germain en Laye."

"The wild boar is dangerous," said Chicot; "King Charles IX., I remember, was nearly killed by one. And then spears are sharp also; is it not so, Henri? and do you know your chief huntsman must have met a wolf not long ago?"

"Why so?"

"Because he has caught the likeness; it is striking."

M. de Monsoreau grew pale, and turning to Chicot, said:

"M. Chicot, I am not used to jesters, having lived little at court, and I warn you that before my king I do not like to be humiliated, above all when I speak of my duties."

"Well, monsieur," said Chicot, "we are not like you, we court people laughed heartily at the last joke."

"And what was that?"

"Making you chief huntsman."

Monsoreau looked daggers at Chicot.

"Come, come," said Henri, "let us speak of something else."

"Yes, let us speak of the merits of Nôtre Dame de Chartres."

"Chicot, no impiety."

"I impious! it is you, on the contrary; there were two chemises accustomed to be together, and you separated them. Join them together and a miracle may happen."

This illusion to the estrangement of the king and queen made every one laugh.

Monsoreau then whispered to Chicot, "Pray withdraw with me into that window, I wish to speak to you." When they were alone, he went on, "Now, M. Chicot, buffoon as you are, a gentleman forbids you; do you understand? forbids you to laugh at him, and to remember that others may finish what M. de Mayenne began."

"Ah! you wish me to become your creditor, as I am his, and to give you the same place in my gratitude."

"It seems to me that, among your creditors, you forget the principal."

"Indeed, I have generally a good memory. Who may it be?"

"M. Nicolas David."

"Oh! you are wrong; he is paid."

At this moment Bussy entered.

"Monsieur," said he to the count, "M. le Duc d'Anjou desires to speak with you."

"With me?"

"With you, monsieur."

"Do you accompany me?"

"No, I go first, to tell the duke you are coming," and he rapidly disappeared.

" Well ? " said the duke.

" He is coming."

" And he suspects nothing ? "

" Nothing ; but if he did, what matter ? is he not your creature ? Does he seem to you less guilty than he did yesterday ? "

" No, a hundred times more so."

" He has carried off, by treason, a noble young girl, and married her equally treasonably ; either he must ask for the dissolution of the marriage himself, or you must do it for him."

" I have promised."

" I have your word ? "

" You have."

" Remember that they know and are anxiously waiting."

" She shall be free, Bussy ; I pledge my word."

Bussy kissed the hand which had signed so many false promises. As he did so, M. de Monsoreau entered, and Bussy went to the corridor, where were several other gentlemen. Here he had to wait as patiently as might be for the result of this interview, on which all his future happiness was at stake. He waited for some time, when suddenly the door of the duke's room opened, and the sound of M. de Monsoreau's voice made Bussy tremble, for it sounded almost joyful. Soon the voices approached, and Bussy could see M. de Monsoreau bowing and retiring, and he heard the duke say :

" Adieu, my friend."

" ' My friend ! ' " murmured Bussy.

Then Monsoreau said, " Your highness agrees with me that publicity is best ? "

" Yes, yes ; an end to all mysteries."

" Then this evening I will present her to the king."

" Do so ; I will prepare him."

" Gentlemen," then said Monsoreau, turning towards those in the corridor, " allow me to announce to you a secret ; monseigneur permits me to make public my marriage with Mademoiselle Diana de Méridor, who has been my wife for more than a month, and whom I intend this evening to present to the court."

Bussy, who had been hidden behind a door, staggered, and almost fell at this unexpected blow. However, he darted a glance of contempt at the duke, towards whom he made a step, but he, in terror, shut his door, and Bussy heard the key turn in the lock. Feeling that if he stayed a moment longer he should betray before every one the violence of his grief, he ran downstairs, got on his horse, and galloped to the Rue St. Antoine. The baron and Diana were eagerly waiting for him, and they saw him enter pale and trembling.

"Madame," cried he, "hate me, despise me ; I believed I could do something and I can do nothing. Madame, you are now the recognized wife of M. de Monsoreau, and are to be presented this evening. I am a fool—a miserable dupe, or rather, as you said, M. le Baron, the duke is a coward and a villain."

And leaving the father and daughter overcome with grief, he rushed wildly away.

CHAPTER XXXV.

WHAT PASSED BETWEEN M. DE MONSOREAU AND THE DUKE.

IT is time to explain the duke's sudden change of intention with regard to M. de Monsoreau. When he first received him, it was with dispositions entirely favorable to Bussy's wishes.

"Your highness sent for me ? " said Monsoreau.

"You have nothing to fear, you who have served me so well, and are so much attached to me. Often you have told me of the plots against me, have aided my enterprises, forgetting your own interests, and exposing your life."

"Your highness——"

"Even lately, in this last unlucky adventure——"

"What adventure, monseigneur ? "

"This carrying off of Mademoiselle de Méridor—poor young creature!"

"Alas!" murmured Monsoreau.

"You pity her, do you not?" said the duke.

"Does not your highness?"

"I! you know how I have regretted this fatal caprice. And, indeed, it required all my friendship for you, and the remembrance of all your good services, to make me forget that without you I should not have carried off this young girl."

Monsoreau felt the blow. "Monseigneur," said he, "your natural goodness leads you to exaggerate, you no more caused the death of this young girl than I did."

"How so?"

"You did not intend to use violence to Mademoiselle de Méridor."

"Certainly not."

"Then the intention absolves you; it is a misfortune, nothing more."

"And besides," said the duke, looking at him, "death has buried all in eternal silence."

The tone of his voice and his look struck Monsoreau. "Monseigneur," said he, after a moment's pause, "shall I speak frankly to you?"

"Why should you hesitate?" said the prince, with astonishment mingled with hauteur.

"Indeed, I do not know, but your highness has not thought fit to be frank with me."

"Really!" cried the duke, with an angry laugh.

"Monseigneur, I know what your highness meant to say to me."

"Speak, then."

"Your highness wished to make me understand that perhaps Mademoiselle de Méridor was not dead, and that therefore those who believed themselves her murderers might be free from remorse."

"Oh, monsieur, you have taken your time before making this consoling reflection to me. You are a faithful servant, on my word; you saw me sad and afflicted, you heard

me speak of the wretched dreams I had since the death of
this woman, and you let me live thus, when even a doubt
might have spared me so much suffering. How must I
consider this conduct, monsieur?"

"Monseigneur, is your highness accusing me?"

"Traitor!" cried the duke, "you have deceived me;
you have taken from me this woman whom I loved——"

Monsoreau turned pale, but did not lose his proud, calm
look. "It is true," said he.

"True, knave!"

"Please to speak lower, monseigneur; your highness
forgets, that you speak to a gentleman and an old servant."

The duke laughed.

"My excuse is," continued he, "that I loved Mademoiselle de Méridor ardently."

"I, also," replied François, with dignity.

"It is true, monseigneur; but she did not love you."

"And she loved you?"

"Perhaps."

"You lie! you know you lie! You used force as I
did; only I, the master, failed, while you, the servant,
succeeded by treason."

"Monseigneur, I loved her."

"What do I care?"

"Monseigneur, take care. I loved her, and I am not a
servant. My wife is mine, and no one can take her from
me, not even the king. I wished to have her, and I took
her."

"You took her! Well! you shall give her up."

"You are wrong, monseigneur. And do not call," continued he, stopping him, "for if you call once—if you do
me a public injury——"

"You shall give up this woman."

"Give her up! she is my wife before God——"

"If she is your wife before God, you shall give her up
before men. I know all, and I will break this marriage, I
tell you. To-morrow, Mademoiselle de Méridor shall be
restored to her father; you shall set off into the exile I

impose on you ; you shall have sold your place ; these are
my conditions, and take care, or I will break you as I
break this glass." And he threw down violently a crystal
cup.

"I will not give up my wife, I will not give up my
place, and I will remain in France," replied Monsoreau.

"You will not ?"

"No, I will ask my pardon of the King of France—of
the king anointed at the Abbey of St. Geneviève; and
this new sovereign will not, I am sure, refuse the first request proffered to him." François grew deadly pale, and
nearly fell.

"Well, well," stammered he, "this request, speak lower
—I listen."

"I will speak humbly, as becomes the servant of your
highness. A fatal love was the cause of all. Love is the
most imperious of the passions. To make me forget that
your highness had cast your eyes on Diana, I must have
been no longer master of myself."

"It was a treason."

"Do not overwhelm me, monseigneur ; I saw you rich,
young and happy, the first Christian prince in the world.
For you are so, and between you and supreme rank there
is now only a shadow easy to dispel. I saw all the splendor
of your future, and, comparing your proud position with
my humble one, I said, 'Leave to the prince his brilliant
prospects and splendid projects, scarcely will he miss the
pearl that I steal from his royal crown.'"

"Comte ! comte !"

"You pardon me, monseigneur, do you not ?"

At this moment the duke raised his eyes, and saw
Bussy's portrait on the wall. It seemed to exhort him to
courage, and he said, "No, I cannot pardon you ; it is
not for myself that I hold out, it is because a father in
mourning—a father unworthily deceived—cries out for his
daughter ; because a woman, forced to marry you, cries
for vengeance against you ; because, in a word, the first
duty of a prince is justice."

"Monseigneur, if justice be a duty, gratitude is not less

13

so ; and a king should never forget those to whom he owes his crown. Now, monseigneur, you owe your crown to me."

" Monsoreau !" cried the duke, in terror.

" But I cling to those only who cling to me."

" I cannot—you are a gentleman, you know I cannot approve of what you have done. My dear count, this one more sacrifice ; I will recompense you for it ; I will give you all you ask."

" Then your highness loves her still ! " cried Monsoreau, pale with jealousy.

" No, I swear I do not."

" Then, why should I ? I am a gentleman ; who can enter into the secrets of my private life ? "

" But she does not love you."

" What matter ? "

" Do this for me, Monsoreau."

" I cannot."

" Then——" commenced the duke, who was terribly perplexed.

" Reflect, sire."

" You will denounce me ? "

" To the king dethroned for you, yes ; for if my new king destroyed my honor and happiness, I would return to the old."

" It is infamous."

" True, sire ; but I love enough to be infamous."

" It is cowardly."

" Yes, your majesty, but I love enough to be cowardly. Come, monseigneur, do something for the man who has served you so well."

" What do you want ? "

" That you should pardon me."

" I will."

" That you should reconcile me with M. de Méridor."

" I will try."

" That you will sign my marriage contract with Mademoiselle de Méridor."

" Yes," said the prince, in a hoarse voice.

"And that you shall honor my wife with a smile when I shall present her to his majesty."

"Yes; is that all?"

"All, monseigneur."

"You have my word."

"And you shall keep the throne to which I have raised you.—There remains now, only," thought Monsoreau, "to find out who told the duke."

CHAPTER XXXVI.

CHICOT AND THE KING.

THAT same evening M. de Monsoreau presented his wife in the queen's circle. Henri, tired, had gone to bed, but after sleeping three or four hours, he woke, and feeling no longer sleepy, proceeded to the room where Chicot slept, which was the one formerly occupied by St. Luc; Chicot slept soundly, and the king called him three times before he woke. At last he opened his eyes and cried out, "What is it?"

"Chicot, my friend, it is I."

"You; who?"

"I, Henri."

"Decidedly, my son, the pheasants must have disagreed with you; I warned you at supper, but you would eat so much of them, as well as of those crabs."

"No; I scarcely tasted them."

"Then you are poisoned, perhaps. Ventre de biche! how pale you are!"

"It is my mask," said the king.

"Then you are not ill?"

"No."

"Then why wake me?"

"Because I am annoyed."

"Annoyed! if you wake a man at two o'clock in the morning, at least you should bring him a present. Have you anything for me?"

" No ; I come to talk to you."

" That is not enough."

" Chicot, M. de Morvilliers came here last evening."

" What for ? "

" To ask for an audience.   What can he want to say to me, Chicot ? "

" What ! it is only to ask that, that you wake me ? "

" Chicot, you know he occupies himself with the police."

" No ; I did not know it."

" Do you doubt his watchfulness ? "

" Yes, I do, and I have my reasons."

" What are they ? "

" Will one suffice you ? "

" Yes, if it be good."

" And you will leave me in peace afterwards ? "

" Certainly."

" Well, one day—no, it was one evening, I beat you in the Rue Foidmentel ; you had with you Quelus and Schomberg."

" You beat me ? "

" Yes, all three of you."

" How, it was you ! wretch ! "

" I, myself," said Chicot, rubbing his hands, " do I not hit hard ? "

" Wretch ! "

" You confess, it was true ? "

" You know it is, villain."

" Did you send for M. de Morvilliers the next day ? "

" You know I did, for you were there when he came."

" And you told him the accident that had happened to one of your friends ? "

" Yes."

" And you ordered him to find out the criminal ? "

" Yes."

" Did he find him ? "

" No."

" Well, then, go to bed, Henri ; you see your police is bad.   And, turning round, Chicot refused to say another word, and was soon snoring again.

The next day the council assembled. It consisted of Quelus, Maugiron, D'Epernon, and Schomberg. Chicot, seated at the head of the table, was making paper boats, and arranging them in a fleet. M. de Morvilliers was announced, and came in, looking grave.

"Am I," said he, "before your majesty's council?"

"Yes, before my best friends; speak freely."

"Well, sire, I have a terrible plot to denounce to your majesty."

"A plot!" cried all.

"Yes, your majesty."

"Oh, is it a Spanish plot?"

At this moment the Duc d'Anjou, who had been summoned to attend the council, entered.

"My brother," said Henri, "M. de Morvilliers comes to announce a plot to us."

The duke threw a suspicious glance round him. "Is it possible?" he said.

"Alas, yes, monseigneur," said M. de Morvilliers.

"Tell us all about it," said Chicot.

"Yes," stammered the duke, "tell us all about it, monsieur."

"I listen," said Henri.

"Sire, for some time I have been watching some malcontents, but they were shopkeepers, or junior clerks, a few monks and students."

"That is not much," said Chicot.

"I know that malcontents always make use either of war or of religion."

"Very sensible!" said the king.

"I put men on the watch, and at last I succeeded in persuading a man from the provosty of Paris to watch the preachers, who go about exciting the people against your majesty. They are prompted by a party hostile to your majesty, and this party I have studied, and now I know their hopes," added he, triumphantly. "I have men in my pay, greedy, it is true, who, for a good sum of money, promised to let me know of the first meeting of the conspirators."

"Oh! never mind money, but let us hear the aim of this conspiracy."

"Sire, they think of nothing less than a second St. Bartholomew."

"Against whom?"

"Against the Huguenots."

"What have you paid for your secret?" said Chicot.

"One hundred and sixty thousand livres."

Chicot turned to the king, saying, "If you like, for one thousand crowns, I will tell you all the secrets of M. de Morvilliers."

"Speak."

"It is simply the League, instituted ten years ago; M. de Morvilliers has discovered what every Parisian knows as well as his *ave*."

"Monsieur," interrupted the chancellor.

"I speak the truth, and I will prove it," cried Chicot.

"Tell me, then, their place of meeting."

"Firstly, the public streets; secondly, the public streets."

"M. Chicot is joking," said the chancellor; "tell me their rallying sign."

"They are dressed like Parisians, and shake their legs when they walk."

A burst of laughter followed this speech; then M. de Morvilliers said, "They have had one meeting-place which M. Chicot does not know of."

"Where?" asked the king.

"The Abbey of St. Geneviève."

"Impossible!" murmured the duke.

"It is true," said M. de Morvilliers, triumphantly.

"What did they decide?" asked the king.

"That the Leaguers should choose chiefs, that every one should arm, that every province should receive a deputy from the conspirators, and that all the Huguenots cherished by his majesty (that was their expression)——"

The king smiled.

"Should be massacred on a given day."

"Is that all?" said the duke.

"No, monseigneur."

"I should hope not," said Chicot; "if the king got only that for one hundred and sixty thousand livres, it would be a shame."

"There are chiefs——"

The Duc d'Anjou could not repress a start.

"What!" cried Chicot, "a conspiracy that has chiefs! how wonderful! But we ought to have more than that for one hundred and sixty thousand livres."

"Their names?" asked the king.

"Firstly, a fanatic preacher; I gave ten thousand livres for his name."

"Very well."

"A monk called Gorenflot."

"Poor devil!" said Chicot."

"Gorenflot?" said the king, writing down the name; "afterwards——"

"Oh!" said the chancellor, with hesitation, "that is all." And he looked round as if to say, "If your majesty were alone, you should hear more."

"Speak, chancellor," said the king, "I have none but friends here."

"Oh! sire, I hesitate to pronounce such powerful names."

"Are they more powerful than I am?" cried the king.

"No, sire; but one does not tell secrets in public."

"Monsieur," said the Duc d'Anjou, "we will retire."

The king signed to the chancellor to approach him, and to the duke to remain. M. de Morvilliers had just bent over the king to whisper his communication, when a great clamor was heard in the court of the Louvre. The king jumped up, but Chicot, running to the window, called out, "It is M. de Guise entering the Louvre."

"The Duc de Guise," stammered the Duc d'Anjou.

"How strange that he should be in Paris," said the king, reading the truth in M. de Morvilliers' look. "Was it of him you were about to speak?" he asked.

"Yes, sire; he presided over the meeting."

"And the others?"

"I know no more."

"You need not write that name on your tablets! you will not forget it," whispered Chicot.

The Duc de Guise advanced, smiling, to see the king.

CHAPTER XXXVII.

WHAT M. DE GUISE CAME TO DO AT THE LOUVRE.

BEHIND M. de Guise there entered a great number of officers, courtiers, and gentlemen, and behind them a concourse of the people ; an escort less brilliant, but more formidable, and it was their cries that had resounded as the duke entered the Louvre.

"Ah ! it 's you, my cousin," said the king ; "what a noise you bring with you ! Did I not hear the trumpets sound ?"

"Sire, the trumpets sound in Paris only for the king, and in campaigns for the general. Here the trumpets would make too much noise for a subject ; there they do not make enough for a prince."

Henri bit his lips. "Have you arrived from the siege of La Charité only to-day ?"

"Only to-day, sire," replied the duke, with a heightened color.

"Ma foi ! your visit is a great honor to us."

"Your majesty jests, no doubt. How can my visit honor him from whom all honor comes ?"

"I mean, M. de Guise," replied Henri, "that every good Catholic is in the habit, on returning from a campaign, to visit God first in one of his temples—the king only comes second. 'Honor God, serve the king,' you know, my cousin."

The heightened color of the duke became now still more distinct ; and the king, happening to turn towards his brother, saw with astonishment, that he was as pale as the duke was red. He was struck by this emotion in each, but he said :

"At all events, duke, nothing equals my joy to see that you have escaped all the dangers of war, although you sought them, I was told in the rashest manner ; but danger knows you and flies you."

The duke bowed.

"But I must beg you, my cousin, not to be so ambitious of mortal perils, for you put to shame sluggards like us, who sleep, eat, and invent new prayers."

"Yes, sire," replied the duke, "we know you to be a pious prince, and that no pleasure can make you forget the glory of God and the interests of the Church. That is why we have come with so much confidence to your majesty."

"With confidence! Do you not always come to me with confidence, my cousin?"

"Sire, the confidence of which I speak refers to the proposition I am about to make to you."

"You have a proposition to make to me! Well, speak, as you say, with confidence. What have you to propose?"

"The execution of one of the most beautiful ideas which has been originated since the Crusades."

"Continue, duke."

"Sire, the title of most Christian king is not a vain one ; it makes an ardent zeal for religion incumbent on its possessor."

"Is the Church menaced by the Saracens once more?"

"Sire, the great concourse of people who followed me, blessing my name, honored me with this reception only because of my zeal to defend the Church. I have already had the honor of speaking to your majesty of an alliance between all true Catholics."

"Yes, yes," said Chicot, "the League ; ventre de biche, Henri, the League. By St. Bartholomew! how can you forget so splendid an idea, my son?"

The duke cast a disdainful glance on Chicot, while D'Anjou, who stood by, as pale as death, tried by signs, to make the duke stop.

"Look at your brother, Henri," whispered Chicot.

"Sire," continued the Duc de Guise, "the Catholics have indeed called this association the Holy League, and its aim is to fortify the throne against the Huguenots, its mortal enemies; but to form an association is not enough, and in a kingdom like France, several millions of men cannot assemble without the consent of the king."

"Several millions!" cried Henri, almost with terror.

"Several millions!" repeated Chicot; "a small number of malcontents, which may bring forth pretty results."

"Sire," cried the duke, "I am astonished that your majesty allows me to be interrupted so often, when I am speaking on serious matters."

"Quite right," said Chicot; "silence there."

"Several millions!" repeated the king; "and against these millions, how many Huguenots are there in my kingdom?"

"Four," said Chicot.

This new sally made the king and his friends laugh, but the duke frowned, and his gentlemen murmured loudly.

Henri, becoming once more serious, said, "Well, duke, what do you wish? To the point."

"I wish, sire—for your popularity is dearer to me than my own—that your majesty should be superior to us in your zeal for religion—I wish you to choose a chief for the League."

"Well!" said the king, to those who surrounded him, "what do you think of it, my friends?"

Chicot, without saying a word, drew out a lion's skin from a corner, and threw himself on it.

"What are you doing, Chicot?" asked the king.

"Sire, they say that night brings good counsel; that must be because of sleep; therefore I am going to sleep, and to-morrow I will reply to my cousin Guise."

The duke cast a furious glance on Chicot, who replied by a loud snore.

"Well, sire!" said the duke, "what does your majesty say?"

"I think that, as usual, you are in the right, my cousin; convoke, then, your principal leaguers, come at their head, and I will choose the chief."

"When, sire?"

"To-morrow."

The Duc de Guise then took leave, and the Duc d'Anjou was about to do the same, when the king said,—

"Stay, my brother, I wish to speak to you."

CHAPTER XXXVIII.

CASTOR AND POLLUX.

THE king dismissed all his favorites, and remained with his brother. The duke, who had managed to preserve a tolerably composed countenance throughout, believed himself unsuspected, and remained without fear.

"My brother," said Henri, after assuring himself that, with the exception of Chicot, no one remained in the room, "do you know that I am a very happy prince?"

"Sire, if your majesty be really happy, it is a recompense from Heaven for your merits."

"Yes, happy," continued the king, "for if great ideas do not come to me, they do to my subjects. It is a great idea which has occurred to my cousin Guise."

The duke make a sign of assent, and Chicot opened his eyes to watch the king's face.

"Indeed," continued Henri, "to unite under one banner all the Catholics, to arm all France on this pretext from Calais to Languedoc, from Bretagne to Burgundy, so that I shall always have an army ready to march against England, Holland, or Spain, without alarming any of them—do you know, François, it is a magnificent idea?"

"Is it not, sire?" said the duke, delighted.

"Yes, I confess I feel tempted to reward largely the author of this fine project."

Chicot opened his eyes, but he shut them again, for he had seen on the face of the king one of his almost imperceptible smiles, and he was satisfied.

"Yes," continued Henri, "I repeat such a project merits recompense, and I will do what I can for the author of this good work, for the work is begun—is it not, my brother?"

The duke confessed that it was.

"Better and better; my subjects not only conceive these good ideas, but, in their anxiety to be of use to me, hasten to put them in execution. But I ask you, my dear François, if it be really to the Duc de Guise that I am indebted for this royal thought?"

"No, sire, it occurred to the Cardinal de Lorraine twenty years ago, only the St. Bartholomew rendered it needless for the time."

"Ah! what a pity he is dead; but," continued Henri, with that air of frankness which made him the first comedian of the day, "his nephew has inherited it, and brought it to bear. What can I do for him?"

"Sire," said François, completely duped by his brother, "you exaggerate his merits. He has, as I say, but inherited the idea, and another man has given him great help in developing it."

"His brother the cardinal?"

"Doubtless he has been occupied with it, but I do not mean him."

"Mayenne, then?"

"Oh! sire, you do him too much honor."

"True, how could any good ideas come to such a butcher? But to whom, then, am I to be grateful for aid to my cousin Guise?"

"To me, sire."

"To you!" cried Henri, as if in astonishment. "How! when I saw all the world unchained against me, the preachers against my vices, the poets against my weaknesses, while my friends laughed at my powerlessness, and my situation was so harassing, that it gave me gray hairs every day: such an idea came to you, François—to you, whom I confess, for man is feeble and kings are blind, I did not always believe to be my friend! Ah! François, how guilty I have been." And Henri, moved even to tears, held out his hand to his brother.

Chicot opened his eyes again,

"Oh!" continued Henri, "the idea is triumphant. Not being able to raise troops without raising an outcry, scarcely to walk, sleep, or love, without exciting ridicule, this idea gives me at once an army, money, friends, and repose. But my cousin spake of a chief?"

"Yes, doubtless."

"This chief, you understand, François, cannot be one of my favorites; none of them has at once the head and the heart necessary for so important a post. Quelus is brave, but is occupied only by his amours. Maugiron is also brave, but he thinks only of his toilette. Schomberg also, but he is not clever. D'Epernon is a valiant man, but he is a hypocrite, whom I could not trust, although I am friendly to him. But you know, François, that one of the heaviest taxes on a king is the necessity of dissimulation; therefore, when I can speak freely from my heart, as I do now, I breathe. Well, then, if my cousin Guise originated this idea, to the development of which you have assisted, the execution of it belongs to him."

"What do you say, sire?" said François, uneasily.

"I say, that to direct such a movement we must have a prince of high rank."

"Sire, take care."

"A good captain and a skilful negotiator."

"The last particularly."

"Well, is not M. de Guise all this?"

"My brother, he is very powerful already."

"Yes, doubtless; but his power makes my strength."

"He holds already the army and the bourgeois; the cardinal holds the Church, and Mayenne is their instrument; it is a great deal of power to be concentrated in one family."

"It is true, François; I had thought of that."

"If the Guises were French princes, their interest would be to aggrandize France."

"Yes, but they are Lorraines."

"Of a house always rival to yours."

"Yes, François; you have touched the sore. I did not think you so good a politician. Yes, there does not pass

a day but one or other of these Guises, either by address
or by force, carries away from me some particle of my
power. Ah! François, if we had but had this explanation sooner, if I had been able to read your heart as I do
now, certain of support in you, I might have resisted
better, but now it is too late."

"Why so?"

"Because all combats fatigue me; therefore I must
make him chief of the League."

"You will be wrong, brother."

"But who could I name, François? who would accept
this perilous post? Yes, perilous; for do you not see
that he intended me to appoint him chief, and that,
should I name any one else to the post, he would treat
him as an enemy?"

"Name some one so powerful that, supported by you,
he need not fear all the three Lorraine princes together."

"Ah, my good brother, I know no such person."

"Look round you, brother."

"I know no one but you and Chicot who are really my
friends."

"Well, brother."

Henri looked at the duke as if a veil had fallen from
his eyes. "Surely you would never consent, brother! It
is not you who could teach all these bourgeois their exercise, who could look over the discourses of the preachers,
who, in case of battle, would play the butcher in the
streets of Paris; for all this, one must be triple, like the
duke, and have a right arm called Charles and a loft
called Louis. What! you would like all this? You, the
first gentleman of our court! Mort de ma vie! how people change with the age!"

"Perhaps I would not do it for myself, brother, but I
would do it for you."

"Excellent brother!" said Henri, wiping away a tear
which never existed.

"Then," said the duke, "it would not displease you
for me to assume this post?"

"Displease me! On the contrary, it would charm me."

François trembled with joy. "Oh! if your majesty thinks me worthy of this confidence."

"Confidence! When you are the chief, what have I to fear? The League itself? That cannot be dangerous, can it, François?"

"Oh, sire!"

"No, for then you would not be chief, or at least, when you are chief, there will be no danger. But, François, the duke is doubtless certain of this appointment, and he will not lightly give way."

"Sire, you grant me the command?"

"Certainly."

"And you wish me to have it?"

"Particularly; but I dare not too much displease M. de Guise."

"Oh, make yourself easy, sire; if that be the only obstacle, I pledge myself to arrange it."

"When?"

"At once."

"Are you going to him? That will be doing him too much honor."

"No, sire; he is waiting for me."

"Where?"

"In my room."

"Your room! I heard the cries of the people as he left the Louvre."

"Yes; but after going out at the great door he came back by the postern. The king had the right to the first visit, but I to the second."

"Ah, brother, I thank you for keeping up our prerogative, which I had the weakness so often to abandon. Go, then, François, and do your best."

François bent down to kiss the king's hand, but he, opening his arms, gave him a warm embrace, and then the duke left the room to go to his interview with the Duc de Guise. The king, seeing his brother gone, gave an angry growl, and rapidly made his way through the secret corridor, until he reached a hiding-place whence he could distinctly hear the conversation between the two dukes.

"Ventre de biche!" cried Chicot, starting up, "how touching these family scenes are! For an instant I believed myself in Olympus, assisting at the reunion of Castor and Pollux after six months' separation."

CHAPTER XXXIX.

IN WHICH IT IS PROVED THAT LISTENING IS THE BEST WAY TO HEAR.

THE Duc d'Aujou was well aware that there were few rooms in the Louvre which were not built so that what was said in them could be heard from the outside; but, completely seduced by his brother's manner, he forgot to take any precautions.

"Why, monseigneur," said the Duc de Guise, "how pale you are!"

"Visibly?"

"Yes, to me."

"The king saw nothing?"

"I think not; but he retained you?"

"Yes."

"And what did he say, monseigneur?"

"He approves the idea, but the more gigantic it appears, the more he hesitates to place a man like you at the head."

"Then we are likely to fail."

"I fear so, my dear duke; the League seems likely to fail."

"Before it begins."

At this moment Henri, hearing a noise, turned and saw Chicot by his side, listening also. "You followed me, knave!" said he.

"Hush, my son," said Chicot; "you prevent me from hearing."

"Monseigneur," said the Duc de Guise, "it seems to me that in this case the king would have refused at once. Does he wish to dispossess me?"

"I believe so."

"Then he would ruin the enterprise?"

"Yes; but I aided you with all my power."

"How, monseigneur?"

"In this—the king has left me almost master, to kill or reanimate the League."

"How so?" cried the duke, with sparkling eyes.

"Why, if, instead of dissolving the League, he named me chief——"

"Ah!" cried the duke, while the blood mounted to his face.

"Ah! the dogs are going to fight over their bones," said Chicot; but to his surprise, and the king's, the Duc de Guise suddenly became calm, and exclaimed, in an almost joyful tone:

"You are an adroit politician, monseigneur, if you did this."

"Yes, I did; but I would not conclude anything without speaking to you."

"Why so, monseigneur?"

"Because I did not know what it would lead us to."

"Well, I will tell you, monseigneur, not to what it will lead us—that God alone knows—but how it will serve us. The League is a second army, and as I hold the first, and my brother the Church, nothing can resist us as long as we are united."

"Without counting," said the Duc d'Anjou, "that I am heir presumptive to the throne."

"True, but still calculate your bad chances."

"I have done so a hundred times."

"There is, first, the King of Navarre."

"Oh! I do not mind him; he is entirely occupied by his amours with La Fosseuse."

"He, monseigneur, will dispute every inch with you; he watches you and your brother; he hungers for the throne. If any accident should happen to your brother, see if he will not be here with a bound from Pau to Paris."

"An accident to my brother," repeated François.

"Listen, Henri," said Chicot.

"Yes, monseigneur," said the Duc de Guise, "an acci-

14

dent. Accidents are not rare in your family; you know that, as well as I do. One prince is in good health, and all at once he falls ill of a lingering malady; another is counting on long years, when, perhaps, he has but a few hours to live."

"Do you hear, Henri?" said Chicot, taking the hand of the king, who shuddered at what he heard.

"Yes, it is true," said the Duc d'Anjou, "the princes of my house are born under fatal influences; but my brother Henri is, thank God, strong and well; he supported formerly the fatigues of war, and now that his life is nothing but recreation——"

"Yes; but, monseigneur, remember one thing; these recreations are not always without danger. How did your father, Henri II., die, for example? He, who also had happily escaped the dangers of war. The wound by M. de Montgomery's lance was an accident. Then your poor brother, François, one would hardly call a pain in the ears an accident, and yet it was one; at least, I have often heard it said that this mortal malady was poured into his ear by some one well known."

"Duke!" murmured François, reddening.

"Yes, monseigneur; the name of king has long brought misfortune with it. Look at Antoine de Bourbon, who died from a spot in the shoulder. Then there was Jeanne d'Albret, the mother of the Béarnais, who died from smelling a pair of perfumed gloves, an accident very unexpected although there were people who had great interest in this death. Then Charles IX., who died neither by the eye, the ear, nor the shoulder, but by the mouth——"

"What do you say?" cried François, starting back.

"Yes, monseigneur, by the mouth. Those hunting books are very dangerous, of which the pages stick together, and can only be opened by wetting the finger constantly."

"Duke! duke! I believe you invent crimes."

"Crimes! who speaks of crimes? I speak of accidents. Was it not also an accident that happened to Charles IX. at the chase? You know what chase I mean; that of the

boar, where, intending to kill the wild boar, which had
turned on your brother, you, who never before had missed
your aim, did so then, and the king would have been killed,
as he had fallen from his horse, had not Henri of Navarre
slain the animal which you had missed."

"But," said the Duc d'Anjou, trying to recover himself,
"what interest could I have had in the death of Charles
IX., when the next king would be Henri III.?"

"Oh! monseigneur, there was already one throne vacant,
that of Poland. The death of Charles IX. would have
left another, that of France; and even the kingdom of
Poland might not have been despised. Besides, the death
of Charles would have brought you a degree nearer the
throne, and the next accident would have benefited you."

"What do you conclude from all this, duke?" said the
Duc d'Anjou.

"Monseigneur, I conclude that each king has his
accident, and that you are the inevitable accident of Henri
III., particularly if you are chief of the League."

"Then I am to accept?"

"Oh! I beg you to do so."

"And you?"

"Oh! be easy; my men are ready, and to-night Paris
will be curious."

"What are they going to do in Paris to-night?" asked
Henri.

"Oh! how foolish you are, my friend; to-night they
sign the League publicly."

"It is well," said the Duc d'Anjou, "till this evening
then."

"Yes, till this evening," said Henri.

"How!" said Chicot, "you will not risk going into
the streets to-night?"

"Yes, I shall."

"You are wrong, Henri; remember the accidents."

"Oh! I shall be well accompanied; will you come with
me?"

"What! do you take me for a Huguenot? I shall go
and sign the League ten times. However, Henri, you have

a great advantage over your predecessors, in being warned,
for you know your brother, do you not?"

"Yes, and, mordieu! before long he shall find it out."

CHAPTER XI.

THE EVENING OF THE LEAGUE.

PARIS presented a fine sight, as through its then narrow
streets thousands of people pressed towards the same point,
for at eight o'clock in the evening, M. le Duc de Guise
was to receive the signatures of the bourgeois to the
League. A crowd of citizens, dressed in their best clothes,
as for a fête, but fully armed, directed their steps towards
the churches. What added to the noise and confusion was
that large numbers of women, disdaining to stay at home
on such a great day, had followed their husbands, and
many had brought with them a whole batch of children.
It was in the Rue de l'Arbre Sec that the crowd was the
thickest. The streets were literally choked, and the crowd
pressed tumultuously towards a bright light suspended below the sign of the Belle Etoile. On the threshold a man,
with a cotton cap on his head and a naked sword in one
hand and a register in the other, was crying out, "Come
come, brave Catholics, enter the hotel of the Belle Etoile,
where you will find good wine; come, to-night the good
will be separated from the bad, and to-morrow morning
the wheat will be known from the tares; come, gentlemen,
you who can write, come and sign;—you who cannot write,
come and tell your names to me, La Hurière; vive la
messe!" A tall man elbowed his way through the crowd,
and in letters half an inch high, wrote his name, 'Chicot.'
Then, turning to La Hurière, he asked if he had not another register to sign. La Hurière did not understand
raillery, and answered angrily. Chicot retorted, and a
quarrel seemed approaching, when Chicot, feeling some
one touch his arm, turned, and saw the king disguised as
a simple bourgeois, and accompanied by Quelus and Mau-

giron, also disguised, and carrying au arquebuse on their shoulders.

"What!" cried the king, "good Catholics disputing among themselves; par la mordieu, it is a bad example."

"Do not mix yourself with what does not concern you," replied Chicot, without seeming to recognize him. But a new influx of the crowd distracted the attention of La Hurière, and separated the king and his companions from the hotel.

"Why are you here, sire?" said Chicot.

"Do you think I have anything to fear?"

"Eh! mon Dieu! in a crowd like this it is so easy for one man to put a knife into his neighbor, and who just utters an oath and gives up the ghost."

"Have I been seen?"

"I think not; but you will be if you stay longer. Go back to the Louvre, sire."

"Oh! oh! what is this new outcry, and what are the people running for?"

Chicot looked, but could at first see nothing but a mass of people crying, howling, and pushing. At last the mass opened, and a monk, mounted on a donkey, appeared. The monk spoke and gesticulated, and the ass brayed.

"Ventre de biche!" cried Chicot, "listen to the preacher."

"A preacher on a donkey!" cried Quelus.

"Why not?"

"He is Silenus," said Maugiron.

"Which is the preacher?" said the king, "for they speak both at once."

"The underneath one is the most eloquent," said Chicot, "but the one at the top speaks the best French; listen, Henri."

"My brethren," said the monk, "Paris is a superb city; Paris is the pride of France, and the Parisians a fine people." Then he began to sing, but the ass mingled his accompaniment so loudly that he was obliged to stop. The crowd burst out laughing.

"Hold your tongue, Panurge, hold your tongue," cried

the monk, "you shall speak after, but let me speak first."

The ass was quiet.

"My brothers," continued the preacher, "the earth is a valley of grief, where man often can quench his thirst only with his tears."

"He is drunk," said the king.

"I should think so."

"I, who speak to you," continued the monk, "I am returning from exile like the Hebrews of old, and for eight days Panurge and I have been living on alms and privations."

"Who is Panurge?" asked the king.

"The superior of his convent, probably; but let me listen."

"Who made me endure this? It was Herod; you know what Herod I speak of. I and Panurge have come from Villeneuve-le-Roi, in three days, to assist at this great solemnity; now we see, but we do not understand. What is passing, my brothers? Is it to-day that they depose Herod? Is it to-day that they put brother Henri in a convent?—Gentlemen," continued he, "I left Paris with two friends; Panurge, who is my ass, and Chicot, who is his majesty's jester. Can you tell me what has become of my friend Chicot?"

Chicot made a grimace.

"Oh," said the king, "he is your friend." Quelus and Maugiron burst out laughing. "He is handsome and respectable," continued the king.

"It is Gorenflot, of whom M. de Morvilliers spoke to you."

"The incendiary of St. Geneviève?"

"Himself!"

"Then I will have him hanged!"

"Impossible!"

"Why?"

"He has no neck."

"My brothers," continued Gorenflot. "I am a true martyr, and it is my cause that they defend at this moment or, rather, that of all good Catholics. You do not know what is passing in the provinces, we have been obliged at Lyons to kill a Huguenot who preached revolt. While one of them remains in France, there will be no tranquillity for us. Let us exterminate them. To arms! to arms!"

Several voices repeated, "To arms!"

"Par la mordieu!" said the king, "make this fellow hold his tongue, or he will make a second St. Bartholomew!"

"Wait," said Chicot, and with his stick he struck Gorenflot with all his force on the shoulders.

"Murder!" cried the monk.

"It is you!" cried Chicot.

"Help me, M. Chicot, help me! The enemies of the faith wish to assassinate me, but I will not die without making my voice heard. Death to the Huguenots!"

"Will you hold your tongue?" cried Chicot. But at this moment a second blow fell on the shoulders of the monk with such force that he cried out with real pain. Chicot, astonished, looked round him, but saw nothing but the stick. The blow had been given by a man who had immediately disappeared in the crowd after administering this punishment.

"Who the devil could it have been?" thought Chicot, and he began to run after the man, who was gliding away, followed by only one companion.

CHAPTER XLI.

THE RUE DE LA FERRONNERIE.

CHICOT had good legs, and he would have made the best use of them to join the man who had beaten Gorenflot if he had not imagined that there might be danger in trying to recognize a man who so evidently wished to avoid it. He thought the best way not to seem to watch them was to pass them; so he ran on, and passed them at the corner of the Rue Tirechappe, and then hid himself

at the end of the Rue des Bourdonnais. The two men
went on, their hats slouched over their eyes, and their
cloaks drawn up over their faces, with a quick and mili-
tary step, until they reached the Rue de la Ferronnerie.
There they stopped and looked round them. Chicot, who
was still ahead, saw in the middle of the street, before a
house so old that it looked falling to pieces, a litter, attached to which were two horses. The driver had fallen
asleep, while a woman, apparently unquiet, was looking
anxiously through the blind. Chicot hid himself behind
a large stone wall, which served as stalls for the vegetable
sellers on the days when the market was held in this street,
and watched. Scarcely was he hidden, when he saw the
two men approach the litter, one of whom, on seeing the
driver asleep, uttered an impatient exclamation, while the
other pushed him to awaken him. "Oh, they are com-
patriots!" thought Chicot. The lady now leaned out of
the window, and Chicot saw that she was young, very pale,
but very beautiful. The two men approached the litter,
and the taller of the two took in both of his the little white
hand which was stretched out to him.

"Well, ma mie," asked he, "how are you ?"

"I have been very anxious," replied she.

"Why the devil did you bring madame to Paris?"
said the other man rudely.

"Ma foi! it is a malediction that you must always have
a petticoat tacked to your doublet!"

"Ah, dear Agrippa," replied the man who had spoken
first, "it is so great a grief to part from one you love."

"On my soul, you make me swear to hear you talk !
Did you come to Paris to make love ?　It seems to me that
Béarn is large enough for your sentimental promenades,
without continuing them in this Babylon, where you have
nearly got us killed twenty times to-day. Go home, if
you wish to make love, but, here, keep to your political
intrigues, my master."

"Let him scold, ma mie, and never mind him ; I think
he would be ill if he did not."

"But, at least, ventre St. Gris, as you say, get into the

litter, and say your sweet things to madame; you will run less risk of being recognized there than in the open street."

"You are right, Agrippa. Give me a place, ma mie, if you permit me to sit by your side."

"Permit, sire; I desire it ardently," replied the lady.

"Sire!" murmured Chicot, who, carried away by an impulse, tried to raise his head, and knocked it against the stone wall. Meanwhile the happy lover profited by the permission given, and seated himself in the litter.

"Oh! how happy I am," he cried, without attending in the least to the impatience of his friend—"ventre St. Gris, this is a good day. Here are my good Parisians, who execrate me with all their souls, and would kill me if they could, working to smooth my way to the throne, and I have in my arms the woman I love. Where are we, D'Aubigné? when I am king, I will erect here a statue to the genius of the Béarnais."

"The Béarn——" began Chicot, but he stopped, for he had given his head a second bump.

"We are in the Rue de la Ferronnerie, sire," said D'Aubigné, "and it does not smell nice."

"Get in then, Agrippa, and we will go on."

"Ma foi, no, I will follow behind; I should annoy you, and, what is worse, you would annoy me."

"Shut the door then, bear of Béarn, and do as you like." Then to the coachman he said, "Lavarrenne, you know where."

The litter went slowly away, followed by D'Aubigné.

"Let me see," said Chicot, "must I tell Henri what I have seen? Why should I? two men and a woman, who hide themselves; it would be cowardly. I will not tell; that I know it myself is the important point, for is it not I who reign? His love was very pretty, but he loves too often, this dear Henri of Navarre. A year ago it was Madame de Sauve, and I suppose this was La Fosseuse. However, I love the Béarnais, for I believe some day he will do an ill turn to those dear Guises. Well! I have seen every one to-day but the Duc d'Anjou; he alone is wanting to my list of princes. Where can my François III. be? Ventre de biche, I must look for the worthy monarch."

Chicot was not the only person who was seeking for the Duc d'Anjou, and unquiet at his absence. The Guises had also sought for him on all sides, but they were not more lucky than Chicot. M. d'Anjou was not the man to risk himself imprudently, and we shall see afterwards what precautions had kept him from his friends. Once Chicot thought he had found him in the Rue Bethisy; a numerous group was standing at the door of a wine-merchant; and in this group Chicot recognized M. de Monsoreau and M. de Guise, and fancied that the Duc d'Anjou could not be far off. But he was wrong. MM. de Monsoreau and Guise were occupied in exciting still more an orator in his stammering eloquence. This orator was Gorenflot, recounting his journey to Lyons, and his duel in an inn with a dreadful Huguenot. M. de Guise was listening intently, for he began to fancy it had something to do with the silence of Nicolas David. Chicot was terrified; he felt sure that in another moment Gorenflot would pronounce his name, which would throw a fatal light on the mystery. Chicot in an instant cut the bridles of some of the horses that were fastened up, and giving them each a violent blow, sent them galloping among the crowd, which opened, and began to disperse in different directions. Chicot passed quickly through the groups, and approaching Gorenflot, took Panurge by the bridle and turned him round. The Duc de Guise was already separated from them by the rush of the people, and Chicot led off Gorenflot to a kind of cul-de-sac by the church of St. Germain l'Auxerrois.

"Ah! drunkard!" said he to him, "ah! traitor! you will then always prefer a bottle of wine to your friend."

"Ah! M. Chicot," stammered the monk.

"What! I feed you, wretch, I give you drink, I fill your pockets and your stomach, and you betray me."

"Ah! M. Chicot!"

"You tell my secrets, wretch."

"Dear friend."

"Hold your tongue; you are but a sycophant, and deserve punishment."

And the monk, vigorous and strong, powerful as a bull, but overcome by wine and repentance, remained without defending himself in the hands of Chicot, who shook him like a balloon full of air.

"A punishment to me, to your friend, dear M. Chicot!"

"Yes, to you," said Chicot, striking him over the shoulders with his stick.

"Ah! if I were but fasting."

"You would beat me, I suppose; I, your friend."

"My friend! and you treat me thus!"

"He who loves well chastises well," said Chicot, redoubling his proofs of friendship. "Now," said he, "go and sleep at the Corne d'Abondance."

"I can no longer see my way," cried the monk, from whose eyes tears were falling.

"Ah!" said Chicot, "if you wept for the wine you have drunk! However, I will guide you."

And taking the ass by the bridle, he led him to the hotel, where two men assisted Gorenflot to dismount, and led him up to the room which our readers already know.

"It is done," said the host, returning.

"He is in bed?"

"Yes, and snoring."

"Very well. But as he will awake some day or other, remember that I do not wish that he should know how he came here; indeed, it will be better that he should not know that he has been out since the famous night when he made such a noise in the convent, and that he should believe that all that has passed since is a dream."

"Very well, M. Chicot; but what has happened to the poor monk?"

"A great misfortune. It appears that at Lyons he quarreled with an agent of M. de Mayenne's and killed him."

"Oh! mon Dieu!"

"So that M. de Mayenne has sworn that he will have
him broken on the wheel."

"Make yourself easy, monsieur; he shall not go out
from here on any pretext."

"Good. And now," said Chicot, as he went away, " I
must find the Duc d'Anjou."

CHAPTER XLII.

THE PRINCE AND THE FRIEND.

WE may remember that the Duc de Guise had invited
the Duc d'Anjou to meet him in the streets of Paris that
evening. However, he determined not to go out of his
palace unless he was well accompanied; therefore the
duke went to seek his sword, which was Bussy d'Amboise.
For the duke to make up his mind to this step he must
have been very much afraid; for since his deception with
regard to M. de Monsoreau he had not seen Bussy, and
stood in great dread of him. Bussy, like all fine natures,
felt sorrow more vividly than pleasure; for it is rare that
a man intrepid in danger, cold and calm in the face of fire
and sword, does not give way to grief more easily than a
coward. Those from whom a woman can draw tears most
easily are those most to be feared by other men. Bussy
had seen Diana received at court as Comtesse de Monsoreau, and as such admitted by the queen into the circle
of her maids of honor; he had seen a thousand curious
eyes fixed on her unrivaled beauty. During the whole
evening he had fastened his ardent gaze on her, who never
raised her eyes to him, and he, unjust, like every man in
love, never thought how she must have been suffering from
not daring to meet his sympathizing glance.

" Oh," said he to himself, seeing that he waited uselessly
for a look, " women have skill and audacity only when
they want to deceive a guardian, a husband, or a mother;
they are awkward and cowardly when they have simply a
debt of gratitude to pay, they fear so much to seem to
love—they attach so exaggerated a value to their least

favor, that they do not mind breaking their lover's heart, if such be their humor. Diana might have said to me frankly, 'I thank you for what you have done for me, but I do not love you.' The blow would have killed or cured me. But no; she prefers letting me love her hopelessly; but she has gained nothing by it, for I no longer love her, I despise her."

And he went away with rage in his heart.

"I am mad," thought he, "to torment myself about a person who disdains me. But why does she disdain me, or for whom? Not, surely, for that long, livid-looking skeleton, who, always by her side, covers her incessantly with his jealous glances. If I wished it, in a quarter of an hour I could hold him mute and cold under my knee with ten inches of steel in his heart, and if I cannot be loved, I could at least be terrible and hated. Oh, her hatred! Rather than her indifference. Yes, but to act thus would be to do what a Quelus or a Maugiron would do if they knew how to love. Better to resemble that hero of Plutarch whom I so much admired, the young Antiochus, dying of love and never avowing it, nor uttering a complaint. Am I not called the brave Bussy?"

He went home, and threw himself on a chair. How long he remained there he did not know, when a man approached him.

"M. le Comte," said he, "you are in a fever."

"Ah, is it you, Rémy?"

"Yes, count. Go to bed."

Bussy obeyed, and all the next day Rémy watched by him, with refreshing drinks for his body and kind words for his mind. But on the day after Bussy missed him.

"Poor lad!" thought he, "he was tired and wanted air; and then doubtless Gertrude expected him; she is but a femme de chambre, but she loves, and a femme de chambre who loves is better than a queen who does not."

The day passed, and Rémy did not return. Bussy was angry and impatient. "Oh!" cried he, "I, who still believed in gratitude and friendship, will henceforth be-

lieve in nothing." Towards evening he heard voices in
his ante-chamber, and a servant entered, saying, "It is
Monseigneur the Duc d'Anjou."

"Let him enter," said Bussy, frowning.

The duke, on entering the room, which was without
lights, said, "It is too dark here, Bussy."

Bussy did not answer; disgust closed his mouth.

"Are you really ill," said the duke, "that you do not
answer?"

"I am very ill."

"Then that is why I have not seen you for two
days?"

"Yes, monseigneur."

The prince, piqued at these short answers, began to
examine the room.

"You seem to me well lodged, Bussy," said he.

Bussy did not reply.

"Bussy must be very ill," said the duke to an attend-
ant who stood by, "why was not Miron called? The
king's doctor is not too good for Bussy." When the
servant was gone, "Are you in grief, Bussy?" said the
duke.

"I do not know."

The duke approached, becoming more and more gracious as he was rebuffed. "Come, speak frankly, Bussy,"
said he.

"What am I to say, monseigneur?"

"You are angry with me?"

"I! for what? besides, it is no use to be angry with
princes." The duke was silent.

"But," said Bussy, "we are losing time in preambles;
to the point, monseigneur. You have need of me, I suppose?"

"Ah, M. de Bussy!"

"Yes, doubtless; do you think I believe that you come
here through friendship; you, who love no one?"

"Oh, Bussy, to say such things to me!"

"Well, be quick, monseigneur, what do you want?
When one serves a prince, and he dissimulates to the

extent of calling you his friend, one must pay for the dissimulation by being ready to sacrifice everything, even life, if necessary."

The duke colored, but it was too dark to see it. "I wanted nothing of you, Bussy, and you deceive yourself in thinking my visit interested. I desire only, seeing the fine evening, and that all Paris is out to sign the League, that you should accompany me a little about the streets."

Bussy looked at him. "Have you not Aurilly to go with you?"

"A lute-player!"

"Ah, monseigneur, you do not mention all his qualities; I believed that he fulfilled other functions for you. Besides, you have a dozen other gentlemen; I hear them in the ante-chamber."

At this moment the door opened. "Who is there?" said the duke, haughtily. "Who enters unannounced where I am?"

"I, Rémy," replied the young man, without any embarrassment.

"Who is Rémy?"

"The doctor, monseigneur," said the young man.

"And my friend," said Bussy. "You heard what monseigneur asks?" continued he, turning to Rémy.

"Yes, that you should accompany him; but——"

"But what?" said the duke.

"But you cannot do it."

"And why so?" cried the duke.

"Because it is too cold out of doors."

"Too cold!" cried the duke, surprised that any one should oppose him.

"Yes, too cold. Therefore I, who answer for M. Bussy's life to himself and to his friends, must forbid him to go out." And he pressed Bussy's hand in a significant manner.

"Very well," said the duke, "if the risk be so great, he must stay." And he turned angrily to the door; but returning to the bed, he said, "Then you have decided not to come?"

"Monseigneur, you hear that the doctor forbids me."

"You ought to see Miron, he is a great doctor."

"I prefer my friend."

"Then adieu."

"Adieu, monseigneur."

No sooner was the duke gone than Rémy said, "Now, monsieur, get up at once, if you please."

"What for?"

"To come out with me. This room is too warm."

"You said just now to the duke that it was too cold outside."

"The temperature has changed since."

"So that——" said Bussy, with curiosity.

"So that now I am convinced that the air will do you good."

"I do not understand."

"Do you understand the medicines I give you? Yet you take them. Come, get up; a walk with M. d'Anjou is dangerous, with me it is healthy. Have you lost confidence in me? If so, send me away."

"Well, as you wish it." And he rose, pale and trembling.

"An interesting paleness," said Rémy.

"But where are we going?"

"To a place where I have analyzed the air to-day."

"And this air?"

"Is sovereign for your complaint, monseigneur."

Bussy dressed, and they went out.

CHAPTER XLIII.

ETYMOLOGY OF THE RUE DE LA JUSSIENNE.

RÉMY took his patient by the arm, and led him by the Rue Coquillière down to the rampart.

"It is strange," said Bussy, "you take me near the marsh of the Grange-Batelier, and call it healthy."

"Oh, monsieur, a little patience; we are going to turn

round the Rue Pagavin, and get into the Rue Montmartre
—you will see what a fine street that is."

"As if I do not know it."

"Well, so much the better; I need not lose time in
showing you its beauties, and I will lead you at once into
a pretty little street."

Indeed, after going a few steps down the Rue Montmartre, they turned to the right.

"This," said Rémy, "is the Rue de la Gypecienne, or
Egyptienne, which you like; often called by the people
the Rue de la Gyssieune, or Jussienne."

"Very likely; but where are we going?"

"Do you see that little church?" said Rémy. "How
nicely it is situated; I dare say you never remarked it before."

"No, I did not know it."

"Well, now that you have seen the exterior, enter and
look at the windows—they are very curious."

There was such a pleased smile on the young man's face,
that Bussy felt sure there must have been some other reason for making him enter than to look at the windows
which it was too dark to see. The chapel was lighted, however, for service, and Rémy began examining a fresco of
the Virgin Mary, which was a continual source of complaint to the women who frequented the church, as they
said that it attracted the attention of the young shopkeepers
away from them.

You had some other object in bringing me here than
that I should admire the St. Marie, had you not?"

"Ma foi! no."

"Then let us go."

"Wait a moment; the service is finishing."

"Now let us go," said Bussy; "they are moving;" and
he walked to the door.

"At least take some holy water."

Bussy obeyed, and Rémy making a sign to a woman
who stood near, she advanced, and Bussy grew suddenly
pale, for he recognized Gertrude. She saluted him and
passed on, but behind her came a figure which, although

15

closely veiled, made his heart beat fast. Rémy looked at
him, and Bussy knew now why he had brought him to this
church. Bussy followed the lady, and Rémy followed
him. Gertrude had walked on before, until she came to
an alley closed by a door. She opened it, and let her
mistress pass. Bussy followed, and the two others disappeared.

It was half-past seven in the evening, and near the beginning of May ; the air began to have the feeling of spring,
and the leaves were beginning to unfold themselves.
Bussy looked round him, and found himself in a little
garden fifty feet square, surrounded by high walls covered
with vines and moss. The first lilacs which had begun
to open in the morning sun sent out their sweet emanations,
and the young man felt tempted to think that so much
perfume and warmth and life came to him only from the
presence of the woman he loved so tenderly.

On a little wooden bench sat Diana, twisting in her
fingers a sprig of wall-flower, which she had picked,
without knowing what she did. As Bussy approached
her, she raised her head, and said timidly, " M. le Comte,
all deception would be unworthy of us ; if you found me
at the church of St. Marie l'Egyptienne, it was not chance
that brought you there."

" No, madame ; Rémy took me out without my knowing where I was going, and I swear to you that I was
ignorant——"

" You do not understand me, monsieur, I know
well that M. Rémy brought you there, by force, perhaps."

" No, madame, not by force ; I did not know that he
was going to take me to see any one."

" That is a harsh speech," said Diana, sadly, and with
tears in her eyes. " Do you mean that had you known,
you would not have come ? "

" Oh, madame ! "

" It would have been but just, monsieur ; you did me
a great service, and I have not thanked you. Pardon me,
and receive all my thanks."

"Madame——" Bussy stopped; he felt so overcome, that he had neither words nor ideas.

"But I wished to prove to you," continued Diana, "that I am not ungrateful, nor forgetful. It was I who begged M. Rémy to procure for me the honor of this interview; it was I who sought for it, forgive me if I have displeased you."

"Oh, madame! you cannot think that."

"I know," continued Diana, who was the strongest, because she had prepared herself for this interview, "how much trouble you had in fulfilling my commission; I know all your delicacy; I know it and appreciate it, believe me. Judge, then, what I must have suffered from the idea that you would misunderstand the sentiments of my heart."

"Madame, I have been ill for three days."

"Oh! I know," cried Diana, with a rising color, "and I suffered more than you, for M. Rémy, he deceived me, no doubt; for he made me believe——"

"That your forgetfulness caused it. Oh! it is true."

"Then I have been right to do as I have done; to see you, to thank you for your kindness, and to swear to you an eternal gratitude. Do you believe that I speak from the bottom of my heart?"

Bussy shook his head sadly, and did not reply.

"Do you doubt my words?" said Diana.

"Madame, those who feel a kindness for you, show it when they can. You knew I was at the palace the night of your presentation, you knew I was close to you, you must have felt my looks fixed on you, and you never raised your eyes to me, you never let me know by a word, a sign, or a gesture, that you were aware of my presence; but perhaps you did not recognize me, madame, you have only seen me twice." Diana replied with so sad a glance of reproach, that Bussy was moved by it.

"Pardon, madame," said he; "you are not an ordinary woman, and yet you act like them. This marriage——"

"I was forced to conclude it."

"Yes, but it was easy to break."

"Impossible, on the contrary."

"Did you not know that near you watched a devoted friend ?"

"Even that made me fear."

"And you did not think of what my life would be, when you belonged to another. But perhaps you kept the name of Monsoreau from choice ?"

"Do you think so ?" murmured Diana ; "so much the better." And her eyes filled with tears. Bussy walked up and down in great agitation.

"I am to become once more a stranger to you," said he.

"Alas !"

"Your silence says enough."

"I can only speak by my silence."

"At the Louvre you would not see me, and now you will not speak to me."

"At the Louvre I was watched by M. de Monsoreau, and he is jealous."

"Jealous! What does he want then ? mon Dieu ! whose happiness can he envy, when all the world is envying his ?"

"I tell you he is jealous ; for the last two or three days he has seen some one wandering round our new abode."

"Then you have quitted the Rue St. Antoine ?"

"How !" cried Diana thoughtlessly, "then it was not you ?"

"Madame, since your marriage was publicly announced, since that evening at the Louvre, where you did not deign to look at me, I have been in bed, devoured by fever, so you see that your husband could not be jealous of me, at least."

"Well ! M. le Comte, if it be true that you had any desire to see me, you must thank this unknown man ; for knowing M. de Monsoreau as I know him, this man made me tremble for you, and I wished to see you and say to you, 'Do not expose yourself so, M. le Comte ; do not make me more unhappy than I am.'"

"Reassure yourself, madame ; it was not I."

"Now, let me finish what I have to say. In the fear

of this man—whom I do not know, but whom M. de
Monsoreau does perhaps—he exacts that I should leave
Paris, so that," said Diana, holding out her hand to Bussy,
"you may look upon this as our last meeting, M. le
Comte. To-morrow we start for Méridor."

"You are going, madame?"

"There is no other way to reassure M. de Monsoreau;
no other way for me to be at peace. Besides, I myself
detest Paris, the world, the court, and the Louvre. I
wish to be alone with my souvenirs of my happy past;
perhaps a little of my former happiness will return to me
there. My father will accompany me, and I shall find
there M. and Madame de St. Luc, who expect me. Adieu,
M. de Bussy."

Bussy hid his face in his hands. "All is over for me,"
he murmured."

"What do you say?" said Diana.

"I say, madame, that this man exiles you, that he takes
from me the only hope left to me, that of breathing the
same air as yourself, of seeing you sometimes, of touching
your dress as you pass. Oh! this man is my mortal
enemy, and if I perish for it, I will destroy him with my
own hands."

"Oh! M. le Comte!"

"The wretch; it is not enough for him that you are
his wife: you, the most beautiful and most charming of
creatures, but he is still jealous. Jealous! The devour-
ing monster would absorb the whole world!"

"Oh! calm yourself, comte; mon Dieu; he is excusable, perhaps."

"He is excusable! you defend him, madame?"

"Oh! if you knew!" cried Diana, covering her face
with her hands.

"If I knew! Oh! madame, I know one thing; he who
is your husband is wrong to think of the rest of the world."

"But!" cried Diana, in a broken voice, "if you were
wrong, M. le Comte, and if he were not."

And the young woman, touching with her cold hand
the burning ones of Bussy, rose and fled among the somber

alleys of the garden, seized Gertrude's arm and dragged her away, before Bussy, astonished and overwhelmed with delight, had time to stretch out his arms to retain her. He uttered a cry and tottered; Rémy arrived in time to catch him in his arms and make him sit down on the bench that Diana had just quitted.

CHAPTER XLIV.

HOW D'EPERNON HAD HIS DOUBLET TORN, AND HOW CHOMBERG WAS STAINED BLUE.

WHILE M. la Hurière piled signature upon signature, while Chicot consigned Gorenflot to the Corne d'Abondance, while Bussy returned to life in the happy little garden full of perfume and love, the king, annoyed at all he had seen in the city, and furious against his brother, whom he had seen pass in the Rue St. Honoré, accompanied by MM. de Guise and Monsoreau, and followed by a whole train of gentlemen, re-entered the Louvre, accompanied by Maugiron and Quelus. He had gone out with all four of his friends, but, at some steps from the Louvre, Schomberg and D'Epernon had profited by the first crush to disappear, counting on some adventures in such a turbulent night. Before they had gone one hundred yards D'Epernon had passed his sword-sheath between the legs of a citizen who was running, and who tumbled down in consequence, and Schomberg had pulled the cap off the head of a young and pretty woman. But both had badly chosen their day for attacking these good Parisians, generally so patient; for a spirit of revolt was prevalent in the streets, and the bourgeois rose, crying out for aid, and the husband of the young woman launched his apprentices on Schomberg. He was brave; therefore he stopped, put his hand on his sword, and spoke in a high tone. D'Epernon was prudent; he fled.

Henri had entered his room at the Louvre, and, seated in his great armchair, was trembling with impatience, and seeking a good pretext for getting into a passion. Maugiron was playing with Narcissus, the large greyhound, and Quelus was sitting near.

"They go on!" cried Henri, "their plot advances; sometimes tigers, sometimes serpents; when they do not spring they glide."

"Oh, sire!" said Quelus, "are there not always plots in a kingdom? What the devil could all the sons, brothers, and cousins of kings do if they did not plot?" And Quelus irreverently turned his back to the king.

"Hear, Maugiron," said the king, "with what nonsense he tries to put me off."

"Well, sire, look at Narcissus; he is a good dog, but when you pull his ears, he growls, and when you tread on his toes he bites."

"Here is the other comparing me to my dog!"

"Not so, sire; I place Narcissus far above you, for he knows how to defend himself, and you do not." And he also turned his back.

"That is right," cried the king, "my good friends, for whom they accuse me of despoiling the kingdom, abandon me, insult me! Ah, Chicot! if you were here."

At this moment, however, the door opened, and D'Epernon appeared, without hat or cloak, and with his doublet all torn.

"Bon Dieu!" cried Henri, "what is the matter?"

"Sire," said D'Epernon, "look at me; see how they treat the friends of your majesty."

"Who has treated you thus?"

"Mordieu, your people; or rather the people of M. le Duc d'Anjou, who cried, 'Vive la Messe!' 'Vive Guise!' 'Vive François!'—vive every one, in fact, except the king."

"And what did you do to be treated thus?"

"I? nothing. What can a man do to a people? They recognized me for your majesty's friend, and that was enough."

"But Schomberg?"

"Well?"

"Did he not come to your aid? did he not defend you?"

"Corbœuf! he had enough to do on his own account."

"How so?"

"I left him in the hands of a dyer whose wife's cap he had pulled off, and who, with his five or six apprentices, seemed likely to make him pass an unpleasant quarter of an hour."

"Par la mordieu! and where did you leave my poor Schomberg? I will go myself to his aid. They may say," continued he, looking at Maugiron and Quelus, "that my friends abandon me, but they shall never say that I abandon them."

"Thanks, sire," said a voice behind Henri; "thanks, but here I am; I extricated myself without assistance; but, mein Gott! it was not without trouble."

"It is Schomberg's voice," cried all, "but where the devil is he?"

"Here I am," cried the voice; and indeed, in the corner of the room they saw something that looked not like a man but a shadow.

"Schomberg," cried the king, "where do you come from, and why are you that color?"

Indeed, Schomberg from head to foot was of a most beautiful blue.

"Der Teufel!" cried he, "the wretches! It is not wonderful that the people ran after me."

"But what is the matter?"

"The matter is, that they dipped me in a vat, the knaves; I believed that it was only water, but it was indigo."

"Oh, mordieu!" cried Quelus, bursting out laughing, "indigo is very dear; you must have carried away at least twenty crowns' worth of indigo."

"I wish you had been in my place."

"And you did not kill any one?"

"I left my poniard somewhere, that is all I know, up to the hilt in a sheath of flesh; but in a second I was taken, carried off, dipped in the vat, and almost drowned."

" And how did you get out of their hands ? "

" By committing a cowardice, sire. "

" What was that ? "

" Crying, ' Vive la Ligue ! ' "

" That was like me ; only they made me add, ' Vive le Duc d'Anjou ! ' " said D'Epernon.

" And I also," cried Schomberg ; " but that is not all."

" What, my poor Schomberg, did they make you cry something else ? "

" No, that was enough, God knows ; but just as I cried, ' Vive le Duc d'Anjou,' guess who passed."

" How can I guess ? "

" Bussy ; his cursed Bussy, who heard me."

" He could not understand."

" Parbleu ! it was not difficult to understand. I had a poniard at my throat, and I was in a vat."

" And he did not come to your rescue ? "

" It seemed as though he was in a dreadful hurry ; he scarcely seemed to touch the ground."

" Perhaps he did not recognize you, as you were blue."

" Ah ! very likely.

" He would be excusable," said the king ; for, indeed, my poor Schomberg, I should hardly have known you myself."

" Never mind ; we shall meet some other time, when I am not in a vat."

" Oh ! as for me," said D'Epernon, " it is his master I should like to punish."

" The Duc d'Anjou, whose praises they are singing all over Paris," said Quelus.

" The fact is, that he is master of Paris to-night," said D'Epernon.

" Ah, my brother ! my brother ! " cried the king.

" Ah ! yes, sire ; you cry, ' my brother,' but you do nothing against him ; and yet it is clear to me that he is at the head of some plot," said Schomberg.

" Eh, mordieu ! that is what I was saying just before you came in, to these gentlemen, and they replied by shrugging their shoulders and turning their backs."

"Not because you said there was a plot, sire, but because you do nothing to suppress it."

"And, now," said Quelus, "we say, 'Save us,' sire; or rather, save yourself; to-morrow M. de Guise will come to the Louvre, and ask you to name a chief for the League; if you name M. d'Anjou, as you promised, he, at the head of one hundred thousand Parisians, excited by this night, can do what he likes."

"Then," said Henri, "if I take a decisive step, you will support me?"

"Yes, sire."

"If, sire, you will only give me time to remodel my dress," said D'Epernon.

"Go to my room, D'Epernon; my valet de chambre will give you what you want."

"And I, sire, must have a bath," said Schomberg.

"Go to my bath."

"Then I may hope, sire, that my insult will not remain unavenged."

Henri remained silent a moment, and then said, "Quelus, ask if M. d'Anjou has returned to the Louvre."

Quelus went, but came back, and said that the duke had not yet returned.

"Well, you, Quelus and Maugiron, go down and watch for his entrance."

"And then?"

"Have all the doors shut."

"Bravo! sire."

"I will be back in ten minutes, sire," said D'Epernon.

"And my stay will depend on the quality of the dye," said Schomberg.

"Come as soon as possible," said the king.

The young men went out, and the king, left alone, kneeled down on his prie-Dieu.

CHAPTER XLV.

CHICOT MORE THAN EVER KING OF FRANCE.

THE gates of the Louvre were generally closed at twelve, but the king gave orders that they should be left open on this night till one. At a quarter to one Quelus came up.

"Sire," said he, "the duke has come in."

"What is Maugiron doing?"

"Watching that he does not go out again."

"There is no danger."

"Then——"

"Let him go to bed quietly. Whom has he with him?"

"M. de Monsoreau and his ordinary gentlemen."

"And M. de Bussy?"

"No; he is not there."

"So much the better."

"What are your orders, sire?"

"Tell Schomberg and D'Epernon to be quick, and let M. de Monsoreau know that I wish to speak to him."

Five minutes after, Schomberg and D'Epernon entered; the former with only a slight blue tint left, which it would take several baths to eradicate, and the latter newly clothed. After them, M. de Monsoreau appeared. "The captain of the guards has just announced to me that your majesty did me the honor to send for me," said he.

"Yes, monsieur; when I was out this evening, I saw the stars so brilliant, and the moon so clear, that I thought it would be splendid weather for the chase to-morrow; so, M. le Comte, set off at once for Vincennes, and get a stag turned out ready for me."

"But, sire, I thought that to-morrow your majesty had given a rendezvous to Monsieur le Duc d'Anjou and M. de Guise, in order to name a chief for the League."

"Well, monsieur?" said the king haughtily.

"Sire, there might not be time."

"There is always time, monsieur, for those who know

how to employ it; that is why I tell you to set off at once, so that you may have all ready for to-morrow morning at ten. Quelus, Schomberg, have the door of the Louvre opened for M. de Monsoreau, and have it 'closed behind him."

The chief huntsman retired in astonishment. "It is a whim of the king's," said he to the young men.

"Yes."

They watched him out, and then returned to the king.

"Now," said Henri, "silence, and all four of you follow me."

"Where are we going, sire ?" said D'Epernon.

"Those who follow will see."

The king took a lantern in his hand, and led the young men along the secret corridor, which led to his brother's rooms. A valet-de-chambre watched here ; but before he had time to warn his master, Henri ordered him to be silent, and the young men pushed him into a room and locked the door.

Henri opened his brother's door. François had gone to bed full of dreams of ambition, which the events of the evening had nourished ; he had heard his name exalted, and the king's abused. Conducted by the Duc de Guise, he had seen the Parisians open everywhere for him and his gentlemen, while those of the king were insulted and hooted. Never since the commencement of his career had he been so popular, and consequently so hopeful. He had placed on the table a letter from M. de Guise, which had been brought to him by M. de Monsoreau. His surprise and terror were great when he saw the secret door open, and still more when he recognized the king. Henri signed to his companions to remain on the threshold, and advanced to the bed, frowning, but silent.

"Sire," stammered the duke, "the honor that your majesty does me is so unlooked for——"

"That it frightens you, does it not ? But stay where you are, my brother ; do not rise."

"But, sire, only—permit me——" and he drew towards him the letter of M. de Guise.

"You are reading ?" asked the king.

"Yes, sire." ·

"Something interesting to keep you awake at this time of night ?"

"Oh, sire, nothing very important; the evening courier——"

"Oh, yes, I understand—Courier of Venus; but no, I see I am wrong—they do not seal billet-doux with seals of that size."

The duke hid the letter altogether.

"How discreet this dear François is !" said the king, with a smile which frightened his brother. However, making an effort to recover himself, he said :

"Did your majesty wish to say anything particular to me ?"

"What I have to say to you, monsieur, I wish to say before witnesses. Here, gentlemen," continued he, turning to the four young men, "listen to us; I order you."

"Sire," said the duke, with a glance full of rage and hatred, "before insulting a man of my rank, you should have refused me the hospitality of the Louvre; in the Hôtel d'Anjou, at least, I should have been free to reply to you."

"Really, you forget, then, that wherever you are, you are my subject ; that I am the king, and that every house is mine."

"Sire, I am at the Louvre, at my mother's."

"And your mother is in my house. But to the point—give me that paper."

"Which ?"

"That which you were reading, which was on your table, and which you hid when I came in."

"Sire, reflect."

"On what ?"

"On this, that you are making a request unworthy of a gentleman, and fit only for a police-officer."

The king grew livid. "That letter, monsieur !"

"A woman's letter, sire,"

" There are some women's letters very good to see, and dangerous not to see—such as those our mother writes."

" Brother !"

" This letter, monsieur !" cried the king, stamping his foot, " or I will have it torn from you by my Swiss !"

The duke jumped out of bed, with the letter crumpled in his hand, evidently with the intention of approaching the fire. But Henri, divining his intention, placed himself between him and the fire.

" You would not treat your brother thus ?" cried the duke.

" Not my brother, but my mortal enemy. Not my brother, but the Duc D'Anjou, who went all through Paris with M. de Guise, who tries to hide from me a letter from one of his accomplices, the Lorraine princes."

" This time," said the duke, " your police are wrong."

" I tell you I saw on the seal the three merlets of Lorraine. Give it to me, mordieu ! or——"

Henri advanced towards his brother and laid his hand on his shoulder. François had no sooner felt the touch of his hand than, falling on his knees, he cried out, " Help ! help ! my brother is going to kill me."

These words, uttered in an accent of profound terror, startled the king and mitigated his rage. The idea passed quickly through his mind that in their family, as by a curse, brother had always assassinated brother.

" No, my brother," said he, " you are wrong ; I do not wish to hurt you, but you cannot contend with me. I am the master, and if you did not know it before, you know it now."

" Yes, my brother, I acknowledge it."

" Very well, then give me that letter ; the king orders it."

The duke let it fall, and the king picked it up, but without reading it put it in his pocket-book.

" Is that all ?" said the duke, with his sinister glance.

" No, monsieur, you must keep your room until my suspicions with respect to you are completely dissipated. The room is commodious, and not much like a prison ;

stay here. You will have good company—at least, outside the door, for this night these four gentlemen will
guard you ; to-morrow they will be relieved by a guard of
Swiss."

"But, my friends—cannot I see them ? "

"Who do you call your friends ? "

"M. de Monsoreau, M. de Ribeirac, M. Antragues, and
M. de Bussy."

"Oh, yes, he, of course."

"Has he had the misfortune to displease your majesty ? "

"Yes."

"When, sire ?"

"Always, but particularly to-night."

"To-night ! what did he do ? "

"Insulted me in the streets of Paris."

"You ? "

"My followers, which is the same thing."

"Bussy ! you have been deceived, sire."

"I know what I say."

"Sire, M. de Bussy has not been out of his hotel for
two days. He is at home, ill in bed, burning with fever."

The king turned to Schomberg, who said, "If he had
fever, at all events he had it in the Rue Coquillière."

"Who told you he was there ? " said the duke.

"I saw him."

"You saw Bussy out of doors ? "

"Yes, looking well and happy, and accompanied by his
ordinary follower, that Rémy."

"Then I do not understand it ; I saw him in bed myself ; he must have deceived me."

"It is well ; he will be punished with the rest," said
the king.

"If M. de Bussy went out alone after refusing to go
out with me——"

"You hear, gentlemen, what my brother says. But we
will talk of him another time ; now I recommend my
brother to your care ; you will have the honor of serving
as guard to a prince of the blood."

"Oh ! sire," said Quelus, "be satisfied ; we know what we owe to M. le Duc."

"It is well ; adieu, gentlemen."

"Sire," cried the duke, "am I really a prisoner, are my friends not to visit me, and am I not to go out ?" And the idea of the next day presented itself to his mind, when his presence would be so necessary to M. de Guise. "Sire," cried he again, "let me at least remain near your majesty ; it is my place, and I can be as well guarded there as elsewhere. Sire, grant me this favor."

The king was about to yield to this request and say, "Yes," when his attention was attracted to the door, where a long body, with its arms, its head, and everything that it could move, was making signs to him to say "No." It was Chicot.

"No," said Henri to his brother ; "you are very well here, and here you must stay."

"Sire——"

"It is my pleasure, and that is enough," said the king, haughtily.

"I said I was the real King of France," murmured Chicot.

CHAPTER XLVI.

HOW CHICOT PAID A VISIT TO BUSSY, AND WHAT FOLLOWED.

THE next morning, about nine, Bussy was eating his breakfast, and talking with Rémy over the events of the previous day.

"Rémy," said he, "did you not think you had seen somewhere that gentleman whom they were dipping in a vat in the Rue Coquillière ?"

"Yes, M. le Comte, but I cannot think of his name."

"I ought to have helped him," said Bussy, "it is a duty one gentleman owes to another ; but, really, Rémy, I was too much occupied with my own affairs."

"But he must have recognized us, for we were our
natural color, and it seemed to me that he rolled his eyes
frightfully, and shook his fist at us."

"Are you sure of that, Rémy? We must find out who
it was; I cannot let such an insult pass."

"Oh!" cried Rémy, "I know now who he was."

"How so?"

"I heard him swear."

"I should think so; any one would have sworn in
such a situation."

"Yes, but he swore in German."

"Bah!"

"Yes, he said, ' Gott verdomme.' "

"Then it was Schomberg?"

"Himself, M. le Comte."

"Then, my dear Rémy, get your salves ready."

"Why so, monsieur?"

"Because, before long, you will have to apply them
either to his skin or to mine."

"You would not be so foolish as to get killed, now you
are so well and so happy; St. Marie l'Egyptienne has
cured you once, but she will get tired of working miracles
for you."

"On the contrary, Rémy, you cannot tell how pleasant
it feels to risk your life when you are happy. I assure
you I never fought with a good heart when I had lost large
sums at play, when things had gone wrong, or when I had
anything to reproach myself with; but when my purse is
full, my heart light, and my conscience clear, I go boldly
to the field, for I am sure of my hand; it is then I am
brilliant. I should fight well to-day, Rémy, for, thanks
to you," said he, extending his hand to the young man,
"I am very happy."

"Stay a moment, however; you will, I hope, deprive
yourself of this pleasure. A beautiful lady of my acquaintance made me swear to keep you safe and sound, under
pretext that your life belongs to her."

"Good Rémy!"

"You call me good Rémy, because I brought you to
16

see Madame de Monsoreau, but shall you call me so when you are separated from her? and unluckily the day approaches, if it be not come."

"What do you mean?"

"Do you not know that she is going to Anjou, and that I myself have the grief of being separated from Gertrude. Ah——"

Bussy could not help smiling at the pretended grief of the young man.

"You love her, then?" he said.

"I should think so; you should see how she beats me."

"And you let her do it?"

"Oh! yes."

"But to return to Diana, Rémy; when shall we set off?"

"Ah! I expected that. On the latest possible day I should say."

"Why so?"

"Firstly, because it seems to me that M. le Duc d'Anjou will want you here."

"After?"

"Because M. de Monsoreau, by a special blessing, does not suspect you in the least, and would suspect something immediately if he saw you disappear from Paris at the same time as his wife."

"What do I care for that?"

"No; but I care. I charge myself with curing the sword strokes received in duels, for, as you manage your sword well, you never receive very serious ones; but not the blows given secretly by jealous husbands; they are animals, who, in such cases, strike hard."

"Well! my dear friend, if it is my destiny to be killed by M. de Monsoreau."

"Well!"

"Well! he will kill me."

"And then, a week after, Madame de Monsoreau will be reconciled to her husband, which will dreadfully enrage your poor soul, which will see it from above or below, without being able to prevent it."

" You are right, Rémy ; I will live."

" Quite right ; but that is not all, you must be charmingly polite to him ; he is frightfully jealous of the Duc d'Anjou, who, while you were ill in bed, promenaded before the house with his Aurilly. Make advances, then, to this charming husband, and do not even ask him what has become of his wife, since you know quite well."

" You are right, Rémy, I believe. Now I am no longer jealous of the bear, I will be civil to him."

At this moment some one knocked at the door.

" Who is there ?" cried Bussy.

" Mousieur," replied a page, " there is a gentleman below who wishes to speak to you."

" To speak to me so early ; who is it ?"

" A tall gentleman, dressed in green velvet."

" Can it be Schomberg ?"

"He said a tall man."

" True, then Monsoreau, perhaps ; well, let him enter."

After a minute the visitor entered.

" M. Chicot !" cried Bussy.

"Himself, M. le Comte."

Rémy retired into another room, and then Chicot said, " Monsieur, I come to propose to you a little bargain."

" Speak, monsieur," said Bussy, in great surprise.

" What will you promise me if I render you a great service ?"

"That depends on the service, monsieur," replied Bussy, disdainfully.

Chicot feigned not to remark this air of disdain. " Monsieur," said he, sitting down and crossing his long legs, I remark that you do not ask me to sit down."

The color mounted to Bussy's face.

" Monsieur," continued Chicot, " have you heard of the League ?"

"I have heard much of it," said Bussy.

" Well, monsieur, you ought to know that it is an association of honest Christians, united for the purpose of religiously massacring their neighbors, the Huguenots. Are you of the League, monsieur ? I am."

"But—monsieur——"

"Say only yes, or no."

"Allow me to express my astonishment——"

"I did myself the honor of asking you if you belonged to the League."

"M. Chicot, as I do not like questions whose import I do not understand, I beg you to change the conversation before I am forced to tell you that I do not like questioners. Come, M. Chicot, we have but a few minutes left."

"Well! in a few minutes one can say a great deal; however, I might have dispensed with asking you the question, as if you do not belong to the League now, you soon will, as M. d'Anjou does."

"M. d'Anjou! Who told you that?"

"Himself, speaking to me in person, as the gentlemen of the law say, or rather write; for example, that dear M. Nicolas David, that star of the Forum Parisiense. Now you understand that as M. d'Anjou belongs to the League, you cannot help belonging to it also; you, who are his right arm. The League knows better than to accept a maimed chief."

"Well, M. Chicot, what then?"

"Why, if you do belong to it, or they think you are likely to do so, what has happened to his royal highness will certainly happen to you."

"And what has happened to him?"

"Monsieur," said Chicot, rising and imitating M. de Bussy's manner of a little before, "I do not love questions, nor questioners, therefore I have a great mind to let them do to you what they have done to-night to the duke."

"M. Chicot," said Bussy, with a smile, "speak, I beg of you; where is the duke?"

"He is in prison?"

"Where?"

"In his own room. Four of my good friends guard him. M. de Schomberg, who was dyed blue yesterday, as you know, since you passed during the operation; M. d'Epernon, who is yellow from the fright he had; M. de

Quelus, who is red with anger ; and M. de Maugiron, who is white with ennui ; it is beautiful to see ; not to speak of the duke, who is going green with terror, so that we shall have a perfect rainbow to delight our eyes."

"Then, monsieur, you think my liberty in danger ?"

"Danger ! monsieur ; suppose that they are already on the way to arrest you."

Bussy shuddered.

".Do you like the Bastile, M. de Bussy ? it is a good place for meditation, and M. Laurent Testu, the governor, keeps a good cook."

"They would send me to the Bastile ?"

"Ma foi ! I ought to have in my pocket something like an order to conduct you there. Would you like to see it ?" and Chicot drew from his pocket an order from the king in due form, to apprehend, wherever he might be, M. Louis de Clermont, Seigneur de Bussy. "Written very nicely by M. Quelus," continued Chicot.

"Then, monsieur," cried Bussy, "you are really rendering me a service ?"

"I think so ; do you agree with me ?"

"Monsieur, I beg you to tell me why you do it ; for you love the king, and he hates me."

"M. le Comte, I save you ; think what you please of my action. But do you forget that I asked for a recompense ?"

"Ah, true."

"Well ?"

"Most willingly, monsieur."

"Then some day you will do what I ask you ?"

"On my honor, if possible."

"That is enough. Now mount your horse and disappear ; I go to carry this order to those who are to use it."

"Then you were not to arrest me yourself ?"

"I ! for what do you take me ?"

"But I should abandon my master."

"Have no scruples ; he abandons you.'

"You are a gentleman, M. Chicot."

Bussy called Rémy. To do him justice, he was listen, ing at the door.

"Rémy, our horses!"

"They are saddled, monsieur."

"Ah!" said Chicot, "this young man knows what he is about."

Bussy thanked Chicot once more, and went down.

"Where are we going?" said Rémy.

"Well——" said Bussy, hesitating.

"What do you say to Normandy?" said Chicot.

"It is too near."

"Flanders, then?"

"Too far."

"Anjou is a reasonable distance, monsieur," said Rémy.

"Well, then, Anjou," said Bussy, coloring.

"Adieu, monsieur!" said Chicot.

"It is destiny," said Rémy, when he was gone.

"Let us be quick, and perhaps we may overtake her," said Bussy.

————

CHAPTER XLVII.

THE CHESS OF M. CHICOT, AND THE CUP AND BALL OF M. QUELUS.

CHICOT returned joyfully to the Louvre. It was a great satisfaction to him to have saved a brave gentleman like Bussy.

M. de Guise, after having received in the morning the principal Leaguers, who came to bring him the registers filled with signatures, and after having made them all swear to recognize the chief that the king should appoint, went out to visit M. d'Anjou, whom he had lost sight of about ten the evening before. The duke found the prince's valet rather unquiet at his master's absence, but he imagined that he had slept at the Louvre.

The Duc de Guise asked to speak to Aurilly, who was most likely to know where his master was. Aurilly came, but stated he had been separated from the prince the evening before by a pressure of the crowd, and had come to the Hôtel d'Anjou to wait for him, not knowing that his highness had intended to sleep at the Louvre. He added that he had just sent to the Louvre to inquire, and that a message had been returned that the duke was still asleep.

"Asleep at eleven o'clock! not likely. You ought to go to the Louvre, Aurilly."

"I did think of it, monseigneur, but I feared that this was only a tale invented to satisfy my messenger, and that the prince was seeking pleasure elsewhere, and might be annoyed at my seeking him."

"Oh, no; the duke has too much sense to be pleasure-seeking on a day like this. Go to the Louvre; you will be sure to find him there."

"I will if you wish it; but what shall I say to him?"

"Say that the convocation at the Louvre is fixed for two o'clock, and that it is necessary that we should have a conference first. It is not at the time when the king is about to choose a chief for the League that he should be sleeping."

"Very well, monseigneur, I will beg his highness to come here."

"And say that I am waiting impatiently for him. Meanwhile I will go and seek M. de Bussy."

"But if I do not find his highness, what am I to do?"

"Then make no further search for him. In any event I shall be at the Louvre at a quarter before two."

Aurilly passed through the courtiers who crowded the Louvre, and made his way to the duke's apartments. At the door he found Chicot playing chess. Aurilly tried to pass, but Chicot, with his long legs blocked up the doorway. He was forced to touch him on the shoulder.

"Ah, it is you, M. Aurilly."

"What are you doing, M. Chicot?"

"Playing chess, as you see."

"All alone?"

"Yes, I am studying; do you play?"

"Very little."

"Yes, I know you are a musician, and music is so difficult an art, that those who give themselves to it must sacrifice all their time."

"You seem very serious over your game."

"Yes, it is my king who disquiets me; you must know, M. Aurilly, that at chess the king is a very insignificant person, who has no will, who can only go one step forward or back, or one to the right or left, while he is surrounded by active enemies, by knights who jump three squares at a time, by a crowd of pawns who surround him, so that if he be badly counseled he is a ruined king in no time, ma foi."

"But, M. Chicot, how does it happen that you are studying this at the door of his royal highness' room?"

"Because I am waiting for M. Quelus, who is in there."

"Where?"

"With his highness."

"With his highness! What is he doing there? I did not think they were such friends."

"Hush!" then he whispered in Aurilly's ear "he is come to ask pardon of the duke for a little quarrel they had yesterday."

"Really!"

"It was the king who insisted on it; you know on what excellent terms the brothers are just now. The king would not suffer an impertinence of Quelus's to pass, and ordered him to apologize."

"Really!"

"Ah! M. Aurilly, I think that we are entering the golden age; the Louvre is about to become Arcadia, and the two brothers Arcades ambo."

Aurilly smiled, and passed into the ante-chamber, where he was courteously saluted by Quelus, between whose hands a superb cup and ball of ebony inlaid with ivory was making rapid evolutions.

"Bravo! M. Quelus," said Aurilly.

"Ah! my dear M. Aurilly, when shall I play cup and ball as well as you play the lute?"

"When you have studied your plaything as long as I

have my instrument. But where is monseigneur? I
thought you were with him."

"I have an audience with him, but Schomberg comes
first."

"What! M. de Schomberg, also!"

"Oh! mon Dieu; yes. The king settled all that. He
is in the next room. Enter, M. Aurilly, and remind the
prince that we are waiting for him.

Aurilly opened the second door and saw Schomberg re-
clining on a kind of couch, from which he amused himself
by sending from a tube little balls of earth through a gold
ring, suspended from the ceiling by a silk thread, while a
favorite dog brought him back the balls as they fell.

"Ah! guten morgen, M. Aurilly, you see I am amusing
myself while I wait for my audience."

"But where is monseigneur?"

"Oh! he is occupied in pardoning D'Epernon and
Maugiron. But will you not enter, you who are priv-
ileged?"

"Perhaps it would be indiscreet."

"Not at all; enter, M. Aurilly, enter." And he pushed
him into the next room, where the astonished musician
perceived D'Epernon before a mirror, occupied in stiffen-
ing his mustachios, while Maugiron, seated near the window, was cutting out engravings, by the side of which
the bas-reliefs on the temple of Venus Aphrodite would
have looked holy.

The duke, without his sword, was in his armchair between these two men, who only looked at him to watch
his movements, and only spoke to him to say something
disagreeable: seeing Aurilly, he got up to meet him.

"Take care monseigneur," said Maugiron, "you are
stepping on my figures."

"Mon Dieu!" cried the musician, "he insults my
master!"

"Dear M. Aurilly," said D'Epernon, still arranging his
mustachois, "how are you?"

"Be so kind as to bring me here your little dagger,"
said Maugiron.

"Gentlemen, gentlemen, do you not remember where you are?"

"Yes, yes, my dear Orpheus, that is why I ask for your dagger; you see M. le Duc has none." ·

"Aurilly!" cried the duke, in a tone full of grief and rage, "do you not see that I am a prisoner?"

"A prisoner! to whom?"

"To my brother; you might know that by my jailers."

"Oh! if I had but guessed it."

"You would have brought your lute to amuse his highness," said a mocking voice behind them, "but I thought of it, and sent for it; here it is."

"How does your chess go on, Chicot?" said D'Epernon.

"I believe I shall save the king, but it is not without trouble. Come, M. Aurilly, give me your poniard in return for the lute; a fair exchange."

The astonished musician obeyed.

"There is one rat in the trap," said Quelus, who returned to his post in the antechamber, only exchanging his cup and ball for Schomberg's shooting tube.

"It is amusing to vary one's pleasures," said Chicot; "so for a change I will go and sign the League."

CHAPTER XLVIII.

THE RECEPTION OF THE CHIEFS OF THE LEAGUE.

THE time for the great reception drew near. Paris, nearly as tumultuous as the evening before, had sent towards the Louvre its deputation of leaguers, its bodies of workmen, its sheriffs, its militia, and its constantly-increasing masses of spectators.

The king, on his throne in the great hall, was surrounded by his officers, his friends, his courtiers, and his family, waiting for all the corporations to defile before him, when M. de Monsoreau entered abruptly.

"Look, Henriquet," said Chicot, who was standing near the king.

"At what?"

"At your chief huntsman; pardieu, he is well worth it. See how pale and dirty he is!"

Henri made a sign to M. de Monsoreau, who approached.

"How is it that you are at the Louvre, monsieur? I thought you at Vincennes."

"Sire, the stag was turned off at seven o'clock this morning, but when noon came, and I had no news, I feared that some misfortune had happened to your majesty, and I returned."

"Really!"

"Sire, if I have done wrong, attribute it to an excess of devotion."

"Yes, monsieur, and I appreciate it."

"Now," said the count, hesitatingly, "if your majesty wishes me to return to Vincennes, as I am reassured——"

"No, no, stay; this chase was a fancy which came into our head, and which went as it came; do not go away, I want near me devoted subjects, and you have just classed yourself as such."

Monsoreau bowed, and said, "Where does your majesty wish me to remain?"

"Will you give him to me for half an hour?" said Chicot to the king, in a low voice.

"What for?"

"To torment him a little. You owe me some compensation for obliging me to be present at this tiresome ceremony."

"Well, take him."

"Where does your majesty wish me to stand?" again asked M. de Monsoreau.

"Where you like; go behind my armchair, that is where I put my friends."

"Come here," said Chicot, making room for M. de Monsoreau, "come and get the scent of these fellows. Here is game which can be tracked without a hound. Here are the shoemakers who pass, or rather, who have passed; then here are the tanners. Mort de ma vie! if you lose their scent, I will take away your place."

M. de Monsoreau listened mechanically; he seemed preoccupied, and looked around him anxiously.

"Do you know what your chief huntsman is hunting for now?" said Chicot, in an undertone, to the king.

"No."

"Your brother."

"The game is not in sight."

"Just ask him where his countess is."

"What for?"

"Just ask."

"M. le Comte," said Henri, "what have you done with Madame de Monsoreau? I do not see her here."

The count started, but replied, "Sire, she is ill, the air of Paris did not agree with her; so having obtained leave from the queen, she set out last night, with her father, for Méridor."

"Paris is not good for women in her situation," said Chicot.

Monsoreau grew pale and looked furiously at him.

"This poor countess!" continued Chicot, "she will die of ennui by the way."

"I said that she traveled with her father."

"A father is very respectable, I allow, but not very amusing; and if she had only that worthy baron to amuse her it would be sad; but luckily——"

"What!" cried the count.

"What?"

"What do you mean by 'luckily'?"

"Ah, it was an ellipsis I used."

The count shrugged his shoulders.

"Oh, but it was. Ask Henri, who is a man of letters."

"Yes," said the king; "but what did your adverb mean?"

"What adverb?"

"'Luckily.'"

"'Luckily' means luckily. Luckily, then, there exist some of our friends, and very amusing ones, who, if they meet the countess, will amuse her, and as they are going the same way, it is probable they will. Oh, I see them from here ; do you not, Henri ; you, who are a man of imagination ? There they go, on a good road, well mounted, and saying sweet things to Madame la Comtesse, which she likes very much, dear lady."

M. de Monsoreau was furious, but he could not show it before the king ; so he said as mildly as he could, "What, have you friends traveling to Anjou ?"

"Good ; pretend to be mysterious."

"I swear to you——"

"Oh! you know they are there, although I saw you 'just' now seeking for them mechanically among the crowd."

"You saw me ?"

"Yes, you, the palest of all chief huntsmen, past, present, and future, from Nimrod to M. d'Aulefort, your predecessor."

"M. Chicot !"

"The palest, I repeat."

"Monsieur, will you return to the friends of whom you spoke, and be so good as to name them, if your superabundant imagination will let you."

"Seek, monsieur. Morbleu, it is your occupation to hunt out animals, witness the unlucky stag whom you deranged this morning, and who thought it very unkind of you. Seek."

The eyes of M. de Monsoreau wandered anxiously again.

"What !" cried he, seeing a vacant place by the king, "not the Duc d'Anjou ?"

"Taïnt ! Taïnt ! the beast is found."

"He is gone to-day."

"He is gone to-day, but it is possible that he set out last night. When did your brother disappear, Henri ?"

"Last night."

"The duke gone !" murmured Monsoreau, paler than ever.

"I do not say he is gone, I say only that he disappeared last night, and that his best friends do not know where he is," said the king.

"Oh !" cried the count, "if I thought so——"

"Well; what should you do? Besides, what harm if he does talk nonsense to Madame de Monsoreau? He is the gallant of the family, you know."

"I am lost !" murmured the count, trying to go away. But Chicot detained him.

"Keep still; mordieu ! you shake the king's chair. Mort de ma vie, your wife will be quite happy with the prince to talk to, and M. Aurilly to play the lute to her."

Monsoreau trembled with anger.

"Quietly, monsieur," continued Chicot; "hide your joy, here is the business beginning; you should not show your feelings so openly; listen to the discourse of the king."

M. de Monsoreau was forced to keep quiet. M. de Guise entered and knelt before the king, not without throwing an uneasy glance of surprise on the vacant seat of M. d'Anjou. The king rose, and the heralds commanded silence.

CHAPTER XLIX.

HOW THE KING NAMED A CHIEF WHO WAS NEITHER THE DUC DE GUISE NOR M. D'ANJOU.

"Gentlemen," said the king, after assuring himself that his four friends, now replaced by ten Swiss, were behind him, "a king hears equally the voices which come to him from above and from below, that is to say, what is commanded by God, or asked by his people. I understand perfectly that there is a guarantee for my people, in the association of all classes which has been formed to defend the Catholic faith, and therefore I approve of the counsels of my cousin De Guise. I declare, then, the Holy League duly constituted, and as so great a body must have a powerful head, and as it is necessary that the chief called to sustain the Church should be one of its most zealous sons, I choose a Christian prince for the chief, and declare that this chief shall be "—he made a slight pause—" Henri de Valois, King of France and Poland."

The Duc de Guise was thunderstruck. Large drops. stood on his forehead, and he looked from one to the other of his brothers. All the leaguers uttered a murmur of surprise and discontent. The cardinal stole up to his brother, and whispered :

"François, I fear we are no longer in safety here. Let us haste to take leave, for the populace is uncertain, and the king whom they execrated yesterday, will be thei. idol for two or three days."

During this time the king had signed the act prepared beforehand by M. de Morvilliers, the only person, with the exception of the queen mother, who was in the secret, then he passed the pen to the Duc de Guise, saying :

"Sign, my cousin ; there, below me, now pass it to M. le Cardinal and M. de Mayenne."

But these two had already disappeared. The king remarked their absence, and added, "Then pass the pen to M. de Monsoreau."

The duke did so, and was about to retire, but the king said, "Wait."

And while the others signed, he added, "My cousin, it was your advice, I believe, to guard Paris with a good army. composed of all the forces of the League. The army is made, and the natural general of the Parisians is the king."

"Assuredly, sire."

"But I do not forget that there is another army to command, and that this belongs of right to the bravest soldier in my kingdom ; therefore go and command the army."

"And when am I to set out, sire ? "

"Immediately."

"Henri, Henri !" whispered Chicot ; but, in spite of his signs and grimaces, the king gave the duke his brevet ready signed. He took it and retired, and was soon out of Paris. The rest of the assembly dispersed gradually, crying, "Vive le Roi ! and Vive la Ligue !"

"Oh, sire !" cried the favorites, approaching the king, "what a sublime idea you have had !"

"They think that gold is going to rain on them like

manna," said Chicot, who followed his master about every-where with lamentations. As soon as they were left alone, "Ah! M. Chicot!" said Henri, "you are never content. Diable! I do not ask even for complaisance, but for good sense."

"You are right, Henri; it is what you want most."

"Confess I have done well."

"That is just what I do not think."

"Ah! you are jealous, M. Roi de France."

"I! Heaven forbid. I shall choose better subjects for jealousy."

"Corbleu."

"Oh! what self-love."

"Am I or not king of the League?"

"Certainly you are; but——"

"But what?"

"You are no longer King of France."

"And who is king then?"

"Everybody, except you; firstly, your brother——"

"My brother!"

"Yes, M. d'Anjou."

"Whom I hold prisoner."

"Yes, but prisoner as he is, he was consecrated."

"By whom was he consecrated?"

"By the Cardinal de Guise. Really, Henri, you have a fine police. They consecrate a king at Paris before thirty-three people, in the church of St. Geneviève, and you do not know of it!"

"Oh! and you do?"

"Certainly I do."

"How can you know what I do not?"

"Ah! because M. de Morvilliers manages your police, and I am my own."

The king frowned.

"Well, then, without counting Henri de Valois, we have François d'Anjou for king," continued Chicot; "and then there is the Duc de Guise."

"The Duc de Guise!"

"Yes, Henri de Guise, Henri le Balafré."

"A fine king! whom I exile, whom I send to the army."

"Good! as if you were not exiled to Poland; and La Charité is nearer to the Louvre than Cracow is. Ah, yes, you send him to the army—that is so clever; that is to say, you put thirty thousand men under his orders, ventre de-biche! and a real army, not like your army of the League; no, no, an army of bourgeois is good for Henri de Valois, but Henri de Guise must have an army of soldiers—and what soldiers? hardened warriors, capable of destroying twenty armies of the League; so that if, being king in fact, Henri de Guise had the folly one day to wish to be so in name, he would only have to turn towards the capital, and say, 'Let us swallow Paris, and Henri de Valois and the Louvre at a mouthful,' and the rogues would do it. I know them."

"You forget one thing in your argument, illustrious politician."

"Ah, diable! it is possible! If you mean a fourth king——"

"No; you forget that before thinking of reigning in France, when a Valois is on the throne, it would be necessary to look back and count your ancestors. That such an idea might come to M. d'Anjou is possible; his ancestors are mine, and it is only a question of primogeniture. But M. de Guise!"

"Ah! that is just where you are in error."

"How so?"

"M. de Guise is of a better race than you think."

"Better than me, perhaps," said Henri, smiling.

"There is no perhaps in it."

"You are mad. Learn to read, my friend."

"Well, Henri, you who can read, read this;" and he drew from his pocket the genealogy which we know already, handing it to Henri, who turned pale as he recognized, near to the signature of the prelate, the seal of St. Peter.

"What do you say, Henri? Are not your fleur-de-lys thrown a little in the background?"

17

"But how did you get this genealogy?"

"I! Do I seek those things? It came to seek me."

"Where?"

"Under the bolster of a lawyer."

"And what was his name?"

"M. Nicolas David."

"Where was he?"

"At Lyons."

"And who took it from under the bolster?"

"One of my good friends."

"Who is he?"

"A monk."

"His name?"

"Gorenflot."

"What! that abominable leaguer, who uttered those incendiary discourses at St. Geneviève, and again yesterday in the streets of Paris?"

"You remember the history of Brutus, who pretended to be a fool?"

"He is, then, a profound politician? Did he take it from the advocate?"

"Yes, by force."

"Then he is brave?"

"Brave as Bayard."

"And having done this, he has not asked for any recompense?"

"He returned humbly to his convent, and only asks me to forget that he ever came out."

"Then he is modest?"

"As St. Crépin."

"Chicot, your friend shall be made a prior on the first vacancy."

"Thanks for him, Henri."

"Ma foi!" said Chicot to himself, "if he escapes being hung by Mayenne, he will have an abbey."

CHAPTER L.

ETEOCLES AND POLYNICES.

THIS day of the League terminated brilliantly and tumultuously, as it began. The friends of the king rejoiced, the preachers proposed to canonize Brother Henri, and spoke everywhere of the great deeds of the Valois. The favorites said, " The lion is roused." The leaguers said, " The fox has discovered the snare."

The three Lorraine princes, as we have seen, had left Paris, and their principal agent, M. de Monsoreau, was ready to start for Anjou. But as he was leaving the Louvre, Chicot stopped him.

" Where are you going in such a hurry ? " said he.

" To his highness."

" His highness ? "

" Yes, I am unquiet about him. We do not live in times when a prince ought to travel without a good escort."

" Well, if you are unquiet, so am I."

" About what ? "

" About his highness also."

" Why ? "

" Do you not know what they say ? "

" That he has gone to Anjou."

" No ; that he is dead."

" Bah ! " said Monsoreau, with a tone of surprise, not unmixed with joy, " you told me he was traveling."

" Diable ! they persuaded me so, but now I have good reason to think that if the poor prince be traveling, it is to another world."

" What gives you these mournful ideas ? "

" He entered the Louvre yesterday, did he not ? "

" Certainly ; I came in with him."

" Well ! he has never been seen to come out."

" From the Louvre ? "

" No."

"Where is Aurilly?"

"Disappeared."

"But his people?"

"Disappeared."

"You are joking, are you not, M. Chicot?"

"Ask!"

"Whom?"

"The king."

"I cannot question his majesty."

"Oh! yes, if you go about it in the right way."

"Well," said the count. "I cannot remain in this un-
certainty." And leaving Chicot, he went to the king's
apartment.

"Where is the king?" he asked. "I have to render
an account to him of the execution of some orders he gave
me."

"With M. le Duc d'Anjou," replied the man.

"With the Duke; then he is not dead?"

"I am not so sure of that."

M. de Monsoreau was thoroughly bewildered; for if M.
d'Anjou were in the Louvre, his absence on such a day
was unaccountable.

Immediately after the sitting, Quelus, Mangiron, Schomberg, and D'Epernon, in spite of the ennui they experienced
there, were so anxious to be disagreeable to the duke that
they returned to him. He, on his part, was mortally ennuyé, as well as anxious, which, it must be confessed, the
conversation of these gentlemen was not calculated to
remove.

"Do you know, Quelus," said Mangiron, "that it is
only now I begin to appreciate our friend Valois; really
he is a great politician."

"Explain yourself," said Quelus,, who was lounging on
a chair.

"While he was afraid of the conspiracy, he kept it
quiet; now he speaks of it openly, therefore he is no
longer afraid of it."

"Well?"

"If he no longer fears it, he will punish it; you know

Valois, he has certainly many good qualities, but clemency is not one of them."

"Granted."

"Then if he punishes these conspirators there will be a trial, and we shall have a fine spectacle."

"Unless, which is possible, on account of the rank of the accused, they arrange it all quietly."

"That would be my advice, certainly ; it is better in family affairs."

Aurilly glanced at the prince.

"Ma foi," said Maugiron, "I know one thing ; that in the king's place I would not spare the high heads, which are always the most guilty. I would make an example of one or two—one, at all events."

"I think it would be well to revive the famous invention of sacks."

"What was that ?"

"A royal fancy in the year 1550 ; they shut up a man in a sack, in company with three or four cats, and threw them into the water. The minute the cats felt the water they attacked the man, and there passed in the sack things which unluckily could never be seen."

"Really, Quelus, you are a well of science, and your conversation is most interesting."

"They could not apply this invention to the chiefs ; they have the right to be beheaded ; but to the small fry, I mean the favorites, squires, and lute-players."

"Gentlemen——" stammered Aurilly.

"Do not reply to them, Aurilly," said François, "it cannot be addressed to me." As he spoke the king appeared on the threshold. The duke rose. "Sire," cried he, "I appeal against the unworthy treatment I meet with from your followers."

Henri did not seem to hear. "Good morning, Quelus," said he kissing his favorite on both cheeks ; "good morning, the sight of you rejoices my soul, and you, my poor Maugiron, how are you ?"

"I am terribly ennuyé, sire ; when I undertook to guard your brother, I thought he was more amusing. Oh ! the

tiresome prince ; are you sure he is the son of your father
and mother ? "

"Sire ! you hear," cried the prince, "is it your wish
that your brother should be insulted ? "

"Silence, monsieur," said Henri, "I do not like my
prisoners to complain."

" Prisoner, or not, I am your——"

" The title which you are about to invoke," interrupted
the king, "is fatal to you. My brother guilty, is doubly
guilty."

" But if he is not ? "

" He is."

" Of what crime ? "

" Of having displeased me."

" Sire, have our family quarrels need of witnesses ? "

" You are right, monsieur. My friends, let me speak a
little to my brother."

" I will take Aurilly," said Maugiron.

" Now we are alone, monsieur," said the king, when
they were gone.

" I waited for this moment impatiently."

" And I also ; ah, you want my crown, my worthy
Eteocles ; you made of the League a means, and of the
throne an aim, and were consecrated in a corner of Paris,
to be able to proclaim yourself to the Parisians shining
with holy oil."

" Alas ! your majesty will not let me speak."

" What for ?—to lie, or to tell me things which I know
already ? But no, you would lie ; for to confess what you
have done, would be to confess that you merit death.
You would lie, and I would spare you that shame."

" My brother, is it your intention to overwhelm me with
outrages ? "

" If what I say is an outrage, it is I who lie, and I ask
no better. Speak then, I listen ; tell me you are not dis-
loyal, and at the same time unskilful."

" I do not know what your majesty means ; you speak
enigmas."

" Then I will explain my words ; you have conspired

against me, as formerly you conspired against my brother Charles, only then it was by the aid of Henri of Navarre, and now it is with the assistance of the Duc de Guise. It is true that formerly you crawled like a serpent; now you wish to spring like the lion; after perfidy, open force; after poison, the sword."

"Poison! what do you mean?" cried François, with flashing eyes.

"The poison with which you assassinated our brother Charles, which you destined for Henry of Navarre, your associate. That fatal poison is known; our mother has used it so often, which is doubtless the reason why you renounced it on this occasion, and preferred rather the part of captain of the League. But look me in the face, François, and learn that a man like you shall never kill me. A sword! Ah! I should like to see you here in this room alone with me, holding a sword. I have conquered you in cunning, and in a combat you would be killed. Dream no longer of struggling against me in any manner, for from this moment I act as king—as master—as despot; I shall watch you everywhere, follow you everywhere, and, at the least suspicion, I will throw you to the axe of my executioner. This is what I had to say to you in private, and I will order you to be left alone to-night to ponder over my words."

"Then, sire, for a suspicion, I have fallen into disgrace with you?"

"Say, under my justice."

"But, at least, sire, fix a term to my captivity, that I may know what to expect?"

"You will know when you hear your sentence read."

"Can I not see my mother?"

"What for? There were but three copies in the world of the famous hunting-book which killed my poor brother, and of the two others, one is in London and the other at Florence. Besides, I am not a Nimrod, like my poor brother; adieu, François."

"Gentlemen," said the king, opening the door, "the Duc d'Anjou has requested to be alone to-night to reflect

on an answer he has to make to me to-morrow morning.
Leave him then alone, except occasional visits of precaution.
If he be troublesome, call me; I have the Bastile
ready, and the governor, M. Laurent Testu, is the best
man in the world to conquer ill tempers."

"Sire," cried François, trying a last effort, "remember
I am your——"

"You were also the brother of Charles IX., I think."

"At least restore me to my friends."

"I deprive myself of mine to give them to you." And
Henri shut the door, while the duke fell in despair into
his armchair.

CHAPTER LI.

HOW PEOPLE DO NOT ALWAYS LOSE THEIR TIME BY SEARCHING EMPTY DRAWERS.

THE scene which the duke had just had with the king
made him regard his position as desperate. The minions
had not allowed him to be ignorant of what had passed,
and he had heard the people cry, "Vive le roi!" He felt
himself abandoned by the other chiefs, who had themselves
to save. In his quarrels with his brother Charles he had
always had for confidants, or rather dupes, those two devoted
men, Coconnas and La Mole, and, for the first time
in his life, feeling himself alone and isolated, he felt a kind
of remorse at having sacrificed them. During that time
his sister Marguerite loved and consoled him. How had
he recompensed her?

He had recently had near him a brave and valiant heart
and sword—Bussy, the brave Bussy. And he had offended
him to please Monsoreau, who had his secret, with which
he always threatened him, and which was now known to
the king. He had therefore quarreled with Bussy gratuitously,
and, above all, uselessly, which as a great politician
once said, "was more than a crime, it was a mistake!"
How he would have rejoiced in his present situation, to
know that Bussy was watching over him; Bussy the loyal,

Bussy the universal favorite. It would have been probable liberty and certain vengeance.

But as we have said, Bussy, wounded to the heart, kept away from the prince, so the prisoner remained fifty feet above the ground, with the four favorites in the corridor, without counting the court full of Swiss. Besides this, one or other of the young men entered from time to time, and, without seeming even to notice the prince, went round the room, examined the doors and windows, looked under the beds and tables, and glanced at the curtains and sheets.

"Ma foi!" said Maugiron, after one of these visits, "I have done; I am not going to look after him any more to-night."

"Yes," said D'Epernon, "as long as we guard him, there is no need of going to look at him."

"And he is not handsome to look at," said Quelus.

"Still," said Schomberg, "I think we had better not relax our vigilance, for the devil is cunning."

"Yes, but not cunning enough to pass over the bodies of four men like us."

"That is true," said Quelus.

"Oh!" said Schomberg, "do you think, if he wants to fly, he will choose our corridor to come through? He would make a hole in the wall."

"With what?"

"Then he has the windows."

"Ah! the windows, bravo, Schomberg; would you jump forty-five feet?"

"I confess that forty-five feet——"

"Yes, and he who is lame, and heavy, and timid as——"

"You," said Schomberg.

"You know I fear nothing but phantoms—that is an affair of the nerves."

"The last phantom was," said Quelus, "that all those whom he had killed in duels appeared to him one night."

"However," said Maugiron, "I have read of wonderful escapes; with sheets, for instance."

"Ah! that is more sensible. I saw myself, at Bordeaux, a prisoner who escaped by the aid of his sheets."

"You see, then?"

"Yes, but he had his leg broken, and his neck, too; his sheets were thirty feet too short, and he had to jump, so that while his body escaped from prison, his soul escaped from his body."

"Besides," said Quelus, "if he escapes, we will follow him, and in catching him some mischief might happen to him."

So they dismissed the subject. They were perfectly right that the duke was not likely to attempt a perilous escape. From time to time his pale face was at the window which overlooked the fosses of the Louvre, beyond which was an open space about fifteen feet broad, and then the Seine rolled calm as a mirror. On the other side rose, like a giant, the tower of Nesle.

He had watched the sunset and the gradual extinction of all the lights. He had contemplated the beautiful spectacle of old Paris, with its roofs gilded by the last rays of the sun, and silvered by the first beams of the moon; then little by little he was seized with a great terror at seeing immense clouds roll over the sky and announce a storm. Among his other weaknesses, the Duc d'Anjou was afraid of thunder, and he would have given anything to have had his guardians with him again, even if they insulted him. He threw himself on his bed, but found it impossible to sleep. Then he began to swear, and break everything near him. It was a family failing, and they were accustomed to it at the Louvre. The young men had opened the door to see what the noise meant, and seeing that it was the duke amusing himself, they had shut it again, which redoubled his anger. He had just broken a chair, when a crashing of glass was heard at the window, and he felt a sharp blow on his thigh. His first idea was that he was wounded by some emissary of the king's.

"Ah! I am dead!" he cried, and fell on the carpet.

But as he fell his hand came in contact with a larger and rougher substance than a ball.

"Oh! a stone," thought he, and feeling his leg, he found it uninjured. He picked up the stone and looked at it, and saw that it was wrapped in a piece of paper. Then the duke's ideas began to change. Might not this stone come from a friend as well as an enemy. He approached the light, cut the silk which tied the paper round the stone and read,—

"Are you tired of keeping your room? Do you love open air and liberty? Enter the little room where the Queen of Navarre hid your poor friend, M. de la Mole, open the cupboard, and, by displacing the lowest bracket, you will find a double bottom; in this there is a silk ladder; attach it yourself to the balcony, two vigorous arms will hold it at the bottom. A horse, swift as thought, will lead you to a safe place.

"A FRIEND."

"A friend!" cried the prince; "oh! I did not know I had a friend. Who is this friend who thinks of me?" And the duke ran to the window, but could see no one.

"Can it be a snare?" thought he; "but first let me see if there is a double bottom and a ladder."

The duke then, leaving the light where it was for precaution, groped his way to the cabinet, which he knew so well. He opened it, felt for the bottom shelf, and, to his great joy, found what he looked for. As a thief escapes with his booty, the duke rushed into the next room with his prey. Ten o'clock struck; the duke thought of his hourly visitors, and hid his ladder under a cushion, on which he sat down. Indeed, five minutes had not passed before Maugiron appeared in a dressing-gown, with a sword in one hand and a light in the other. As he came in one of his friends said to him, "The bear is furious, he was breaking everything just now; take care he does not devour you, Maugiron."

Maugiron made his usual examination; he saw a broken window, but thought the duke had done it in his rage.

"Maugiron!" cried Schomberg, from outside, "are you already eaten that you do not speak? In that case, sigh, at least, that we may know and avenge you."

The duke trembled with impatience.

"No, no," said Maugiron, "on the contrary, my bear is quite conquered."

And so saying he went out and locked the door. When the key had ceased to turn in the lock the duke murmured,—

"Take care, gentlemen, or the duke will be too much for you."

CHAPTER LII.

VENTRE ST. GRIS.

LEFT alone, the duke, knowing he had at least an hour before him, drew out his ladder and carefully examined the fastenings.

"The ladder is good," said he, at length, "and will not break."

Then he unrolled it all, and counted thirty-eight rounds of fifteen inches each.

"The length is sufficient," said he, "there is nothing to fear on that point. Ah! but if it were some of those cursed minions who sent me to the ladder? If I attach it to the balcony they will let me do it, and while I am descending they will cut the cords. But, no; they could not be foolish enough to think I would fly without barricading the door, and I should have time to fly before they could force it. But what person in the world, except my sister herself, could know of a ladder hidden in her dressing-room? What friend of mine can it be?"

Suddenly an idea struck him, and he cried, "Bussy!"

Indeed, Bussy, whom so many ladies adored, Bussy was a hero to the Queen of Navarre, and his only true friend— was it Bussy? Everything made him think so. The duke, of course, did not know all his motives for being angry with him, for he did not know his love for Diana.

and believed him to be too noble to think of resentment
when his master was a prisoner. He approached the window again, and fancied he could see in the fog the indis-
tinct forms of three horses and two men by the river.
Two men. These must be Bussy and Rémy. He then
looked through the keyhole, and saw his four guardians;
two were asleep, and two had inherited Chicot's chess-
board and were playing. He extinguished his light.

Then he opened his window, and looked over the balcony; the gulf below him looked dreadful in the darkness, and he drew back. But air and liberty have an attraction so irresistible to a prisoner, that François, on
withdrawing from the window, felt as if he were being
stifled, and for an instant something like disgust of life
and indifference to death passed through his mind. He
fancied he was growing courageous, and, profiting by this
moment of excitement, he seized the ladder, fixed it to the
balcony, then barricaded the door as well as he could, and
returned to the window. The darkness was now great,
and the first growlings of the storm began to make themselves heard; a great cloud with silver fringes extended
itself like a recumbent elephant from one side to the other
of the river. A flash of lightning broke the immense cloud
for a moment, and the prince fancied that he saw below
him in the fosse the same figures he had imagined before.
A horse neighed; there was no more doubt—he was waited
for.

He shook the ladder to see if it was firm, then he put
his leg over the balustrade and placed his foot on the first
step. Nothing can describe the anguish of the prisoner at
this moment, placed between a frail silk cord on the one
hand and his brother's cruel menaces on the other. But
as he stood there he felt the ladder stiffened; some one
held it. Was it a friend or an enemy? Were they open
arms or armed ones which waited for him? An irresistible terror seized him; he still held the balcony with his
left hand, and made a movement to remount, when a very
slight pull at the ladder came to him like a solicitation.
He took courage, and tried the second step. The ladder

was held as firm as a rock, and he found a steady support for
his foot. He descended rapidly, almost gliding down, when
all at once, instead of touching the earth, which he knew
to be near, he felt himself seized in the arms of a man
who whispered, "You are saved." Then he was carried
along the fosse till they came to the end, when another
man seized him by the collar and drew him up, and after
having aided his companion in the same way, they ran to
the river, where stood the horses. The prince knew he
was at the mercy of his saviours, so he jumped at once on
a horse, and his companions did the same. The same
voice now said, "Quick!" And they set off at a gallop.

"All goes well at present," thought the prince, "let
us hope it will end so. Thanks, my brave Bussy," said he
to his companion on the right, who was entirely covered
with a large cloak.

"Quick!" replied the other.

They arrived thus at the great ditch of the Bastile,
which they crossed on a bridge improvised by the Leaguers
the night before. The three cavaliers rode towards
Charenton, when all at once the man on the right entered
the forest of Vincennes, saying only, "Come." The
prince's horse neighed, and several others answered from
the depths of the forest. François would have stopped if
he could, for he feared they were taking him to an ambush,
but it was too late, and in a few minutes he found himself
in a small open space, where eight or ten men on horseback
were drawn up.

"Oh! oh!" said the prince, "what does this mean,
monsieur?"

"Ventre St. Gris! it means that we are saved."

"You! Henri!" cried the duke, stupefied, "you! my
liberator?"

"Does that astonish you? Are we not related, Agrippa?"
continued he, looking round for his companion.

"Here I am," said D'Aubigné.

"Are there two fresh horses, with which we can go a
dozen leagues without stopping?"

"But where are you taking me, my cousin?"

"Where you like, only be quick, for the King of France has more horses than I have, and is rich enough to kill a dozen if he wishes to catch us."

"Really, then, I am free to go where I like?"

"Certainly, I wait your orders."

"Well, then, to Angers."

"To Angers; so be it, there you are at home."

"But you?"

"I! when we are in sight of Angers I shall leave you, and ride on to Navarre, where my good Margot expects me, and must be much ennuyée at my absence."

"But no one knew you were here?"

"I came to sell three diamonds of my wife's."

"Ah! very well."

"And also to know if this League was really going to ruin me."

"You see there is nothing in it."

"Thanks to you, no."

"How! thanks to me?"

"Certainly. If, instead of refusing to be chief of the League, when you knew it was directed against me, you had accepted, I was ruined. Therefore, when I heard that the king had punished your refusal with imprisonment, I swore to release you, and I have done so."

"Always so simple-minded," thought François, "really, it is easy to deceive him."

"Now for Anjou," thought the king. "Ah! M. de Guise, I send you a companion you do not want."

CHAPTER LIII.

THE FRIENDS.

WHILE Paris was in this ferment, Madame de Monsoreau, escorted by her father and two servants, pursued their way to Méridor. She began to enjoy her liberty, precious to those who have suffered. The azure of the sky, compared to that which hung always menacingly over the black towers of the Bastile, the trees already green, all appeared to her fresh and young, beautiful and new, as if she had really come out of the tomb where her father had believed her. He, the old baron, had grown young again. We will not attempt to describe their long journey, free from incidents. Several times the baron said to Diana,—

"Do not fear, my daughter."

"Fear what?"

"Were you not looking if M. de Monsoreau was following us?"

"Yes, it was true, I did look," replied she, with a sigh and another glance behind.

At last, on the eighth day, they reached the château of Méridor, and were received by Madame de St. Luc and her husband. Then began for these four people one of those existences of which every man has dreamed in reading Virgil or Theocritus. The baron and St. Luc hunted from morning till evening; you might have seen troops of dogs rushing from the hills in pursuit of some hare or fox, and startling Diana and Jeanne, as they sat side by side on the moss, under the shade of the trees.

"Recount to me," said Jeanne, "all that happened to you in the tomb, for you were dead to us. See, the hawthorn is shedding on us its last flowers, and the elders send out their perfume. Not a breath in the air, not a human being near us; recount, little sister."

"What can I say?"

"Tell me, are you happy? That beautiful eye often swimming in tears, the paleness of your cheeks, that mouth which tries a smile which it never finishes—Diana, you must have many things to tell me."

"No, nothing."

"You are, then, happy with M. de Monsoreau?"

Diana shuddered.

"You see!" said Jeanne.

"With M. de Monsoreau! Why did you pronounce that name? why do you evoke that phantom in the midst of our woods, our flowers, our happiness?"

"You told me, I think," said Jeanne, "that M. de Bussy showed much interest in you."

Diana reddened, even to her round pretty ears.

"He is a charming creature," continued Jeanne, kissing Diana.

"It is folly," said Diana; "M. de Bussy thinks no more of Diana de Méridor."

"That is possible; but I believe he pleases Diana de Monsoreau a little."

"Do not say that."

"Does it displease you?"

"I tell you he thinks no more of me; and he does well —oh, I was cowardly."

"What do you say?"

"Nothing, nothing."

"Now, Diana, do not cry, do not accuse yourself. You cowardly! you, my heroine! you were constrained."

"I believed it; I saw dangers, gulfs under my feet. Now, Jeanne, these dangers seem to me chimerical, these gulfs as if a child could cross them. I was cowardly, I tell you; oh, I had no time to reflect."

"You speak in enigmas."

"No," cried Diana, rising, "it was not my fault, it was his. The Duc d'Anjou was against him; but when one wishes a thing, when one loves, neither prince nor master should keep you back. See, Jeanne, if I loved——"

"Be calm, dear friend."

"I tell you, _we_ were cowardly."

"'We!' of whom do you speak? That 'we' is eloquent, my dearest Diana."

"I mean my father and I; you did not think anything else, did you? My father is a nobleman—he might have spoken to the king; I am proud, and do not fear a man when I hate him. But _he_ did not love me."

"You lie to yourself! you know the contrary, little hypocrite!"

"You may believe in love, Jeanne, you, whom M. de St. Luc married in spite of the king; you, whom he carried away from Paris; you, who pay him by your caresses for proscription and exile."

"And he thinks himself richly repaid,"

18

" But I—reflect a little, do not be egotistical—I, whom that fiery young man pretended to love—I, who fixed the regards of that invincible Bussy, he who fears no one—I was alone with him in the cloister of l'Egyptienne—we were alone; but for Gertrude and Rémy, our accomplices, he could have carried me off. At that moment I saw him suffering because of me; I saw his eyes languishing, his lips pale and parched with fever. If he had asked me to die to restore the brightness to his eyes, and the freshness to his lips, I should have died. Well, I went away, and he never tried to detain me. Wait still. He knew that I was leaving Paris, that I was returning to Méridor; he knew that M. de Monsoreau—I blush as I tell it—was only my husband in name; he knew that I traveled alone; and along the road, dear Jeanne, I kept turning, thinking I heard the gallop of his horse behind us. But no, it was only the echo of my own. I tell you he does not think of me. I am not worth a journey to Anjou while there are so many beautiful women at the court of France, whose smiles are worth a hundred confessions from the provincial, buried at Méridor. Do you understand now? Am I forgotten, despised——"

She had not finished when the foliage of the oak rustled, a quantity of mortar and moss fell from the old wall, and a man threw himself at the feet of Diana, who uttered an affrighted cry.

Jeanne ran away—she recognized him.

"Here I am!" cried Bussy, kissing the dress of Diana.

She too recognized him, and, overcome by this unexpected happiness, fell unconscious into the arms of him whom she had just accused of indifference.

CHAPTER LIV.

BUSSY AND DIANA.

FAINTINGS from love seldom last any length of time, nor are they very dangerous. Diana was not long in opening her eyes, and finding herself supported by Bussy.

"Oh!" murmured she, "it was shocking, count, to surprise us thus."

Bussy expected other words, men are so exacting, but Diana said no more, and, disengaging herself gently from his arms, ran to her friend, who, seeing her faint, had returned softly, and stood a little way off.

"Is it thus that you receive me, madame?"

"No, M. de Bussy, but——"

"Oh! no 'but,' madame," sighed Bussy, drawing near again.

"No, no, not on your knees!"

"Oh! let me pray to you an instant, thus!" cried the count. "I have so longed for this place."

"Yes, but to come to it, you jumped over the wall. Not only is it not suitable for a man of your rank, but it is very imprudent."

"How so?"

"If you had been seen?"

"Who could have seen me?"

"Our hunters, who, a quarter of an hour ago, passed by this wall."

"Do not be uneasy, madame, I hide myself too carefully to be seen."

"Hidden! really!" said Jeanne, "tell us how, M. de Bussy."

"Firstly, if I did not join you on the road, it was not my fault, I took one route and you another. You came by Rambouillet, and I by Chartres. And then judge if your poor Bussy be not in love; I did not dare to join you. It was not in the presence of your father and your servants that I wished to meet you again, for I did not desire to compromise you, so I made the journey stage by stage, devoured by impatience. At last you arrived. I had taken a lodging in the village, and, concealed behind the window, I saw you pass."

"Oh! mon Dieu! are you then at Angers under your own name?"

"For what do you take me? I am a traveling merchant; look at my costume, it is of a color much worn among drapers and goldsmiths. I have not been remarked."

"Bussy, the handsome Bussy, two days in a provincial town and not remarked; who would believe that at court?" said Jeanne.

"Continue, count," said Diana, blushing; "how do you come here from the town?"

"I have two horses of a chosen race; I leave the village on one, stopping to look at all the signs and writings, but when out of sight my horse takes to a gallop, which brings him the four miles in half an hour. Once in the wood of Méridor I ride to the park wall, but it is very long, for the park is large. Yesterday I explored this wall for more than four hours, climbing up here and there, hoping to see you. At last, when I was almost in despair, I saw you in the evening returning to the house; the two great dogs of the baron were jumping round you. When you had disappeared, I jumped over, and saw the marks on the grass where you had been sitting. I fancied you might have adopted this place, which is charming, during the heat of the sun, so I broke away some branches that I might know it again, and sighing, which hurts me dreadfully——"

"From want of habit," said Jeanne.

"I do not say no, madame; well, then, sighing, I retook my way to the town. I was very tired, I had torn my dress in climbing trees, but I had seen you, and I was happy."

"It is an admirable recital," said Jeanne, "and you have surmounted dreadful obstacles; it is quite heroic;

but in your place I would have preserved my doublet, and above all, have taken care of my white hands. Look at yours, how frightful they are with scratches."

"Yes, but then I should not have seen her whom I came to see."

"On the contrary, I should have seen her better than you did."

"What would you have done then?"

"I would have gone straight to the Château de Méridor. M. le Baron would have pressed me in his arms, Madame de Monsoreau would have placed me by her at table, M. de St. Luc would have been delighted to see me, and his wife also. It was the simplest thing in the world, but lovers never think of what is straight before them."

Bussy smiled at Diana. "Oh, no," he said, "that would not have done for me."

"Then I no longer understand what good manners are."

"No," said Bussy, "I could not go to the castle; M. le Baron would watch his daughter."

"Good!" said Jeanne, "here is a lesson for me," and kissing Diana on the forehead, she ran away. Diana tried to stop her, but Bussy seized her hands, and she let her friend go. They remained alone.

"Have I not done well, madame," said Bussy, "and do you not approve?"

"I do not desire to feign," said Diana, "besides, it would be useless; you know I approve; but here must stop my indulgence; in calling for you as I did just now I was mad—I was guilty."

"Mon Dieu! What do you say?"

"Alas! count, the truth; I have a right to make M. de Monsoreau unhappy, to withhold from him my smiles and my love, but I have no right to bestow them on another: for, after all, he is my master."

"Now, you will let me speak, will you not?"

"Speak!"

"Well! of all that you have just said, you do not find one word in your heart."

"How!"

"Listen patiently; you have overwhelmed me with sophisms. The commonplaces of morality do not apply here; this man is your master, you say, but did you choose him? No; fate imposed him on you, and you submitted. Now, do you mean to suffer all your life the consequences of this odious constraint? I will deliver you from it."

Diana tried to speak, but Bussy stopped her.

"Oh! I know what you are going to say; that if I provoke M. de Monsoreau and kill him, you will see me no more. So be it; I may die of grief, but you will live free and happy, and you may render happy some gallant man, who in his joy will sometimes bless my name, and cry, 'Thanks, Bussy, thanks, for having delivered us from that dreadful Monsoreau;' and you, yourself, Diana, who will not dare to thank me while living, will thank me dead."

Diana seized his hand.

"You have not yet implored me, Bussy; you begin with menaces."

"Menace you! oh! could I have such an intention, I, who love you so ardently, Diana. I know you love me; do not deny it, I know it, for you have avowed it. Here, on my knees before you, my hand on my heart, which has never lied, either from interest or from fear, I say to you, Diana, I love you, for my whole life. Diana, I swear to you, that if I die for you, it will be in adoring you. If you still say to me, 'go,' I will go without a sigh, or complaint, from this place where I am so happy, and I should say, 'this woman does not love me, and never will love me.' Then I should go away, and you would see me no more, but as my devotion for you is great, my desire to see you happy would survive the certainty that I could never be happy myself."

Bussy said this with so much emotion, and, at the same time firmness, that Diana felt sure that he would do all he said, and she cried,—

"Thanks, count, for you take from me all remorse by your threats."

Saying these words, she gave him her hand, which he

kissed passionately. Then they heard the light steps of Jeanne, accompanied by a warning cough. Instinctively the clasped hands parted. Jeanne saw it.

"Pardon, my good friends, for disturbing you," said she, "but we must go in if we do not wish to be sent for. M. le Comte, regain, if you please, your excellent horse, and let us go to the house. See what you lose by your obstinacy, M. de Bussy, a dinner at the château, which is not to be despised by a man who has had a long ride, and has been climbing trees, without counting all the amusement we could have had, or the glances that might have passed. Come, Diana, come away."

Bussy looked at the two friends with a smile. Diana held out her hand to him.

"Is that all?" said he; "have you nothing to say?"

"Till to-morrow," replied she.

"Only to-morrow."

"To-morrow, and always."

Bussy uttered a joyful exclamation, pressed his lips to her hand, and ran off. Diana watched him till he was out of sight.

"Now!" said Jeanne, when he had disappeared, "will you talk to me a little?"

"Oh! yes."

"Well! to-morrow I shall go to the chase with St. Luc and your father."

"What, you will leave me alone at the château!"

"Listen, dear friend; I also have my principles, and there are certain things that I cannot consent to do."

"Oh, Jeanne!" cried Diana, growing pale, "can you say such things to me?"

"Yes, I cannot continue thus."

"I thought you loved me, Jeanne. What cannot you continue?"

"Continue to prevent two poor lovers from talking to each other at their ease." Diana seized in her arms the laughing young woman.

"Listen!" said Jeanne, "there are the hunters calling us, and poor St. Luc is impatient."

CHAPTER LV.

HOW BUSSY WAS OFFERED THREE HUNDRED PISTOLES FOR
HIS HORSE, AND PARTED WITH HIM FOR NOTHING.

THE next day, Bussy left Angers before the most wakeful
bourgeois had had their breakfast. He flew along the road,
and Diana, mounted on a terrace in front of the castle,
saw him coming, and went to meet him. The sun had
scarcely risen over the great oaks, and the grass was still wet
with dew, when she heard from afar, as she went along,
the horn of St. Luc, which Jeanne incited him to sound.
She arrived at the meeting-place just as Bussy appeared
on the wall. The day passed like an hour. What had
they to say? That they loved each other. What had they
to wish for ? They were together.

"Diana," said Bussy at length, "it seems to me as
though my life had begun only to-day. You have shown
me what it is to live."

"And I," replied she, "who not long ago would have
willingly thrown myself into the arms of death, would now
tremble to die and lose your love. But why do you not
come to the castle ? My father would be glad to see you,
and M. de St. Luc is your friend."

"Alas, Diana, if I came once, I should be always there ;
all the province would know it, and if it came to the ears
of that ogre, your husband, he would hasten here. You
forbid me to deliver you from him——"

"Oh, yes ! "

"Well, then, for the safety of our happiness, we must
guard our secret. Madame de St. Luc knows it, and her
husband soon will. I have written him a line this morning,
asking him for an interview at Angers, and when he comes
I will make him promise never to breathe a word of this.
It is the more important, dear Diana, as doubtless they are

seeking me everywhere. Things looked grave when I left Paris."

"You are right; and then my father is so scrupulous that, in spite of his love for me, he is capable of denouncing me to M. de Monsoreau."

"Let us hide ourselves well, then; I fear some evil spirit, jealous of our happiness."

"Say adieu to me, then; and do not ride so fast—your horse frightens me."

"Fear nothing; he knows the way, and is the gentlest and safest horse I ever rode. When I return to the city, buried in sweet thoughts, he takes the way without my touching the bridle."

At last the sound of the returning chase was heard, the horns playing an air agreed upon with Jeanne, and Bussy left. As he approached the city, he remarked that the time was approaching when the gates of the city would be closed. He was preparing to ride on quickly, when he heard behind him the gallop of horses. For a lover who wishes to remain concealed, as for a robber, everything seems a menace. Bussy asked himself whether he should ride on or draw up and let them pass, but their course was so rapid that they were up to him in a moment. There were two.

"Here is the city," said one, with a Gascon accent; "three hundred more blows with the whip, and one hundred with the spur; courage and vigor!"

"The beast has no more breath—he shivers and totters; he will not go on; and yet I would give a hundred horses to be in my city before nightfall."

"It is some Angers man out late," thought Bussy. "But look, the horse is falling; take care, monsieur," cried he; "quit your horse—he is about to fall."

Indeed, as he spoke the animal fell heavily on his side, shook his legs convulsively, then suddenly his breath stopped, his eyes grew dim, and he was dead.

"Monsieur!" cried the cavalier to Bussy, "three hundred pistoles for your horse!"

"Ah, mon Dieu!" cried Bussy, drawing near.

"Do you hear me, monsieur? I am in haste."

"Ah! my prince, take it for nothing," cried Bussy, who had recognized the Duc d'Anjou.

At the same moment they heard the click of a pistol, which was cocked by the duke's companion.

"Stop, M. d'Aubigné," cried the duke, "it is Bussy, I believe."

"Oh! yes, my prince, it is I. But what, in Heaven's name are you doing, killing horses on the road at this hour?"

"Ah! is it M. de Bussy?" said D'Aubigné, "then you do not want me any more. Permit me to return to him who sent me?"

"Not without receiving my sincere thanks and the promise of a lasting friendship."

"I accept it, monseigneur, and will recall your words to you some day."

"M. D'Aubigné! I am in the clouds," murmured Bussy.

"Did you not know? As you are here, did you not expect me?" said the prince, with an air of suspicion which did not escape Bussy, who began to reflect that his secret residence in Anjou might seem very strange to the prince.

"I did better than expect you," said Bussy, "and as you wish to enter the town before the gates are closed, jump into the saddle, monseigneur."

The prince accepted, and Bussy mounted behind him, asking himself if this prince, dressed in black, were not the evil spirit sent already to disturb his happiness.

"Where do we go now, monseigneur?" said he, as they entered the city.

"To the castle. Let them hoist my banner and convoke the nobility of the district."

"Nothing more easy," said Bussy, full of surprise, but willing to be docile. The news was soon spread through the city that the duke had arrived, and a crowd soon collected.

"Gentlemen!" cried the duke, "I have come to throw myself into my good city of Angers. At Paris the most terrible dangers have menaced my life—I had lost even my liberty. I succeeded in escaping, thanks to some good friends, and now I am here I feel my tranquillity and my life assured."

The people cried, "Long live our seigneur."

"Now let me sup," said the prince, "I have had nothing since the morning."

The city was illuminated, guns were fired, the bells of the cathedral were rung, and the wind carried to Méridor the noisy joy of the good Angevins.

CHAPTER LVI.

THE DIPLOMACY OF THE DUC D'ANJOU.

WHEN the duke and Bussy were left alone, the duke said, "Let us talk."

François, who was very quick, had perceived that Bussy had made more advances to him than usual, therefore he judged that he was in some embarrassing situation, and that he might, by a little address, get an advantage over him. But Bussy had had time to prepare himself, and he was quite ready.

"Yes, let us talk, monseigneur," replied he.

"The last day I saw you, my poor Bussy, you were very ill."

"It is true, monseigneur, I was very ill, and it was almost a miracle that saved me."

"There was near you a doctor very devoted to you, for he growled at every one who approached you."

"True, prince, Rémy loves me."

"He kept you rigorously to your bed, did he not?"

"At which I was in a great rage, as your highness might have seen."

"But, if that were the case, why did you not send the doctor to the devil, and come out with me as I begged you to do? But as it was a grave affair, you were afraid to compromise yourself."

"Did you say I was afraid?"

"I did say so."

"Well, then, it was a lie!" said Bussy, jumping up from his chair; "you lied to yourself, monseigneur, for you do not believe a single word of what you say. There are twenty scars on my body, which prove the contrary. I never knew fear, and, ma foi, I know people who cannot say the same."

"You have always unanswerable arguments, M. de Bussy," cried the duke, turning very pale; "when you are accused, you cry louder than your accuser, and then you think you are right."

"Oh! I am not always right, I know well, but I know on what occasions I am wrong."

"And what are they?"

"When I serve ungrateful people."

"Really, monsieur, I think you forget yourself," said the duke, with some dignity. Bussy moved towards the door, but the prince stopped him.

"Do you deny, monsieur," said he, "that after refusing to go out with me, you went out immediately after?"

"I deny nothing, monseigneur, but I will not be forced to confession."

"Tell me why you would not go out with me."

"I had business."

"At home?"

"Or elsewhere."

"I thought that when a gentleman was in the service of a prince, his principal business was that of the prince."

"And who does your business generally, monseigneur, if not I?"

"I do not say no; generally I find you faithful and devoted, and, I will say more, I excuse your bad humor."

"You are very good."

"Yes, for you had some reason to be angry."

"Ah! you confess it."

"Yes, I promised you the disgrace of M. de Monsoreau. It seems you hate him very much."

"I! not at all. I find him very ugly, and should have liked him away from court, not to have had to look at him. It seems, however, that you admire him, and there is no accounting for tastes."

"Well, then, as that was your sole excuse, you were doubly wrong to refuse to accompany me, and then to go out after, and commit follies."

"Follies! what did I do?"

"Doubtless, you do not like MM. d'Epernon and Schomberg, neither do I, but one must have some prudence. Kill them, and I should be grateful to you, but do not exasperate them."

"What did I do to them?"

"Why, you had D'Epernon stoned."

"I!"

"Yes, so that his clothes were torn to pieces."

"Good! and what about M. Schomberg?"

"You will not deny that you had him dyed indigo color? When I saw him three hours after, he was still bright blue. Do you call that a joke?" And the prince laughed in spite of himself, and Bussy joined him.

"Then," said he, "they think it was I who played them these tricks!"

"Perhaps it was I."

"And you have the conscience to reproach a man who had such fine ideas."

"Well, I pardon you. But I have another complaint to make. What did you do to deliver me from my unlucky situation?"

"You see, I came to Anjou."

"It seems to me that you would have been more useful nearer."

"Ah! there we differ; I preferred coming to Anjou."

"Your caprice is a bad reason."

"But, if I came to gather your partisans?"

"Ah! that is different. What have you done?"

"I will explain that to you to-morrow; at present I must leave you."

"Why!"

"I have to see an important person."

"Oh, very well; but be prudent."

" Prudent ! are we not the strongest here ? "

" Never mind, risk nothing. Have you done much ? "

" I have only been here two days."

" But you keep yourself concealed, I hope."

" I should think so. Look at my dress; am I in the habit of wearing cinnamon-colored clothes ? "

" And where are you lodging ? "

" Ah ! I hope you will appreciate my devotion ; in a tumble-down old house, near the ramparts. But you, my prince, how did you get out of the Louvre ? How was it that I found you on the road, with M. d'Aubigné for a companion ? "

" Because I have friends."

" You ! friends ! "

" Yes, friends that you do not know."

" Well, and who are they ? "

" The King of Navarre and D'Aubigné, whom you saw."

" The King of Navarre ! Ah ! true, did you not conspire together ? "

" I never conspired, M. de Bussy."

" No ; ask poor La Mole and Coconnas."

" La Mole," said the prince, gloomily, " died for another crime than the one alleged against him."

" Well, never mind him. How the devil did you get out of the Louvre ? "

" Through the window."

" Which window ? "

" That of my bedroom."

" Then you knew of the rope-ladder ? "

" What rope-ladder ? "

" In the cupboard."

" Ah ! it seems you knew it," cried the prince, turning pale.

" Oh ! your highness knows I have sometimes had the happiness of entering that room."

" In the time of my sister Margot. Then you came in by the window ? "

" As you came out. All that astonishes me is, that you knew of the ladder."

"It was not I who found it."

"Who then ?"

"I was told of it."

"By whom ?"

"By the King of Navarre."

"Ah ! the King of Navarre knew of it ; I should not have thought so. However, now you are here safe and sound, we will put Anjou in flames, and Béarn and Angoumois will catch the light, so we shall have a fine blaze."

"But did you not speak of a rendezvous ?"

"It is true ; the interest of the conversation was making me forget. Adieu, monseigneur."

"Do you take your horse ?"

"If it will be useful to you, monseigneur, you may keep it, I have another."

"Well ! I accept ; we will settle that later."

The duke gave Bussy his hand, and they separated.

CHAPTER LVII.

THE IDEAS OF THE DUC D'ANJOU.

BUSSY returned home, but instead of St. Luc, whom he expected, he found only a letter fixing their meeting for the next day. About six in the morning St. Luc started, and rode straight to Bussy's house.

"Accept the hospitality of my poor hut, St. Luc," said Bussy, "I am encamped here."

"Yes, like a conqueror on the field of battle."

"What do you mean ?"

"I mean, dear Bussy, that my wife has no secrets from me, and has told me all. Receive my compliments, but, since you have sent for me, permit me to give you a piece of advice."

"Well."

"Get rid as soon as possible of that abominable Monsoreau ; no one at the court knows of your love for his wife, so when you marry the widow, no one will say you killed him on purpose."

"There is but one obstacle to this project, which presented itself to my mind, as to yours."

"What is it?"

"That I have sworn to Diana to respect the life of her husband, as long as he does not attack me."

"You were very wrong."

"Why so?"

"Because if you do not take the initiative, he will discover you, and will kill you."

"I cannot break my oath to Diana. Besides, he who is now a monster in all eyes, would be thought an angel in his tomb."

"Therefore I do not advise you to kill him yourself."

"Oh, St. Luc, no assassins."

"Who spoke of assassins?"

"Of what then?"

"Nothing; an idea passed through my mind; I will tell you what it was at another time. I do not love this Monsoreau much more than you, although I have not the same reason to detest him, so let us speak of the wife instead of the husband."

Bussy smiled. "You are a capital companion, St Luc," said he, "and you may count on my friendship. Now my friendship consists of three things, my purse, my sword, and my life. Now, what about Diana?"

"I wished to ask if you were not coming to Méridor."

"My dear friend, I thank you, but you know my scruples."

"I know all. At Méridor you fear to meet Monsoreau, although he is eighty leagues off; fear to have to shake his hand, and it is hard to shake the hand of the man you wish to strangle; you fear to see him embrace Diana, and it is hard to see that of the woman you love."

"Ah! how well you understand!" cried Bussy, with rage; "but, my dear friend, did you not hear last night the noise of bells and guns?"

"Yes; and we wondered what it meant."

"It meant that the Duc d'Anjou arrived last night."

St. Luc jumped up. "The duke here! We heard he was imprisoned at the Louvre."

"That is just why he is now at Angers. He managed to escape through a window, and came here."

"Well?"

"Well, here is an excellent opportunity to revenge yourself for the king's persecutions. The prince has already a party, he will soon have troops, and we shall have something like a little civil war."

"Oh! oh!"

"And I reckoned on you to help us."

"Against the king?" said St. Luc, with sudden coldness.

"Not precisely against the king, but against those who fight against us."

"My dear Bussy, I came here for country air, not to fight against his majesty."

"But let me present you to monseigneur."

"Useless, my dear Bussy, I do not like Angers."

"My dear St. Luc, you will do me a great service by consenting; the duke asked me what I came here for, and, not being able to tell because of his own passion for Diana, I said that I had come to draw to his cause all the gentlemen in the Canton; I even told him I had a rendezvous with one this morning."

"Well! tell him you have seen the gentleman, and that he asks six months to consider. Listen, I will always help you to defend Diana, you shall help me to defend my wife. We will make a treaty for love, but not for politics."

"I see, I must yield to you, St. Luc, for you have the advantage over me. I want you, and you do not want me."

"On the contrary, it is I who claim your protection."

"How so?"

"Suppose the rebels besiege and sack Méridor."

The two friends laughed; then, as the duke had sent to inquire for Bussy, they separated with renewed promises of friendship, and charmed with each other.

19

Bussy went to the ducal palace, where already all the nobility of the provinces were arriving. He hastened to arrange an official reception, a repast and speeches, and having thus cut out some hours' occupation for the prince, mounted his other horse, and galloped to Méridor. The duke made some good speeches, and produced a great effect, giving himself out for a prince persecuted by the king on account of the love of the Parisians for him. When Bussy returned, it was four in the afternoon; he dismounted, and presented himself to the duke all covered with dust.

"Ah! my brave Bussy, you have been at work?"

"You see, monseigneur."

"You are very hot."

"I have ridden fast."

"Take care not to get ill again."

"There is no danger."

"Whence do you come?"

"From the environs. Is your highness content? have you had a numerous assemblage?"

"Yes, I am pretty well satisfied, but I missed some one."

"Who?"

"Your protégé, the Baron de Méridor."

Bussy changed color.

"And yet we must not neglect him," continued the duke, "he is influential here."

"You think so?"

"I am sure of it. He was the correspondent of the League at Angers, chosen by M. de Guise, and the Guises choose their men well. He must come, Bussy."

"But if he does not come?"

"I will go to him."

"To Méridor?"

"Why not?"

"Oh, why not, certainly," cried Bussy, with flashing eyes, "a prince may do anything."

"Then you think he is still angry with me?"

"How should I know?"

" You have not seen him ?"

" No."

" As one of the great men of the province, I thought——"

" I was not sufficiently fortunate in the former promises I made him to be in a hurry to present myself to him."

" Has he not attained his object ?"

" How so ?"

" He wanted his daughter to marry the count, and she has done so."

Bussy turned his back on the duke, who, at the same moment, moved towards another gentleman who entered the room. Bussy began to reflect on what the duke's projects were with regard to the baron—whether they were purely political, or whether he was still seeking to approach Diana ; but he imagined that, embroiled with his brother, banished from the Louvre, and the chief of a provincial insurrection, he had sufficiently grave interests at stake to outweigh his love fancies. He passed the night banqueting with the duke and the Angevin gentlemen, then in dancing with the Angevin ladies. It is needless to say that he was the admiration of the latter, and the hatred of the husbands, several of whom looked at him in a way which did not please him, so that, curling his mustachios, he invited three or four of them to take a walk with him by moonlight ; but his reputation had preceded him, and they all declined.

At the door Bussy found a laughing face waiting for him, which he believed to be eighty leagues off.

" Ah," cried he joyfully, " it is you, Rémy."

" Yes, monsieur."

" I was going to write to you to join me."

" Really !"

" On my word."

" That is capital ; I was afraid you would scold me."

" For what ?"

" For coming without leave. But I heard that Monsieur le Duc d'Anjou had escaped, and had fled here. I knew you were here also, and I thought there might be civil war, and many holes made in skins, so I came."

" You did well, Rémy ; I wanted you."

" How is Gertrude, monsieur ? "

" I will ask Diana the first time I see her."

" And, in return, every time I see her I will ask for news of Madame de Monsoreau."

" You are charming."

Meanwhile they had reached Bussy's lodging.

" Here is my palace ; you must lodge as you can."

" It will not be difficult ; I could sleep standing, I am so tired."

. Bussy rose early the next morning, and went to the ducal palace, leaving word for Rémy to follow him. The duke had prepared a list of important things to be done : firstly, a walk round the walls to examine the fortifications ; secondly, a review of the inhabitants and their arms ; thirdly, a visit to the arsenal ; fourthly, correspondence.

" Ah !" cried the duke, " you already !"

" Ma foi ! yes, monseigneur ; I could not sleep, your highness's interests were so much on my mind. What shall we do this morning ? Shall we hunt ?"

" How !" said the duke, " you pretend to have been thinking all night of my interests, and the result of so much meditation is to propose to me a hunt !"

" True," said Bussy ; " besides, we have no hounds."

" And no chief huntsman."

" Ah, ma foi ! the chase would be more agreeable without him."

" Ah, I am not like you—I want him ; he would have been very useful to us here."

" How so ? "

" He has property here."

" He !"

" He or his wife."

Bussy bit his lips.

" Méridor is only three leagues off, you know that," continued the duke, " you, who brought the old baron to me."

" Dame ! I brought him because he hung on to my cloak. However, my protection did not do him much good."

"Listen," said the duke, "I have an idea."

"Diable!" said Bussy, who was always suspicious of the duke's ideas.

"Yes; it is that, if Monsoreau had the advantage over you at first, you shall have it now."

"What do you mean?"

"It is very simple; you know me, Bussy?"

"I have that misfortune."

"Think you I am the man to submit to an affront with impunity?"

"Explain yourself, monseigneur."

"Well, he stole the young girl I loved to make her his wife; now I will steal his wife!"

Bussy tried to smile, but made a grimace instead. "Steal his wife!" stammered he.

"Nothing more easy, she is here, and you told me she hated her husband; therefore, without too much vanity, I may flatter myself she will give me the preference, if I promise her——"

"What, monseigneur?"

"To get rid of her husband for her."

"You will do that?"

"You shall see. Meanwhile I will pay a visit to Méridor."

"You will dare?"

"Why not?"

"You will present yourself before the old baron, whom you abandoned after promising me——"

"I have an excellent excuse to give him."

"Where the devil will you find it?"

"Oh! I will say to him, I did not break this marriage, because Monsoreau, who knew that you were one of the principal agents to the League, threatened to denounce you to the king."

"Has your highness invented that?"

"Not entirely."

"Then I understand."

"Yes, I shall make him believe that by marrying his daughter I saved his life."

"It is superb."

"Well! order the horses, and we will go to Méridor."

"Immediately, monseigneur." Bussy then went to the door, but turned back and said, ' How many horses will your highness have ?"

"Oh, four or five, what you like."

"If you leave it to me, I shall take a hundred."

"What for ?" cried the prince, surprised.

"To have at least twenty-five I can rely on in case of attack."

"Attack !"

"Yes, I have heard that there are thick woods in that neighborhood, and it would not surprise me if we fell into some ambush."

"Ah, do you think so ?"

"Monseigneur knows that true courage does not exclude prudence; I will order one hundred and fifty." And he moved towards the door.

"A moment," said the prince. "Do you think I am in safety at Angers ?"

"Why, the town is not very strong, but well defended——"

"Yes, but it may be badly defended; however brave you are, you can be but in one place at a time."

"True."

"Then if I am not in safety here—and I am not if Bussy doubts——"

"I did not say I doubted."

"If I am not safe, I had better make myself so. I will go to the castle and entrench myself."

"You are right, monseigneur."

"And then another idea."

"The morning is fruitful."

"I will make the Méridors come here."

"Monseigneur, you are grand to-day. Now let us visit the castle."

Bussy went out while the prince was getting ready, and found Rémy waiting. He wrote hastily a little note, picked a bunch of roses from the conservatory, rolled the note round the stems, went to the stable, brought out his horse, and, putting Rémy on it, and giving him the bouquet, led him out of the city.

"Now," said he, "let Roland go; at the end of this road you will find the forest, in the forest a park, round the park a wall, and at that part of the wall where Roland stops, throw over this bouquet."

"He whom you expect does not come," said the note, "because he who was not expected has come, and is more menacing than ever, for he loves still. Take with the lips and the heart all that is invisible to the eyes in this paper."

In half an hour Rémy reached his destination, carried by his horse, and threw over the bouquet; a little cry from the other side told him it had been received. Then Rémy returned, in spite of his horse, which seemed much put out at losing its accustomed repast on the acorns. Rémy joined Bussy as he was exploring a cave with the prince.

"Well," said he to his messenger, "what did you hear or see?"

"A wall, a cry, seven leagues," replied Rémy laconically.

CHAPTER LVIII.

A FLIGHT OF ANGEVINS.

BUSSY contrived to occupy the duke so well with his preparations for war during two days, that he found no time to think of Méridor, and from time to time, under pretext of examining the outer fortifications, jumped on Roland, and arrived at a certain wall, which he got over all the more quickly because each time he made some stone fall, and was, in fact, gradually making a breach.

Towards the end of the third day, as an enormous convoy of provisions was entering the city, the produce of a tax levied by the duke on his good Angevins, as M. d'Anjou, to make himself popular, was tasting the black bread and salt fish of the soldiers, they heard a great noise at one of the gates of the city, where a man, mounted on a white horse, had presented himself. Now Bussy had had himself named Captain-General of Anjou, and had established the most severe discipline in Angers; no one could go out of or enter the town without a password; all which had no other aim than to prevent the duke from sending a messenger to Méridor without his knowledge.

The man on the white horse had arrived at a furious gallop, and had attempted to enter, but had been stopped.

"I am Antragues," said he, "and desire to speak to the Duc d'Anjou."

"We do not know Antragues," they replied, "but as for seeing the duke, you shall be satisfied, for we shall arrest you, and conduct you to him."

"You are a nice fellow, truly, to talk of arresting Charles Balzac d'Antragues, Baron de Cuneo, and Comte de Graville."

"We will do so, however," replied the bourgeois, who had twenty men behind him.

"Wait a little, my good friends. You do not know the Parisians. Well, I will show you a specimen of what they can do."

"Let us arrest him!" cried the furious militia.

"Softly, my little lambs of Anjou; it is I who will have that pleasure."

"What does he say?" asked the bourgeois.

"He says that his horse has only gone ten leagues, and will ride over you all." And drawing his sword and swinging it furiously round, he cut off in his passage the blades of the nearest halberts, and in less than ten minutes fifteen or twenty of them were changed into broom-handles.

"Ah! this is very amusing!" cried he, laughing, and as he spoke stunning one of the bourgeois with a blow on the head with the flat of his sword. However, as more and more bourgeois crowded to the attack, and Antragues began to feel tired, he said, "Well, you are as brave as lions; I will bear witness to it; but, you see, you have nothing left but the handles of your halberts, and you do not know how to load your muskets. I had resolved to enter the city, but I did not know it was guarded by an army of Cæsars. I renounce my victory over you. Good evening, I am going away; only tell the prince that I came here expressly to see him."

However, the captain had managed to communicate the fire to the match of his musket, but just as he was raising it to his shoulder, Antragues gave him such a furious blow upon the fingers that he dropped it.

"Kill him! kill him!" cried several voices, "do not let him escape!"

"Ah!" said Antragues, "just now you would not let me come in, now you will not let me go out. Take care, that will change my tactics, and instead of the flat of my sword, I will use the point—instead of cutting the halberts, I will cut the wrists. Now, will you let me go?"

"No, no, he is tired, kill him!"

"Well, then, take care of your hands!"

Scarcely had he spoken when another cavalier appeared, riding furiously also, and who cried out as he approached:

"Antragues, what are you doing among all these bourgeois?"

"Livarot!" cried Antragues. "Mon Dieu, you are welcome; Montjoie and St. Denis, to the rescue!"

"I heard four hours ago that you were before me, and I have been trying to catch you. But what is the matter; do they want to massacre you?"

"Yes, they will neither let me in nor out."

"Gentlemen!" said Livarot, "will you please to step either to the right or left, and let us pass."

"They insult us! kill them!" cried the people.

"Oh! this is Angers' manners!" said Livarot, drawing his sword.

"Yes, you see; unluckily, there are so many of them."

"If there were but three of us!"

"And here is Ribeirac coming."

"Do you hear him?"

"I see him. Here, Ribeirac!"

"Are you fighting?" cried Ribeirac.

"Good morning, Livarot; good morning, Antragues."

"Let us charge them," said Antragues.

The bourgeois looked in stupefaction at this reinforcement that was about to join the attacking party.

"They are a regiment," said the captain of the militia.

"This is only the advanced guard," cried another.

"We are fathers of families, and our lives belong to our children," said others, and they all tried to fly, fighting with each other to get out of the way.

At this stage of the affair Bussy and the prince arrived, followed by twenty cavaliers, to ascertain the cause of the tumult. They were told that it was three incarnate devils from Paris who were making all the disturbance.

"Three men, Bussy; see who they are."

Bussy raised himself in his stirrups, and his quick eye soon recognized Livarot.

"Mort de ma vie, monseigneur," cried he, "they are our friends from Paris who are besieging us."

"No!" cried Livarot, "on the contrary, it is these people who are killing us."

"Down with your arms, knaves," cried the duke, "these are friends."

"Friends!" cried the bourgeois, "then they should have had the password; for we have been treating them like Pagans and they us like Turks."

Livarot, Antragues, and Ribeirac advanced in triumph to kiss the duke's hand.

"Monseigneur," said Bussy, "how many militia do you think there were here?"

"At least one hundred and fifty."

"You have not very famous soldiers, since three men beat them."

"True, but I shall have the three men who did beat them."

CHAPTER LIX.

ROLAND.

THANKS to the reinforcement which had arrived, M. le Duc d'Anjou could go where he pleased; he explored the ramparts of the surrounding country and castles. The Angévin gentlemen found liberty and amusement at the court of the duke, and the three friends were soon intimate with many of these nobles, especially those who had pretty wives. The general joy was at its height when twenty-two riding horses, thirty carriage horses, and forty mules, together with litters, carriages and wagons, arrived at Angers, all the property of the duke. We must allow that the saddles were not paid for, and that the coffers were empty, but still it made a magnificent effect. The duke's reputation for wealth was henceforward solidly established, and all the province remained convinced that he was rich enough to war against all Europe if need were, therefore they did not grudge the new tax which the prince imposed upon them. People never mind giving or lending to rich people, only to poor ones; therefore the worthy prince lived like a patriarch on all the fat of the land. Numerous cavaliers arrived to offer to him their adhesions, or their offers of service. One afternoon, however, about four o'clock, M. de Monsoreau arrived on horseback at the gates of Angers. He had ridden eighteen leagues that day; therefore his spurs were red, and his horse covered with foam, and half dead. They no longer made difficulties about letting strangers enter, therefore M. de Monsoreau went straight through the city to the palace, and asked for the duke.

"He is out reconnoitering," replied the sentinel.

"Where?"

"I do not know."

"Diable! What I have to say to him is very pressing."

"First put your horse in the stable, or he will fall."

" The advice is good ; where are the stables ? "

" As he spoke a man approached and asked for his name.
M. de Monsoreau gave it. The major-domo (for it was
he) bowed respectfully, for the chief huntsman's name
was well known in Anjou.

" Monsieur," said he, " please to enter and take some
repose. Monseigneur has not been out more than ten
minutes, and will not be back till eight o'clock."

" Eight o'clock ! I cannot wait so long ; I am the bearer
of news which cannot be too soon known to his highness.
Can I not have a horse and a guide ? "

" There are plenty of horses, but a guide is a different
thing, for his highness did not say where he was going."

" Well, I will take a fresh horse, and try to discover
him."

" Probably you will hear where he has passed, monsieur."

" Do they ride fast ? "

" Oh no."

" Well, get me a horse then."

" Will monsieur come into the stables and choose one ?
they all belong to the duke." Monsoreau entered. Ten
or twelve fine horses, quite fresh, were feeding from the
manger, which was filled with grain.

Monsoreau looked over them, and then said, "I will
take this bay." .

" Roland ? "

" Is that his name ? "

" Yes, and it is his highness's favorite horse. M. de
Bussy gave him to the duke, and it is quite a chance that
it is here to-day."

Ronald was soon saddled, and Monsoreau rode out of
the stable.

" In which direction did they start ? " asked he.

The man pointed it out.

" Ma foi ! " said Monsoreau, " the horse seems to know
the way."

Indeed, the animal set off without being urged, and
went deliberately out of the city, took a short cut to the
gate, and then began to accelerate his pace : Monsoreau

let him go. He went along the boulevard, then turned into a shady lane, which cut across the country, passing gradually from a trot to a gallop.

"Oh!" thought Monsoreau, as they entered the woods, "one would say we were going to Méridor. Can his highness be there?" and his face grew black at the thought.

"Oh!" murmured he, "I who was going to see the prince, and putting off till to-morrow to see my wife, shall I see them both at the same time?"

The horse went on, turning always to the right.

"We cannot be far from the park," said he.

At that moment his horse neighed, and another answered him. In a minute Monsoreau saw a wall, and a horse tied to a neighboring tree.

"There is some one," thought he, turning pale.

CHAPTER LX.

WHAT M. DE MONSOREAU CAME TO ANNOUNCE.

As M. de Monsoreau approached, he remarked the dilapidation of the wall; it was almost in steps, and the brambles had been torn away, and were lying about. He looked at the horse standing there. The animal had a saddle-cloth embroidered in silver, and in one corner an F. and an A. There was no doubt, then, that it came from the prince's stables; the letters stood for François d'Anjou. The count's suspicions at this sight became real alarm; the duke had come here, and had come often, for, besides the horse waiting there, there was a second that knew the way. He tied up his horse near to the other, and began to scale the wall. It was an easy task; there were places for both feet and hands, and the branches of an oak-tree, which hung over, had been carefully cut away. Once up, he saw at the foot of a tree a blue mantilla and a black cloak, and not far off a man and woman, walking hand in hand, with their backs turned to the wall, and nearly hidden by the trees. Unluckily, with

M. de Monsoreau's weight a stone fell from the wall on
the crackling branches with a great noise.

At this noise the lovers must have turned and seen him,
for the cry of a woman was heard, and a rustling of the
branches as they ran away like startled deer. At this cry,
Monsoreau felt cold drops on his forehead, for he recognized Diana's voice. Full of fury, he jumped over the
wall, and with his drawn sword in his hand, tried to follow the fugitives, but they had disappeared, and there
was not a trace or a sound to guide him. He stopped,
and considered that he was too much under the influence
of passion to act with prudence against so powerful a
rival. Then a sublime idea occurred to him; it was to
climb back again over the wall, and carry off with his own
the horse he had seen there. He retraced his steps to the
wall and climbed up again; but on the other side no horse
was to be seen; his idea was so good, that before it came
to him it had come to his adversary. He uttered a howl
of rage, clenching his fists, but started off at once on foot.
In two hours and a half, he arrived at the gates of the city,
dying with hunger and fatigue, but determined to interrogate every sentinel, and find out by what gate a man
had entered with two horses. The first sentinel he ap-
plied to said that, about two hours before, a horse without a rider had passed through the gate, and had taken
the road to the palace; he feared some accident must have
happened to his rider. Monsoreau ground his teeth with
passion, and went on to the castle. There he found great
life and gaiety, windows lighted up, and animation everywhere. He went first to the stable, and found his horse
in the stall he had taken him from; then, without chang-
ing his dress, he went to the dining-room. The prince
and all his gentlemen were sitting round a table magnificently served and lighted. The duke, who had been told
of his arrival, received him without surprise, and told him
to sit down and sup with him.

"Monseigneur," replied he, "I am hungry, tired, and
thirsty; but I will neither eat, drink, nor sit down till I
have delivered my important message."

" You come from Paris ? "

" Yes, in great haste."

" Well, speak."

Monsoreau advanced, with a smile on his lips and hatred in his heart, and said, " Monseigneur, your mother is advancing hastily to visit you."

The duke looked delighted. " It is well," said he; " M. de Monsoreau, I find you to-day, as ever, a faithful servant ; let us continue our supper, gentlemen."

Monsoreau sat down with them, but gloomy and preoccupied. He still seemed to see the two figures among the trees, and to hear the cry of Diana.

" You are overcome with weariness," said the prince to him, " really, you had better go to bed."

" Yes," said Livarot, " or he will go to sleep in his chair."

" Pardon, monseigneur, I am tired out."

" Get tipsy," said Antragues ; " there is nothing so good when you are tired. To your health, count ! "

" You must give us some good hunts," said Ribeirac, " you know the country."

" You have horses and woods here," said Antragues.

" And a wife," added Livarot.

" We will hunt a boar, count," said the prince.

" Oh, yes, to-morrow ! " cried the gentlemen.

" What do you say, Monsoreau ? "

" I am always at your highness's orders, but I am too much fatigued to conduct a chase to-morrow; besides which, I must examine the woods."

" And we must leave him time to see his wife," cried the duke.

" Granted," cried the young men ; " we give him twenty-four hours to do all he has to do."

" Yes, gentlemen, I promise to employ them well."

" Now go to bed," said the duke, and M. de Monsoreau bowed, and went out, very happy to escape.

CHAPTER LXI.

HOW THE KING LEARNED THE FLIGHT OF HIS BELOVED BROTHER, AND WHAT FOLLOWED.

WHEN Monsoreau had retired, the repast continued, and was more gay and joyous than ever.

"Now, Livarot," said the duke, "finish the recital of your flight from Paris, which Monsoreau interrupted."

Livarot began again, but as our title of historian gives us the privilege of knowing better than Livarot himself what had passed, we will substitute our recital for that of the young man.

Towards the middle of the night Henri III. was awoke by an unaccustomed noise in the palace. It was oaths, blows on the wall, rapid steps in the galleries, and, amidst all, these words continually sounding, "What will the king say?"

Henri sat up and called Chicot, who was asleep on the couch.

Chicot opened one eye.

"Ah, you were wrong to call me, Henri," said he; "I was dreaming that you had a son."

"But listen."

"To what? You say enough follies to me by day, without breaking in on my nights."

"But do you not hear?"

"Oh, oh! I do hear cries."

"Do you hear, 'What will the king say?'"

"It is one of two things—either your dog Narcissus is ill, or the Huguenots are taking their revenge for St. Bartholomew."

"Help me to dress."

"If you will first help me to get up."

"What a misfortune!" sounded from the antechamber.

"Shall we arm ourselves?" said the king.

"We had better go first and see what is the matter."

And almost immediately they went out by the secret door into the gallery. "I begin to guess," said Chicot; "your unlucky prisoner has hanged himself."

"Oh, no; it cannot be that."

"So much the worse."

"Come on;" and they entered the duke's chamber.

The window was open, and the ladder still hung from it. Henri grew as pale as death.

"Oh, my son, you are not so blasé as I thought!" said Chicot.

"Escaped!" cried Henri, in such a thundering voice that all the gentlemen who were crowded round the window turned in terror. Schomberg tore his hair, Quelus and Maugiron struck themselves like madmen; as for D'Epernon, he had vanished. This sight calmed the king.

"Gently, my son," said he, laying hold of Maugiron.

"No! mordieu!" cried he, "I will kill myself!" and he knocked his head against the wall.

"Hola! help me to hold him."

"It would be an easier death to pass your sword through your body!" said Chicot.

"Quelus, my child," said the king, "you will be as blue as Schomberg when he came out of the indigo."

Quelus stopped, but Schomberg still continued to tear at his hair.

"Schomberg, Schomberg, a little reason, I beg."

"It is enough to drive one mad!"

"Indeed, it is a dreadful misfortune; there will be a civil war in my kingdom. Who did it—who furnished the ladder? Mordieu! I will hang all the city! Who was it? Ten thousand crowns to whoever will tell me his name, and one hundred thousand to whoever will bring him to me, dead or alive!"

"It must have been some Angevin," said Maugiron.

"Oh yes! we will kill all the Angevins!" cried Quelus.

However, the king suddenly disappeared; he had thought of his mother, and, without saying a word, went to her. When he entered, she was half lying in a great armchair. She heard the news without answering.

20

"You say nothing, mother. Does not this flight seem
to you criminal, and worthy of punishment?"

"My dear son, liberty is worth as much as a crown;
and remember, I advised you to fly in order to gain a
crown."

"My mother, he braves me—he outrages me!"

"No; he only saves himself."

"Ah! this is how you take my part."

"What do you mean, my son?"

"I mean that with age the feelings grow calm—that
you do not love me as much as you used to do."

"You are wrong, my son," said Catherine coldly;
"you are my beloved son, but he of whom you complain
is also my son."

"Well, then, madame, I will go to find other counselors capable of feeling for me and of aiding me."

"Go, my son; and may God guide your counselors,
for they will have need of it to aid you in this strait."

"Adieu, then, madame!"

"Adieu, Henri! I do not pretend to counsel you—you
do not need me, I know—but beg your counselors to reflect well before they advise, and still more before they
execute."

"Yes, madame, for the position is difficult."

"Very grave," replied she, raising her eyes to heaven.
"Have you any idea who it was that carried him off?"
Catherine did not reply.

"I think it was the Angevins," continued the king.
Catherine smiled scornfully.

"The Angevins!"

"You do not think so?"

"Do you, really?"

"Tell me what you think, madame."

"Why should I?"

"To enlighten me."

"Enlighten you! I am but a doting old woman, whose
only influence lies in her prayers and repentance."

"No, mother; speak, you are the cleverest of us
all."

"Useless; I have only ideas of the last century; at my age it is impossible I should give good counsel."

"Well, then, mother, refuse me your counsel, deprive me of your aid. In an hour I will hang all the Angevins in Paris."

"Hang all the Angevins!" cried Catherine, in amazement.

"Yes, hang, slay, massacre, burn; already, perhaps, my friends are out to begin the work."

"They will ruin themselves, and you with them."

"How so?"

"Blind! Will kings eternally have eyes, and not see?"

"Kings must avenge their injuries, it is but justice, and in this case all my subjects will rise to defend me."

"You are mad."

"Why so?"

"You will make oceans of blood flow. The standard of revolt will soon be raised; and you will arm against you a host who never would rise for François."

"But if I do not revenge myself they will think I am afraid."

"Did any one ever think I was afraid? Besides, it was not the Angevins."

"Who was it then? it must have been my brother's friends."

"Your brother has no friends."

"But who was it then?"

"Your enemy."

"What enemy?"

"O! my son, you know you have never had but one; yours, mine, your brother Charles's; always the same."

"Henri of Navarre, you mean?"

"Yes, Henri of Navarre."

"He is not at Paris."

"Do you know who is at Paris, and who is not? No, you are all deaf and blind."

"Can it have been he?"

"My son, at every disappointment you meet with, at

every misfortune that happens to you of which the author
is unknown, do not seek or conjecture ; it is useless. Cry
out, it is Henri of Navarre, and you will be sure to be
right. Strike on the side where he is, and you will be
sure to strike right.   Oh ! that man, that man ; he is the
sword suspended over the head of the Valois."

"Then you think I should countermand my orders
about the Angevins ? "

" At once, without losing an instant.   Hasten ; perhaps
you are already too late."

Henry flew out of the Louvre to find his friends, but
found only Chicot drawing figures in the sand with a stone.

CHAPTER LXII.

HOW, AS CHICOT AND THE QUEEN MOTHER WERE AGREED, THE KING BEGAN TO AGREE WITH THEM.

"Is this how you defend your king ? " cried Henri.

"Yes, it is my manner, and I think it is a good one."

"Good, indeed ! "

" I maintain it, and I will prove it."

" I am curious to hear this proof."

"It is easy ; but first, we have committed a great folly."

" How so ? " cried Henri, struck by the agreement between Chicot and his mother.

"Yes," replied Chicot, "your friends are crying
through the city, 'Death to the Angevins ! ' and now that
I reflect, it was never proved that they had anything to do
with the affair.   And your friends, crying thus through
the city, will raise that nice little civil war of which MM.
de Guise have so much need, and which they did not
succeed in raising for themselves.   Besides which, your
friends may get killed, which would not displease me, I
confess, but which would afflict you, or else they will
chase all the Angevins from the city, which will please
M. d'Anjou enormously."

"Do you think things are so bad?"

"Yes, if not worse.

"But all this does not explain what you do here, sitting on a stone."

"I am tracing a plan of all the provinces that your brother will raise against you, and the number of men each will furnish to the revolt."

"Chicot, Chicot, you are a bird of bad augury."

"The owl sings at night, my son, it is his hour. Now it is dark, Henri, so dark that one might take the day for the night, and I sing what you ought to hear. Look!"

"At what?"

"My geographical plan. Here is Anjou, something like a tartlet, you see; there your brother will take refuge. Anjou, well managed, as Monsoreau and Bussy will manage it, will alone furnish to your brother ten thousand combatants."

"Do you think so?"

"That is the minimum; let us pass to Guyenne; here it is, this figure like a calf walking on one leg. Of course, you will not be astonished to find discontent in Guyenne; it is an old focus for revolt, and will be enchanted to rise. They can furnish 8,000 soldiers; that is not much, but they are well trained. Then we have Béarn and Navarre; you see these two compartments, which look like an ape on the back of an elephant—they may furnish about 16,000. Let us count now—10,000 for Anjou, 8,000 for Guyenne, 16,000 for Béarn and Navarre; making a total of 34,000."

"You think, then, that the King of Navarre will join my brother?"

"I should think so."

"Do you believe that he had anything to do with my brother's escape?"

Chicot looked at him. "That is not your own idea, Henri."

"Why not?"

"It is too clever, my son."

"Never mind whose idea it was; answer my question."

"Well! I heard a 'Ventre St. Gris' in the Rue de la Ferronnerie."

"You heard a 'Ventre St. Gris!' But it might not have been he."

"I saw him."

"You saw Henri of Navarre in Paris?"

"Yes."

"You saw my mortal enemy here, and did not tell me?"

"I am not a spy. Then there are the Guises; 20,000 or 25,000 men under the orders of the Duc de Guise will make up altogether a nice little army."

"But Henri of Navarre and the Duc de Guise are enemies."

"Which will not prevent them from uniting against you; they will be free to fight with each other when they have conquered you."

"You are right, Chicot, and my mother is right. I will call the Swiss."

"Oh, yes! Quelus has got them."

'My guards, then."

"Schomberg has them."

"My household at least."

"They have gone with Maugiron."

"Without my orders?"

"And when do you ever give orders, except, perhaps, to flagellate either your own skin, or that of others?—But about government.—Bah! allow me to observe that you have been a long time finding out that you rank seventh or eighth in this kingdom."

"Here they are!" cried the king, as three cavaliers approached, followed by a crowd of men on foot and on horseback.

"Schomberg! Quelus! come here," cried the king.

They approached.

"I have been seeking you, and waiting for you impatiently. What have you done? Do not go away again without my permission."

"There is no more need," said Maugiron, who now approached, "since all is finished."

" All is finished ? "

" Heaven be praised," said D'Epernon, appearing all at once, no one knew from whence.

" Then you have killed them ? " cried the king ; " well, at least the dead do not return."

" Oh ! we had not that trouble ; the cowards ran away, we had scarcely time to cross our swords with them."

Henri grew pale. " With whom ? " said he.

" With Antragues ? "

" On the contrary, he killed a lackey of Quelus's."

" Oh ! " murmured the king, " here is a civil war lighted up."

Quelus started. " It is true," said he.

" Ah " said Chicot. " You begin to perceive it, do you ? "

" But, M. Chicot, you cried with us, ' Death to the Angevins ! ' "

" Oh ! that is a different thing ; I am a fool, and you are clever men."

" Come, peace, gentlemen ; we shall have enough of war soon."

" What are your majesty's orders ? "

" That you employ the same ardor in calming the people as you have done in exciting them, and that you bring back all the Swiss, my guards, and my household, and have the doors of the Louvre closed, so that perhaps to-morrow the bourgeois may take the whole thing for a sortie of drunken people."

The young men went off, and Henri returned to his mother.

" Well," said she, " what has passed ? "

" All you foresaw, mother."

" They have escaped ? "

" Alas ! yes."

" What else ? "

" Is not that enough ? "

" The city ? "

" Is in tumult ; but that is not what disquiets me."

" No, it is the provinces."

"Which will revolt."

"What shall you do?"

"I see but one thing."

"What is that?"

"To withdraw the army from La Charité, and march on Anjou."

"And M. de Guise?"

"Oh, I will arrest him if necessary."

"And you think violent measures will succeed?"

"What can I do, then?"

"Your plan will not do."

"Well, what is your idea?"

"Send an ambassador."

"To whom?"

"To your brother."

"An ambassador to that traitor! You humiliate me, mother."

"This is not a moment to be proud."

"An ambassador will ask for peace?"

"Who will buy it if necessary."

"With what? mon Dieu!"

"If it were only to secure quietly, afterwards, those who have gone to make war on you."

"I would give much for that."

"Well, then, the end is worth the means."

"I believe you are right, mother; but whom shall I send?"

"Seek among your friends."

"My mother, I do not know a single man to whom I could confide such a mission."

"Confide it to a woman, then."

"My mother, would you consent?"

"My son, I am very old, and very weak, and death will perhaps await me on my return; but I will make this journey so rapidly that your brother and his friends will not have had time to learn their own power."

"Oh, my good mother!" cried Henri, kissing her hands, "you are my support, my benefactress!"

"That means that I am still Queen of France," murmured she.

CHAPTER LXIII.

IN WHICH IT IS PROVED THAT GRATITUDE WAS ONE OF ST. LUC'S VIRTUES.

THE next morning, M. de Monsoreau rose early, and descended into the courtyard of the palace. He entered the stable, where Roland was in his place.

"Are the horses of monseigneur taught to return to their stable alone?" asked he of the man who stood there.

"No, M. le Comte."

"But Roland did so yesterday."

"Oh, he is remarkably intelligent."

"Has he ever done it before?"

"No, monsieur; he is generally ridden by the Duc d'Anjou, who is a good rider, and never gets thrown."

"I was not thrown," replied the count, "for I also am a good rider; no, I tied him to a tree while I entered a house, and at my return he had disappeared. I thought he had been stolen, or that some passer-by had played a bad joke by carrying him away; that was why I asked how he returned to the stable."

"He returned alone, as monsieur said just now."

"It is strange. Monseigneur often rides this horse, you say?"

"Nearly every day."

"His highness returned late last night?"

"About an hour before you."

"And what horse did he ride? was it a bay with a white star on his forehead?"

"No, monsieur, he rode Isolin, which you see here."

"And in the prince's escort is there any one who rides such a horse as I describe?"

"I know of no one."

"Well," said Monsoreau, impatiently, "saddle me Roland."

" Roland ? "

" Yes, are there any orders against it ? "

" No ; on the contrary, I was told to let you have any horse you pleased."

When Roland was saddled, Monsoreau said to the man, " What are your wages ? "

" Twenty crowns, monsieur."

" Will you earn ten times that sum at once ? "

" I ask no better.   But how ? "

" Find out who rode yesterday the horse I described."

" Ah, monsieur, what you ask is very difficult, there are so many gentlemen come here."

" Yes, but two hundred crowns are worth some trouble."

" Certainly, M. le Comte, and I will do my best to discover."

" That is right, and here are ten crowns to encourage you."

" Thanks, M. le Comte."

" Well, tell the prince I have gone to reconnoiter the wood for the chase."

As he spoke he heard steps behind him, and turned. " Ah, M. de Bussy ! " he cried.

" Why, M. le Comte, who would have thought of seeing you here ! "

" And you, who they said was so ill."

" So I am ; my doctor orders absolute rest, and for a week I have not left the city.   Ah ! you are going to ride Roland; I sold him to the duke, who is very fond of him."

" Yes, he is an excellent animal ; I rode him yesterday."

" Which makes you wish for him again to-day ? "

" Yes."

" You were speaking of a chase."

" Yes, the prince wishes for one."

" Whereabouts is it to be ? "

" Near Méridor.   Will you come with me ? "

" No, thank you, I do not feel well."

" Oh ! " cried a voice from behind, " there is M. de Bussy out without permission."

"Ah! there is my doctor scolding. Adieu, comte."

Bussy went away, and Monsoreau jumped into the saddle.

"What is the matter?" said Rémy; "you look so pale, I believe you are really ill."

"Do you know where he is going?"

"No."

"To Méridor."

"Well, did you hope he would not?"

"Mon Dieu! what will happen, after what he saw yesterday?"

"Madame de Monsoreau will deny everything."

"But he saw her."

"She will say he did not."

"She will never have the courage."

"Oh, M. de Bussy, is it possible you do not know women better than that!"

"Rémy, I feel very ill."

"So I see. Go home, and I will prescribe for you."

"What?"

"A slice of fowl and ham, and some lobster."

"Oh, I am not hungry."

"The more reason I should order you to eat."

"Rémy, I fear that that wretch will make a great scene at Méridor. I ought to have gone with him when he asked me."

"What for?"

"To sustain Diana."

"Oh, she will sustain herself. Besides, you ought not to be out; we agreed you were too ill."

"I could not help it, Rémy, I was so unquiet."

Rémy carried him off, and made him sit down to a good breakfast.

M. de Monsoreau wished to see if it were chance or habit that had led Roland to the park wall; therefore he left the bridle on his neck. Roland took precisely the same road as on the previous day, and before very long M. de Monsoreau found himself in the same spot as before. Only now the place was solitary, and no horse was there. The count climbed the wall again, but no one was to be

seen ; therefore, judging that it was useless to watch for
people on their guard, he went on to the park gates. The
baron, seeing his son-in-law coming over the drawbridge,
advanced ceremoniously to meet him. Diana, seated
under a magnificent sycamore, was reading poetry, while
Gertrude was embroidering at her side. The count, seeing them, got off his horse, and approached them.

"Madame," said he, "will you grant me the favor of
an interview ? "

"Willingly, monsieur."

"What calm, or rather what perfidy!" thought the
count.

"Do you do us the honor of remaining at the chât   ?"
asked the baron.

"Yes, monsieur, until to-morrow, at least."

The baron went away to give orders, and Diana reseated
herself, while Monsoreau took Gertrude's chair, and, with
a look sufficient to intimidate most people, said :

"Madame, who was in the park with you yesterday ?"

"At what time ?" said Diana, in a firm voice.

"At six."

"Where ?"

"Near the copse."

"It must have been some one else, it was not I."

"It was you, madame."

"What do you know about it ?"

"Tell me the man's name !" cried Monsoreau, furiously.

"What man ?"

"The man who was walking with you."

"I cannot tell, if it was some other woman."

"It was you, I tell you."

"You are wrong, monsieur."

"How dare you deny it ? I saw you."

"You, monsieur ?"

"Yes, madame, myself. And there is no other lady
here."

"You are wrong again ; there is Jeanne de Brissac."

"Madame de St. Luc ?"

"Yes, my friend."

"And M. de St. Luc ?"

"Never leaves her; theirs was a love-match; you must have seen them."

"It was not them; it was you, with some man whom I do not know, but whom I will know, I swear. I heard your cry."

"When you are more reasonable, monsieur, I shall be ready to hear you; at present I will retire."

"No, madame, you shall stay."

"Monsieur, here are M. and Madame de St. Luc, I trust you will contain yourself."

Indeed, M. and Madame de St. Luc approached. She bowed to Monsoreau, and St. Luc gave him his hand; then, leaving his wife to Monsoreau, took Diana, and after a walk they returned, warned by the bell for dinner, which was early at Méridor, as the baron preserved the old customs. The conversation was general, and turned naturally on the Duc d'Anjou, and the movement his arrival had caused. Diana sat far from her husband, between St. Luc and the baron.

CHAPTER LXIV.

THE PROJECT OF M. DE ST. LUC.

WHEN the repast was over, Monsoreau took St. Luc's arm and went out. "Do you know," said he, "that I am very happy to have found you here, for the solitude of Méridor frightened me."

"What, with your wife? As for me, with such a companion I should find a desert delightful."

"I do not say no, but still——"

"Still, what?"

"I am very glad to have met you here."

"Really, monsieur, you are very polite, for I cannot believe that you could possibly fear ennui with such a companion, and such a country."

"Bah! I pass half my life in the woods."

"The more reason for being fond of them, it seems to

me. I know I shall be very sorry to leave them ; unluckily, I fear I shall be forced to do so before long."

" Why so ? "

" Oh ! monsieur, when is man the arbiter of his own destiny ? He is like the leaf of the tree, which the wind blows about. You are very fortunate."

" Fortunate ; how ? "

" To live amongst these splendid trees."

" Oh ! I do not think I shall stay here long ; I am not so fond of nature, and I fear these woods ; I think they are not safe."

" Why ? on account of their loneliness, do you mean ? "

" No, not that, for I suppose you see friends here."

" Not a soul."

" Ah ! really. How long is it since you had any visitor ? "

" Not since I have been here."

" Not one gentleman from the court at Angers ? "

" Not one."

" Impossible."

" It is true."

" Then I am wrong."

" Perfectly ; but why is not the park safe, are there bears here ? "

" Oh, no."

" Wolves ? "

" No."

" Robbers ? "

" Perhaps. Tell me, monsieur, Madame de St. Luc seemed to me very pretty ; is she not ? "

" Why, yes."

" Does she often walk in the park ? "

" Often ; she adores the woods, like myself."

" And do you accompany her ? "

" Always."

" Nearly always ? "

" What the devil are you driving at ? "

" Oh ; mon Dieu, nothing ; or, at least, a trifle."

" I listen."

"They told me——"

"Well?"

"You will not be angry?"

"I never am so."

"Besides, between husbands, these confidences are right; they told me a man had been seen wandering in the park."

"A man."

"Yes."

"Who came for my wife?"

"Oh! I do not say that."

"You would be wrong not to tell me, my dear Monsoreau. Who saw him? pray tell me."

"Oh! to tell you the truth, I do not think it was for Madame de St. Luc that he came."

"For whom, then?"

"Ah! I fear it is for Diana."

"Oh! I should like that better."

"What?"

"Certainly; you know we husbands are an egotistical set. Every one for himself, and God for us all."

"The devil rather."

"Then you think a man entered here?"

"I think so."

"And I do more than think," said St. Luc, "for I saw him."

"You saw a man in the park?"

"Yes."

"When?"

"Yesterday."

"Alone?"

"With Madame de Monsoreau."

"Where?"

"Just here to the left." And as they had walked down to the old copse, St. Luc pointed out the spot where Bussy always came over.

"Ah!" continued he, "here is a wall in a bad state; I must warn the baron."

"Whom do you suspect?"

"Of what?"

"Of climbing over here to talk to my wife."

St. Luc seemed to reflect.

"Diable!" said he, "it could only have been——"

"Whom?"

"Why, yourself."

"Are you joking, M. de St. Luc?"

"Ma foi, no; when I was first married I did such things."

"Come! you are trying to put me off; but do not fear, I have courage. Help me to seek, you will do me an immense favor."

St. Luc shook his head. "It must have been you," said he.

"Do not jest, I beg of you; the thing is serious."

"Do you think so?"

"I am sure of it."

"Oh! and how does this man come?"

"Secretly."

"Often?"

"I fear so; look at the marks in the wall."

"Well, I suspected it, but I always fancied it was you."

"But I tell you, no!"

"Oh, I believe you, my dear sir."

"Well, then——"

"It must have been some one else."

Monsoreau began to look black, but St. Luc preserved his easy nonchalance.

"I have an idea," said he.

"Tell me."

"If it were——"

"Well!"

"But, no."

"Pray speak."

"The Duc d'Anjou."

"I thought so at first, but I have made inquiries, and it could not have been he."

"Oh! he is very cunning."

"Yes, but it was not he."

"Wait, then."

"Well!"

"I have another idea; if it was neither you nor the duke, it must have been I."

"You?"

"Why not?"

"You to come on horseback to the outside of the park, when you live inside!"

"Oh, mon Dieu! I am such a capricious being."

"You, who fled away when you saw me!"

"Oh! any one would do that."

"Then you were doing wrong," cried the count, no longer able to keep in his anger.

"I do not say so."

"You are mocking me," cried the count, growing very pale, "and have been doing so for a quarter of an hour."

"You are wrong, monsieur," said St. Luc, drawing out his watch, and looking steadily at him; "it has been twenty minutes."

"You insult me."

"And you insult me with your questions like a constable."

"Ah! now I see clearly."

"How wonderful, at ten o'clock in the morning. But what do you see?"

"I see that you act in concert with the traitor, the coward, whom I saw yesterday."

"I should think so; he is my friend."

"Then I will kill you in his place."

"Bah! in your own house, and without crying, gare. Ah! M. de Monsoreau, how badly you have been brought up, and how living among beasts spoils the manners."

"Do you not see that I am furious?" howled the count.

"Yes, indeed, I do see it, and it does not become you at all; you look frightful."

The count drew his sword.

"Ah!" said St. Luc, "you try to provoke me; you see I am perfectly calm."

31

"Yes, I do provoke you."

"Take the trouble to get over the wall; on the other side we shall be on neutral ground."

"What do I care!"

"I do; I do not want to kill you in your own house."

"Very well!" said Monsoreau, climbing over.

"Take care; pray do not hurt yourself, my dear count; those stones are loose," said St. Luc. Then he also got over.

CHAPTER LXV.

HOW M. DE ST. LUC SHOWED M. DE MONSOREAU THE THRUST THAT THE KING HAD TAUGHT HIM.

"ARE you ready?" cried Monsoreau.

"No; I have the sun in my eyes."

"Move then; I warn you I shall kill you."

"Shall you really? Well, man proposes, and God disposes. Look at that bed of poppies and dandelions."

"Well!"

"Well, I mean to lay you there." And he laughed as he drew his sword. Monsoreau began the combat furiously, but St. Luc parried his thrusts skilfully.

"Pardieu! M. de Monsoreau," said he, "you use your sword very well; you might kill any one but Bussy or me."

Monsoreau grew pale.

"As for me," continued St. Luc, "the king, who loves me, took the trouble to give me a great many lessons, and showed me, among other things, a thrust, which you shall see presently. I tell you, that you may have the pleasure of knowing you are killed by the king's method; it is very flattering." And then suddenly he rushed furiously on Monsoreau, who, half wild with rage as he was, parried five thrusts, but received the sixth full in his chest.

"Ah!" said St. Luc, "you will fall just where I told you," as Monsoreau sank down on the poppies. Then, wiping his sword, he stood quietly by, watching the changes which came over the face of the dying man.

"Ah, you have killed me!" cried Monsoreau.

"I intended to do so, but now I see you dying, devil take me if I am not sorry for what I have done. You are horribly jealous, it is true, but you were brave. Have you any last wish? If so, tell it to me; and, on the faith of a gentleman, it shall be executed. Are you thirsty? Shall I get you water?"

Monsoreau did not reply. He turned over with his face to the earth, biting the ground, and struggling in his blood. Then he tried to raise his head, but fell back with a groan.

"Come, he is dead; let me think no more about him. Ah! but that is not so easy, when you have killed a man." And jumping back over the wall, he went to the château. The first person he saw was Diana talking to his wife.

"How well she will look in black," thought he. Then, approaching them, "Pardon me," said he, "but may I say a few words to Jeanne?"

"Do so; I will go to my father."

"What is it?" said Jeanne, when Diana was gone; "you look rather gloomy."

"Why, yes."

"What has happened?"

"Oh, mon Dieu! an accident."

"To you?"

"Not precisely to me, but to a person who was near me."

"Who was it?"

"The person I was walking with."

"M. de Monsoreau?"

"Alas! yes; poor dear man."

"What has happened to him?"

"I believe he is dead."

"Dead!" cried Jeanne, starting back in horror.

"Just so."

"He who was here just now talking——"

"Yes, that is just the cause of his death; he talked too much."

"St. Luc, you are hiding something from me!" cried Jeanne, seizing his hands.

"I! Nothing; not even the place where he lies."

"Where is it?"

"Down there behind the wall; just where Bussy used to tie his horse."

"It was you who killed him."

"Parbleu! that is not very difficult to discover."

"Unlucky that you are!"

"Ah, dear friend! he provoked me, insulted me, drew the sword first."

"It is dreadful! the poor man!"

"Good; I was sure of it; before a week is over he will be called St. Monsoreau."

"But you cannot stay here in the house of the man you have killed."

"So I thought at once, and that is why I came to ask you to get ready."

"He has not wounded you?"

"No, I am perfectly unhurt."

"Then, we will go."

"As quickly as possible, for you know the accident may be discovered at any moment."

"Then Diana is a widow."

"That is just what I thought of."

"After you killed him?"

"No, before."

"Well, I will go and tell her."

"Spare her feelings."

"Do not laugh. Meanwhile you get the horses saddled. But where shall we go?"

"To Paris."

"But the king?"

"Oh! he will have forgotten everything by this time; besides, if there is to be war, as seems probable, he will be glad of me. But I must have pen and ink."

"For what?"

"To write to Bussy; I cannot leave Anjou without telling him why."

"No, of course not; you will find all that you require in my room." St. Luc went in, and wrote,—

"DEAR FRIEND,

"You will learn, by report, ere long, the accident which has happened to M. de Monsoreau; we had together, by-the old copse, a discussion on broken-down walls and horses that go home alone. In the heat of the argument, he fell on a bed of poppies and dandelions so hard that he died there.

"Your friend for life,
"ST. LUC.

"P. S. As you may think this rather improbable, I must add that we had our swords in our hands. I set off at once for Paris to make peace with the king, Anjou not seeming to me very safe after what has occurred."

Ten minutes after a servant set off for Angers with this letter, while M. and Madame de St. Luc went out by another door, leaving Diana much grieved at their departure, and much embarrassed how to tell the baron what had occurred. She had turned away her eyes from St. Luc as he passed.

"That is the reward for serving your friends," said he to his wife; "decidedly all people are ungrateful excepting me."

CHAPTER LXVI.

IN WHICH WE SEE THE QUEEN-MOTHER ENTER THE TOWN OF ANGERS, BUT NOT TRIUMPHANTLY.

AT the same time that M. de Monsoreau fell under the sword of St. Luc, a flourish of trumpets sounded at the closed gates of Angers. It was Catherine de Medicis, who arrived there with rather a large suite. They sent to tell Bussy, who rose from his bed, and went to the prince, who immediately got into his. Certainly the airs played by the trumpets were fine, but they had not the virtue of those which made the walls of Jericho fall, for the gates

did not open. Catherine leaned out of her litter to show
herself to the guards, hoping the sight of her would do
more than the sound of the trumpets. They saw her, and
saluted her courteously, but did not open the gates. Then
she sent a gentleman to demand admittance, but they replied that Angers being in a state of war, the gates could
not be opened without some necessary formalities. Catherine was furious. At last Bussy appeared, with five
other gentlemen.

"Who is there?" cried he.

"It is her majesty the queen mother, who has come to
visit Angers."

"Very well, go to the left, and about eighty steps off
you will find the postern."

"A postern for her majesty!" cried the gentleman.

But Bussy was no longer there to hear, he and his friends
had ridden off towards the indicated spot.

"Did your majesty hear?" asked the gentleman.

"Oh! yes, monsieur, I heard; let us go there, if that
be the only way to get in."

The cortége turned to the left, and the postern opened.

"Your majesty is welcome to Angers," said Bussy.

"Thank you, M. de Bussy," said the queen, descending
from her litter, and advancing towards the little door.
Bussy stopped her. "Take care, madame," said he, "the
door is low, and you will hurt yourself."

"Must I then stoop?" replied she; "it is the first
time I ever entered a city so."

Once through the gate she re-entered her litter to go to
the palace, Bussy and his friends escorting her.

"Where is my son?" cried she; "why do I not see
M. d'Anjou?"

"Monseigneur is ill, madame, or else your majesty cannot doubt that he would have come himself to do the
honors of *his* city."

Catherine was sublime in hypocrisy.

"Ill—my poor child, ill!" cried she; "ah! let us
hasten to him; is he well taken care of?"

"Yes, madame, we do our best."

"Does he suffer?"

"Horribly, he is subject to these sudden indispositions."

"It was sudden, then?"

"Mon Dieu! yes, madame."

When they arrived at the palace, Bussy ran up first to the duke.

"Here she is!" cried he.

"Is she furious?"

"Exasperated."

"Does she complain?"

"No, she does worse, she smiles."

"What do the people say?"

"They looked at her in mute terror; now, monseigneur, be careful."

"We stick to war?"

"Pardien, ask one hundred to get ten, and with her you will only get five."

"Bah! you think me very weak. Are you all here? Where is Monsorean?"

"I believe he is at Méridor."

"Her majesty the queen mother!" cried the usher at the door.

Catherine entered, looking pale. The duke made a movement to rise, but she threw herself into his arms and half stifled him with kisses. She did more—she wept.

"We must take care," said Antragues to Ribeirac, "each tear will be paid for by blood."

Catherine now sat down on the foot of the bed. At a sign from Bussy every one went away but himself.

"Will you not go and look after my poor attendants, M. de Bussy? you who are at home here," said the queen.

It was impossible not to go, so he replied, "I am happy to please your majesty," and he also retired.

Catherine wished to discover whether her son were really ill or feigning. But he, worthy son of such a mother, played his part to perfection. She had wept, he had a fever. Catherine, deceived, thought him really ill, and hoped to have more influence over a mind weakened by suffering. She overwhelmed him with tenderness, em-

braced him, and wept so much that at last he asked her
the reason.

"You have run so great a risk," replied she.

"In escaping from the Louvre, mother?"

"No, after."

"How so?"

"Those who aided you in this unlucky escape——"

"Well?"

"Were your most cruel enemies."

"She wishes to find out who it was," thought he.

"The King of Navarre," continued she, "the eternal
scourge of our race——"

"Ah! she knows."

"He boasts of having gained much by it."

"That is impossible, for he had nothing to do with it;
and if he had, I am quite safe, as you see.   I have not
seen the King of Navarre for two years."

"It was not only of danger I spoke!"

"Of what, then?" replied the duke, smiling, as he saw
the tapestry shake behind the queen.

"The king's anger," said she, in a solemn voice; "the
furious anger which menaces you——"

"This danger is something like the other, madame;
he may be furious, but I am safe here."

"You believe so?"

"I am sure of it; your majesty has announced it to me
yourself."

"How so?"

"Because if you had been charged only with menaces,
you would not have come, and the king in that case would
have hesitated to place such a hostage in my hands."

"A hostage! I I!" cried she, terrified.

"A most sacred and venerable one," replied the duke,
with a triumphant glance at the wall.

Catherine was baffled, but she did not know that Bussy
was encouraging the duke by signs.

"My son," said she at length, "you are quite right;
they are words of peace I bring to you."

"I listen, mother, and I think we shall now begin to
understand each other."

CHAPTER LXVII.

LITTLE CAUSES AND GREAT EFFECTS.

CATHERINE had, as we have seen, had the worst of the argument. She was surprised, and began to wonder if her son were really as decided as he appeared to be, when a slight event changed the aspect of affairs. Bussy had been, as we said, encouraging the prince secretly at every word that he thought dangerous to his cause. Now his cause was war at any price, for he wished to stay in Anjou, watch M. de Monsoreau, and visit his wife. The duke feared Bussy, and was guided by him. Suddenly, however, Bussy felt himself pulled by his cloak; he turned and saw Rémy, who drew him gently towards him.

"What is it, Rémy?" said he impatiently. "Why disturb me at such a moment?"

"A letter."

"And for a letter you take me from this important conversation."

"It is from Méridor."

"Oh! thank you, my good Rémy."

"Then I was not wrong?"

"Oh, no; where is it?"

"That is what made me think it of importance; the messenger would only give it to you yourself."

"Is he here?"

"Yes."

"Bring him in."

Rémy opened the door, and a servant entered.

"Here is M. de Bussy," said Rémy.

"Oh, I know him well," said the man, giving the letter.

"Did she give it to you?"

"No; M. de St. Luc."

As Bussy read, he grew first pale, then crimson.

Rémy dismissed the servant, and Bussy, with a bewildered look, held out the letter to him.

"See," said he, "what St. Luc has done for me."

"Well," said Rémy, "this appears to me to be very good and St. Luc is a gallant fellow."

"It is incredible!" cried Bussy.

"Certainly; but that is nothing. Here is our position quite changed; I shall have a Comtesse de Bussy for a patient."

"Yes, she shall be my wife. So he is dead."

"So, you see, it is written."

"Oh, it seems like a dream, Rémy. What! shall I see no more that specter, always coming between me and happiness? It cannot be true."

"It is true; read again, 'he died there.'"

"But Diana cannot stay at Méridor—I do not wish it; she must go where she will forget him."

"Paris will be best; people soon forget at Paris."

"You are right; we will return to the little house in the Rue des Tournelles, and she shall pass there her months of widowhood in obscurity."

"But to go to Paris you must have——"

"What?"

"Peace in Anjou."

"True; oh, mon Dieu! what time lost."

"That means that you are going at once to Méridor."

"No, not I, but you; I must stay here; besides, she might not like my presence just now."

"How shall I see her? Shall I go to the castle?"

"No; go first to the old copse and see if she is there; if she is not then go to the castle."

"What shall I say to her?"

"Say that I am half mad." And pressing the young man's hand, he returned to his place behind the tapestry.

Catherine had been trying to regain her ground.

"My son," she had said, "it seemed to me that a mother and son could not fail to understand each other."

"Yet you see that happens sometimes."

" Never when she wishes it."

" When they wish it, you mean," said the duke, seeking a sign of approbation from Bussy for his boldness.

" But I wish it, my son, and am willing to make any sacrifices to attain peace."

" Oh ! "

" Yes, my dear child. What do you ask ?—what do you demand ? Speak."

" Oh, my mother ! " said François, almost embarrassed at his own easy victory.

" Listen, my son. You do not wish to drown the kingdom in blood—it is not possible ; you are neither a bad Frenchman nor a bad brother."

" My brother insulted me, madame, and I owe him nothing, either as my brother or king."

" But I, François—you cannot complain of me ? "

" Yes, madame, you abandoned me."

" Ah ! you wish to kill me. Well, a mother does not care to live to see her children murder each other ! " cried Catherine, who wished very much to live.

" Oh, do not say that, madame, you tear my heart ! " cried François, whose heart was not torn at all.

Catherine burst into tears. The duke took her hands, and tried to reassure her, not without uneasy glances towards the tapestry.

" But what do you want or ask for, mother ? I will listen," said he.

" I wish you to return to Paris, dear child, to return to your brother's court, who will receive you with open arms."

" No, madame, it is not he whose arms are open to receive me—it is the Bastile."

" No ; return, and on my honor, on my love as a mother, I solemnly swear that you shall be received by the king as though you were king and he the Duc d'Anjou."

The duke looked to the tapestry.

" Accept, my son ; you will have honors, guards."

" Oh, madame, your son gave me guards—his four minions ! "

" Do not reply so ; you shall choose your own guards, and M. de. Bussy shall be their captain, if you like."

Again the duke glanced to the wall, and, to his surprise, saw Bussy smiling and applauding by every possible method.

" What is the meaning of this change ?" thought the duke ; " is it that he may be captain of my guards ? Then must I accept ?" said he aloud, as though talking to himself.

" Yes, yes !" signed Bussy, with head and hands.

" Quit Anjou, and return to Paris ?"

" Yes !" signed Bussy, more decidedly than ever.

" Doubtless, dear child," said Catherine, " it is not disagreeable to return to Paris."

" Well, I will reflect," said the duke, who wished to consult with Bussy.

" I have won," thought Catherine.

They embraced once more, and separated.

CHAPTER LXVIII.

HOW M. DE MONSOREAU OPENED AND SHUT HIS EYES, WHICH PROVED THAT HE WAS NOT DEAD.

RÉMY rode along, wondering in what humor he should find Diana, and what he should say to her. He had just arrived at the park wall, when his horse, which had been trotting, stopped so suddenly that, had he not been a good rider, he would have been thrown over his head. Rémy, astonished, looked to see the cause, and saw before him a pool of blood, and a little further on, a body, lying against the wall. " It is Monsoreau !" cried he ; " how strange ! he lies dead there, and the blood is down here. Ah ! there is the track ; he must have crawled there, or rather that good M. de St. Luc leaned him up against the wall that the blood might not fly to his head. He died with his eyes open, too."

All at once Rémy started back in horror ; the two eyes, that he had seen open, shut again, and a paleness more

livid than ever spread itself over the face of the defunct.
Rémy became almost as pale as M. de Monsoreau, but, as
he was a doctor, he quickly recovered his presence of
mind, and said to himself that if Monsoreau moved his
eyes, it showed he was not dead. "And yet I have read,"
thought he, "of strange movements after death. This
devil of a fellow frightens one even after death. Yes, his
eyes are quite closed; there is one method of ascertaining
whether he is dead or not, and that is to shove my sword
into him, and if he does not move, he is certainly dead."
And Rémy was preparing for this charitable action, when
suddenly the eyes opened again. Rémy started back, and
the perspiration rolled off his forehead as he murmured,
"He is not dead; we are in a nice position. Yes, but if
I kill him he will be dead." And he looked at Monsoreau,
who seemed also to be looking at him earnestly.

"Oh!" cried Rémy, "I cannot do it. God knows that
if he were upright before me I would kill him with all
my heart; but as he is now, helpless and three parts dead,
it would be an infamy."

"Help!" murmured Monsoreau, "I am dying."

"Mordieu!" thought Rémy, "my position is embarrassing. I am a doctor, and, as such, bound to succor
my fellow-creatures when they suffer. It is true that
Monsoreau is so ugly that he can scarcely be called a
fellow-creature, still he is a man. Come, I must forget
that I am the friend of M. de Bussy, and do my duty as a
doctor."

"Help!" repeated the wounded man.

"Here I am," said Rémy.

"Fetch me a priest and a doctor."

"The doctor is here, and perhaps he will dispense with
the priest."

"Rémy," said Monsoreau, "by what chance——"

Rémy understood all the question might mean. This
was no beaten road, and no one was likely to come without particular business.

"Pardieu!" he replied, "a mile or two off I met M. de
St. Luc——"

"Ah! my murderer."

"And he said, 'Rémy, go to the old copse, there you will find a man dead.' "

"Dead?"

"Yes, he thought so; well, I came here and saw you."

"And now, tell me frankly, am I mortally wounded?"

"I will try to find out."

Rémy approached him carefully, took off his cloak, his doublet and shirt. The sword had penetrated between the sixth and seventh ribs.

"Do you suffer much?"

"In my back, not in my chest."

"Ah, let me see; where?"

"Below the shoulder bone."

"The steel must have come against a bone." And he began to examine. "No, I am wrong," said he, "the sword came against nothing, but passed right through." Monsoreau fainted after this examination.

"Ah! that is all right," said Rémy, "syncope, low pulse, cold in the hands and legs: Diable! the widowhood of Madame de Monsoreau will not last long, I fear."

At this moment a slight bloody foam rose to the lips of the wounded man.

Rémy drew from his pocket his lancet case; then tearing off a strip from the patient's shirt, bound it round his arm.

"We shall see," said he, "if the blood flows. Ah, it does! and I believe that Madame de Monsoreau will not be a widow. Pardon, my dear M. de Bussy, but I am a doctor."

Presently the patient breathed, and opened his eyes.

"Oh!" stammered he, "I thought all was over."

"Not yet, my dear monsieur; it is even possible——"

"That I live!"

"Oh, mon Dieu! yes; but let me close the wound. Stop; do not move; nature at this moment is aiding my work. I make the blood flow, and she stops it. Ah! nature is a great doctor, my dear sir. Let me wipe your lips. See the bleeding has stopped already. Good; all goes well, or rather badly."

" Badly ! "

" No, not for you ; but I know what I mean."

" You think I shall get well ? "

" Alas ! yes."

- " You are a singular doctor, M. Rémy."

" Never mind, as long as I cure you," said he, rising.

" Do not abandon me," said the count.

" Ah ! you talk too much. Diable ! I ought to tell him to cry out."

" What do you mean ? "

" Never mind ; your wound is dressed. Now I will go to the castle and fetch assistance."

" And what must I do meanwhile ? "

" Keep quite still ; do not stir ; breathe lightly, and try not to cough. Which is the nearest house ? "

" The château de Méridor."

" Which is the way to it ? " said Rémy, affecting ignorance.

" Get over the wall, and you will find yourself in the park."

" Very well ; I go."

" Thanks, generous man."

" Generous, indeed, if you only knew all."

He soon arrived at the château, where all the inhabitants were busy looking for the body of the count ; for St. Luc had given them a wrong direction. Rémy came among them like a thunderbolt, and was so eager to bring them to the rescue, that Diana looked at him with surprise,

" I thought he was Bussy's friend," murmured she, as Rémy disappeared, carrying with him a wheelbarrow, lint and water.

CHAPTER LXIX.

HOW M. LE DUC D'ANJOU WENT TO MÉRIDOR TO CONGRATU-
LATE MADAME DE MONSOREAU ON THE DEATH OF HER
HUSBAND, AND FOUND HIM THERE BEFORE HIM.

As soon as the duke left his mother, he hastened to
Bussy to know the meaning of all his signs. Bussy, who
was reading St. Luc's letter for the fifth time, received the
prince with a gracious smile.

"How! monseigneur takes the trouble to come to my
house to seek me."

"Yes mordieu, I want an explanation."

"From me?"

"Yes, from you."

"I listen, monseigneur."

"You tell me to steel myself against the suggestions of
my mother, and to sustain the attack valiantly. I do so;
and in the hottest of the fight you tell me to surrender."

"I gave you all those charges, monseigneur, because I
was ignorant of the object for which your mother came;
but now that I see that she has come to promote your
highness's honor and glory——"

"How! what do you mean?"

"Doubtless: what does your highness want? To triumph over your enemies, do you not? For I do not believe, as some people say, that you wish to become King
of France."

The duke looked sullen.

"Some might counsel you to it, but believe me they are
your most cruel enemies. Consider for yourself, monseigneur; have you one hundred thousand men—ten
millions of livres—alliance with foreigners—and, above all,
would you turn against your king?"

"My king did not hesitate to turn against me."

"Ah! there you are right. Well! declare yourself—

get crowned—take the title of King of France—and if
you succeed, I ask no better; I should grow great with
you."

" Who speaks of being king ? " cried the duke, angrily;
" you discuss a question which I have never proposed,
even to myself."

" Well, then, that is settled. Let them give you a
guard and five hundred thousand livres. Obtain, before
peace is signed, a subsidy from Anjou, to carry on the
war. Once you have it, you can keep it. So, we should
have arms and money, and we could do——God knows
what."

" But once they have me at Paris, they will laugh
at me."

" Oh ! impossible, monseigneur; did you not hear what
the queen mother offered you ? "

" She offered me many things."

" That disquiets you ? "

" Yes."

" But, among other things, she offered you a company
of guards, even if I commanded it."

" Yes, she offered that."

" Well, accept; I will be captain; Antragues and Livarot lieutenants; and Ribeirac ensign. Let us get up
your company for you, and see if they dare to laugh at
you then."

" Ma foi ! I believe you are right, Bussy; I will think
of it."

" Do so, monseigneur."

" What were you reading so attentively when I came in ? "

" Oh ! a letter, which interests you still more than
me. Where the devil were my brains, that I did not show
it to you ? "

" What is it ? "

" Sad news, monseigneur; Monsoreau is dead."

" What ! " cried the duke, with a surprise which Bussy
thought was a joyful one.

" Dead, monseigneur."

" M. de Monsoreau ! "

22

"Mon Dieu! yes; are we not all mortal?"

"Yes; but so suddenly."

"Ah! but if you are killed?"

"Then, he was killed?"

"So it seems; and by St. Luc, with whom he quarreled."

"Oh, that dear St. Luc!"

"I did not think he was one of your highness's friends."

"Oh, he is my brother's, and, since we are to be reconciled, his friends are mine. But are you sure?"

"As sure as I can be. Here is a letter from St. Luc, announcing it; and I have sent Rémy, my doctor, to present my condolences to the old baron."

"Oh, Monsoreau!" cried the prince, with his malignant smile.

"Why monseigneur, one would say you hated the poor count."

"No, it was you."

"Of course I did; did he not humiliate me through you?"

"You remember it still."

"But you, monseigneur, whose friend and tool he was——"

"Well, well, get my horse saddled, Bussy."

"What for?"

"To go to Méridor; I wish to pay a visit to Madame Monsoreau. I have been projecting one for some time, and I do not know why it has not taken place sooner."

"Now Monsoreau is dead," thought Bussy, "I do not care; I will protect Diana. I will go with him, and see her."

A quarter of an hour after, the prince, Bussy, and ten gentlemen rode to Méridor, with that pleasure which fine weather, turf, and youth always inspire in men on horseback.

The porter at the château came to ask the names of the visitors.

"The Duc d'Anjou," replied the prince.

The porter blew his horn, and soon windows were opened,

and they heard the noise of bolts and bars as the door was unfastened, and the old baron appeared on the threshold, holding in his hand a bunch of keys. Immediately behind him stood a lady.

"Ah, there is the beautiful Diana!" cried the duke; "do you see her, Bussy?"

Diana, indeed, came out of the house, and behind her came a litter, on which lay Monsoreau, his eyes shining with fever and jealousy as he was carried along.

"What does this mean?" cried the duke to his companion, who had turned whiter than the handkerchief with which he was trying to hide his emotion.

"Long live the Duc d'Anjou!" cried Monsoreau, raising his hand in the air by a violent effort.

"Take care, you will hurt yourself," said a voice behind him. It was Rémy.

Surprise does not last long at court, so, with a smile, the duke said, "Oh, my dear count, what a happy surprise! Do you know we heard you were dead?"

"Come near, monseigneur, and let me kiss your hand. Thank God, not only I am not dead, but I shall live; I hope to serve you with more ardor than ever."

As for Bussy, he felt stunned, and scarcely dared to look at Diana. This treasure, twice lost to him, belonged still to his rival.

"And you, M. de Bussy," said Monsoreau, "receive my thanks, for it is almost to you that I owe my life."

"To me!" stammered the young man, who thought the count was mocking him.

"Yes, indirectly, it is true, for here is my saviour," said he, turning to Rémy, who would willingly have sunk into the earth. Then, in spite of his signs, which he took for precautions to himself, he recounted the care and skill which the young doctor had exhibited towards him.

The duke frowned, and Bussy looked thunders. The poor fellow raised his hands to heaven.

"I hear," continued the count, "that Rémy one day found you dying, as he found me. It is a tie of friendship between us, M. de Bussy, and when Monsoreau loves, ie loves well ; it is true that when he hates, it is also with all his heart."

"Come, then," said the duke, getting off his horse, "deign, beautiful Diana, to do us the honors of the house, which we thought to find in grief, but which we find still the abode of joy. As for you, Monsoreau, rest—you require it."

"Monseignour !" said the count, "it shall never be said that Monsoreau, while he lived, allowed another to do the honors of his house to you ; my servants will carry me, and wherever you go, I shall follow."

Bussy approached Diana, and Monsoreau smiled ; he took her hand, and he smiled again. It was only the duke he feared.

"Here is a great change, M. le Comte," said Diana.

"Alas ! why is it not greater !"

CHAPTER LXX.

THE INCONVENIENCE OF LARGE LITTERS AND NARROW DOORS.

BUSSY did not quit Diana ; the smiles of Monsoreau gave him a liberty which he was only too glad to make use of.

"Madame," said he to Diana, "I am in truth the most miserable of men. On the news of his death, I advised the prince to return to Paris, and to come to terms with his mother ; he did so, and now you remain in Anjou."

"Oh, Louis," replied she, "we dare not say that we are unhappy ; so many happy days, so many joys—do you forget them all ?"

"I forget nothing, madame ; on the contrary, I remember but too much, and that is why I suffer as I do at losing this happiness. What shall I do if I return to Paris, a hundred leagues from you ? My heart sinks at the thought, Diana."

Diana looked at him, and saw so much grief in his eyes, that she said, "Well, if you go to Paris, I will go also."

"How! will you quit M. de Monsoreau?"

"No, he would not allow me to do so; he must come with us."

"Wounded, ill as he is? Impossible!"

"He will come, I tell you." And, leaving Bussy, she went to the prince. The count frowned dreadfully.

"Monseigneur," said she, "they say your highness is fond of flowers; if you will come with me, I will show you the most beautiful in Anjou."

The duke offered her his hand.

"Where are you about to take monseigneur?" asked Monsoreau uneasily.

"Into the greenhouse."

"Ah! well, carry me there."

"Ma foi!" thought Rémy, "I was right not to kill him, for he will soon kill himself."

Diana smiled on Bussy, and said to him, in a low voice, "Do not let M. de Monsoreau suspect that you are about to leave Anjou, and I will manage all."

"Good!" said Bussy, and approaching the prince, he whispered, "Do not let Monsoreau know that we intend to make peace."

"Why not?"

"Because he might tell the queen-mother, to make a friend of her."

"You suspect him, then?"

"Yes, I do."

"Well, so do I; I believe he only counterfeited death to deceive us."

"No, he really received a sword-thrust through his body, and but for that fool of a Rémy, he would have died; I believe his soul must be glued to his body."

They arrived at the conservatory, and Diana continued to smile charmingly on the prince. He passed first, then Diana, and Monsoreau wished to follow, but it was impossible. His litter was too large to go through the door. At this sight he uttered a groan. Diana went on quietly, without looking at him, but Bussy, who understood her, said to him:

"It is useless to try, M. le Comte, your litter will not pass."

"Monseigneur!" cried Monsoreau, "do not go into that conservatory, some of the flowers exhale dangerous perfumes."

Then he fainted, and was carried to his room.

Bussy went to tell Diana what had happened, and she left the duke to go to the castle.

"Have we succeeded?" said Bussy to her as she passed.

"I hope so; do not go away without having seen Gertrude."

When Monsoreau opened his eyes again, he saw Diana standing at his bedside.

"Ah! it is you, madame," said he, "to-night we leave for Paris."

Rémy cried out in horror, but Monsoreau paid no attention.

"Can you think of such a thing, with your wound?" said Diana, quietly.

"Madame, I would rather die than suffer, and were I to die on the road, we start to-night."

"As you please, monsieur."

"Then make your preparations."

"My preparations are soon made, but may I ask the reason of this sudden determination?"

"I will tell you, madame, when you have no more flowers to show to the prince, and when my doors are large enough to admit litters."

Diana bowed.

"But, madame——" said Rémy.

"M. le Comte wishes it," replied she, "and my duty is to obey." And she left the room.

As the duke was making his adieux to the Baron de Méridor, Gertrude appeared, and said aloud to the duke that her mistress regretted that she could not have the honor of saying farewell to his highness; and softly to Bussy that Diana would set off for Paris that evening.

As they went home again, the duke felt unwilling to leave

Anjou now that Diana smiled on him. Therefore he said, "I have been reflecting, Bussy," said he.

"On what, monseigneur?"

"That it is not wise to give in at once to my mother."

"You are right, she thinks herself clever enough without that."

"But by dragging it on for a week, and giving fêtes, and calling the nobility around us, she will see how strong we are."

"Well reasoned, but still——"

"I will stay here a week; depend upon it I shall draw new concessions from the queen."

Bussy appeared to reflect. "Well, monseigneur," said he, "perhaps you are right, but the king, not knowing your intentions, may become annoyed; he is very irascible."

"You are right, but I shall send some one to the king to announce my return in a week."

"Yes, but that some one will run great risks."

"If I change my mind, you mean."

"Yes, and in spite of your promise, you would do so if you thought it your interest."

"Perhaps."

"Then they will send your messenger to the Bastile."

"I will give him a letter, and not let him know what he is carrying."

"On the contrary, give him no letter, and let him know."

"Then no one will go."

"Oh! I know some one."

"Who?"

"I, myself."

"You!"

"Yes, I like difficult negotiations."

"Bussy, my dear Bussy, if you will do that, I shall be eternally grateful."

Bussy smiled. The duke thought he hesitated.

"And I will give you ten thousand crowns for your journey," added he.

" Thanks, monseigneur, but these things cannot be paid for."

" Then you will go ? "

" Yes."

" When ? "

" Whenever you like."

" The sooner the better."

" This evening if you wish it."

" Dear Bussy."

" You know I would do anything for your highness. I will go to-night ; you stay here and enjoy yourself, and get me something good from the queen-mother."

" I will not forget."

Bussy then prepared to depart as soon as the signal arrived from Méridor. It did not come till the next morning, for the count had felt himself so feeble that he had been forced to take a night's rest. But early in the morning a messenger came to announce to Bussy that the count had set off for Paris in a litter, followed on horseback by Rémy, Diana, and Gertrude. Bussy jumped on his horse, and took the same road.

CHAPTER LXXI.

WHAT TEMPER THE KING WAS IN WHEN ST. LUC REAPPEARED AT THE LOUVRE.

SINCE the departure of Catherine, Henri, however, confident in his ambassador, had thought only of arming himself against the attacks of his brother. He amused, or rather ennuyéd, himself by drawing up long lists of proscriptions, in which were inscribed in alphabetical order all who had not shown themselves zealous for his cause. The lists became longer every day, and at the S—— and the L——, that is to say, twice over, was inscribed the name of M. de St. Luc. Chicot, in the midst of all this, was, little by little, and man by man, enrolling an army for his master. One evening Chicot entered the room where the king sat at supper.

"What is it?" asked the king.

"M. de St. Luc."

"M. de St. Luc?"

"Yes."

"At Paris?"

"Yes."

"At the Louvre?"

"Yes."

The king rose, red and agitated.

"What has he come for? The traitor!"

"Who knows?"

"He comes, I am sure, as deputy from the states of Anjou—as an envoy from my rebellious brother. He makes use of the rebellion as a safe conduct to come here and insult me."

"Who knows?"

"Or perhaps he comes to ask me for his property, of which I have kept back the revenues, which may have been rather an abuse of power, as, after all, he has committed no crime."

"Who knows?"

"Ah, you repeat eternally the same thing; mort de ma vie! you tire my patience out with your eternal 'Who knows?'"

"Eh! mordieu! do you think you are very amusing with your eternal questions?"

"At least you might reply something."

"And what should I reply? Do you take me for an ancient oracle? It is you who are tiresome with your foolish suppositions."

"M. Chicot?"

"M. Henri."

"Chicot, my friend, you see my grief and you laugh at me."

"Do not have any grief."

"But every one betrays me."

"Who knows? Ventre de biche! who knows?"

Henri went down to his cabinet, where, at the news of his return, a number of gentlemen had assembled, who were looking at St. Luc with evident distrust and animosity. He, however, seemed quite unmoved by this. He had brought his wife with him also, and she was seated, wrapped in her traveling-cloak, when the king entered in an excited state.

"Ah, monsieur, you here!" he cried.

"Yes, sire," replied St. Luc.

"Really, your presence at the Louvre surprises me."

"Sire, I am only surprised that, under the circumstances, your majesty did not expect me."

"What do you mean, monsieur?"

"Sire, your majesty is in danger."

"Danger!" cried the courtiers.

"Yes, gentlemen, a real, serious danger, in which the king has need of the smallest as well as the greatest of those devoted to him; therefore I come to lay at his feet my humble services."

"Ah!" said Chicot, "you see, my son, that I was right to say, 'who knows.'"

Henri did not reply at once; he would not yield immediately. After a pause, he said, "Monsieur, you have only done your duty; your services are due to us."

"The services of all the king's subjects are due to him, I know, sire; but in these times many people forget to pay their debts. I, sire, come to pay mine, happy that your majesty will receive me among the number of your creditors."

"Then," said Henri, in a softer tone, "you return without any other motive than that which you state; without any mission, or safe-conduct?"

"Sire, I return simply and purely for that reason. Now, your majesty may throw me into the Bastile, or have me shot, but I shall have done my duty. Sire, Anjou is on fire; Touraine is about to revolt; Guienne is rising. M. le Duc d'Anjou is hard at work."

"He is well supported, is he not?"

"Sire, M. de Bussy, firm as he is, cannot make your brother brave."

"Ah! he trembles, then, the rebel."

"Let me go and shake St. Luc's hand," said Chicot, advancing.

The king followed him, and going up to his old favorite, and laying his hand on his shoulder, said,—

"You are welcome, St. Luc!"

"Ah! sire," cried St. Luc, kissing the king's hand, "I find again my beloved master."

"Yes, but you, my poor St. Luc, you have grown thin."

"It is with grief at having displeased your majesty," said a feminine voice. Now, although the voice was soft and respectful, Henri frowned, for it was as distasteful to him as the noise of thunder was to Augustus.

"Madame de St. Luc!" said he. "Ah! I forgot."

Jeanne threw herself at his feet.

"Rise, madame," said he, "I love all that bear the name of St. Luc." Jeanne took his hand and kissed it, but he withdrew it quickly.

"You must convert the king," said Chicot to the young woman, "you are pretty enough for it."

But Henri turned his back to her, and passing his arm round St. Luc's neck, said,—

"Then we have made peace, St. Luc?"

"Say rather, sire, that the pardon is granted."

"Madame!" said Chicot, "a good wife should not leave her husband," and he pushed her after the king and St. Luc.

CHAPTER LXXII.

IN WHICH WE MEET TWO IMPORTANT PERSONAGES WHOM WE HAVE LOST SIGHT OF FOR SOME TIME.

THERE are two of the personages mentioned in this story, about whom the reader has the right to ask for information. We mean an enormous monk, with thick eyebrows and large lips, whose neck was diminishing every day; and a large donkey whose sides were gradually swelling out like a balloon. The monk resembled a hogshead;

and the ass was like a child's cradle, supported by four posts.

The one inhabited a cell at St. Geneviève, and the other the stable at the same convent. The one was called Gorenflot, and the other Panurge. Both were enjoying the most prosperous lot that ever fell to a monk and an ass.

The monks surrounded their illustrious brother with cares and attentions, and Panurge fared well for his master's sake.

If a missionary arrived from foreign countries, or a secret legate from the Pope, they pointed out to him Brother Gorenflot, that double model of the church preaching and militant; they showed Gorenflot in all his glory, that is to say, in the midst of a feast, seated at a table in which a hollow had been cut on purpose for his sacred stomach, and they related with a noble pride that Gorenflot consumed the rations of eight ordinary monks. And when the newcomer had piously contemplated this spectacle, the prior would say, " See how he eats! And if you had but heard his sermon one famous night, in which he offered to devote himself for the triumph of the faith. It is a mouth which speaks like that of St. Chrysostom, and swallows like that of Gargantua."

Every time that any one spoke of the sermon, Gorenflot sighed and said :

" What a pity I did not write it !

" A man like you has no need to write," the prior would reply. " No, you speak from inspiration; you open your mouth, and the words of God flow from your lips."

" Do you think so ? " sighed Gorenflot.

However, Gorenflot was not perfectly happy. He, who at first thought his banishment from the convent an immense misfortune, discovered in his exile infinite joys before unknown to him. He sighed for liberty ; liberty with Chicot, the joyous companion, with Chicot, whom he loved without knowing why. Since his return to the convent, he had never been allowed to go out. He never attempted to combat this decision, but he grew sadder from day to day. The prior saw this, and at last said to him:

"My dear brother, no one can fight against his vocation; yours is to fight for the faith; go then, fulfil your mission, only watch well over your precious life, and return for the great day."

"What great day?"

"That of the Fête Dieu."

"Ita," replied Gorenflot; it was the only Latin word he knew, and used it on all occasions. "But give me some money to bestow in alms in a Christian manner."

"You have your text, have you not, dear brother?"

"Yes, certainly."

"Confide it to me."

"Willingly, but to you alone; it is this: 'The flail which threshes the corn.'"

"Oh, magnificent! sublime!" cried the prior.

"Now, my father, am I free?"

"Yes, my son, go and walk in the way of the Lord."

Gorenflot saddled Panurge, mounted him with the aid of two vigorous monks, and left the convent about seven in the evening. It was the same day on which St. Luc arrived at Paris from Méridor.

Gorenflot, having passed through the Rue St. Etienne, was going to have turned to the right, when suddenly Panurge stopped; a strong hand was laid on his croup.

"Who is there?" cried Gorenflot, in terror.

"A friend."

Gorenflot tried to turn, but he could not.

"What do you want?" said he.

"Will my venerable brother show me the way to the Corne d'Abondance?"

"Morbleu! it is M. Chicot," cried Gorenflot, joyfully.

"Just so; I was going to seek you at the convent, when I saw you come out, and followed you until we were alone. Ventre de biche! how thin you are!"

"But what are you carrying, M. Chicot?" said the monk, "you appear laden."

"It is some venison which I have stolen from the king."

"Dear M. Chicot! and under the other arm?"

"A bottle of Cyprus wine sent by a king to my king."

"Let me see!"

"It is my wine, and I love it much; do not you, brother?"

"Oh! oh!" cried Gorenflot, raising his eyes and hands to Heaven, and beginning to sing in a voice which shook the neighboring windows. It was the first time he had sung for a month.

CHAPTER LXXIII.

DIANA'S SECOND JOURNEY TO PARIS.

LET us leave the two friends entering the Corne d'Abondance, and return to the litter of M. Monsoreau and to Bussy, who set out with the intention of following them. Not only is it not difficult for a cavalier well mounted to overtake foot travelers, but it is difficult not to pass them. This happened to Bussy.

It was the end of May, the heat was great, and about noon M. de Monsoreau wished to make a halt in a little wood, which was near the road, and as they had a horse laden with provisions, they remained there until the great heat of the day had gone by. During this time Bussy passed them, but he had not traveled, as we may imagine, without inquiring if a party on horseback, and a litter carried by peasants, had been seen. Until he had passed the village of Durtal, he had obtained the most satisfactory information, and, convinced that they were before him, had ridden on quickly. But he could see nothing of them, and suddenly all traces of them vanished, and on arriving at La Flèche he felt certain he must have passed them on the road. Then he remembered the little wood, and doubted not that they had been resting there when he passed. He installed himself at a little inn, which had the advantage of being opposite the principal hotel, where he doubted not that Monsoreau would stop; and he remained at the window watching. About four o'clock he saw a courier arrive, and half an hour afterwards the whole party. He waited till nine o'clock, and then he saw the courier set out again, and after him the litter, then Diana, Rémy, and Gertrude on horseback. He mounted his horse and followed them, keeping them in sight. Monsoreau scarcely allowed Diana to move from his side, but kept calling her every instant. After a little while, Bussy gave a long, shrill whistle, with which he had been in the habit of calling his servants at his hotel. Rémy recognized it in a moment. Diana started, and looked at the young man, who made an affirmative sign; then he came up to her and whispered:

"It is he!"

"Who is speaking to you, madame?" said Monsoreau.

"To me, monsieur?"

"Yes, I saw a shadow pass close to you, and heard a voice."

"It is M. Rémy; are you also jealous of him?"

"No, but I like people to speak out, it amuses me."

"There are some things which cannot be said aloud before M. le Comte, however," said Gertrude, coming to the rescue.

"Why not?"

"For two reasons; firstly, because some would not interest you, and some would interest you too much."

"And of which kind is what M. Rémy has just whispered?"

"Of the latter."

"What did Rémy say to you, madame?"

"I said, M. le Comte, that if you excite yourself so much, you will be dead before we have gone a third of the way."

Monsoreau grew deadly pale.

"He is expecting you behind," whispered Rémy, again, "ride slowly, and he will overtake you."

Monsoreau, who heard a murmur, tried to rise and look back after Diana.

"Another movement like that, M. le Comte, and you will bring on the bleeding again," said Rémy.

Diana turned and rode back a little way, while Rémy walked by the litter to occupy the count. A few seconds after, Bussy was by her side.

"You see I follow you," said he, after their first embrace.

"Oh! I shall be happy, if I know you are always so near to me."

"But by day he will see us."

"No; by day you can ride afar off, it is only I who will see you, Louis. From the summit of some hill, at the turn of some road, your plume waving, your handkerchief fluttering in the breeze, would speak to me in your name, and tell me that you love me."

"Speak on, my beloved Diana; you do not know what music I find in your voice."

"And when we travel by night, which we shall often do, for Rémy has told him that the freshness of the evening is good for his wounds, then, as this evening, from time to time, I will stay behind, and we will tell each other, with a rapid pressure of the hands, all our thoughts of each other during the day."

"Oh! I love you! I love you!" murmured Bussy. "Oh! to see you, to press your hand, Diana."

Suddenly they heard a voice which made them both tremble, Diana with fear, and Bussy with anger.

"Diana!" it cried, "where are you? Answer me."

"Oh! it is he! I had forgotten him," said Diana. "Sweet dream, frightful awaking."

"Listen, Diana; we are together. Say one word, and nothing can separate us more; Diana, let us fly! What prevents us? Before us is happiness and liberty. One word, and we go; one word, and lost to him, you belong to me forever."

"And my father?"

"When he shall know how I love you?"

"Oh! a father!"

"I will do nothing by violence, dear Diana; order, and I obey."

"It is our destiny, Bussy ; but be strong, and you shall see if I know how to love."

"Must we then separate ?"

"Comtesse ! " cried the voice, " reply, or, if I kill myself in doing it, I will jump from this infernal litter."

" Adieu, Bussy, he will do as he says."

"You pity him ? "

"Jealous ! " said Diana, with an adorable smile.

Bussy let her go.

In a minute she was by the litter, and found the count half fainting.

"Ah ! " cried he, " where were you, madame ? "

" Where should I have been ? Behind you."

" At my side, madame ; do not leave me again."

From time to time this scene was renewed. They all hoped he would die with rage ; but he did not die : on the contrary, at the end of ten days, when they arrived at Paris, he was decidedly better. During these ten days Diana had conquered all Bussy's pride, and had persuaded him to come and visit Monsoreau, who always showed him much friendship. Rémy watched the husband and gave notes to the wife.

"Esculapius and Mercury," said he ; " my functions accumulate."

CHAPTER LXXIV.

HOW THE AMBASSADOR OF THE DUC D'ANJOU ARRIVED AT THE LOUVRE, AND THE RECEPTION HE MET WITH.

As neither Catherine nor the Duc d'Anjou reappeared at the Louvre, the dissension between the brothers became apparently every day more and more certain. The king thought, "No news, bad news." The minions added, "François, badly counseled, has detained the queen-mother."

Badly counseled. In these words were comprised all the policy of this singular reign, and the three preceding

23

354 CHICOT, THE JESTER.

ones. Badly counseled was Charles IX. when he author-
ized the massacre of St. Bartholomew. Badly counseled
was François II. when he ordered the massacre at Amboise.
Badly counseled had been Henri II. when he burned so
many heretics and conspirators. And now they dared not
say, " Your brother has the family blood in his veins ;
he wishes, like the rest, to dethrone or poison ; he would
do to you what you did to your elder brother ; what your
elder brother did to his, what your mother has taught
you to do to one another." Therefore they said, "Your
brother is badly counseled."

Now, as only one person was able to counsel François,
it was against Bussy that the cry was raised, which became
every day more and more furious. At last the news was
spread that the duke had sent an ambassador. At this
the king grew pale with anger, and the minions swore that
he should be cut to pieces, and a piece sent to all the provinces of France as a specimen of the king's anger.

Chicot said nothing, but he reflected. Now the king
thought much of Chicot's reflections, and he questioned
him about them.

"Sire," replied he, " if your brother sends an ambassador, it is because he feels himself strong enough to do
so ; he who is prudence itself. Now, if he is strong, we
must temporize with him. Let us respect his ambassador,
and receive him with civility. That engages you to nothing. Do you remember how your brother embraced Ad-
miral Coligny, who came as ambassador from the Huguenots ? "

" Then you approve of the policy of my brother
Charles ? "

"Not so, but I cite a fact ; and I say to you, do not
hurt a poor devil of a herald, or ambassador ; perhaps we
may find the way to seize the master, the mover, the chief,
the great Duc d'Anjou, with the three Guises ; and if you
can shut them up in a place safer than the Louvre, do it."

" That is not so bad."

" Then why do you let all your friends bellow so ? "

" Bellow ! "

"Yes; I would say, roar, if they could be taken for lions, but they are more like bearded apes."

"Chicot, they are my friends."

"Friends! I would lay any bet to make them all turn against you before to-morrow."

"Well, what do you advise?"

"To wait, my son. Half the wisdom of Solomon lies in that word. If an ambassador arrive, receive him courteously. And as to your brother, kill him if you can and like, but do not degrade him. He is a great knave, but he is a Valois; besides, he can do that well enough for himself."

"It is true, Chicot."

"One more lesson that you owe me. Now let me sleep, Henri; for the last week I have been engaged in fuddling a monk."

"A monk! the one of whom you have already spoken to me?"

"Just so. You promised him an abbey."

"I?"

"Pardieu! it is the least you can do for him, after all he has done for you."

"He is then still devoted to me?"

"He adores you. Apropos, my son——"

"What?"

"In three weeks it will be the Fête Dieu."

"Well!"

"Are we to have some pretty little procession?"

"I am the most Christian king, and it is my duty to set an example to my subjects."

"And you will, as usual, stop at the four great convents of Paris?"

"Yes."

"At St. Geneviève?"

"Yes, that is the second I stop at."

"Good."

"Why do you ask?"

"Oh, nothing—I was curious. Now I know all I want, so good night, Henri!"

" But just as Chicot prepared to leave, a great noise was
heard.

" What is that noise ? " said the king.

" It is ordained that I am not to sleep. Henri, you must
get me a room in the town, or I must leave your service ;
the Louvre becomes insupportable."

At this moment the captain of the guards entered, saying, " Sire, it is an envoy from M. le Duc d'Anjou."

" With a suite ?"

" No, sire, alone."

" Then you must receive him doubly well, Henri, for he
is a brave fellow."

" Well," said the king, very pale, but trying to look
calm, " let all my court assemble in the great hall."

CHAPTER LXXV.

WHICH IS ONLY THE END OF THE PRECEDING ONE.

HENRI sat on his throne in the great hall, and around
him was grouped an eager crowd. He looked pale and
frowning.

. " Sire," said Quelus to the king, " do you know the name
of the ambassador ? "

" No ; but what does it matter ? "

" Sire, it is M. de Bussy ; the insult is doubled."

" I see no insult," said the king, with affected sang-froid.

" Let him enter," continued he. Bussy, with his hat in
his hand, and his head erect, advanced straight to the king,
and waited, with his usual look of pride, to be interrogated.

" You here, M. de Bussy ! " said the king ; " I thought
you were in Anjou."

" Sire, I was, but you see I have quitted it."

" And what brings you here ? "

" The desire of presenting my humble respects to your
majesty."

The king and courtiers looked astonished ; they expected
a different answer.

" And nothing else ? " said the king.

" I will add, sire, the orders I received from the Duc d'Anjou to join his respects to mine."

" And the duke said nothing else ? "

" Only that he was on the point of returning with the queen-mother, and wished me to apprise your majesty of the return of one of your most faithful subjects."

The king was choked with surprise.

" Good morning, M. de Bussy," said Chicot.

Bussy turned, astonished to find a friend in that place.

"Good day, M. Chicot ; I am delighted to see you."

" Is that all you have to say, M. de Bussy ?" asked the king.

"Yes, sire; anything that remains to be said, will be said by the duke himself."

The king rose and went away, and Bussy continued to converse with Chicot, until the king called to him. As soon as Bussy was alone, Quelus approached him.

" Good morning, M. Quelus," said Bussy graciously ; " may I have the honor of asking how you are ? "

"Very bad."

"Oh, mon Dieu ! what is the matter ? "

"Something annoys me infinitely."

"Something ! And are you not powerful enough to get rid of it ? "

"It is not something, but some one, that M. Quelus means," said Maugiron, advancing.

" And whom I advise him to get rid of," said Schomberg, coming forward on the other side.

"Ah, M. de Schomberg ! I did not recognize you."

" Perhaps not ; is my face still blue ? "

" Not so ; you are very pale. Are you not well ? "

" Yes, it is with anger."

" Oh ! then you have also some one who annoys you ? "

" Yes, monsieur."

" And I also," said Maugiron.

" Really, gentlemen, you all look very gloomy."

" You forget me," said D'Epernon, planting himself before Bussy.

" Pardon me, M. d'Epernon, you were behind the others,

as usual, and I have so little the pleasure of knowing you, that it was not for me to speak first."

It was strange to see Bussy smiling and calm among those four furious faces, whose eyes spoke with so terrible an eloquence, that he must have been blind or stupid not to have understood their language.

But Bussy never lost his smile.

"It seems to me that there is an echo in this room," said he quietly.

"Look, gentlemen," said Quelus, "how provincial M. de Bussy has become; he has a beard, and no knot to his sword; he has black boots and a gray hat."

"It is an observation that I was just making to myself, my dear sir; seeing you so well dressed, I said to myself, 'How much harm a few weeks' absence does to a man; here am I, Louis de Clermont, forced to take a little Gascon gentleman as a model of taste.' But let me pass; you are so near to me that you tread on my feet, and I feel it in spite of my boots."

And turning away, he advanced towards St. Luc, whom he saw approaching.

"Incredible!" cried all the young men, "we insulted him; he took no notice."

"There is something in it," said Quelus.

"Well!" said the king, advancing, "what were you and M. de Bussy saying?"

"Do you wish to know what M. de Bussy said, sire?"

"Yes, I am curious."

"Well, I trod on his foot, and insulted him, and he said nothing."

"What, gentlemen," cried Henri, feigning anger, "you dared to insult a gentleman in the Louvre!"

"Alas! yes, sire, and he said nothing."

"Well! I am going to the queen."

As the king went out of the great door, St. Luc re-entered by a side one, and advanced towards the four gentlemen.

"Pardon, M. Quelus," said he, "but do you still live in the Rue St. Honoré?"

" Yes, my dear friend ; why do you ask ? "

" I have two words to say to you."

" Ah ! "

" And you, M. de Schomberg ? "

" Rue Béthisy," said Schomberg, astonished.

." D'Epernon's address I know."

" Rue de Grenelle."

" You are my neighbor.   And you, Maugiron ? "

" Near the Louvre.   But I begin to understand ; you come from M. de Bussy."

" Never mind from whom I come ; I have to speak to you, that is all."

" To all four of us ? "

" Yes."

" Then if you cannot speak here, let us all go to Schomberg's ; it is close by."

" So be it."

And the five gentlemen went out of the Louvre arm in arm.

<hr>

CHAPTER LXXVI.

HOW M. DE ST. LUC ACQUITTED HIMSELF OF THE COMMISSION GIVEN TO HIM BY BUSSY.

LET us leave St. Luc a little while in Schomberg's room, and see what had passed between him and Bussy.

Once out of the hall, St. Luc had stopped, and looked anxiously at his friend.

" Are you ill ? " said he, " you are so pale ; you look as though you were about to faint."

" No, I am only choking with anger."

" You do not surely mind those fellows ? "

" You shall see."

" Come, Bussy, be calm."

" You are charming, really ; be calm, indeed ! if you had had half said to you that I have had, some one would have been dead before this."

" Well, what do you want ? "

"You are my friend; you have already given me a terrible proof of it."

"Ah! my dear friend," said St. Luc, who believed Monsoreau dead and buried, "do not thank me, it is not worth while; certainly the thrust was a good one, and succeeded admirably, but it was the king who showed it me, when he kept me here a prisoner at the Louvre."

"Dear friend."

"Never mind Monsoreau; tell me about Diana. Was she pleased at last? Does she pardon me? When will the wedding take place?"

"Oh! my dear friend, we must wait till Monsoreau is dead."

"What!" cried St. Luc, starting back as though he had put his foot on a pointed nail."

"Yes; poppies are not such dangerous plants as you thought; he did not die from his fall on them, but is alive and more furious than ever."

"Really?"

"Yes, and he talks of nothing but vengeance, and of killing you on the first occasion."

"And I have announced his death to every one; he will find his heirs in mourning. But he shall not give me the lie; I shall meet him again, and if he escapes me a second time——"

"Calm yourself, my dear St. Luc; really, I am better off than you would think; it is the duke whom he suspects, and of whom he is jealous. I am his dear Bussy—his precious friend. That is only natural, for it was that fool of a Rémy who cured him.

"What an idiot he must have been!"

"He has an idea that, as an honest man and a doctor, it is his duty to cure people. However, Monsoreau says he owes his life to me, and confides his wife to my care."

"Ah! I understand that this makes you wait more patiently for his death. However, I am quite thunderstruck at the news."

"But now, my friend, let us leave Monsoreau."

"Yes, let us enjoy life while he is still ill; but once he

is well, I shall order myself a suit of mail, have new locks
put on my doors, and you must ask the Duc d'Anjou if
his mother has not given him some antidote against
poison. Meanwhile, let us amuse ourselves."

"Well, my dear friend, you see you have only rendered
me half a service."

"Do you wish me to finish it ?"

"Yes, in another way."

"Speak."

"Are you great friends with those four gentlemen ?"

"Ma foi ! we are something like cats and dogs in the
sun ; as long as we all get the heat, we agree, but if one of
us took the warmth from another, then I do not answer
for the consequences."

"Well, will you go for me to M. Quelus, first ?"

"Ah !"

"And ask him what day it will please him that I should
cut his throat, or he mine ?"

"I will."

"You do not mind it ?"

"Not the least in the world. I will go at once if you
wish it."

"One moment ; as you go, just call on M. Schomberg
and make him the same proposal."

"Schomberg too ? Diable, how you go on ! Well, as
you wish."

"Then, my dear St. Luc, as you are so amiable, go also
to M. Maugiron, and ask him to join the party."

"What, three ! Bussy, you cannot mean it. I hope
that is all."

"No ; from him go to D'Epernon."

"Four !"

"Even so, my dear friend ; I need not recommend to
a man like you to proceed with courtesy and politeness
towards these gentlemen. Let the thing be done in gallant fashion."

"You shall be content, my friend. What are your conditions ?"

"I make none ; I accept theirs."

" Your arms ? "

" What they like."

" The day, place, and hour ? "

" Whatever suits them."

" But——"

" Oh ! never mind such trifles, but do it quickly ; I will walk in the little garden of the Luxembourg ; you will find me there when you have executed your commission."

" You will wait, then ? "

" Yes."

" It may be long."

" I have time."

We know how St. Luc found the four young men, and accompanied them to Schomberg's house. St. Luc remained in the ante-chamber, waiting until, according to the etiquette of the day, the four young men were installed in the saloon ready to receive him. Then an usher came and saluted St. Luc, who followed him to the threshold of the saloon, where he announced M. d'Espinay de St. Luc.

Schomberg then rose and saluted his visitor, who, to mark the character of the visit, instead of returning it, put on his hat. Schomberg then, turning towards Quelus, said,

" I have the honor to present to you M. Jacques de Levis, Comte de Quelus."

The two gentlemen bowed, and then the same ceremony was gone through with the others. This done, the four friends sat down, but St. Luc remained standing and said to Quelus,

" M. le Comte, you have insulted M. le Comte Louis de Clermont d'Amboise, Seigneur de Bussy, who presents to you his compliments, and calls you to single combat on any day and hour, and with such arms as may please you. Do you accept ? "

" Certainly ; M. de Bussy does me much honor."

" Your day and hour, M. le Comte ? "

" To-morrow morning at seven o'clock."

" Your arms ? "

"Rapier and dagger, if that suits M. de Bussy."

St. Luc bowed. Then he addressed the same questions to the others, and received the same answers.

"If we all choose the same day and hour, M. de Bussy will be rather embarrassed," said Schomberg.

"Certainly," replied St. Luc, "M. de Bussy may be embarrassed, but he says that the circumstance would not be new to him, as it has already happened at the Tournelles."

"And he would fight us all four?"

"All four."

"Separately?"

"Separately, or at once."

The four young men looked at each other; then Quelus, red with anger, said:

"It is very fine of M. de Bussy, but however little we may be worth, we can each do our own work; we will accept, therefore, the count's proposal, fighting separately, or rather, which will be still better, as we do not seek to assassinate a gallant man, chance shall decide which of us shall fight M. de Bussy."

"And the three others?"

"Oh! M. de Bussy has too many friends, and we too many enemies, for them to remain with folded arms. Do you agree to this, gentlemen?"

"Yes!" cried all.

"If MM. Riberac, Antragues, and Livarot would join the party, it would be complete."

"Gentlemen," said St. Luc, "I will transmit your desires to M. de Bussy, and I believe I may promise that he is too courteous not to agree to your wishes. It therefore only remains for me to thank you in his name."

Then he took his leave, after throwing his purse to the four lackeys, whom he found outside, to drink to their masters' healths.

CHAPTER LXXVII.

IN WHAT RESPECT M. DE ST. LUC WAS MORE CIVILIZED
THAN M. DE BUSSY, THE LESSONS WHICH HE GAVE
HIM, AND THE USE WHICH M. DE BUSSY MADE OF
THEM.

St. Luc returned, proud of having executed his commission so well. Bussy thanked him, but looked sad,
which was not natural to him.

"Have I done badly?" said St. Luc.

"Ma foi, my dear friend, I only regret you did not say,
'at once.'"

"Why! what is the hurry?"

"I wish to die as soon as possible."

St. Luc looked at him in astonishment.

"Die! at your age, with your name, and Diana!"

"Yes, I shall kill them, I know, but I shall receive
some good blow which will tranquilize me forever."

"What black ideas, Bussy!"

"A husband whom I thought dead, and who has returned to life; a wife who can scarcely quit the bedside
of the pretended dying man. Not to see her, smile on
her, touch her hand. Mon Dieu!——"

St. Luc interrupted him with a burst of laughter.
"Oh!" cried he, "the innocent man. Why, no lover
can be more fortunate than you."

"Prove that to me."

"You are the friend of M. de Monsoreau."

"Yes, I am ashamed to say, he calls me his friend."

"Well! be his friend."

"Oh! and abuse this title!"

"Is he really your friend?"

"He says so."

"No; for he makes you unhappy. Now the end of
friendship is to make one another happy. At least, so his

majesty says, and he is learned in friendship. So, if he makes you unhappy, he is not your friend ; therefore you may treat him either as a stranger, and take his wife from him, or as an enemy, and kill him if he murmurs."

"In fact, I hate him. But do you not think he loves me ?"

"Diable ! Take away his wife and see."

"I must continue to be a man of honor."

"And let Madame de Monsoreau cure her husband both physically and morally. For it is certain that if you get yourself killed, she will attach herself to the only man who remains to her."

Bussy frowned.

"But," added St. Luc, "here is my wife ; she always gives good advice. She has been picking herself a bouquet in the gardens of the queen-mother, and will be in a good humor. Listen to her ; she speaks gold."

Jeanne arrived radiant, full of happiness and fun. Bussy saluted her in a friendly manner, and she held out her hand to him, saying, with a smile, "How go on the love affairs ?"

"They are dying."

"They are wounded and fainting ; perhaps you can restore them, Jeanne ?"

"Let me see ; show me the wound."

In two words, this is it : M. de Bussy does not like smiling on M. de Monsoreau, and he thinks of retiring."

"And leaving Diana to him ?"

"Oh ! madame, St. Luc does not tell you that I wish to die."

"Poor Diana !" murmured Jeanne, "decidedly men are ungrateful."

"Good ! this is the conclusion my wife draws."

"I, ungrateful !' cried Bussy, "because I fear to render my love vile, by practising a disgraceful hypocrisy ?"

"Oh ! monsieur, that is only a pretext. If you were really in love, you would fear but one thing—not to be loved in return."

"But, madame, there are sacrifices——"

"Not another word. Confess that you love Diana no longer; it will be more worthy of a gallant man."

Bussy grew pale.

"You do not dare to tell her; well, I will."

"Madame! madame!"

"You are rich, you men, with your sacrifices. And does she make none? What! expose herself to be massacred by that tiger of a Monsoreau, preserve her position only by employing a strength of will of which Samson or Hannibal would have been incapable. Oh! I swear, Diana is sublime, I could not do a quarter of what she does every day."

"Thank you!" said St. Luc.

"And he hesitates!" continued she, "he does not fall on his knees and say his mea culpa."

"You are right," said Bussy, "I am but a man, that is to say, an imperfect creature, inferior to the most commonplace woman."

"It is lucky you are convinced of it."

"What do you order me?"

"To go at once and pay a visit——"

"To M. de Monsoreau?"

"Who speaks of him?—to Diana."

"But he never leaves her."

"When you went so often to see Madame de Barbezieux, had she not always near her that great ape who bit you because he was jealous?"

Bussy began to laugh, and St. Luc and Jeanne followed his example.

"Madame," then said Bussy, "I am going to M. de Monsoreau's house; adieu."

He went there, and found the count in bed; he was delighted to see him, and told him that Rémy promised that his wound would be cured in three weeks. Bussy recounted to him the commission with which he had been charged, and his visit to the court.

"The duke has still projects on foot, has he not?

"I believe so."

"Do not compromise yourself for that bad man; I

know him : he is perfidious, and will not hesitate to betray you."

"I know it."

"You are my friend, and I wish to put you on your guard."

"You must sleep after the dressing of your wound," said Rémy.

"Yes, my dear doctor. My friend, take a turn in the garden with Madame de Monsoreau."

"I am at your orders," replied Bussy.

CHAPTER LXXVIII.

THE PRECAUTIONS OF M. DE MONSOREAU.

St. Luc was right, and Jeanne was right, and Bussy soon acknowledged it. As for Diana, she gave herself up to the two instincts that Figaro recognizes as inborn in mankind, to love and to deceive. M. de Monsoreau grew better and better. He had escaped from fever, thanks to the application of cold water, that new remedy which Providence had discovered to Ambrose Paré, when all at once he received a great shock at hearing of the arrival in Paris of the duke with the queen-mother. The day after his arrival, the duke, under the pretext of asking after him, presented himself at his hotel, and it was impossible to close his door against a prince who showed so much interest in him. M. de Monsoreau therefore was obliged to receive the prince, who was most amiable to him and to his wife. As soon as he was gone, M. de Monsoreau took Diana's arm, and in spite of Rémy's remonstrances walked three times round his armchair; and, from his satisfied air, Diana was sure he was meditating on some project.

The next day the duke came again, and this time Monsoreau walked round his room. That evening Diana warned Bussy that her husband had certainly some project in his head. A few minutes after, when Bussy and Monsoreau were alone, "When I think," said Monsoreau,

" that this prince, who smiles on me, is my mortal enemy, and tried to have me assassinated by M. de St. Luc——"

" Oh, assassinated ! take care, M. le Comte. St. Luc is a gentleman, and you confess yourself that you provoked him, drew the sword first, and received your wound in fair fight."

" Certainly ; but it is not the less true that he obeyed the wishes of M. d'Anjou."

" Listen ! I know M. de St. Luc, and I can assure you he is devoted to the king, and hates the duke. If your wound had come from Autragues, Livarot, or Ribeirac, it might be so ; but not from St. Luc."

" You do not know," replied Monsoreau, obstinate in his opinion. At last he was able to go down into the garden. "That will do," said he ; " now we will move."

" Why move ? " said Rémy. " The air is good here, and there is plenty of amusement."

" Too much ; M. d'Anjou fatigues me with his visits, and he always brings with him a crowd of gentlemen, and the noise of their spurs destroys my nerves."

" But where are you going ? "

" I have ordered them to get ready my little house at the Tournelles."

Bussy and Diana exchanged a look of loving remembrance.

" What, that little place ? " cried Rémy, imprudently.

" What ! do you know it ? "

" Who does not know the houses of the chief huntsman ? particularly I, who lived in the Rue Beautrellis."

" Yes, yes, I will go there. It is a fortress, and one can see from the window, three hundred yards off, who is coming to visit you, and avoid them if you like, particularly when you are well ! "

Bussy bit his lips ; he feared a time might come when Monsoreau might avoid him. Diana thought of the time when she had seen Bussy in that house, lying fainting on the bed.

" You cannot do it," said Rémy.

" Why not, if you please, monsieur ? "

"Because the chief huntsman of France must hold receptions—must keep valets and equipages. Let him have a palace for his dogs, if he likes, but not a dog-kennel for himself."

"It is true, but——"

"But I am the doctor of the mind as of the body ; it is not your residence here that displeases you."

"What then ?"

"That of madame ; therefore send her away."

"Separate ?" cried Monsoreau, fixing on Diana a look, more of anger than love.

"Then give up your place—send in your resignation. I believe it would be wise ; if you do not do your duty, you will displease the king, and if you do——"

"I will do anything but quit the countess," said Monsoreau, with closely-shut teeth. As he spoke, they heard in the courtyard a noise of voices and horses' feet.

"The duke again !" cried he.

"Yes," said Rémy.

Immediately after the prince entered, and Monsoreau saw his first glance given to Diana. He brought to her, as a present, one of those masterpieces, of which the artists of that day were in the habit of producing two or three in the course of a lifetime. It was a poniard, with a handle of chased gold. This handle was a smelling-bottle, and on the blade a chase was carved with admirable skill ; horses, dogs, trees, game, and hunters, mingled together in an harmonious pêle-mêle, on this blade of azure and gold.

"Let me see," cried Monsoreau, who feared there was a note hidden in the handle.

The prince separated the two parts. "To you, who are a hunter," said he, "I give the blade : to the countess, the handle. Good-morning, Bussy, you are then a friend of the count's, now ?"

Diana reddened, but Bussy said :

"Your highness forgets that you asked me to inquire after M. de Monsoreau."

"It is true."

24

The prince sat down, and began to talk to Diana. In a few minutes he said, "Count, it is dreadfully warm in your rooms. I see the countess is stifling. I will give her my arm for a turn in the garden."

The husband looked furious.

"Give me an arm," said he to Bussy, and he got up and followed his wife.

"Ah!" said the duke, "it seems you are better."

"Yes, monseigneur, and I hope soon to be able to accompany Madame de Monsoreau wherever she goes."

"Good; but meanwhile, do not fatigue yourself."

Monsoreau was obliged to sit down, but he kept them in view.

"Count," said he to Bussy, "will you be amiable enough to escort Madame de Monsoreau this evening to my house at the Tournelles?"

"You cannot do that, monsieur," said Rémy.

"Why not?"

"Because M. d'Anjou would never forgive you if you helped to play him such a trick."

Bussy was about to cry, "What do I care?" but a glance from Rémy stopped him.

"Rémy is right," said Monsoreau, "it would injure you; to-morrow I will go myself."

"You will lose your place."

"It is possible; but I shall keep my wife."

The next day they went to the old house; Diana took her old room, with the bed of white and gold damask. A corridor only separated it from that of the count. Bussy tore his hair with rage.

CHAPTER LXXIX.

A VISIT TO THE HOUSE AT LES TOURNELLES.

THE duke became more and more in love with Diana, as she seemed always to escape him, and with his love for her, his hatred of Monsoreau increased. On the other side he had not renounced his political hopes, but had recommenced his underhand machinations. The moment was favorable, for many wavering conspirators had been encouraged by the kind of triumph which the weakness of the king, and the cunning of Catherine, had given to the duke ; however, he no longer confided his projects to Bussy, and showed him only a hypocritical friendship. He was vaguely uneasy at seeing him at Monsoreau's house, and envious of the confidence that Monsoreau, so suspicious of himself, placed in him. He was frightened also at the joy and happiness which shone in Diana's face. He knew that flowers only bloom in the light of the sun, and women in that of love. She was visibly happy, and this annoyed him. Determined to use his power, both for love and vengeance, he thought it would be absurd to be stayed in this purpose by such ridiculous obstacles as the jealousy of a husband, and the repugnance of a wife. One day he ordered his equipages, intending to visit Monsoreau. He was told that he had moved to his house in the Rue St. Antoine.

"Let us go there," said he to Bussy. Soon the place was in commotion at the arrival of the twenty-four handsome cavaliers, each with two lackeys, who formed the prince's suite. Both Bussy and the prince knew the house well ; they both went in, but while the prince entered the room, Bussy remained on the staircase. It resulted from this arrangement that the duke was received by Monsoreau alone, while Bussy was received by Diana, while Gertrude kept watch. Monsoreau, always pale, grew livid at sight of the prince.

"Monseigneur, here ! really it is too much honor for my poor house !" cried he, with a visible irony.

The prince smiled. "Wherever a suffering friend goes, I follow him," replied he. "How are you ?"

"Oh, much better ; I can already walk about, and in a week I shall be quite well."

"Was it your doctor who prescribed for you the air of the Bastile ?" asked the prince, with the most innocent air possible.

"Yes, monseigneur."

"Did you not like the Rue des Petits-Pères ?"

"No, monseigneur ; I had too much company there—they made too much noise. "

"But you have no garden here."

"I did not like the garden."

The prince bit his lips. "Do you know, comte," said he, "that many people are asking the king for your place ?"

"On what pretext, monseigneur ?"

"They say you are dead."

"Monseigneur, you can answer for it that I am not."

"I answer for nothing ; you bury yourself as though you were dead."

It was Monsoreau's turn to bite his lips.

"Well, then, I must lose my place," said he.

"Really ? "

"Yes ; there are things I prefer to it."

"You are very disinterested."

"It is my character, monseigneur."

"Then of course you will not mind the king's knowing your character ?"

"Who will tell him ?"

"Diable ! if he asks me about you, I must repeat our conversation."

"Ma foi ! monseigneur, if all they say in Paris were reported to the king, his two ears would not be enough to listen with."

"What do they say at Paris, monsieur ?" asked the prince sharply.

Monsoreau tried to calm himself. "How should a poor invalid, as I am, know ?" said he. "If the king is angry at seeing his work badly done, he is wrong."

"How so ?"

"Because, doubtless, my accident proceeds, to some extent, from him."

"Explain yourself."

"M. de St. Luc, who wounded me, is a dear friend of the king's. It was the king who taught him the thrust by which he wounded me, and it might have been the king who prompted him."

"You are right; but still the king is the king."

"Until he is so no longer."

The duke trembled. "Is not Madame de Monsoreau here?" said he.

"Monseigneur, she is ill, or she would have come to present her respects to you."

"Ill! poor woman! it must be grief at seeing you suffer."

"Yes, and the fatigue of moving."

"Let us hope it will be a short indisposition. You have so skilful a doctor."

"Yes, that dear Rémy——"

"Why, he is Bussy's doctor."

"He has lent him to me."

"You are, then, great friends?"

"He is my best, I might say my only, friend."

"Adieu, come!"

As the duke raised the tapestry, he fancied he saw the skirt of a dress disappear into the next room, and immediately Bussy appeared at his post in the middle of the corridor. Suspicion grew stronger with the duke.

"We are going," said he to Bussy, who ran down-stairs without replying; while the duke, left alone, tried to penetrate the corridor where he had seen the silk dress vanish. But, turning, he saw that Monsoreau had followed, and was standing at the door.

"Your highness mistakes your way," said he.

"True," said the duke, "thank you." And he went down with rage in his heart. When he returned home, Aurilly glided into his room.

"Well," said the duke, "I am baffled by the husband!"

"And, perhaps, also by the lover, monseigneur."

"What do you say?"

"The truth."

"Speak, then."

"I hope your highness will pardon me—it was in your service."

"I pardon you in advance. Go on."

"After your highness had gone up-stairs, I watched under a shed in the courtyard."

"Ah! What did you see?"

"I saw a woman's dress; I saw this woman lean forward, and then I heard the sound of a long and tender kiss."

"But who was the man?"

"I cannot recognize arms."

"No, but you might gloves."

"Indeed, it seemed to me——"

"That you recognized them?"

"It was only a guess."

"Never mind."

"Well, monseigneur, they looked like the gloves of M. de Bussy."

"Buff, embroidered with gold, were they not?"

"Yes, monseigneur."

"Ah! Bussy! yes, it was Bussy. Oh, I was blind and yet not blind; but I could not believe in so much audacity."

"But your highness must not believe it too lightly; might there not have been a man hidden in her room?"

"Yes, doubtless, but Bussy, who was in the corridor, would have seen him."

"That is true."

"And then the gloves——"

"Yes, and besides the kiss, I heard——"

"What?"

"Three words, 'Till to-morrow evening.'"

"Oh! mon Dieu!"

"So that, if you like, we can make sure."

"Aurilly, we will go."

"Your highness knows I am at your orders."

"Ah! Bussy, a traitor! Bussy, the honest man—Bussy, who does not wish me to be King of France;" and the duke, smiling with an infernal joy, dismissed Aurilly.

CHAPTER LXXX.

THE WATCHERS.

THE duke kept Bussy near him all day, so as not to lose sight of his movements. Bussy did not care, so that he had his evenings free. At ten o'clock he wrapped himself in his cloak, and with a rope ladder under his arm went towards the Bastile. The duke, who did not know that he had a ladder, and could not believe in any one walking alone at night through the streets of Paris, thought Bussy would certainly call at his hotel for a horse and a servant, and lost ten minutes in preparations. During those ten minutes, Bussy, active and in love, had already gone three-fourths of the distance. He was lucky, as brave people generally are, and met with no accident by the way, and on arriving saw a light in the windows. It was the signal agreed on between him and Diana. He threw his ladder up to the balcony, it had six hooks to it, and was sure to fasten itself somewhere. At the noise, Diana put out her light and opened the window to fasten the ladder. The thing was done in a moment. Diana looked all around; the street seemed deserted. Then she signed to Bussy to mount, and he was up in five seconds. The moment was happily chosen, for while he got in at the window, M. de Monsoreau, after having listened patiently for a quarter of an hour at his wife's door, descended the stairs painfully, leaning on the arm of a confidential valet, and it so happened that he opened the street-door just as the ladder was drawn up, and the window closed. He looked around, but the streets were deserted.

" You have been badly informed," said he to the servant.

" No, monsieur, I have just left the Hôtel d'Anjou, and they told me that the duke had ordered two horses for this evening. But perhaps it was not to come here."

" Where else should he go ? " said Monsoreau, with a

somber air. He, like all jealous persons, thought the whole world had nothing to do but to torment him.

"Perhaps I should have done better to stay in her room," murmured he. "But they probably have signals for corresponding; she would have warned him of my presence, and I should have learned nothing. It is better to watch outside. Come, conduct me to the hiding-place, whence you say one can see everything."

"Come, monsieur."

About twenty-five steps from the door was an enormous heap of stones belonging to demolished houses, and serving for fortifications to the children of the neighborhood when they played at battles. In the midst was a space, which could contain two people. The valet spread a cloak, on which Monsoreau sat down, while his servant sat at his feet, with a loaded musket placed beside him. Diana had prudently drawn her thick curtains, so that scarcely a ray of light showed through, to betray that there was life in this gloomy house.

They had been watching about ten minutes, when two horses appeared at the end of the street. The valet pointed to them.

"I see," said Monsoreau.

The two men got off their horses, and tied them up at the corner of the Hôtel des Tournelles.

"Monseigneur," said Aurilly, "I believe we have arrived too late; he must have gone straight from your hotel, and must have entered."

"Perhaps so; but if we did not see him go in, we can see him come out."

"Yes, but when?"

"When we please."

"Would it be too curious to ask how you mean to manage?"

"Nothing is more easy; we have but to knock at the door, and ask after M. de Monsoreau. Our lover will be frightened at the noise, and as you enter the house he will come out at the window, and I, who am hidden outside, shall see him."

"And Monsoreau?"

"What can he say? I am his friend, and was uneasy about him, as he looked so ill yesterday; nothing can be more simple."

"It is very ingenious, monseigneur."

"Do you hear what they say?" asked Monsoreau of his valet.

"No, monsieur, but we soon shall, for they are coming nearer."

"Monseigneur," said Aurilly, "here is a heap of stones which seems made on purpose for us."

"Yes, but wait a moment, perhaps we can see through the opening of the curtain." And they stood for some minutes trying to find a place to peep through. Meanwhile, Monsoreau was boiling with impatience, and his hand approached the musket.

"Oh! shall I suffer this?" murmured he, "shall I devour this affront also? No, my patience is worn out. Mordieu! that I can neither sleep, nor wake, nor even suffer quietly, because a shameful caprice has lodged in the idle brain of this miserable prince. No, I am not a complaisant valet; I am the Comte de Monsoreau, and if he comes near, on my word, I will blow his brains out. Light the match, René."

At this moment, just as the prince was about to seek his hiding-place, leaving his companion to knock at the door, Aurilly touched his arm.

"Well, monsieur, what is it?" asked the prince.

"Come away, monseigneur, come."

"Why so?"

"Do you not see something shining there to the left?"

"I see a spark among that heap of stones."

"It is the match of a musket, or arquebuse."

"Ah! who the devil can be in ambush there?"

"Some friend or servant of Bussy's. Let us go and make a detour, and return another way. The servant will give the alarm, and we shall see Bussy come out of the window."

"You are right; come;" and they went to their horses.

"They are going," said the valet.

"Yes. Did you recognize them?"

"They seemed to me to be the prince and Aurilly."

"Just so. But I shall soon be more sure still."

"What will monsieur do?"

"Come."

Meanwhile, the duke and Aurilly turned into the Rue St. Catherine, intending to return by the boulevard of the Bastile.

Monsoreau went in, and ordered his litter.

What the duke had foreseen happened. At the noise that Monsoreau made, Bussy took the alarm, the light was extinguished, the ladder fixed, and Bussy, to his great regret, was obliged to fly, like Romeo, but without having, like him, seen the sun rise and heard the lark sing. Just as he touched the ground, and Diana had thrown him the ladder, the duke and Aurilly arrived at the corner of the Bastile. They saw a shadow suspended from Diana's window, but this shadow disappeared almost instantaneously at the corner of the Rue St. Paul.

"Monsieur," said the valet to Monsoreau, "we shall wake up the household."

"What do I care?" cried Monsoreau, furiously. "I am master here, I believe, and I have at least the right to do what M. d'Anjou wished to do."

The litter was got ready, and, drawn by two stout horses, it was soon at the Hôtel d'Anjou.

The duke and Aurilly had so recently come in that their horses were not unsaddled. Monsoreau, who had the entrée, appeared on the threshold just as the duke, after having thrown his hat on a chair, was holding out his boots to a valet to pull off. A servant, preceding him by some steps, announced M. de Monsoreau. A thunderbolt breaking his windows, could not have astonished the prince more.

"M. de Monsoreau!" cried he, with an uneasiness he could not hide.

"Myself, monseigneur," replied he, trying to repress his emotion, but the effort he made over himself was so violent that his legs failed him, and he fell on to a chair which stood near.

"But you will kill yourself, my dear friend," said the duke; "you are so pale, you look as though you were going to faint."

"Oh, no ; what I have to say to your highness is of too much importance ; I may faint afterwards."

"Speak, then, my dear comte."

"Not before your people, I suppose."

The duke dismissed every one.

"Your highness has just come in ?" said Monsoreau.

"As you see, comte."

"It is very imprudent of your highness to go by night in the streets."

"Who told you I had been in the streets ?"

"The dust on your clothes."

"M. de Monsoreau, have you another employment besides that of chief huntsman ?"

"Yes, that of spy, monseigneur ; all the world follow that calling now, more or less, and I, like the rest."

"And what does this profession bring you, monsieur ?"

"Knowledge."

"It is curious."

"Very curious."

"Well, tell me what you have to say."

"I came for that."

"You permit me to sit down ?" said the duke.

"No irony, monseigneur, towards an old and faithful servant, who comes at this hour and in this state to do you a service. If I sat down, on my honor, it was because I could not stand."

"A service ! to do me a service ?"

"Yes."

"Speak, then."

"Monseigneur, I come on the part of a great prince."

"From the king ?"

"No ; M. le Duc de Guise."

"Ah ! that is quite a different thing. Approach, and speak low."

CHAPTER LXXXI.

HOW M. LE DUC D'ANJOU SIGNED, AND, AFTER HAVING SIGNED, SPOKE.

THERE was a moment's silence. Then the duke said :
" Well, M. le Comte, what have you to say to me from
the Duc de Guise ? "

" Much, monseigneur."

" They have written to you ? "

" No ; the duke writes no more since that strange dis-
appearance of Nicholas David. They have come to Paris."

" MM. de Guise are at Paris ? "

" Yes, monseigneur."

" I have not seen them."

" They are too prudent to expose themselves or your
highness to any risk."

" And I was not told ! "

" I tell you now."

" What have they come for ? "

" They come, monseigneur, to the rendezvous you gave
them."

" That I gave them ! "

" Doubtless ; on the day when your highness was arrested
you received a letter from M. de Guise, and replied to it
verbally, through me, that they were to come to Paris
from the thirty-first of May to the second of June. It is
now the thirty-first of May, and if your highness has forgotten them, they have not forgotten you."

François grew pale. So many events had passed since,
that he had forgotten the rendezvous. " It is true," said
he, at length, " but the relations which then existed between us exist no longer."

" If that be so, monseigneur, you would do well to tell
them, for I believe they think differently."

" How so ? "

"You, perhaps, think yourself free as regards them, but they feel bound to you."

"A snare, my dear comte, in which a man does not let himself be taken twice."

"And where was monseigneur taken in a snare?"

"Where? at the Louvre, mordieu."

"Was it the fault of MM. de Guise?"

"I do not say so, but they never assisted me to escape."

"It would have been difficult; they were flying themselves."

"It is true."

"But when you were in Anjou, did they not charge me to tell you that you could always count on them, as they on you, and that the day you marched on Paris, they would do the same?"

"It is true, but I did not march on Paris."

"You are here."

"Yes; but as my brother's ally."

"Monseigneur will permit me to observe that he is more than the ally of the Guises."

"What then?"

"Their accomplice."

The duke bit his lips.

"And you say they charged you to announce their arrival to me?"

"They did me that honour."

"But they did not tell you the motive of their return?"

"They told me all, knowing me to be the confidant of your highness."

"Then they have projects. What are they?"

"The same always."

"And they think them practicable?"

"They look upon them as certain."

"And these projects have for an aim——"

The duke stopped, not daring to finish.

"To make you King of France; yes, monseigneur."

The duke felt the flush of joy mount to his face.

" But," said he, "is the moment favorable ? "

" Your wisdom must decide."

" My wisdom ? "

" Yes, the facts cannot be contradicted.   The nomina-
tion of the king as head of the League was only a comedy,
quickly seen through and appreciated.   Now the reaction
has commenced, and the entire state is rising against the
tyranny of the king and his creatures.   Sermons are a call
to arms, and churches are places where they curse the
king, instead of praying to God.   The army trembles
with impatience ; the bourgeois league together ; our
emissaries bring in nothing but signatures and new adherents to the League.   In a word, the king's reign
touches on its close.   Now, do you renounce your former
projects ? "

The duke did not reply.

" Monseigneur knows that he may speak frankly to
me."

" I think," said the duke, " that considering my brother
has no children, that his health is uncertain, and that after
him the crown will come naturally to me, there is no
reason why I should compromise my name and my dignity,
in a useless struggle, and try to take, with danger, what
will come to me in due course."

" Your highness is in error ; your brother's throne will
only come to you if you take it.   MM. de Guise cannot
be kings themselves, but they will only allow to reign a
king of their own making, a king whom they substitute
for the reigning one.   They count on your highness, but
if you refuse, they will seek another."

" And who will dare to seat himself on the throne of
Charlemagne ? "

" A Bourbon instead of a Valois, monseigneur ; a son
of St. Louis, instead of a son of St. Louis."

" The king of Navarre ? "

" Why not ?   He is young, and brave."

" He is a Huguenot."

" Was he not converted at the St. Bartholomew ? "

" Yes, and he abjured afterwards."

"Oh, monseigneur, what he did for his wife, he will do again for the crown."

"They think, then, that I will yield my rights without a struggle."

"The case is provided for."

"I will fight."

"They are men of war."

"I will put myself at the head of the League."

"They are the soul of it."

"I will join my brother."

"Your brother will be dead."

"I will call the kings of Europe to my aid."

"They will think twice before making war on a people."

"My party will stand by me."

"Your party, I believe, consists of M. de Bussy and myself."

"Then I am tied.".

"Nearly so. You can do nothing without the Guises; with them, everything. Say the word, and you are king."

The duke walked about for a few minutes, in great agitation, then stopped, and said, "Go on, count."

"This, then, is the plan. In eight days the Fête Dieu will take place, and the king meditates on that day a great procession to the convents of Paris. There, the guards will remain at the door, the king will stop before each altar, kneel down, and say five paters and five aves."

"I know all that."

"He will go to St. Geneviève——"

"Yes."

"He will enter with a suite of five or six persons, and behind them, the doors will be closed."

"And then——"

"Your highness knows the monks who will do the honors of the Abbey to his majesty."

"They will be the same——"

"Who were there when your highness was crowned."

"They will dare to lay hands on the Lord's anointed?"

" Oh ! to shave him, only."

" They will never dare to do that to a king."

" He will not be a king then."

" How so ? "

" Have you never heard of a holy man who preaches sermons, and is going to perform miracles ? "

" Brother Gorenflot ? "

" Just so."

" The one who wished to preach the League with his arquebuse on his shoulder ? "

" The same."

" Well ! they will conduct the king into his cell ; once there, he will be asked to sign his abdication, then, when he has signed, Madame de Montpensier will enter, scissors in hand. She wears them now, hanging to her side ; they are charming scissors, made of gold, and admirably chased, to do him honor. You understand the rest. We announced to the people that the king, experiencing a holy repentance for his sins, has announced his intention of never more leaving the convent. If there are any who doubt, M. de Guise holds the army, M. le Cardinal the Church, and M. de Mayenne the bourgeois ; and with these three powers you can make the people believe what you like."

" But they will accuse me of violence," said the duke.

" You need not be there."

" They will look on me as a usurper."

" Monseigneur forgets the abdication."

" The king will refuse."

" It seems that Brother Gorenflot is not only clever, but strong."

" The plan is then settled ? "

" Quite."

" And they do not fear that I shall denounce it ? "

" No, monseigneur ; for in that case, they have another, not less sure."

" Ah ! "

" Yes."

" And this one ? "

"I do not know; they thought me too much your friend to trust me with it."

"Well, I yield, count. What must I do?"

"Approve."

"I do."

"Words are not enough."

"What then?"

"Writing."

"It is a folly to suppose I will ever consent to that."

"And why not?"

"If the conspiracy fail——"

"It is just in case it should, that they ask for your signature."

"Then they wish to shelter themselves behind my name?"

"Just so."

"Then I refuse."

"You cannot."

"I cannot refuse?"

"No."

"Are you mad?"

"To refuse is to betray."

"Let them think as they like; at all events I will choose my own danger."

"Monseigneur, you choose badly."

"I will risk it," cried François, endeavoring to keep firm.

"For your own interest I advise you not to do so."

"But I shall compromise myself by signing."

"In refusing, you assassinate yourself."

François shuddered.

"They would dare?" said he.

"They would dare anything, monseigneur. The conspirators have gone so far, that they must succeed at any cost."

The duke, with his usual indecision, felt terribly perplexed.

"I will sign," said he, at last.

"When?"

" To-morrow."

" No, monseigneur ; if you sign, it must be at once."

" But M. de Guise must draw up the agreement."

" It is already drawn—here it is ; " and Monsoreau drew
a paper from his pocket : it was a full adhesion to the
scheme. The duke read it through, growing more and
more pale as he did so.

" Here is the pen, monseigneur."

" Then I must sign ? "

" If you wish to do so ; no one forces you."

" Yes, they do, since they menace me with assassination."

" I do not menace you, monseigneur—I only warn
you."

" Give me the pen."

And, snatching it eagerly, he signed the paper. Monsoreau watched him with an eye full of hatred and hope,
and no sooner had the duke finished than, exclaiming
" Ah ! " he seized the paper, buttoned it into his doublet,
and wrapped his cloak over it.

François looked at him with astonishment, for a flash
of ferocious joy played over his face.

" And now, monseigneur, be prudent," said he.

" How so ? "

" Do not run about the streets with Aurilly, as you did
just now."

" What do you mean ? "

" I mean that, this evening, you pursued with your love
a woman whom her husband adores, and whom he is jealous of, enough to kill any one who approaches her without
permission."

" Is it of you and your wife that you are speaking ? "

" Yes, monseigneur. I have married Diana de Méridor ;
she is mine, and no one shall have her while I live—not
even a prince ; I swear it by my name and on this poniard ! "
and he touched with his poniard the breast of the prince,
who started back.

" Monsieur, you menace me ! " cried François, pale with
rage,

"No, monseigneur; once more, I say, I only warn you."

"Of what?"

"That no one shall make love to my wife."

"And I warn you that you are too late, and that some one makes love to her already."

Monsoreau uttered a terrible cry. "Is it you?" cried he.

"You are mad, count!"

"No, I am not; prove your words."

"Who was hidden this evening, twenty steps from your door, with a musket?"

"I."

"Well, comte, during that time there was a man with your wife."

"You saw him go in?"

"I saw him come out."

"By the door?"

"No, by the window."

"Did you recognize him?"

"Yes."

"Name him, monseigneur, or I do not answer for myself."

The duke half smiled.

"M. le Comte," said he, "on my faith as a prince, on my soul, within a week I will tell you his name."

"You swear it."

"I swear it."

"Well, monseigneur, you have a week; but——" said he, touching the paper in his breast.

"Come back in eight days."

"Good! in eight days I shall have regained all my strength, ready for vengeance."

CHAPTER LXXXII.

A PROMENADE AT THE TOURNELLES.

In course of time the Angevin gentlemen had returned to Paris, although not with much confidence. They knew too well the king, his brother, and mother, to hope that all would terminate in a family embrace. They returned, therefore, timidly, and glided into the town armed to the tooth, ready to fire on the least suspicion, and drew their swords fifty times before the Hôtel d'Anjou on harmless bourgeois, who were guilty of no crime but of looking at them. They presented themselves at the Louvre, magnificently dressed in silk, velvet, and embroidery. Henri III. would not receive them; they waited vainly in the gallery. It was MM. Quelus, Maugiron, Schomberg, and D'Epernon who came to announce this news to them, with great politeness, and expressing all the regrets in the world.

"Ah, gentlemen," said Antragues, "the news is sad, but, coming from your mouths, it loses half its bitterness."

"Gentlemen," said Schomberg, "you are the flower of grace and courtesy. Would it please you to change the reception which you have missed into a little promenade?"

"Ah! gentlemen, we were about to propose it."

"Where shall we go?" said Quelus.

"I know a charming place near the Bastile," said Schomberg.

"We follow you, go on."

Then the eight gentlemen went out, arm in arm, talking gaily on different subjects, until Quelus said, "Here is a solitary place, with a good footing."

"Ma foi, yes."

"Well! we thought that you would one day accompany us here to meet M. de Bussy, who has invited us all here."

"It is true," said Bussy.

"Do you accept?" said Maugiron.

"Certainly; we rejoice at such an honor."

"That is well," said Schomberg; "shall we each choose an opponent?"

"No," said Bussy, "that is not fair; "let us trust to chance, and the first one that is free can join the others."

"Let us draw lots then," said Quelus.

"One moment," said Bussy, "first let us settle the rules of the game."

"They are simple; we will fight till death ensues!"

"Yes, but how?"

"With sword and dagger."

"On foot?"

"Oh, yes! on horseback one's movements are not so free."

"Then, on foot."

"What day?"

"The soonest possible."

"No," said D'Epernon, "I have a thousand things to settle and a will to make; I would rather wait five or six days."

"So be it."

"Then draw lots."

"One moment! divide the ground into four compartments, each for a pair."

"Well said."

"I propose for number one, the long square between the chestnuts; it is a fine place."

"Agreed."

"But the sun? one would be turned to the east."

"No," said Bussy, "that is not fair;" and he proposed a new position, which was agreed to.

Schomberg and Ribeirac came first. They were the first pair; Quelus and Antragues the second; then Livarot and Maugiron the third. D'Epernon, who saw himself left to Bussy, grew very pale.

"Now, gentlemen," said Bussy, "until the day of the combat, let us be friends. Will you accept a dinner at the Hôtel Bussy?"

All agreed, and returned with Bussy to his hotel, where a sumptuous banquet united them till morning.

CHAPTER LXXXIII.

IN WHICH CHICOT SLEEPS.

THE movements of the young men had been remarked by the king and Chicot. The king walked up and down, waiting impatiently for his friends to return ; but Chicot followed them at a distance, and saw enough to be satisfied of their intentions. When he returned to the house he found the king, walking up and down, muttering.

"Ah ! my dear friend ! do you know what has become of them ?" cried Henri.

"Whom ? your minions ?"

"Alas ! yes, my poor friends."

"They must lie very low by this time."

"Have they been killed ?" cried Henri ; "are they dead ?"

"Dead, I fear——"

"And you laugh, wretch ?"

"Oh ! my son, dead drunk."

"Oh ! Chicot, how you terrified me. But why do you calumniate these gentlemen ?"

"On the contrary, I praise them."

"Be serious, I beg ; do you know that they went out with the Angevins ?"

"Of course, I know it."

"What was the result ?"

"What I tell you ; that they are dead drunk."

"But Bussy !"

"He is intoxicating them ; he is a dangerous man."

"Chicot, for pity's sake——"

"Yes ; Bussy has given a dinner to your friends ; how do you like that ?"

"Impossible ! They are sworn enemies."

"Have you good legs ?"

"What do you mean ?"

"Will you go to the river ?"

"I would go to the end of the world to see such a thing."

"Well! go only to the Hôtel Bussy."

"Will you accompany me?"

"Thank you, I have just come from there."

"But——"

"Oh! no; I, who have seen, do not need to be convinced. Go, my son, go. You disquiet yourself about your friends; you first pity them as if they were dead, and when you hear they are not dead, you are uneasy still——"

"You are intolerable, M. Chicot."

"Would you have preferred that they should each have had seven or eight wounds by a rapier?"

"I should like to be able to depend on my friends."

"Oh! ventre de biche, depend upon me; I am here, my son, only feed me. I want pheasant and truffles."

Henri and his only friend went to bed early, the king still sighing.

The next day, at the petite levée of the king, MM. Quelus, Schomberg, Maugiron, and D'Epernon presented themselves. Chicot still slept. The king jumped from his bed in a fury, and tearing off the perfumed mask from his face, cried, "Go out from here."

The young men looked at each other in wonder.

"But, sire, we wished to say to your majesty——"

"That you are no longer drunk, I suppose."

Chicot opened his eyes.

"Your majesty is in error," said Quelus, gravely.

"And yet I have not drunk the wine of Anjou."

"Oh! I understand," said Quelus, smiling.

"What?"

"If your majesty will remain alone with us, we will tell you."

"I hate drunkards and traitors."

"Sire," cried three of the gentlemen.

"Patience, gentlemen," said Quelus, "his majesty has slept badly, and had unpleasant dreams. A few words will set all right."

" Speak then, but be brief."

"It is possible, sire, but difficult."

" Yes ; one turns long round certain accusations."

" No, sire, we go straight to it," replied Quelus, looking again at Chicot and the usher, as though to reiterate his request that they might be left alone. The king signed to the usher to leave the room, but Chicot said, " Never mind me, I sleep like a top," and closing his eyes again, he began to snore with all his strength.

CHAPTER LXXXIV.

WHERE CHICOT WAKES.

" YOUR majesty," said Quelus, " knows only half the business, and that the least interesting half. Assuredly, we have all dined with M. de Bussy, and to the honor of his cook, be it said, dined well. There was, above all, a certain wine from Austria or Hungary, which really appeared to me marvelous. But during the repast, or rather after it, we had the most serious and interesting conversation concerning your majesty's affairs."

"You make the exordium very long."

" How talkative you are, Valois !" cried Chicot.

"Oh! oh! M. Gascon," said Henri, "if you do not sleep, you must leave the room."

" Pardieu, it is you who keep me from sleeping, your tongue clacks so fast."

Quelus, seeing it was impossible to speak seriously, shrugged his shoulders, and rose in anger.

" We were speaking of grave matters," said he.

" Grave matters ?"

" Yes," said D'Epernon, "if the lives of eight brave gentlemen are worth the trouble of your majesty's attention."

" What does it mean, my son ?" said Henri, placing his hand on Quelus's shoulder.

" Well, sire, the result of our conversation was, that royalty is menaced—weakened, that is to say, that all the world is conspiring against you. Sire, you are a great king, but you have no horizon before you ; the nobility have raised so many barriers before your eyes, that you can see nothing, if it be not the still higher barriers that the people have raised. When, sire, in battle one battalion places itself like a menacing wall before another, what happens ? Cowards look behind them, and seeing an open space, they fly ; the brave lower their heads and rush on."

"Well, then forward !" cried the king, " mordieu ! am I not the first gentleman in my kingdom ? Were they not great battles that I fought in my youth ? Forward, then, gentlemen, and I will take the lead ; it is my custom in the mêlée."

"Oh ! yes, sire," cried the young men, with one voice.

" And," said Quelus, "against these ramparts which are closing round your majesty, four men will march, sure to be applauded by you, and glorified by posterity."

" What do you mean, Quelus ? " cried the king, with eyes in which joy was tempered by solicitude; " who are these four men ? "

"I, and these other gentlemen," replied Quelus, with pride ; " we devote ourselves, sire."

" To what ? "

" To your safety."

" Against whom ?"

" Against your enemies."

" Private enmities of young men ? "

" Oh ! sire, that is the expression of vulgar prejudice ; speak like a king, sire, not like a bourgeois. Do not profess to believe that Maugiron detests Antragues, that Schomberg dislikes Livarot, that D'Epernon is jealous of Bussy, and that I hate Ribeirac. Oh ! no. They are all young, and agreeable, and might love each other like brothers : it is not, therefore, a rivalry between man and man, which places the swords in our hands ; it is the quarrel of France with Anjou, the dispute as to the rights of the populace against the prerogatives of the king. We present ourselves as champions of royalty in those lists,

CHICOT, THE JESTER.

where we shall be met by the champions of the League, and we came to say, 'Bless us, sire, smile on those who are going to die for you.' Your blessing will, perhaps, give us the victory, your smile will make us die happy."

Henri, overcome with emotion, opened his arms to Quelus and the others. He united them in his heart; and it was not a spectacle without interest, a picture without expression, but a scene in which manly courage was allied to softer emotions, sanctified by devotion. Chicot looked on, and his face, ordinarily indifferent or sarcastic, was not the least noble and eloquent of the six.

"Ah!" cried the king, "I am proud to-day, not of being King of France, but of being your friend; at the same time, as I know my own interests best, I will not accept a sacrifice, of which the result will deliver me up, if you fall, into the hands of my enemies. France is enough to make war on Anjou; I know my brother, the Guises, and the League, and have often conquered more dangerous foes."

"But, sire, soldiers do not reason thus, they never take ill luck into their calculations."

"Pardon me, Maugiron; a soldier may act blindly, but the captain reflects."

"Reflect, then, sire, and let us act, who are only soldiers," said Schomberg: "besides, I know no ill luck; I am always successful."

"Friend, friend," said the king, sadly, "I wish I could say as much. It is true, you are but twenty."

"Sire," said Quelus, "on what day shall we meet MM. Bussy, Livarot, Antragues and Ribeirac?"

"Never; I forbid it absolutely."

"Sire, excuse us, the rendezvous was arranged before the dinner, words were said which cannot be retracted."

"Excuse me, monsieur," said Henri, "the king absolves from oaths and promises by saying, 'I will, or I will not,' for the king is all-powerful. Tell these gentlemen, therefore, that I have menaced you with all my anger if you come to blows; and that you may not doubt it yourselves, I swear to exile you, if——"

"Stop! sire; do not swear; because, if for such a cause we have merited your anger, and this anger shows itself by exiling us, we will go into exile with joy, because, being no longer on your majesty's territories, we can then keep our promises, and meet our adversaries."

"If these gentlemen approach you within range of an arquebuse, I will throw them all into the Bastile."

"Sire, if you do so we will all go barefooted, and with cords round our necks, to M. Testu, the governor, and pray to be incarcerate with them."

"I will have them beheaded, then; I am king, I hope."

"We will cut our throats at the foot of their scaffold."

Henri kept silent for a long time; then, raising his eyes, said, "God will surely bless a cause defended by such noble hearts."

"Yes, they are noble hearts," said Chicot, rising; "do what they wish, and fix a day for their meeting. It is your duty, my son."

"Oh! mon Dieu! mon Dieu!" murmured Henri.

"Sire, we pray you," cried all the four gentlemen, bending their knees.

"Well! so be it. Let us trust that God will give us the victory. But let us prepare for the conflict in a Christian manner. If I had time, I would send all your swords to Rome, that the Pope might bless them. But we have the shrine of St. Geneviève, which contains most precious relics: let us fast, and do penance, and keep holy the great day of the Fête Dieu, and then the next day——"

"Ah! sire, thanks; that is in eight days!" cried the young men.

And they seized the hands of the king, who embraced them all once more, and, going into his oratory, melted into tears.

"Our cartel is ready," said Quelus, "we have but to add the day and hour. Write, Maugiron, the day after the Fête Dieu. Here is a table."

"It is done," said Maugiron, "now who will carry the letter?"

"I will, if you please," said Chicot, approaching, "but I wish to give you a piece of advice. His majesty speaks of fasts and macerations. That is all very well after the combat, but before, I prefer good nourishment, generous wine, and eight hours' sleep every night."

"Bravo, Chicot!"

"Adieu, my little lions," replied the Gascon, "I go to the Hôtel Bussy." He went three steps and returned, and said, "Apropos, do not quit the king during the Fête Dieu; do not go to the country, any of you, but stay by the Louvre. Now, I will do your commission."

CHAPTER LXXXV.

THE FÊTE DIEU.

DURING these eight days events were preparing themselves, as a tempest gathers in the heavens during the calm days of summer. Monsoreau had an attack of fever for twenty-four hours, then he rallied, and began to watch himself; but as he discovered no one, he became more than ever convinced of the hypocrisy of the Duc d'Anjou, and of his bad intentions with regard to Diana.

Bussy did not discontinue his visits by day, but, warned by Rémy of this constant watchfulness, came no more at night to the window.

Chicot divided his time between the king, whom he watched like a child, and his friend Gorenflot, whom he had persuaded to return to his convent. He passed hours with him in his cell, always bringing with him large bottles in his pocket, and the report began to be spread that Gorenflot had nearly persuaded him to turn monk.

As for the king, he gave constant lessons in fencing to his friends, teaching them new thrusts, and, above all, exercising D'Epernon, to whom fate had given so skilful an adversary, that he was visibly preoccupied by it.

Any one walking in the streets of Paris at certain hours, might have met the strange monks, of whom our first chapters furnished some description, and who resembled troopers more than monks. Then, to complete the picture, we must add that the Hôtel de Guise had become at once mysterious and turbulent, the most peopled within and the most deserted without that can be imagined; that meetings were held every night in the great hall, and with all the blinds and windows hermetically closed, and that these meetings were preceded by dinners, to which none but men were invited, and which were presided over by Madame de Montpensier. Of all these meetings, however, important though they were, the police suspected nothing. On the morning of the great day, the weather was superb, and the flowers which filled the streets sent their perfumes through the air. Chicot, who for the last fortnight had slept in the king's room, woke him early; no one had yet entered the royal chamber.

"Oh, Chicot!" cried the king, "you have woke me from one of the sweetest dreams I ever had in my life."

"What was it, my son?"

"I dreamed that Quelus had run Antragues through the body, and was swimming in the blood of his adversary. Let us go and pray that my dream may be realized. Call, Chicot, call."

"What do you want?"

"My hair-cloth and my scourge."

"Would you not prefer a good breakfast?"

"Pagan, would you go to hear mass on the Fête Dieu with a full stomach?"

"Even so."

"Call, Chicot."

"Patience; it is scarcely eight o'clock, and you will have plenty of time to scourge yourself. Let us talk first. Converse with your friend; you will not repent it, Valois, on the faith of a Chicot."

"Well, talk; but be quick."

"How shall we divide our day, my son?"

"Into three parts."

"In honor of the Trinity; very well, let me hear these three parts."

" First, mass at St. Germain l'Auxerrois."

" Well ? "

" Return to the Louvre, for a collation."

" Very good."

" Then, a procession of penitents through the streets, stopping at the principal convents of Paris, beginning at the Jacobins and finishing at St. Geneviève, where I have promised the prior to stay till to-morrow in the cell of a saint, who will pray for the success of our arms."

" I know him."

" The saint ? "

" Yes, perfectly."

" So much the better ; you shall accompany me, and we will pray together."

" Yes ; make yourself easy."

" Then dress yourself, and come."

" Wait a little."

" What for ? "

" I have more to ask."

" Be quick, then, for time passes."

" What is the court to do ? "

" Follow me."

" And your brother ? "

" Will accompany me."

" Your guard ? "

" The French guard wait for me at the Louvre, and the Swiss at the door of the Abbey."

" That will do ; now I know all."

" Then I may call ? "

" Yes."

Henri struck on his gong.

" The ceremony will be magnificent," said Chicot.

" God will accept our homage; I hope."

" But tell me, Henri, before any one comes in, have you nothing else to say to me ? "

" No, I have given you all the details."

" Have you settled to sleep at St. Geneviève ? "

" Doubtless."

" Well, my son, I do not like that part of the program."

"How so?"

"When we have dined I will tell you. another plan that has occurred to me."

"Well, I consent."

"Whether you consent or not, it will be all the same thing."

"What do you mean?"

"Hush! here are your valets."

As he spoke, the ushers opened the door, and the barber, perfumer, and valet of the king entered, and commenced to execute upon his majesty one of those toilets which we have described elsewhere. When the king was dressing, the Duc d'Anjou was announced. He was accompanied by M. de Monsoreau, D'Epernon, and Aurilly. Henri, at the sight of Monsoreau, still pale and looking more frightful than ever, could not repress a movement of surprise.

"You have been wounded, comte, have you not?" said he.

"Yes, sire."

"At the chase, they told me."

"Yes, sire."

"But you are better now?"

"I am well."

"Sire," said the duke, "would it please you that, after our devotions, M. de Monsoreau should go and prepare a chase for us in the woods of Compiègne?"

"But do you not know that to-morrow——"

He was going to say, "Four of your friends are to fight four of mine;" but he stopped, for he remembered that it was a secret.

"I know nothing" said the duke; "but if your majesty will inform me——"

"I meant that, as I am to pass the night at the Abbey of St. Geneviève, I should perhaps not be ready for to-morrow; but let the count go; if it be not to-morrow, it shall be the day after."

"You hear?" said the duke to Monsoreau.

"Yes, monseigneur."

At this moment Quelus and Schomberg entered. The king received them with open arms.

Monsoreau said softly to the duke, "You exile me, monseigneur."

"Is it not your duty to prepare the chase for the king?"

"I understand—this is the last of the eight days fixed by your highness, and you prefer sending me to Compiègne to keeping your promise."

"No, on the contrary; I keep my promise."

"Explain yourself."

"Your departure will be publicly known."

"Well?"

"Well, do not go, but hide near your house; then, believing you gone, the man you wish to know will come; the rest concerns yourself: I engage for no more."

"Ah! if that be so——"

"You have my word."

"I have better than that, I have your signature."

"Oh, yes, mordieu! I know that."

Aurilly touched D'Epernon's arm and said, "It is done; Bussy will not fight to-morrow."

"Not fight!"

"I answer for it."

"Who will prevent it?"

"Never mind that."

"If it be so, my dear sorcerer, there are one thousand crowns for you."

"Gentlemen," said the king, who had finished his toilet, "to St. Germain l'Auxerrois."

"And from there to St. Geneviève?" asked the duke.

"Certainly," replied Henri, passing into the gallery where all his court were waiting for him.

CHAPTER LXXXVI.

WHICH WILL ELUCIDATE THE PREVIOUS CHAPTER.

THE evening before M. de Monsoreau had returned to his home from the Hôtel Guise, and had found Bussy there. Then, in his friendship for this brave gentleman, he had taken him aside, and said:

"Will you permit me to give you a piece of advice?"

"Pray do."

"If I were you, I should leave Paris to-morrow."

"I! and why so?"

"All that I can tell you is, that your absence may save you from great embarrassment."

"How so?"

"Are you ignorant of what is to take place to-morrow?"

"Completely."

"On your honor?"

"On my word as a gentleman."

"M. d'Anjou has confided nothing to you?"

"Nothing; M. d'Anjou confides nothing to me beyond what all the world knows."

"Well! I, who am not the Duc d'Anjou, who love my friends for their own sakes, and not for mine, I will tell you, my dear count, that he is preparing for grave events to-morrow, and that the parties of Guise and Anjou meditate a stroke which may end in the fall of the king."

Bussy looked at M. de Monsoreau with suspicion, but his whole manner expressed so much sincerity that it was impossible to doubt him.

"Count," replied he, "my sword belongs to the Duc d'Anjou. The king, against whom I have done nothing, hates me, and has never let slip an occasion of doing or saying something wounding to me; and to-morrow I tell you—but you alone, remember—I am about to risk my

26

life to humiliate Henri de Valois, in the person of his favorites."

"Then you are resolved to risk all the consequences of your adherence to the duke?"

"Yes."

"You know where it may lead you?"

"I know where I will stop; whatever complaints I have against the king, I will never lift a hand against him; but I will let others do what they like, and I will follow M. d'Anjou to protect him in case of need."

"My dear comte," said Monsoreau, "the Duc d'Anjou is perfidious and a traitor; a coward, capable, from jealousy or fear, of sacrificing his most faithful servant—his most devoted friend; abandon him, take a friend's counsel, pass the day in your little house at Vincennes, go where you like, except to the procession of the Fête Dieu."

"But why do you follow the duke yourself?"

"For reasons which concern my honor. I have need of him for a little while longer."

"Well! that is like me; for things which concern my honor I must follow the duke."

The Comte de Monsoreau pressed his hand, and they parted.

The next morning Monsoreau announced to his wife his approaching departure for Compiègne, and gave all the necessary orders. Diana heard the news with joy. She knew from her husband of the duel which was arranged between Bussy and D'Epernon, but had no fear for the result, and looked forward to it with pride. Bussy had presented himself in the morning to the Duc d'Anjou, who, seeing him so frank, loyal, and devoted, felt some remorse; but two things combated this return of good feeling—firstly, the great empire Bussy had over him, as every powerful mind has over a weak one, and which annoyed him; and, secondly, the love of Bussy for Diana, which awoke all the tortures of jealousy in his heart. Monsoreau, it was true, inspired him with equal dislike and fear, but he thought, "Either Bussy will accompany me and aid my triumph, and then if I triumph, I do not care for

Monsoreau, or Bussy will abandon me, and then I owe him nothing, and I will abandon him in return."

When they were in the church, the duke saw Rémy enter, and going up to his master, slide a note into his hand.

"It is from her," thought he; "she sends him word that her husband is leaving Paris."

Bussy put the note into his hat, opened, and read it, and the prince saw his face radiant with joy and love.

The duke looked round; if Monsoreau had been there, perhaps he would not have had patience to wait till the evening to denounce Bussy.

The mass over, they returned to the Louvre, where a collation waited for the king in his room, and for his gentlemen in the gallery. On entering the Louvre, Bussy approached the duke.

"Pardon, monseigneur," said he, "but can I say two words to you?"

"Are you in a hurry?"

"Very much so."

"Will it not do during the procession? we shall walk side by side."

"Monseigneur must excuse me, but what I wished to ask is, that I need not accompany you."

"Why so?"

"Monseigneur, to-morrow is a great day, and I would wish to retire to-day to my little house at Vincennes."

"Then you do not join the procession with the king and court?"

"No, monseigneur, if you will excuse me."

"Will you not rejoin me at St. Geneviève?"

"Monseigneur, I wish to have the whole day to myself."

"But if anything should occur when I have need of my friends?"

"As monseigneur would only want me to draw my sword against my king, it is a double reason for excusing myself," replied Bussy; "my sword is engaged against M. d'Epernon." —

Monsoreau had told the duke the night before that he might reckon on Bussy; this change, therefore, must have been occasioned by Diana's note."

"Then," said the duke, "you abandon your chief and master?"

"Monseigneur, he who is about to risk his life in a bloody duel, as ours will be, has but one master, and it is to Him my last devotions will be paid."

"You know that I am playing for a throne, and you leave me."

"Monseigneur, I have worked enough for you; I will work again to-morrow, do not ask me for more than my life."

"It is well!" said the duke, in a hollow voice, "you are free; go, M. de Bussy."

Bussy, without caring for the prince's evident anger, ran down the staircase of the Louvre, and went rapidly to his own house.

The duke called Aurilly. "Well! he has condemned himself," said he.

"Does he not follow you?"

"No."

"He goes to the rendezvous?"

"Yes."

"Then it is for this evening?"

"It is."

"Is M. de Monsoreau warned?"

"Of the rendezvous—yes; but not yet of the man."

"Then you have decided to sacrifice the count?"

"I have determined to revenge myself; I fear now but one thing."

"What is that?"

"That Monsoreau will trust to his strength, and that Bussy will escape him."

"Reassure yourself, monseigneur."

"Why?"

"Is M. de Bussy irrevocably condemned?"

"Yes, mordieu! A man who dictates to me—who takes away from me her whom I was seeking for—who is a sort of lion, of whom I am less the master than the keeper—yes, Aurilly, he is condemned without mercy."

"Well, then, be easy, for if he escape Monsoreau, he will not escape from another."

"And who is that ?"

"Does your highness order me to name him ?"

"Yes, I do."

"It is M. d'Epernon."

"D'Epernon ! who was to fight him to-morrow ?"

"Yes, monseigneur."

"How is that ?"

Aurilly was about to reply, when the duke was summoned ; for the king was at table, and had sent for his brother.

"You shall tell me during the procession," said the duke.

We will now tell our readers what had passed between Aurilly and D'Epernon. They had long known each other, for Aurilly had taught D'Epernon to play on the lute, and, as he was fond of music, they were often together. He called upon Aurilly to tell him of his approaching duel, which disquieted him not a little. Bravery was never one of D'Epernon's prominent qualities, and he looked on a duel with Bussy as certain death. When Aurilly heard it, he told D'Epernon that Bussy practised fencing every morning with an artist, lately arrived, who was said to have borrowed from all nations their best points, until he had become perfect. During this recital D'Epernon grew livid with terror.

"Ah ! I am doomed," said he.

"Well ?"

But it is absurd to go out with a man who is sure to kill me."

"You should have thought of that before making the engagement."

"Peste ! I will break the engagement."

"He is a fool who gives up his life willingly at twenty-five. But, now I think of it——"

"Well."

"M. de Bussy is sure to kill me."

"I do not doubt it."

"Then it will not be a duel, but an assassination."

"Perhaps so."

"And if it be, it is lawful to prevent an assassination by——"

"By?"

"A murder."

"Doubtless."

"What prevents me, since he wishes to kill me, from killing him first?"

"Oh, mon Dieu! nothing; I thought of that myself."

"It is only natural."

"Very natural."

"Only, instead of killing him with my own hands, I will leave it to others."

"That is to say, you will hire assassins?"

"Ma foi! yes, like M. de Guise for St. Megrim."

"It will cost you dear."

"I will give three thousand crowns."

"You will only get six men for that, when they know who they have to deal with."

"Are not six enough?"

"M. de Bussy would kill four before they touched him. Do you remember the fight in the Rue St. Antoine?"

"I will give six thousand; if I do the thing, I will take care he does not escape."

"Have you your men?"

"Oh, there are plenty of unoccupied men—soldiers of fortune."

"Very well; but take care."

"Of what?"

"If they fail they will denounce you."

"I have the king to protect me."

"That will not hinder M. de Bussy from killing you."

"That is true."

"Should you like an auxiliary?"

"I should like anything which would aid me to get rid of him."

"Well, a certain enemy of your enemy is jealous."

"And he is now laying a snare for him ?"

"Ah !"

"Well ?"

"But he wants money ; with your six thousand crowns he will take care of your affair as well as his own. You do not wish the honor of the thing to be yours, I suppose ?"

"Mon Dieu ! no ; I only ask to remain in obscurity."

"Send your men, and he will use them."

"But I must know who it is."

"I will show you in the morning."

"Where ?"

"At the Louvre."

"Then he is noble ?"

"Yes :"

"Aurilly, you shall have the six thousand crowns."

"Then it is settled ?"

"Irrevocably."

"At the Louvre, then ?"

"Yes, at the Louvre."

We have seen in the preceding chapter how Aurilly said to D'Epernon, "Be easy, Bussy will not fight to-morrow."

CHAPTER LXXXVII

THE PROCESSION.

As soon as the collation was over, the king had entered his room with Chicot, to put on his penitent's robe and had come out an instant after, with bare feet, a cord round his waist, and his hood over his face ; the courtiers had made the same toilet. The weather was magnificent, and the pavements were strewn with flowers ; an immense crowd lined the roads to the four places where the king was to stop. The clergy of St. Germain led the procession, and the Archbishop of Paris followed, carrying the holy sacrament ; between them walked young boys, shaking

censers, and young girls scattering roses. Then came the
king, followed by his four friends, barefooted and frocked
like himself.

The Duc d'Anjou followed in his ordinary dress, accompanied by his Angevins. Next came the principal
courtiers, and then the bourgeois. It was one o'clock
when they left the Louvre. Crillon and the French
guards were about to follow, but the king signed to them
to remain. It was near six in the evening before they
arrived before the old abbey, where they saw the prior and
the monks drawn up on the threshold to wait for his
majesty. The Duc d'Anjou, a little before, had pleaded
great fatigue, and had asked leave to retire to his hotel,
which had been granted to him. His gentlemen had retired with him, as if to proclaim that they followed the
duke and not the king, besides which, they did not wish
to fatigue themselves before the morrow. At the door of
the abbey the king dismissed his four favorites, that they
also might take some repose. The archbishop also, who
had eaten nothing since morning, was dropping with
fatigue, so the king took pity on him and on the other
priests and dismissed them all. Then, turning to the
prior, Joseph Foulon, "Here I am, my father," said he ;
"I come, sinner as I am, to seek repose in your solitude."

The prior bowed, and the royal penitent mounted the
steps of the abbey, striking his breast at each step, and
the door was immediately closed behind him.

"We will first," said the prior, "conduct your majesty
into the crypt, which we have ornamented in our best
manner to do honor to the King of heaven and earth."

No sooner had the king passed through the somber
arcade, lined with monks, and turned the corner which
led to the chapel, than twenty hoods were thrown into the
air, and eyes were seen brilliant with joy and triumph.
Certainly, they were not monkish or peaceful faces displayed, but bristling mustaches and embrowned skins,
many scarred by wounds, and by the side of the proudest
of all, who displayed the most celebrated scar, stood a
woman covered with a frock, and looking triumphant and

happy. This woman, shaking a pair of golden scissors which hung by her side, cried :

"Ah ! my brothers, at last we have the Valois !"

"Ma foi, sister, I believe so."

"Not yet," murmured the cardinal.

"How so ?"

"Shall we have enough bourgeois guards to make head against Crillon and his guards ?"

"We have better than bourgeois guards ; and, believe me, there will not be a musket-shot exchanged."

"How so ?" said the duchess. "I should have liked a little disturbance."

"Well, sister, you will be deprived of it. When the king is taken he will cry out, but no one will answer ; then, by persuasion or by violence, but without showing ourselves, we shall make him sign his abdication. The news will soon spread through the city, and dispose in our favor both the bourgeois and the troops."

"The plan is good, and cannot fail," said the duchess.

"It is rather brutal," said the Duc de Guise ; "besides which, the king will refuse to sign the abdication. He is brave, and will rather die."

"Let him die, then."

"Not so," replied the duke, firmly. "I will mount the throne of a prince who abdicates and is despised, but not of an assassinated man who is pitied. Besides, in your plans you forget M. le Duc d'Anjou, who will claim the crown."

"Let him claim, mordieu !" said Mayenne ; "he shall be comprised in his brother's act of abdication. He is in connection with the Huguenots, and is unworthy to reign."

"Are you sure of that ?"

"Pardieu ! did he not escape from the Louvre by the aid of the King of Navarre ?"

"Well ?"

"Then another clause in favor of our house shall follow ; this clause shall make you lieutenant-general of the kingdom, from which to the throne is only a step."

"Yes, yes," said the cardinal, "all that is settled ; but

it is probable that the French guards, to make sure that
the abdication is a genuine one, and above all, a voluntary
one, will insist upon seeing the king, and will force the
gates of the abbey if they are not admitted.   Crillon does
not understand joking, and he is just the man to say to
the king, ' Sire, your life is in danger ; but, before everything, let us save our honor.'"

"The general has taken his precautions.   If it be
necessary to sustain a siege, we have here eighty gentlemen, and I have distributed arms to a hundred monks.
We could hold out for a month against the army ; besides,
in case of danger, we have the cave to fly to with our
prey."

"What is the Duc d'Anjou doing ?"

"In the hour of danger he has failed, as usual.   He has
gone home, no doubt, waiting for news of us, through
Bussy or Monsoreau."

"Mon Dieu ! he should have been here ; not at home."

"You are wrong, brother," said the cardinal ; "the
people and the nobles would have seen in it a snare to en-
trap the family.   As you said just now, we must, above
all things, avoid playing the part of usurper.   We must
inherit.   By leaving the Duc d'Anjou free, and the queen-
mother independent, no one will have anything to accuse
us of.   If we acted otherwise, we should have against us
Bussy, and a hundred other dangerous swords."

"Bah ! Bussy is going to fight against the king's
minions."

"Pardieu ! he will kill them, and then he will join us,"
said the Duc de Guise ; "he is a superior man, and one
whom I much esteem, and I will make him general of the
army in Italy, where war is sure to break out."

"And I," said the duchess, " if I become a widow, will
marry him."

"Who is near the king ? " asked the duke.

"The prior and Brother Gorenflot."

"Is he in the cell ?"

"Oh, no ! he will look first at the crypt and the relics."
At this moment a bell sounded.

" The king is returning," said the Duc de Guise ; "let us become monks again." And immediately the hoods covered ardent eyes and speaking scars, and twenty or thirty monks, conducted by the three brothers, went towards the crypt.

CHAPTER LXXXVIII.

CHICOT THE FIRST.

THE king visited the crypt, kissed the relics—often striking his breast, and murmuring the most doleful psalms. At last the prior said, " Sire, will it please you now to depose your earthly crown at the feet of the eternal king ? "

" Let us go ! " said the king.

They arrived at the cell, on the threshold of which stood Gorenflot, his eyes brilliant as carbuncles.

Henri entered. " Hic portus salutis ! " murmured he.

" Yes," replied Foulon.

" Leave us ! " said Gorenflot, with a majestic gesture ; and immediately the door shut, and they were left alone.

" Here you are, then, Herod ! pagan ! Nebuchadnezzar ! " cried Gorenflot, suddenly.

" Is it to me you speak, my brother ? " cried the king, in surprise.

" Yes, to you. Can one accuse you of anything so bad, that it is not true ? "

" My brother ! "

" Bah ! you have no brother here. I have long been meditating a discourse, and now you shall have it. I divide it into three heads. First, you are a tyrant ; second, you are a satyr ; third, you are dethroned."

" Dethroned ! "

" Neither more or less. This abbey is not like Poland, and you cannot fly."

" Ah ! a snare ! "

" Oh, Valois, learn that a king is but a man."

" You are violent, my brother."

" Pardieu ! do you think we imprison you to flatter you ? "

" You abuse your religious calling."

" There is no religion.'

" Oh, you are a saint, and say such things ! "

" I have said it."

" You speak dreadfully, my brother."

" Come, no preaching ; are you ready ? "

" To do what ? "

" To resign your crown ; I am charged to demand it of you."

" You are committing a mortal sin."

" Oh ! I have right of absolution, and I absolve myself in advance.   Come, renounce, Brother Valois."

" Renounce what ? "

" The throne of France."

" Rather death ! "

" Oh ! then you shall die !   Here is the prior returning. Decide ! "

" I have my guards—my friends ; they will defend me."

" Yes, but you will be killed first."

" Leave me at least a little time for reflection."

" Not an instant ! "

" Your zeal carries you away, brother," said the prior, opening the door ; and saying to the king, " Your request is granted," he shut it again.

Henri fell into a profound reverie.   " I accept the sacrifice," he said, after the lapse of ten minutes.

" It is done—he accepts ! " cried Gorenflot.

The king heard a murmur of joy and surprise.

" Read him the act," said a voice, and a monk passed a paper to Gorenflot.

Gorenflot read it to the king, who listened with his head buried in his hands.

" If I refuse to sign ? " cried he, shedding tears.

" It will be doubly your ruin," said the Duc de Guise, from under his hood.   " Look on yourself as dead to the world, and do not force your subjects to shed the blood of a man who has been their king."

"I will not be forced."

"I feared so," said the duke to his sister. Then, turning to his brother, "Let every one arm and prepare," said he.

"For what?" cried the king, in a miserable tone.

'For anything."

he king's despair redoubled.

"Corbleu!" cried Gorenflot, "I hated you before, Valois, but now I despise you! Sign, or you shall perish by my hand!"

"Have patience," said the king; "let me pray to my divine Master for resignation."

"He wishes to reflect again," said Gorenflot.

"Give him till midnight," said the cardinal.

"Thanks, charitable Christian!" cried the king.

"His brain is weak," said the duke; "we serve France by dethroning him."

"I shall have great pleasure in clipping him!" said the duchess.

Suddenly a noise was heard outside, and soon they distinguished blows struck on the door of the abbey, and Mayenne went to see what it was. "My brothers," said he, "there is a troop of armed men outside."

"They have come to seek him," said the duchess.

"The more reason that he should sign quickly."

"Sign, Valois, sign!" roared Gorenflot.

"You gave me till midnight," said the king, piteously.

"Ah! you hoped to be rescued."

"He shall die if he does not sign!" cried the duchess.

Gorenflot offered him the pen. The noise outside redoubled.

"A new troop!" cried a monk; "they are surrounding the abbey!"

"The Swiss," cried Foulon, "are advancing on the right!"

"Well, we will defend ourselves; with such a hostage in our hands, we need not surrender."

"He has signed!" cried Gorenflot, tearing the paper from Henri, who buried his face in his hands.

"Then you are king!" cried the cardinal to the duke; "take the precious paper."

The king overturned the little lamp which alone lighted the scene, but the duke already held the parchment.

"What shall we do?" said a monk. "Here is Crillon, with his guards, threatening to break in the doors!"

"In the king's name!" cried the powerful voice of Crillon.

"There is no king!" cried Gorenflot through the window.

"Who says that?" cried Crillon.

"I! I! I!"

"Break in the doors, Monsieur Crillon!" said, from outside, a voice which made the hair of all the monks, real and pretended, stand on end.

"Yes, sire," replied Crillon, giving a tremendous blow with a hatchet on the door.

"What do you want?" said the prior, going to the window.

"Ah! it is you, M. Foulon," replied the same voice, "I want my jester, who is in one of your cells. I want Chicot, I am ennuyé at the Louvre."

"And I have been much amused, my son," said Chicot, throwing off his hood, and pushing his way through the crowd of monks, who recoiled, with a cry of terror.

At this moment the Duc de Guise, advancing to a lamp, read the signature obtained with so much labor. It was "Chicot I."

"Chicot!" cried he; "thousand devils!"

"Let us fly!" said the cardinal, "we are lost."

"Ah!" cried Chicot, turning to Gorenflot, who was nearly fainting, and he began to strike him with the cord he had round his waist.

CHAPTER LXXXIX.

INTEREST AND CAPITAL.

As the king spoke and the conspirators listened, they passed from astonishment to terror. Chicot I. relinquished his rôle of apparent terror, threw back his hood, crossed his arms, and, while Gorenflot fled at his utmost speed, sustained, firm and smiling, the first shock. It was a terrible moment, for the gentlemen, furious at the mystification of which they had been the dupes, advanced menacingly on the Gascon. But this unarmed man, his breast covered only by his arms—this laughing face, stopped them still more than the remonstrance of the cardinal, who said to them that Chicot's death could serve no end, but, on the contrary, would be terribly avenged by the king, who was the jester's accomplice in this scene of terrible buffoonery.

The result was, that daggers and rapiers were lowered before Chicot, who continued to laugh in their faces.

However, the king's menaces and Crillon's blows became more vehement, and it was evident that the door could not long resist such an attack. Thus, after a moment's deliberation, the Duc de Guise gave the order for retreat. This order made Chicot smile, for, during his nights with Gorenflot, he had examined the cave and found out the door, of which he had informed the king, who had placed there Torquenot, lieutenant of the Swiss guards. It was then evident that the leaguers, one after another, were about to throw themselves into the trap. The cardinal made off first, followed by about twenty gentlemen. Then Chicot saw the duke pass with about the same number, and afterwards Mayenne. When Chicot saw him go he laughed outright. Ten minutes passed, during which he listened earnestly, thinking to hear the noise of the leaguers sent back into the cave, but to his astonishment,

the sound continued to go further and further off. His
laugh began to change into oaths. Time passed, and the
leaguers did not return; had they seen that the door was
guarded and found another way out? Chicot was about
to rush from the cell, when all at once the door was ob-
structed by a mass which fell at his feet, and began to tear
its hair.

"Ah! wretch that I am!" cried the monk. "Oh!
my good M. Chicot, pardon me, pardon me!"

How did Gorenflot, who went first, return now alone?
was the question that presented itself to Chicot's mind.

"Oh! my good M. Chicot!" he continued to cry,
"pardon your unworthy friend, who repents at your
knees."

"But how is it you have not fled with the others?"

"Because the Lord in His anger has struck me with
obesity, and I could not pass where the others did. Oh!
unlucky stomach! Oh! miserable paunch!" cried the
monk, striking with his two hands the part he apostro-
phized. "Ah! why am not I thin like you, M. Chicot?"

Chicot understood nothing of the lamentations of the
monk.

"But the others are flying, then?" cried he, in a voice
of thunder.

"Pardieu! what should they do? Wait to be hung?
Oh! unlucky paunch!"

"Silence, and answer me."

"Interrogate me, M. Chicot; you have the right."

"How are the others escaping?"

"As fast as they can."

"So I imagine; but where?"

"By the hole."

"Mordieu! what hole?"

"The hole in the cemetery cellar."

"Is that what you call the cave?"

"Oh! no; the door of that was guarded outside. The
great cardinal, just as he was about to open it, heard a
Swiss say, 'Mich dwistel,' which means, 'I am thirsty.'"

"Ventre de biche! so then they took another way?"

"Yes, dear M. Chicot, they are getting out through the cellar."

"How does that run?"

"From the crypt to the Porte St. Jacques."

"You lie; I should have seen them repass before this cell."

"No, dear M. Chicot; they thought they had not time for that, so they are creeping out through the air-hole."

"What hole?"

"One which looks into the garden, and serves to light the cellar."

"So that you——"

"I was too big, and could not pass, and they drew me back by my legs, because I intercepted the way for the others."

"Then he who is bigger than you?"

"He! who?"

"Oh! Holy Virgin, I promise you a dozen wax candles, if he also cannot pass."

"M. Chicot!"

"Get up."

The monk raised himself from the ground as quickly as he could.

"Now lead me to the hole."

"Where you wish."

"Go on, then, wretch."

Gorenflot went on as fast as he was able, while Chicot indulged himself by giving him a few blows with the cord. They traversed the corridor, and descended into the garden.

"Here! this way," said Gorenflot.

"Hold your tongue, and go on."

"There it is," and exhausted by his efforts, the monk sank on the grass, while Chicot, hearing groans, advanced, and saw something protruding through the hole. By the side of this something lay a frock and a sword. It was evident that the individual in the hole had taken off successively all the loose clothing which increased his size;

and yet, like Gorenflot, he was making useless efforts to get through.

"Mordieu! ventrebleu! sangdieu!" cried a stifled voice. "I would rather pass through the midst of the guards. Do not pull so hard, my friends; I shall come through gradually; I feel that I advance, not quickly, it is true, but I do advance."

"Ventre de biche!" murmured Chicot, "it is M. de Mayenne. Holy Virgin, you have gained your candles."

And he made a noise with his feet like some one running fast.

"They are coming," cried several voices from inside.

"Ah!" cried Chicot, as if out of breath, "it is you, miserable monk!"

"Say nothing, monseigneur!" murmured the voices, "he takes you for Gorenflot."

"Ah! it is you, heavy mass—pondus immobile; it is you, indigesta moles!"

And at each apostrophe, Chicot, arrived at last at his desired vengeance, let fall the cord with all the weight of his arm on the body before him.

"Silence!" whispered the voices again; "he takes you for Gorenflot."

Mayenne only uttered groans, and made immense efforts to get through.

"Ah! conspirator!" cried Chicot again; "ah! unworthy monk, this is for your drunkenness, this for idleness, this for anger, this for greediness, and this for all the vices you have."

"M. Chicot, have pity," whispered Gorenflot.

"And here, traitor, this is for your treason," continued Chicot.

"Ah! why did it not please God to substitute for your vulgar carcass the high and mighty shoulders of the Duc de Mayenne, to whom I owe a volley of blows, the interest of which has been accumulating for seven years!"

"Chicot!" cried the duke.

"Yes, Chicot, unworthy servant of the king, who wishes he had the hundred arms of Briareus for this occasion,"

And he redoubled his blows with such violence, that the sufferer, making a tremendous effort, pushed himself through, and fell torn and bleeding into the arms of his friends. Chicot's last blow fell into empty space. He turned, and saw that the true Gorenflot had fainted with terror.

CHAPTER XC.

WHAT WAS PASSING NEAR THE BASTILE WHILE CHICOT WAS PAYING HIS DEBT TO M. DE MAYENNE.

It was eleven at night, and the Duc d'Anjou was waiting impatiently at home for a messenger from the Duc de Guise. He walked restlessly up and down, looking every minute at the clock. All at once he heard a horse in the courtyard, and thinking it was the messenger, he ran to the window, but it was a groom leading up and down a horse which was waiting for its master, who almost immediately came out. It was Bussy, who, as captain of the duke's guards, came to give the password for the night. The duke, seeing this handsome and brave young man, of whom he had never had reason to complain, experienced an instant's remorse, but on his face he read so much joy, hope, and happiness, that all his jealousy returned. However, Bussy, ignorant that the duke was watching him, jumped into his saddle and rode off to his own hotel, where he gave his horse to the groom. There he saw Rémy.

"Ah! you Rémy?"

"Myself, monsieur."

"Not yet in bed?"

"I have just come in. Indeed, since I have no longer a patient, it seems to me that the days have forty-eight hours."

"Are you ennuyé?"

"I fear so."

"Then Gertrude is abandoned?"

"Perfectly."

"You grew tired?"

"Of being beaten. That was how her love showed itself."

"And does your heart not speak for her to-night?"

"Why to-night?"

"Because I would have taken you with me."

"To the Bastile?"

"Yes."

"You are going there?"

"Yes."

"And Monsoreau?"

"Is at Compiègne, preparing a chase for the king."

"Are you sure, monsieur?"

"The order was given publicly this morning."

"Ah, well; Jourdain, my sword."

"You have changed your mind?"

"I will accompany you to the door, for two reasons."

"What are they?"

"Firstly, lest you should meet any enemies."

Bussy smiled.

"Oh! mon Dieu, I know you fear no one, and that Rémy the doctor is but a poor companion; still, two men are not so likely to be attacked as one. Secondly, because I have a great deal of good advice to give you."

"Come, my dear Rémy, come. We will speak of her; and next to the pleasure of seeing the woman you love, I know none greater than talking of her."

Bussy then took the arm of the young doctor, and they set off. Rémy on the way tried hard to induce Bussy to return early, insisting that he would be more fit for his duel on the morrow.

Bussy smiled. "Fear nothing," said he.

"Ah! my dear master, to-morrow you ought to fight like Hercules against Antæus—like Theseus against the Minotaur—like Bayard—like something Homeric, gigantic, impossible; I wish people to speak of it in future times as the combat, par excellence, and in which you had not even received a scratch."

"Be easy, my dear Rémy, you shall see wonders. This

morning I put swords in the hands of four fencers, who during eight minutes could not touch me once, while I tore their doublets to pieces."

So conversing, they arrived in the Rue St. Antoine.

" Adieu ! here we are," said Bussy.

"Shall I wait for you ? "

"Why ? "

" To make sure that you will return before two o'clock, and have at least five or six hours' sleep before your duel."

"If I give you my word ? "

"Oh ! that will be enough ; Bussy's word is never doubted."

" You have it then."

" Then, adieu, monsieur."

" Adieu, Rémy."

Rémy watched, and saw Bussy enter, not this time by the window, but boldly through the door, which Gertrude opened for him.   Then Rémy turned to go home ; but he had only gone a few steps, when he saw coming towards him five armed men, wrapped in cloaks.   When they arrived about ten yards from him, they said good night to each other, and four went off in different directions, while the fifth remained stationary.

"M. de St. Luc ! " said Rémy.

" Rémy ! "

" Rémy, in person.   Is it an indiscretion to ask what your lordship does at this hour so far from the Louvre ? "

" Ma foi ! I am examining, by the king's order, the physiognomy of the city.   He said to me, ' St. Luc, walk about the streets of Paris, and if you hear any one say I have abdicated, contradict him.' "

" And have you heard it ? "

" Nowhere ; and as it is just midnight, and I have met no one but M. de Monsorean, I have dismissed my friends, and am about to return."

" M. de Monsorean ? "

" Yes."

" You met him ? "

" With a troop of armed men ; ten or twelve at least."

"Impossible !"

"Why so ?"

"He ought to be at Compiègne."

"He ought to be, but he is not."

"But the king's order ?"

"Bah ! who obeys the king ?"

"Did he know you ?"

"I believe so."

"You were but five ?"

"My four friends and I."

"And he did not attack you ?"

"On the contrary, he avoided me, which astonished me, as on seeing him, I expected a terrible battle."

"Where was he going ?"

"To the Rue de la Tixanderie."

"Ah ! mon Dieu !"

"What ?"

"M. de St. Luc, a great misfortune is about to happen."

"To whom?"

"To M. de Bussy."

"Bussy ! speak, Rémy ; I am his friend, you know."

"Oh ! M. de Bussy thought him at Compiègne."

"Well ?"

"And, profiting by his absence, is with Madame de Monsoreau."

"Ah !"

"Do you not see ? he has had suspicions, and has feigned to depart, that he might appear unexpectedly."

"Ah ! it is the Duc d'Anjou's doing, I believe. Have you good lungs, Rémy"

"Corbleu ! like a blacksmith's bellows."

"Well ! let us run. You know the house ?"

"Yes."

"Go on then." And the young men set off like hunted deer.

"Is he much in advance of us ?" said Rémy.

"About a quarter of an hour."

"If we do but arrive in time !"

CHAPTER XCI.

THE ASSASSINATION.

BUSSY, himself without disquietude or hesitation, had been received by Diana without fear, for she believed herself sure of the absence of M. de Monsoreau. Never had this beautiful woman been more beautiful, nor Bussy more happy. She was moved, however, by fears for the morrow's combat, now so near, and she repeated to him, again and again, the anxiety she felt about it, and questioned him as to the arrangements he had made for flight. To conquer was not all ; there was afterwards the king's anger to avoid, for it was not probable that he would ever pardon the death or defeat of his favorites.

"And then, said she, "are you not acknowledged to be the bravest man in France ? Why make it a point of honor to augment your glory ? You are already superior to other men, and you do not wish to please any other woman but me, Louis. Therefore, guard your life, or rather—for I think there is not a man in France capable of killing you, Louis—I should say, 'take care of wounds, for you may be wounded. Indeed, it was through a wound received in fighting with these same men, that I first made your acquaintance."

"Make yourself easy," said Bussy, smiling ; "I will take care of my face—I shall not be disfigured."

"Oh, take care of yourself altogether. Think of the grief you would experience if you saw me brought home wounded and bleeding, and that I should feel the same grief on seeing your blood. Be prudent, my too courageous hero—that is all I ask. Act like the Roman of whom you read to me the other day : let your friends fight, aid the one who needs it most, but if three men—if two men attack you, fly ; you can turn, like Horatius, and kill them one after another."

" Yes, my dear Diana."

" Oh, you reply without hearing me, Louis; you look at me, and do not listen."

· " But I see you, and you are beautiful."

" Do not think of my beauty just now! Mon Dieu! it is your life I am speaking of. Stay, I will tell you something that will make you more prudent—I shall have the courage to witness this duel."

" You!"

" I shall be there."

" Impossible, Diana!"

" No; listen. There is, in the room next to this, a window looking into a little court, but with a side-view of the Tournelles."

" Yes, I remember—the window from which I threw crumbs to the birds the other day."

" From there I can have a view of the ground; therefore, above all things, take care to stand so that I can see you ; you will know that I am there, but do not look at me, lest your enemy should profit by it."

" And kill me, while I had my eyes fixed upon you. If I had to choose my death, Diana, that is the one I should prefer."

" Yes; but now you are not to die, but live."

" And I will live ; therefore tranquilize yourself, Diana. Besides, I am well seconded—you do not know my friends ; Antragues uses his sword as well as I do, Ribeirac is so steady on the ground that his eyes and his arms alone seem to be alive, and Livarot is as active as a tiger. Believe me, Diana, I wish there were more danger, for there would be more honor."

" Well, I believe you, and I smile and hope; but listen, and promise to obey me."

" Yes, if you do not tell me to leave."

" It is just what I am about to do. I appeal to your reason."

" Then you should not have made me mad."

" No nonsense, but obedience—that is the way to prove your love."

"Order, then."

"Dear friend, you want a long sleep; go home "

"Not already."

"Yes, I am going to pray for you."

"Pray now, then."

As he spoke, a pane of the window flew into pieces, then the window itself, and three armed men appeared on the balcony while a fourth was climbing over. This one had his face covered with a mask, and held in his right hand a sword, and in his left a pistol.

Bussy remained paralyzed for a moment by the dreadful cry uttered by Diana at this sight. The masked man made a sign, and the three others advanced. Bussy put Diana back, and drew his sword.

"Come, my brave fellows!" said a sepulchral voice from under the mask; "he is already half-dead with fear."

"You are wrong," said Bussy; "I never feel fear."

Diana drew near him.

"Go back, Diana," said he. But she threw herself on his neck. "You will get me killed," said he; and she drew back.

"Ah!" said the masked man, "it is M. de Bussy, and I would not believe it, fool that I was! Really, what a good and excellent friend! He learns that the husband is absent, and has left his wife alone, and fears she may be afraid, so he comes to keep her company, although on the eve of a duel. I repeat, he is a good and excellent friend!"

"Ah! it is you, M. de Monsoreau!" said Bussy; "throw off your mask."

"I will," said he, doing so.

Diana uttered another cry; the comte was as pale as a corpse, but he smiled like a demon.

"Let us finish, monsieur," said Bussy; "it was very well for Homer's heroes, who were demigods, to talk before they fought; but I am a man—attack me, or let me pass."

Monsoreau replied by a laugh which made Diana shudder, but raised Bussy's anger.

"Let me pass!" cried he.

"Oh, oh!"

"Then, draw and have done; I wish to go home and I live far off."

During this time two other men mounted into the balcony.

"Two and four make six," said Bussy, "where are the others?"

"Waiting at the door."

Diana fell on her knees, and in spite of her efforts Bussy heard her sobs.

"My dear comte," said he, "you know I am a man of honor."

"Yes, you are, and madame is a faithful wife."

"Good, monsieur; you are severe, but, perhaps, it is deserved; only as I have a prior engagement with four gentlemen, I beg to be allowed to retire to-night, and I pledge my word, you shall find me again, when and where you will."

Monsoreau shrugged his shoulders.

"I swear to you, monsieur," said Bussy, "that when I have satisfied MM. Quelus, Schomberg, D'Epernon, and Maugiron, I shall be at your service. If they kill me, your vengeance will be satisfied, and if not——"

Monsoreau turned to his men. "On, my brave fellows," said he.

"Oh!" said Bussy, "I was wrong; it is not a duel, but an assassination."

"Yes."

"We were each deceived with regard to the other; but remember, monsieur, that the Duc d'Anjou will avenge me."

"It was he who sent me."

Diana groaned.

Instantaneously Bussy overturned the prie-Dieu, drew a table towards him, and threw a chair over all, so that in a second he had formed a kind of rampart between himself and his enemies. This movement had been so rapid, that the ball fired at him from the arquebuse only struck the prie-Dieu. Diana sobbed aloud. Bussy glanced at her, and then at his assailants, crying, "Come on, but take care, for my sword is sharp."

The men advanced, and one tried to seize the prie-Dieu, but before he reached it, Bussy's sword pierced his arm. The man uttered a cry, and fell back.

Bussy then heard rapid steps in the corridor, and thought he was surrounded. He flew to the door to lock it, but before he could reach it, it was opened, and two men rushed in.

"Ah! dear master!" cried a well-known voice, "are we in time?"

"Rémy!"

"And I?" cried a second voice, "it seems they are attempting assassination here."

"St. Luc!" cried Bussy, joyfully. "Ah! M. de Monsoreau, I think now you will do well to let us pass, for if you do not, we will pass over you."

"Three more men," cried Monsoreau. And they saw three new assailants appear on the balcony.

"They are an army," cried St. Luc.

"Oh! God protect him!" cried Diana.

"Wretch!" cried Monsoreau, and he advanced to strike her. Bussy saw the movement. Agile as a tiger, he bounded on him, and touched him in the throat; but the distance was too great, it was only a scratch. Five or six men rushed on Bussy, but one fell beneath the sword of St. Luc.

"Rémy!" cried Bussy, "carry away Diana."

Monsoreau uttered a yell and snatched a pistol from one of the men.

Rémy hesitated. "But you?" said he.

"Away! away! I confide her to you."

"Come, madame," said Rémy.

"Never! I will never leave him."

Rémy seized her in his arms.

"Bussy, help me! Bussy!" cried Diana. For any one who separated her from Bussy, seemed an enemy to her.

"Go," cried Bussy, "I will rejoin you."

At this moment Monsoreau fired, and Bussy saw Rémy

totter, and then fall, dragging Diana with him. Bussy uttered a cry, and turned.

"It is nothing, master," said Rémy. "It was I who received the ball. She is safe."

As Bussy turned, three men threw themselves on him ; St. Luc rushed forward, and one of them fell. The two others drew back.

"St. Luc," cried Bussy, "by her you love, save Diana."

"But you ?"

"I am a man."

St. Luc rushed to Diana, seized her in his arms, and disappeared through the door.

"Here, my men, from the staircase," shouted Monsoreau.

"Ah ! coward !" cried Bussy.

Monsoreau retreated behind his men. Bussy gave a back stroke and a thrust ; with the first he cleft open a head, and with the second pierced a breast.

"That clears !" cried he.

"Fly, master !" cried Rémy.

"Diana must save herself first," murmured he.

"Take care," cried Rémy again, as four men rushed in through the door from the staircase. Bussy saw himself between two troops, but his only cry was, "Ah ! Diana !"

Then, without losing a second, he rushed on the four men ; and taken by surprise, two fell, one dead, one wounded.

Then, as Monsoreau advanced, he retreated again behind his rampart.

"Push the bolts, and turn the key," cried Monsoreau, "we have him now." During this time, by a great effort, Rémy had dragged himself before Bussy, and added his body to the rampart.

There was an instant's pause. Bussy looked around him. Seven men lay stretched on the ground, but nine remained. And seeing these nine swords, and hearing Monsoreau encouraging them, this brave man, who had never known fear, saw plainly before him the image of death, beckoning him with its gloomy smile.

"I may kill five more," thought he, "but the other four will kill me. I have strength for ten minutes' more combat; in that ten minutes let me do what man never did before."

And rushing forward, he gave three thrusts, and three times he pierced the leather of a shoulder-belt, or the buff of a jacket, and three times a stream of blood followed.

During this time he had parried twenty blows with his left arm, and his cloak, which he had wrapped round it, was hacked to pieces.

The men changed their tactics; seeing two of their number fall and one retire, they renounced the sword, and some tried to strike with the butt-ends of their muskets, while others fired at him with pistols. He avoided the balls by jumping from side to side, or by stooping; for he seemed not only to see, hear, and act, but to divine every movement of his enemies, and appeared more than a man, or only man because he was mortal. Then he thought that to kill Monsoreau would be the best way to end the combat, and sought him with his eyes among his assailants, but he stood in the background, loading the pistols for his men. However, Bussy rushed forward, and found himself face to face with him. He, who held a loaded pistol, fired, and the ball, striking Bussy's sword, broke it off six inches from the handle.

"Disarmed!" cried Monsoreau.

Bussy drew back, picking up his broken blade, and in an instant it was fastened to the handle with a handkerchief; and the battle recommenced, presenting the extraordinary spectacle of a man almost without arms, but also almost without wounds, keeping six enemies at bay, and with ten corpses at his feet for a rampart. When the fight began again, Monsoreau commenced to draw away the bodies, lest Bussy should snatch a sword from one of them. Bussy was surrounded; the blade of his sword bent and shook in his hand, and fatigue began to render his arm heavy, when suddenly, one of the bodies raising itself, pushed a rapier into his hand. It was Rémy's last act of devotion. Bussy uttered a cry of joy, and threw

away his broken sword : at the same moment Monsoreau
fired at Rémy, and the ball entered his brain. This time
he fell to rise no more.

Bussy uttered a cry. His strength seemed to return to
him, and he whirled round his sword in a circle, cutting
through a wrist at his right hand, and laying open a
cheek at his left. Exhausted by the effort, he let his
right arm fall for a moment, while with his left he tried
to undraw the bolts behind him. During this second, he
received a ball in his thigh, and two swords touched his
side. But he had unfastened the bolt, and turned the
key. Sublime with rage, he rushed on Monsoreau, and
wounded him in the breast.

"Ah!" cried Bussy, "I begin to think I shall escape."

The four men rushed on him, but they could not touch
him, and were repulsed with blows. Monsoreau approached him twice more, and twice more was wounded.
But three men seized hold of the handle of his sword, and
tore it from him. He seized a stool of carved wood, and
struck three blows with it, and knocked down two men ;
but it broke on the shoulder of the third, who sent his
dagger into Bussy's breast.

Bussy seized him by the wrist, forced the dagger from
him, and stabbed him to the heart. The last man
jumped out of the window. Bussy made two steps to follow him, but Monsoreau, raising himself from the floor,
where he was lying, wounded him in the leg with his
dagger. The young man seized a sword which lay near,
and plunged it so vigorously into his breast, that he pinned
him to the floor.

"Ah!" cried Bussy, "I do not know if I shall live,
but at least I shall have seen you die!"

Bussy dragged himself to the corridor, his wounds
bleeding fearfully. He threw a last glance behind him.
The moon was shining brilliantly, and its light penetrated
this room inundated with blood, and illuminated the walls
pierced by balls, and hacked by blows, and lighted up the
pale faces of the dead, which even then seemed to preserve
the fierce look of assassins.

Bussy, at the sight of this field of battle, peopled by him with slain, nearly dying as he was, experienced a feeling of pride. As he had intended, he had done what no man had done before him. There now remained to him only to fly.

But all was not over for the unfortunate young man. On arriving on the staircase, he saw arms shine in the courtyard ; some one fired, and the ball pierced his shoulder.; The court being guarded, he thought of the little window, where Diana had said she would sit to see the combat, and as quickly as he could he dragged himself there, and locked the door behind him ; then he mounted the window with great difficulty, and measured the distance with his eyes, wondering if he could jump to the other side.

"Oh, I shall never have the strength !" cried he.

But at that moment he heard steps coming up the staircase ; it was the second troop mounting. He collected all his strength, and made a spring ; but his foot slipped, and he fell on the iron spikes, which caught his clothes, and he hung suspended.

He thought of his only friend.

"St. Luc !" cried he, "help ! St. Luc !"

" Ah, it is you, M. de Bussy," answered a voice from behind some trees.

Bussy shuddered, for it was not the voice of St. Luc.

"St. Luc !" cried he again, "come to me ! Diana is safe ! I have killed Monsoreau !"

" Ah ! Monsoreau is killed ? " said the same voice.

" Yes." Then Bussy saw two men come out from behind the trees.

" Gentlemen," cried he, " in heaven's name, help an unfortunate nobleman, who may still escape if you aid him."

" What do you say, monseigneur ? " said one.

" Imprudent ! " said the other.

" Monseigneur," cried Bussy, who heard the conversation, "deliver me, and I will pardon you for betraying me."

" Do you hear ? " said the duke.

"What do you order ?"

"That you deliver him from his sufferings," said he, with a kind of laugh.

Bussy turned his head to look at the man who laughed at such a time, and at the same instant an arquebuse was discharged into his breast.

"Cursed assassin ! oh, Diana !" murmured he, and fell back dead.

"Is he dead ?" cried several men who, after forcing the door, appeared at the windows.

"Yes," said Aurilly. "But fly; remember that his highness the Duc d'Anjou was the friend and protector of M. de Bussy."

The men instantly made off, and when the sound of their steps was lost, the duke said, "Now, Aurilly, go up into the room and throw out of the window the body of Monsoreau."

Aurilly obeyed, and the blood fell over the clothes of the duke, who, however, raised the coat of the dead man, and drew out the paper which he had signed.

"This is all I wanted," said he ; "so now let us go."

"And Diana ?"

"Ma foi ! I care no more for her. Untie her and St. Luc, and let them go."

Aurilly disappeared.

"I shall not be king of France," murmured the duke, "but, at all events, I shall not be beheaded for high treason."

CHAPTER XCII.

HOW BROTHER GORENFLOT FOUND HIMSELF MORE THAN EVER BETWEEN A GALLOWS AND AN ABBEY.

THE guard placed to catch the conspirators got none of them ; they all escaped, as we have seen ; therefore, when Crillon at last broke open the door, he found the place deserted and empty. In vain they opened doors and windows; in vain the king cried, "Chicot!" No one answered.

"Can they have killed him?" said he. "Mordieu! if they have they shall pay for it!"

Chicot did not reply, because he was occupied in beating M. de Mayenne, which gave him so much pleasure that he neither heard nor saw what was passing. However, when the duke had disappeared, he heard and recognized the royal voice.

"Here, my son, here!" he cried, trying at the same time to raise Gorenflot, who, beginning to recover himself, cried, "Monsieur Chicot!"

"You are not dead, then?"

"My good M. Chicot, you will not give me up to my enemies?"

"Wretch!"

Gorenflot began to howl and wring his hands.

"I, who have had so many good dinners with you," continued Gorenflot; "I, who drank so well, that you always called me the king of the sponges; I, who loved so much the capons you used to order at the Corne d'Abondance, that I never left anything but the bones."

This climax appeared sublime to Chicot, and determined him to clemency.

"Here they are! Mon Dieu," cried Gorenflot, vainly trying to rise, "here they come, I am lost! Oh! good M. Chicot, help me!" and finding he could not rise, he threw himself with his face to the ground.

"Get up," said Chicot.

"Do you pardon me?"

"We shall see."

"You have beaten me so much."

Chicot laughed; the poor monk fancied he had received the blows given to Mayenne.

"You laugh, M. Chicot."

"I do, animal."

"Then I shall live?"

"Perhaps."

28

"You would not laugh if your Gorenflot was about to die."

"It does not depend upon me, but on the king ; he alone has the power of life and death."

At this moment lights appeared, and a crowd of embroidered dresses and swords shining in the light of the torches.

"Ah ! Chicot ! my dear Chicot, how glad I am to see you," cried the king.

"You hear, good M. Chicot," whispered Gorenflot, "this great prince is glad to see you."

"Well ?"

"Well ! in his happiness he would not refuse you a favor ; ask for my pardon."

"What ! from Herod ?"

"Oh ! silence, dear M. Chicot."

"Well ! sire, how many have you caught ?" said Chicot, advancing.

"Confiteor," said Gorenflot.

"Not one," said Crillon, "the traitors must have found some opening unknown to us."

"It is probable."

"But you saw them ?" said the king.

"All."

"You recognized them, no doubt ?"

"No, sire."

"Not recognized them ?"

"That is to say, I recognized only one. "

"Who was that ?"

"M. de Mayenne."

"M. de Mayenne, to whom you owed——"

"Yes, sire ; we are quits."

"Ah ! tell me about that, Chicot."

"Afterwards, my son ; now let us think of the present.

"Confiteor," repeated Gorenflot.

"Ah ! you have made a prisoner," said Crillon, laying his large hand on the monk's shoulder.

Chicot was silent for a minute, leaving Gorenflot a prey

to all the anguish of such profound terror that he nearly
fainted again.

At last Chicot said, "Sire, look well at this monk."

"The preacher Gorenflot," cried Henri.

"Confiteor, confiteor," repeated he.

"Himself," said Chicot.

"He who——"

"Just so," interrupted Chicot.

"Ah, ah!"

Gorenflot shook with terror, for he heard the sounds of
swords clashing.

"Wait," said Chicot, "the king must know all." And,
taking him aside, "My son," said he, "thank God for
having permitted this holy man to be born thirty-five years
ago, for it is he who has saved us all."

"How so?"

"It was he who recounted to me the whole plot, from
the alpha to the omega."

"When?"

"About a week ago; so that if ever your majesty's
enemies catch him he will be a dead man."

Gorenflot heard only the last words, "a dead man";
and he covered his face with his hands.

"Worthy man," said the king, casting a benevolent look
on the mass of flesh before him, "we will cover him with
our protection."

Gorenflot perceived the nature of the look, and began to
feel relieved.

"You will do well, my king," said Chicot.

"What must we do with him?"

"I think that as long as he remains in Paris he will be
in danger."

"If I gave him guards."

Gorenflot heard this proposition of Henri's. "Well!"
thought he, "I shall get off with imprisonment; I prefer
that to beating, if they only feed me well."

"Oh! no, that is needless," said Chicot, "if you will
allow me to take him with me."

"Where?"

" Home."

" Well ! take him, and then return to the Louvre."

" Get up, reverend father," said Chicot.

" He mocks me," murmured Gorenflot.

" Get up, brute," whispered Chicot, giving him a sly kick.

" Ah ! I have deserved it," cried Gorenflot.

" What does he say ? " asked the king.

" Sire, he is thinking over all his fatigues and his tortures, and when I promised him your protection, he said, ' Oh ! I have well merited that.' "

" Poor devil ! " said the king, " take good care of him."

" Oh ! be easy, sire, he will want for nothing with me."

" Oh ! M. Chicot, dear M. Chicot," cried Gorenflot, " where am I to be taken to ? "

" You will know soon. Meanwhile, monster of iniquity, thank his majesty."

" What for ? "

" Thank him, I tell you."

" Sire," stammered Gorenflot, "since your gracious majesty——"

" Yes," interrupted Henri, "I know all you did for me, in your journey from Lyons, on the evening of the League, and again to-day. Be easy, you shall be recompensed according to your merits."

Gorenflot sighed.

" Where is Panurge ? " said Chicot.

" In the stable, poor beast."

" Well ! go and fetch him, and return to me."

" Yes, M. Chicot."

And the monk went away as fast as he could, much astonished not to be followed by guards.

" Now, my son," said Chicot, " keep twenty men for your own escort, and send ten with M. Crillon to the Hôtel d'Anjou and let them bring your brother here."

" Why ? "

" That he may not escape a second time."

" Did my brother——"

" Have you repented following my advice to-day ? "

"No, par le mordieu."

"Then do what I tell you."

Henri gave the order to Crillon, who set off at once.

"And you?" said Henri.

"Oh! I am waiting for my saint."

"And you will rejoin me at the Louvre?"

"In an hour; go, my son."

Henri went; and Chicot, proceeding to the stables, met Gorenflot coming out on his ass. The poor devil had not an idea of endeavoring to escape from the fate that he thought awaited him.

"Come, come," said Chicot, "we are waited for."

Gorenflot made no resistance, but he shed many tears.

CHAPTER XCIII.

WHERE CHICOT GUESSES WHY D'EPERNON HAD BLOOD ON HIS FEET AND NONE IN HIS CHEEKS.

THE king, returning to the Louvre, found his friends peacefully asleep, except D'Epernon, whose bed was empty.

"Not come in yet; how imprudent," murmured the king to Chicot, who had also returned, and was standing with them by their beds. "The fool; having to fight tomorrow with a man like Bussy, and to take no more care than this. Let them seek M. d'Epernon," said he, going out of the room, and speaking to an usher.

"M. d'Epernon is just coming in, sire," replied the man.

Indeed, D'Epernon came softly along, thinking to glide unperceived to his room.

On seeing the king he looked confused.

"Ah! here you are at last," said Henri; "come here and look at your friends. They are wise! they understand the importance of the duel to-morrow; but you, instead of praying and sleeping like them, have been running about the streets. Corbleu; how pale you are! What will you look like to-morrow?"

D'Epernon was indeed pale, but at the king's remark he colored.

"Now go to bed," continued Henri, "and sleep if you can."

"Why not?"

"Much time you will have. You are to fight at daybreak; and at this time of year the sun rises at four. It is now two; you have but two hours to sleep."

"Two hours well employed go a long way."

"You will sleep, then?"

"Well, sire!"

"I do not believe it."

"Why not?"

"Because you are agitated; you think of to-morrow."

"I will sleep, sire, if your majesty will only let me."

"That is just," said Chicot.

Indeed D'Epernon undressed and got into bed, with a calm and satisfied look, that seemed, both to the king and Chicot to augur well.

"He is as brave as a Cæsar," said the king.

"So brave that I do not understand it," said Chicot.

"See, he sleeps already."

Chicot approached the bed to look.

"Oh!" said he.

"What is it?"

"Look," and he pointed to D'Epernon's boots.

"Blood!"

"He has been walking in blood."

"Can he be wounded?" said the king, anxiously.

"Bah! he would have told us; and, besides, unless he had been wounded like Achilles in the heel——"

"See, the sleeve of his doublet is also spotted. What can have happened to him?"

"Perhaps he has killed some one to keep his hand in."

"It is singular. Well, to-morrow, at least——"

"To-day, you mean."

"Well! to-day I shall be tranquil."

"Why so?"

"Because those cursed Angevins will be killed."

"You think so, Henri?"

"I am sure of it; my friends are brave."

"I never heard that the Angevins were cowards."

"No, doubtless; but my friends are so strong; look at Schomberg's arm; what muscle!"

"Ah! if you saw Antragues's! Is that all that reassures you?"

"No; come, and I will show you something."

"Where?"

"In my room."

"And this something makes you confident of victory?"

"Yes."

"Come, then."

"Wait, and let me take leave of them. Adieu, my good friends," murmured the king, as he stooped and imprinted a light kiss on each of their foreheads.

Chicot was not superstitious, but as he looked on, his imagination pictured a living man making his adieux to the dead.

"It is singular," thought he. "I never felt so before—poor fellows."

As soon as the king quitted the room, D'Epernon opened his eyes; and, jumping out of bed, began to efface, as well as he could, the spots of blood on his clothes. Then he went to bed again.

As for Henri, he conducted Chicot to his room, and opened a long ebony coffer lined with white satin.

"Look!" said he.

"Swords!"

"Yes! but blessed swords, my dear friend."

"Blessed! by whom?"

"By our holy father the Pope, who granted me this favor. To send this box to Rome and back, cost me twenty horses and four men."

"Are they sharp?"

"Doubtless; but their great merit is that they are blessed."

"Yes, I know that; but still I should like to be sure they are sharp."

"Pagan!"

" Let us talk of something else."

" Well, be quick."

" You want to sleep ?"

" No, to pray."

" In that case we will talk. Have you sent for M. d'Anjou ?"

" Yes, he is waiting below."

" What are you going to do with him ?"

" Throw him into the Bastile."

" That is very wise ; only choose a dungeon that is deep and safe—such for example, as those which were occupied by the Constable de St. Paul, or Armagnac."

" Oh ! be easy."

" I know where they sell good black velvet, my son."

" Chicot ! he is my brother."

" Ah ! true ; the family mourning is violet. Shall you speak to him ?"

" Yes, certainly ; if only to show him that his plots are discovered."

" Hum !"

" Do you disapprove ?"

" In your place I should cut short the conversation, and double the imprisonment."

" Let them bring here the Duc d'Anjou," said the king.

A minute after the duke entered, very pale and disarmed. Crillon followed him.

" Where did you find him ?" asked the king.

" Sire, his highness was not at home, but I took possession of his hotel in the king's name, and soon after he returned, and we arrested him without resistance."

" That is fortunate." Then, turning to the prince, he said, " Where were you, monsieur ?"

" Wherever I was, sire, be sure it was on your business."

" I doubt it."

François bowed.

" Come, tell me where you were while your accomplices were being arrested."

" My accomplices !"

" Yes ; your accomplices."

"Sire, your majesty is making some mistake."

"Oh! this time you shall not escape me; your measure of crime is full."

"Sire, be moderate; there is certainly some one who slanders me to you."

"Wretch! you shall die of hunger in a cell of the Bastile!"

"I bow to your orders, whatever they may be."

"Hypocrite! But where were you?"

"Sire, I was serving your majesty, and working for the glory and tranquillity of your reign."

"Really! your audacity is great."

"Bah!" said Chicot, "tell us about it, my prince; it must be curious."

"Sire, I would tell your majesty, had you treated me as a brother, but as you have treated me as a criminal, I will let the event speak for itself."

Then, bowing profoundly to the king, he turned to Crillon and the other officers, and said, "Now, which of you gentlemen will conduct the first prince of the blood to the Bastile?"

Chicot had been reflecting, and a thought struck him.

"Ah!" murmured he, "I believe I guess now why M. d'Epernon had so much blood on his feet and so little in his cheeks."

CHAPTER XCIV.

THE MORNING OF THE COMBAT.

THE king did not sleep all night, and very early in the morning he set off, accompanied by Chicot, to examine the ground where the combat was to take place.

"Quelus will be exposed to the sun," said he; "he will have it at his right, just in his only eye; whereas Maugiron, who has good eyes, will be in the shade. That is badly managed. As for Schomberg, his place is good; but Quelus, my poor Quelus!"

"Do not torment yourself so, my king, it is useless."

"And D'Epernon; I am really unjust not to think of him; he, who is to fight Bussy. Look at his place, Chicot, he who will have to give way constantly, for Bussy is like a tiger, he has a tree on his right and a ditch on his left."

"Bah!" said Chicot, "I am not concerned about D'Epernon."

"You are wrong; he will be killed."

"Not he; be sure he has taken precautions."

"How so?"

"He will not fight."

"Did you not hear what he said before going to bed?"

"That is just why I think he will not fight."

"Incredulous and distrustful!"

"I know my Gascon, Henri; but if you will take my advice, you will return to the Louvre."

"Do you think I can stay there during the combat?"

"I do not wish you not to love your friends, but I do wish you not to leave M. d'Anjou alone at the Louvre."

"Is not Crillon there?"

"Crillon is only a buffalo—a rhinoceros—a wild boar; while your brother is the serpent, whose strength lies in his cunning."

"You are right; I should have sent him to the Bastile."

When Chicot and the king entered, the young men were being dressed by their valets.

"Good morning, gentlemen," said he; "I find you all in good spirits, I hope?"

"Yes, sire," said Quelus.

"You look gloomy, Maugiron."

"Sire, I am superstitious, and I had bad dreams last night, so I am drinking a little wine to keep up my spirits."

"My friend, remember that dreams are the impressions of the previous day, and have no influence on the morrow."

"Yes, sire," said D'Epernon, "I also had bad dreams last night; but, in spite of that, my hand is steady and fit for action."

"Yes," said Chicot, "you dreamed you had blood on

your boots ; that is not a bad dream, for it signifies that you will be a conqueror, like Alexander or Cæsar."

"My friends," said Henri, "remember you fight only for honor ; the past night has seated me firmly on my throne, therefore do not think of me ; and, above all things, no false bravery ; you wish to kill your enemies, not to die yourselves."

The gentlemen were now ready, and it only remained to take leave of their master.

"Do you go on horseback ? " asked he.

"No, sire, on foot."

They each kissed his hand, and D'Epernon said, "Sire, bless my sword."

"Not so, D'Epernon ; give up your sword—I have a better one for each of you. Chicot, bring them here."

"No, sire, send your captain of the guards ; I am but a Pagan, and they might lose their virtue by coming through my hands."

"What are these swords, sire ? " said Schomberg.

"Italian swords, my son, forged at Milan."

"Thanks, sire."

"Now go, it is time," said the king, who could hardly control his emotion.

"Sire," said Quelus, "shall we not have your majesty's presence to encourage us ? "

"No, that would not be right ; you will be supposed to fight without any one being cognizant of it, and without my sanction. Let it appear to be the result of a private quarrel."

When they were gone, the king threw himself down in tears.

"Now," said Chicot, "I will go to see this duel, for I have an idea that something curious will happen with regard to D'Epernon." And he went off.

Henri shut himself up in his own room, first saying to Crillon, who knew what was to take place, "If we are conquerors, Crillon, come and tell me ; if not, strike three blows on the door."

CHAPTER XCV.

THE FRIENDS OF BUSSY.

THE friends of the Duc d'Anjou had passed as good and tranquil a night as those of the king, although their master had not taken the same care of them. After a good supper, they had all retired to sleep at Autragues's house, which was nearest to the field of battle. Autragues, before supper, had gone to take leave of a little milliner whom he adored, Ribeirac had written to his mother, and Livarot had made his will. They were up early in the morning, and dressed themselves in red breeches and socks, that their enemies might not see their blood, and they had doublets of gray silk. They wore shoes without heels, and their pages carried their swords, that their arms might not be fatigued.

The weather was splendid, for love, war, or walking; and the sun gilded the roofs, on which the night dew was sparkling. The streets were dry, and the air delightful.

Before leaving the house, the young men had sent to the Hôtel d'Anjou to inquire for Bussy, and had received a reply that he had gone out the evening before and had not yet returned.

"Oh!" said Autragues, "I know where he is; the king ordered a grand chase at Compiègne, and M. de Monsoreau was to set off yesterday. It is all right, gentlemen; he is nearer the ground than we are, and may be there before us. We will call for him in passing."

The streets were empty as they went along; no one was to be seen except peasants coming from Montreuil or Vincennes, with milk or vegetables.

The young men went on in silence until they reached the Rue St. Antoine.

Then, with a smile, they glanced at Monsoreau's house

"One could see well from there, and I am sure poor

Diana will be more than once at the window," said Antragues.

"I think she must be there already," said Ribeirac,
"for the window is open."

"True, but what can be the meaning of that ladder
before it?"

"It is odd."

"We are not the only ones to wonder," said Livarot,
"see those peasants, who are stopping their carts to
look."

The young men arrived under the balcony. "M. de
Monsoreau," they cried, "do you intend to be present at
our combat? if so, be quick, for we wish to arrive first."

They waited, but no one answered.

"Did you put up that ladder?" asked Antragues of a
man who was examining the ground.

"God forbid!" replied he.

"Why so?"

"Look up."

"Blood!" cried Ribeirac.

"The door has been forced," said Antragues; and seizing the ladder, he was on the balcony in a moment.

"What is it?" cried the others, seeing him turn pale.

A terrible cry was his only answer. Livarot mounted
behind him. "Corpses! death everywhere!" cried he.
And they both entered the room. It bore horrible traces
of the terrible combat of the previous night. A river of
blood flowed over the room; and the curtains were hanging in strips from sword cuts.

"Oh! poor Rémy!" cried Antragues, suddenly.

"Dead!"

"Yes."

"But a regiment of troopers must have passed through
the room," cried Livarot. Then, seeing the door of the
corridor open, and traces of blood indicating that one or
more of the combatants had also passed through there, he
followed it. Meanwhile, Antragues went into the adjoining room; there also blood was everywhere, and this blood
led to the window. He leaned out and looked into the

little garden. The iron spikes still held the livid corpse of the unhappy Bussy. At this sight, it was not a cry, but a yell, that Antragues uttered. Livarot ran to see what it was, and Ribeirac followed.

"Look!" said Antragues, "Bussy dead! Bussy assassinated and thrown out of window."

They ran down.

"It is he," cried Livarot.

"His wrist is cut."

"He has two balls in his breast."

"He is full of wounds."

"Ah! poor Bussy! we will have vengeance!"

Turning round they came against a second corpse. "Monsoreau!" cried Livarot.

"What! Monsoreau also."

"Yes, pierced through and through."

"Ah! they have assassinated all our friends."

"And his wife? Madame de Monsoreau!" cried Antragues; but no one answered.

"Bussy, poor Bussy."

"Yes, they wished to get rid of the most formidable of us all."

"It is cowardly! it is infamous!"

"We will tell the duke."

"No," said Antragues, "let us not charge any one with the care of our vengeance. Look, my friends, at the noble face of the bravest of men; see his blood, that teaches that he never left his vengeance to any other person. Bussy! we will act like you, and we will avenge you."

Then, drawing his sword, he dipped it in Bussy's blood.

"Bussy," said he, "I swear on your corpse, that this blood shall be washed off by the blood of your enemies."

"Bussy," cried the others, "we swear to kill them or die."

"No mercy," said Antragues.

"But we shall be but three."

"True, but we have assassinated no one, and God will strengthen the innocent. Adieu, Bussy!"

"Adieu, Bussy!" repeated the others; and they went out, pale but resolute, from that cursed house, around which a crowd had begun to collect.

Arriving on the ground, they found their opponents waiting for them.

"Gentlemen," said Quelus, rising and bowing, "we have had the honor of waiting for you."

"Excuse us," said Antragues, "but we should have been here before you, but for one of our companions."

"M. de Bussy," said D'Epernon, "I do not see him. Where is he?"

"We can wait for him," said Schomberg.

"He will not come."

All looked thunderstruck; but D'Epernon exclaimed:

"Ah! the brave man par excellence—is he, then, afraid?"

"That cannot be," said Quelus.

"You are right, monsieur," said Livarot.

"And why will he not come?"

"Because he is dead."

"Dead!" cried they all, but D'Epernon turned rather pale.

"And dead because he has been assassinated," said Antragues. "Did you not know it, gentlemen?"

"No; how should we?"

"Besides, is it certain?"

Antragues drew his sword. "So certain that here is his blood," said he.

"M. de Bussy assassinated!"

"His blood cries for vengeance! do you not hear it, gentlemen?" said Ribeirac.

"What do you mean?"

"'Seek whom the crime profits,' the law says," replied Ribeirac.

"Ah! gentlemen, will you explain yourselves?" cried Maugiron.

"That is just what we have come for."

"Quick! our swords are in our hands!" said D'Eper-non.

"Oh! you are in a great hurry, M. le Gascon; you did not crow so loud when we were four against four!"

"Is it our fault, if you are only three?"

"Yes, it is your fault; he is dead because you preferred him lying in his blood to standing here; he is dead, with his wrist cut, that that wrist might no longer hold a sword; he is dead, that you might not see the lightning of those eyes, which dazzled you all. Do you understand me? am I clear?"

"Enough, gentlemen!" said Quelus. "Retire, M. d'Epernon! we will fight three against three. These gentlemen shall see if we are men to profit by a misfortune which we deplore as much as themselves. Come, gentlemen," added the young man, throwing his hat behind him, and raising his left hand, while he whirled his sword with the right, "God is our judge if we are assassins!"

"Ah! I hated you before," cried Schomberg, "and now I execrate you!"

"On your guard, gentlemen!" cried Antragues.

"With doublets or without?" said Schomberg.

"Without doublets, without shirts; our breasts bare, our hearts uncovered!"

The young men threw off their doublets and shirts.

"I have lost my dagger," said Quelus; "it must have fallen on the road."

"Or else you left it at M. de Monsoreau's, in the Place de la Bastile," said Antragues.

Quelus gave a cry of rage, and drew his sword.

"But he has no dagger, M. Antragues," cried Chicot, who had just arrived.

"So much the worse for him; it is not my fault," said Antragues.

CHAPTER XCVI.

THE COMBAT.

THE place where this terrible combat was to take place was sequestered and shaded by trees. It was generally frequented only by children, who came to play there during the day, or by drunkards or robbers, who made a sleeping-place of it by night.

Chicot, his heart palpitating, although he was not of a very tender nature, seated himself before the lackeys and pages, on a wooden balustrade.

He did not love the Angevins, and detested the minions, but they were all brave young men, and in their veins flowed a generous blood, which he was probably destined to see flow before long.

D'Epernon made a last bravado, "What! you are all afraid of me?" he cried.

"Hold your tongue," said Antragues.

"Come away, bravest of the brave," said Chicot, "or else you will lose another pair of shoes."

"What do you mean?"

"I mean that there will soon be blood on the ground, and that you will walk in it, as you did last night."

D'Epernon became deadly pale, and, moving away, he seated himself at some distance from Chicot.

The combat began as five o'clock struck, and for a few minutes nothing was heard but the clashing of swords; not a blow was struck. At last Schomberg touched Ribeirac in the shoulder, and the blood gushed out; Schomberg tried to repeat the blow, but Ribeirac struck up his sword, and wounded him in the side.

"Now let us rest a few seconds, if you like," said Ribeirac.

Quelus, having no dagger, was at a great disadvantage; for he was obliged to parry with his left arm, and, as it was bare, on each occasion it cost him a wound. His hand was soon bleeding in several places, and Antragues had also wounded him in the breast; but at each wound he repeated, "It is nothing."

Livarot and Maugiron were still unwounded.

Ribeirac and Schomberg recommenced; the former was pierced through the breast, and Schomberg was wounded in the neck.

Ribeirac was mortally wounded, and Schomberg rushed on him and gave him another; but he, with his right hand, seized his opponent's, and with his left plunged his dagger into his heart.

Schomberg fell back, dragging Ribeirac with him. Livarot ran to aid Ribeirac to disengage himself from the grasp of his adversary, but was closely pursued by Maugiron, who cut open his head with a blow of his sword. Livarot let his sword drop, and fell on his knees; then Maugiron hastened to give him another wound, and he fell altogether.

Quelus and Maugiron remained against Antragues. Quelus was bleeding, but from slight wounds.

Antragues comprehended his danger; he had not the least wound, but he began to feel tired, so he pushed aside Quelus' sword and jumped over a barrier; but at the same moment, Maugiron attacked him behind; Antragues turned, and Quelus profited by this movement to get under the barrier.

"He is lost!" thought Chicot.

"Vive le roi!" cried D'Epernon.

"Silence, if you please, monsieur," said Antragues.

At this instant Livarot, of whom no one was thinking, rose on his knees, hideous from the blood with which he was covered, and plunged his dagger between the shoulders of Maugiron, who fell, crying out, "Mon Dieu! I am killed!"

Livarot fell back again, fainting.

"M. de Quelus," said Antragues, "you are a brave man; yield—I offer you your life."

"And why yield?"

" You are wounded, and I am not."

" Vive le roi ! " cried Quelus ; " I have still my sword ! " And he rushed on Antragues, who parried the thrust, and, seizing his arm, wrested his sword from him, saying, " Now you have it no longer."

" Oh, a sword ! " cried Quelus ; and, bounding like a tiger on Antragues, he threw his arms round him.

Antragues struck him with his dagger again and again, but Quelus managed to seize his hands, and twisted round him like a serpent, with arms and legs. Antragues, nearly suffocated, reeled and fell, but on the unfortunate Quelus. He managed to disengage himself, for Quelus' powers were failing him, and, leaning on one arm, gave him a last blow.

" Vive le r——" said Quelus, and that was all. The silence and terror of death reigned everywhere.

Antragues rose, covered with blood, but it was that of his enemy.

D'Epernon made the sign of the cross, and fled as if he were pursued by demons.

Chicot ran and raised Quelus, whose blood was pouring out from nineteen wounds.

The movement roused him, and he opened his eyes.

" Antragues," said he, " on my honor, I am innocent of the death of Bussy."

" Oh ! I believe you, monsieur," cried Antragues, much moved.

" Fly ! " murmured Quelus ; " the king will never forgive you."

" I cannot abandon you thus, even to escape the scaffold."

" Save yourself, young man," said Chicot ; " do not tempt Providence twice in one day."

Antragues approached Ribeirac, who still breathed.

" Well ? " asked he.

" We are victors," said Antragues, in a low tone, not to offend Quelus.

" Thanks," said Ribeirac ; " now go."

And he fainted again.

Antragues picked up his own sword, which he had dropped, then that of Quelus, which he presented to him. A tear shone in the eyes of the dying man. "We might have been friends," he murmured.

"Now fly," said Chicot; "you are worthy of being saved."

"And my companions?"

"I will take care of them, as of the king's friends."

Antragues wrapped himself in a cloak which his squire handed to him, so that no one might see the blood with which he was covered, and, leaving the dead and wounded, he disappeared through the Porte St. Antoine.

CHAPTER XCVII.

THE END.

THE king, pale with anxiety, and shuddering at the slightest noise, employed himself in conjecturing, with the experience of a practised man, the time that it would take for the antagonists to meet and that the combat would last.

"Now," he murmured first, "they are crossing the Rue St. Antoine—now they are entering the field—now they have begun." And at these words, the poor king, trembling, began to pray.

Rising again in a few minutes, he cried:

"If Quelus only remembers the thrust I taught him! As for Schomberg, he is so cool that he ought to kill Ribeirac; Maugiron, also, should be more than a match for Livarot. But D'Epernon, he is lost; fortunately he is the one of the four whom I love least. But if Bussy, the terrible Bussy, after killing him, falls on the others! Ah, my poor friends!"

"Sire!" said Crillon, at the door.

"What! already?"

"Sire, I have no news but that the Duc d'Anjou begs to speak to your majesty."

"What for?"

"He says that the moment has come for him to tell you what service he rendered your majesty, and that what he has to tell you will calm a part of your fears."

"Well, let him come."

At this moment they heard a voice crying, "I must speak to the king at once!"

The king recognized the voice, and opened the door.

"Here, St. Luc!" cried he. "What is it? But, mon Dieu! what is the matter? Are they dead?"

Indeed, St. Luc, pale, without hat or sword, and spotted with blood, rushed into the king's room.

"Sire!" cried he, "vengeance! I ask for vengeance!"

"My poor St. Luc, what is it? You seem in despair."

"Sire, one of your subjects, the bravest, noblest, has been murdered this night—traitorously murdered!"

"Of whom do you speak?"

"Sire, you do not love him, I know; but he was faithful, and, if need were, would have shed all his blood for your majesty, else he would not have been my friend."

"Ah!" said the king, who began to understand; and something like a gleam of joy passed over his face.

"Vengeance, sire, for M. de Bussy!"

"M. de Bussy?"

"Yes, M. de Bussy, whom twenty assassins poniarded last night. He killed fourteen of them."

"M. de Bussy dead?"

"Yes, sire."

"Then he does not fight this morning?"

St. Luc cast a reproachful glance on the king, who turned away his head, and, in doing so, saw Crillon still standing at the door. He signed to him to bring in the duke.

"No, sire, he will not fight," said St. Luc; "and that is why I ask, not for vengeance—I was wrong to call it so —but for justice. I love my king, and am, above all things, jealous of his honor, and I think that it is a deplorable service which they have rendered to your majesty by killing M. de Bussy."

The Duc d'Anjou had just entered, and St. Luc's words

had enlightened the king as to the service his brother had boasted of having rendered him.

"Do you know what they will say?" continued St. Luc. "They will say, if your friends conquer, that it is because they first murdered Bussy."

"And who will dare to say that?"

"Pardieu! every one," said Crillon.

"No, monsieur, they shall not say that," replied the king, "for you shall point out the assassin."

"I will name him, sire, to clear your majesty from so heinous an accusation," said St. Luc.

"Well! do it."

The Duc d'Anjou stood quietly by.

"Sire," continued St. Luc, "last night they laid a snare for Bussy, while he visited a woman who loved him; the husband, warned by a traitor, came to his house with a troop of assassins; they were everywhere—in the street—in the courtyard, even in the garden."

In spite of his power over himself, the duke grew pale at these last words.

"Bussy fought like a lion, sire, but numbers overwhelmed him, and——"

"And he was killed," interrupted the king, "and justly; I will certainly not revenge an adulterer."

"Sire, I have not finished my tale. The unhappy man, after having defended himself for more than half an hour in the room, after having triumphed over his enemies, escaped, bleeding, wounded, and mutilated: he only wanted some one to lend him a saving hand, which I would have done had I not been seized by his assassins, and bound, and gagged. Unfortunately, they forgot to take away my sight as well as my speech, for I saw two men approach the unlucky Bussy, who was hanging on the iron railings. I heard him entreat them for help, for in these two men he had the right to reckon on two friends. Well, sire, it is horrible to relate—it was still more horrible to see and hear—one ordered him to be shot, and the other obeyed."

"And you know the assassins?" cried the king, moved in spite of himself.

"Yes," said St. Luc, and turning to the prince, with an expression of intense hatred, he cried, "the assassin, sire, was the prince, his friend."

The duke stood perfectly quiet and answered, "Yes, M. de St. Luc is right; it was I, and your majesty will appreciate my action, for M. de Bussy was my servant, it is true; but this morning he was to fight against your majesty."

"You lie, assassin!" cried St. Luc. "Bussy, full of wounds, his hands cut to pieces, a ball through his shoulder, and hanging suspended on the iron trellis-work, might have inspired pity in his most cruel enemies; they would have succored him. But you, the murderer of La Mole and of Coconnas, you killed Bussy, as you have killed, one after another, all your friends. You killed Bussy, not because he was the king's enemy, but because he was the confidant of your secrets. Ah! Monsoreau knew well your reason for this crime."

"Cordieu!" cried Crillon, "why am I not king?"

"They insult me before you, brother," said the duke, pale with terror.

"Leave us, Crillon," said the king.

The officer obeyed.

"Justice, sire, justice!" cried St. Luc again.

"Sire," said the duke, "will you punish me for having served your majesty's friends this morning?"

"And I," cried St. Luc, "I say that the cause which you espouse is accursed, and will be pursued by the anger of God. Sire, when your brother protects our friends, woe to them."

The king shuddered.

Then they heard hasty steps and voices, followed by a deep silence; and then, as if a voice from heaven came to confirm St. Luc's words, three blows were struck slowly and solemnly on the door by the vigorous arm of Crillon.

Henri turned deadly pale.

"Conquered," cried he; "my poor friends!"

"What did I tell you, sire?" cried St. Luc. "See now murder succeeds."

But the king saw nothing, heard nothing; he buried his face in his hands, and murmured, "Oh! my poor friends; who will tell me about them?"

"I, sire," said Chicot.

"Well!" cried Henri.

"Two are dead, and the third is dying."

"Which is the third?"

"Quelus."

"Where is he?"

"At the Hôtel Boissy."

The king said no more, but rushed from the room. St. Luc had taken Diana home to his wife, and this had kept him from appearing sooner at the Louvre. Jeanne passed three days and nights watching her through the most frightful delirium.

On the fourth day, Jeanne, overcome by fatigue, went to take a little rest: two hours after, when she returned, Diana was gone.

Quelus died at the Hôtel Boissy, in the king's arms, after lingering for thirty days.

Henri was inconsolable. He raised three magnificent tombs for his friends, on which their effigies were sculptured, life-size, in marble. He had innumerable masses said for them, and prayed for their souls himself night and morning.

For three months Chicot never left his master, and consoled him as well as he could. In the month of September, Chicot received the following letter, dated from the Priory of Beaume:

"DEAR M. CHICOT,

"The air is soft in this place, and the vintage promises to be good this year. They say that the king, whose life I saved, still grieves much. Bring him to the priory, dear M. Chicot; we will give him wine of 1550, which I have discovered in my cellar, and which is enough to make one forget the greatest grief; for I find in the Holy Writ these words, 'Good wine rejoices the heart of man.' It is in Latin. I will show it you. Come, then, dear M. Chicot;

come, with the king, M. d'Epernon, and M. de St. Luc, and we will fatten them all.

"The reverend prior,

"DOM GORENFLOT,

"Your humble servant and friend.

"P.S.—Tell the king that I have not yet had time to pray for the souls of his friends; but when the vintage is over, I shall not fail to do so."

"Amen," said Chicot; "here are poor devils well recommended to Heaven."

THE END.

NOTE:—For the information of the reader The Valois Romances should read in the chronological order as follows; 1st, Marguerite de Valois; 2d, Chicot the Jester, 3d, The Forty-five Guardsmen.

CPSIA information can be obtained at www.ICGtesting.com
Printed in the USA
LVOW090053290911

248326LV00001B/84/P